LOST IN
TRANSLATION

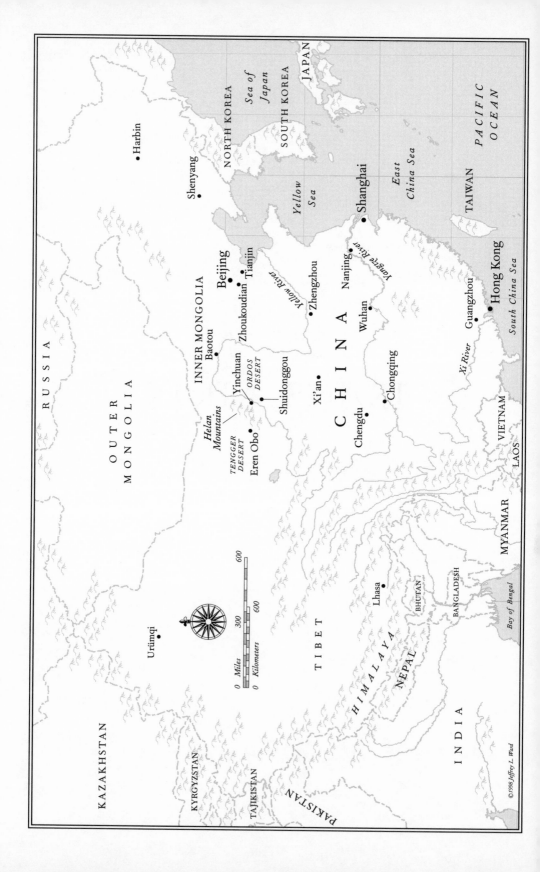

LOST IN
TRANSLATION

Nicole Mones

Delacorte Press

Published by
Delacorte Press
Bantam Doubleday Dell Publishing Group, Inc.
1540 Broadway
New York, New York 10036

Permissions follow on p. v

Library of Congress Cataloging in Publication Data

Mones, Nicole.
    Lost in translation / by Nicole Mones.
      p.   cm.
    ISBN 0-385-31934-7
    I. Title.
  PS3563.0519L67 1998
  813'.54—dc21   97-51654
                                                                         CIP

Manufactured in the United States of America
Published simultaneously in Canada

September 1998

10   9   8   7   6   5   4   3   2   1

BVG

Author's Note

This is a work of fiction. It includes references to real people and events, which are used to give the fiction a historical reality. In particular, although many of the facts concerning Teilhard de Chardin and Lucile Swan are accurate and the quotations from their letters come directly from published sources, their lives are used fictitiously in this work. Names, characters, and incidents relating to nonhistorical figures are the product of the author's imagination. Please see the Historical Note for more information.

Material from the following sources has been reprinted by permission:

The Phenomenon of Man, by Pierre Teilhard de Chardin. Copyright 1955 by Editions de Seuil. Copyright © 1959 in the English translation by William Collins Sons & Co. Ltd., London, and Harper and Row, Publishers, Inc., New York. Reprinted by permission of HarperCollins Publishers, Inc.

The Phenomenon of Man, by Pierre Teilhard de Chardin. © Editions du Seuil, 1951. Reprinted by permission.

"As the sun rose over the mountain . . ." reprinted by permission of Philomel Books from *Chinese Mother Goose Rhymes*, selected and edited by Robert Wyndham, © 1968 by Robert Wyndham.

Brief segments have also been quoted from the following works:

Letters From a Traveller, by Pierre Teilhard de Chardin, Copyright © 1962 in the English translation by William Collins Sons & Co. Ltd., London, and Harper and Row, Publishers, Inc., New York.

Letters to Léontine Zanta, by Pierre Teilhard de Chardin in the English translation by William Collins Sons & Co. Ltd., London, and Harper and Row, Publishers, Inc., New York, 1969.

The Letters of Teilhard de Chardin and Lucile Swan, Thomas M. King and Mary Wood Gilbert, editors. Copyright © 1993 by Mary Wood Gilbert.

Since the inner face of the world is manifest deep within our human consciousness, and there reflects upon itself, it would seem that we have only got to look at ourselves in order to understand the dynamic relationships existing between the *within* and the *without* of things at a given point in the universe.

In fact so to do is one of the most difficult of all things.

—Pierre Teilhard de Chardin
The Phenomenon of Man

LOST IN
TRANSLATION

1

IN THE LOBBY of the Minzu Hotel, Second Night Clerk Huang glanced out through the great glass doors just as the foreign interpreter wheeled her bicycle past. He stared, fascinated. He knew what it meant when she left, late at night, wearing a short skirt. There were no secrets in China. He smiled and turned back to his computer.

Outside, Alice Mannegan pedaled down Changan Dajie. She flew past the cobbled sidewalks, the storefronts crowded with Chinese *paizi*, signboards in arty, propulsive italic characters: Happy Fortune and Flying Crane and Propitious Wind. Knives and shoes and beauty supplies, bicycle parts and baling wire, all screaming for attention.

But their metal shutters had clanged down for the night. The black-headed crowd was gone. In daytime the boulevard throbbed with *renao* life, but now the bubbling volcano of Pekingese and frantically jingling bike bells was silent. It still smelled like Beijing, though. The air was ripe, opulent, sewerish—and thick with history.

Beyond the low row of storefronts she glimpsed the squat,

massive official buildings—the institutes and bureaus and admin-
istrations which lined the boulevard. Changan was the main
spoke of Beijing's wheel. Broad and straight, built for parades, it
roared right to the heart of the capital, and of all China, the
Forbidden City. The *Danei*, people used to call it. The Great
Within. And now there it was: the massive ocher bulwarks, the
medieval walls, closed, faceless; all *qi* pointing inward, to what
was concealed, powerful, and endlessly complex. Its entrance was
crowned with the huge red-cheeked portrait of Chairman Mao,
smiling down from atop the Gate of Heavenly Peace.

Alice turned, skirting Tiananmen Square. A breeze rustled
leaves above her head and sent an empty fast-food container
skipping across the pavement. She glanced right and left at the
sound. No one.

She pedaled harder, the summer night wind silky on her face.
Past the great stone Qianmen arch, then south on Qianmen Boulevard into the old Chinese City with its riot of shops, restaurants, theaters. She veered off the boulevard, through the tangle
of narrow *hutong*s. She loved this ancient maze of dirt-packed
lanes. To her this was the true heart of the capital, not the
colossal high-walled palace behind her. Here in the gracefully
repeating pattern of silvery stone walls and tile roofs, Alice
sometimes felt China in her grasp. Sometimes. She turned again,
right, then left. Now she crossed the familiar intersection, with
the old capped-over stone well in the center. She steered into a
brick-paved, stone-walled alley so narrow, her bicycle could
barely pass. There. The Brilliant Coffee.

The neon sign screamed COFFEE in English, English being
very fashionable in Beijing just now, but of course coffee had
very little to do with the purposes of this establishment. She
chained her bike to the crowded metal rack. There was one door,
painted black, and a row of windows sealed over to make the
place appear closed. There were no signs of life. But it was
Friday night, almost midnight, and Alice knew better.

She pushed open the door. Instantly she was hit with the pounding, insistent karaoke bass and above that the roaring stutter of a smoking, chattering crowd. Hip, dazzlingly dressed Chinese, fresh out of their cultural confinement and keening to be part of the exploding *yangqi,* the now, crammed in shoulder to shoulder. Not a seat anywhere, she thought, looking around. Hardly a place to stand.

Across the low-ceilinged room she watched a slight man with a closely cropped black head and antique round glasses take the stage and begin belting a nineteen fifties R&B tune. He lurched from one foot to the other, out of time with the music, swinging the microphone stand from side to side as he shouted out each syllable.

She smiled. God, she loved Beijing. Tomorrow she would meet her new client. Tonight was free. She scanned the packed tables as the horns took off in a smart, prerecorded flourish.

A man slid into place beside her. He had wide shoulders, a deep waist, and black eyes flat in his head. "You await someone?" he said in Chinese.

"Wo zai deng, wo bu zai deng," she shrugged, her intonation almost perfect. I'm waiting, but then again I'm not. "What about you?"

He smiled, pleased with her subtlety, and it warmed her all over, because it was an uncontrolled streak of pleasure that opened his ivory-colored face suddenly into something unprotected, almost innocent—though innocence, in a place like the Brilliant Coffee, would be impossible. People kept themselves well concealed in places like this. Which suited Alice fine.

He laughed softly. "I wait for you," he said. "And an outside person too. Imagine."

"Yes. An outside person." Behind his smile she caught the usual male reserve, the relaxed sense of his own racial superiority which always made her tremble with fear and hope and excitement.

"Please." He signaled with a sidelong glance, then turned and threaded through the crowd away from her, not leading her, not even looking back at her, but knowing she would follow. A waiter jostled past them with a full tray. She felt the Chinese eyes: Look, a Western woman in a short black dress, red hair, birdlike, freckled. She liked being noticed. It heightened the satisfaction of nights like these, nights she allowed herself because, after all, she was a woman and when there wasn't real love in her life she needed, at least, some attention. Now—a miracle. The man was producing two empty chairs.

"How are you called?" He leaned close to shut out the wall of music.

She answered "Yulian," the Chinese name she currently used for these situations. Yulian was an old-fashioned name; it meant Fragrant Lotus. It was a name that rang on many levels. The bound feet had been called lotuses, and there was also that famous heroine of Chinese erotic fiction, the Golden Lotus.

These allusions were not lost on him. He pressed his mouth together in amusement. "I'm Lu Ming."

A hollow-chested young waiter with a sharp, acne-cratered face materialized. *"Bai jiu,"* Lu Ming told him, slang for the steamroller 120-proof rice spirits popular in China. Then he turned to Alice: "Unless you'd rather have a"—he interrupted his Chinese to try to pronounce it the English way—"Coca-Cola?"

"Bai jiu ye xing," she answered. Good, she thought, rice spirits, one shot, maybe two. It was better to be high. "Good. *Bai jiu.*"

The spirits arrived, clear liquid in two tiny glasses. Lu Ming toasted their friendship with a standard phrase, and then added, *"Gan-bei,"* dry glass, and they both drained it and laughed. The fire burned through her stomach and rose instantly to her head. How long since she'd eaten?

"What are you doing in Beijing?" Lu Ming asked, circling his empty glass on the wet tabletop.

She paused. Sometimes she invented professions; tonight, on a whim, she decided to tell the truth. "I'm an interpreter."

"Trade?"

"Freelance. I'm about to start a job with an archaeologist. Something to do with *Homo erectus*."

"Eh?" he squinted.

"You know, *Homo erectus,* our ancestors, the missing link? Like Peking Man."

"You mean the ape-man?" he chortled, using the street word, *yuanren.* "I doubt very much if the Chinese people could be descended from the ape-man!"

"Well"—she tensed slightly at this prejudice—"I don't know anything about it, really. I'm just a translator."

Still Lu Ming did not let it go. "But such an expedition must cost huge money!" He raised his hand in a two-fingered signal to the passing waiter. "And for what? For history? Eh, it's a waste!" Two new, full glasses appeared in front of them. The music blasted away. "History is but a hobby. It's for old men with no *yang* left."

"I like history," she said defensively. "I think old things are beautiful."

"What counts now and for the future is modernization. Commerce." He leaned into her. "Money."

"To money." She forced a smile. It was no use arguing with Chinese men. Especially if you were a woman. And a foreigner. Their probing interest in her—the free American mind, the direct laughter, the pale, willing body—always held the potential for an edge of contempt. If she could stay back from that edge, though, the excitement was unmatched. The two of them drank. "And you, Lu Ming? What do you do?"

"I'm in business," he said simply, as if no further explanation

5

were needed of this most glorious word. Gracefully he withdrew a white card from his black jacket.

She glanced at the characters. "Lu Investment Consulting Group?"

He touched his forelock in mock salute.

"Well, Chairman Lu, to your profits." She smiled, pleased to see that there was now yet another tiny, full glass in front of her. *"Gan-bei."* They drank and gasped together. The booming room shuddered. "These must be good times for you," she said, rolling the empty glass between her palms. "The current leaders."

"Eh, it's so. It's because of old Deng Xiao-ping we have all this." He paused and with a rapid sweep of his eyes managed to include the frenzied crowd, the recorded tidal wave of guitar and saxophones, the rolling static of laughter, and, last and most pointedly, his square white business card half splashed now with rice brandy on the table. *"Ta-de kai fang zheng che, liufang bai shi; danshi Liu-Si ye jiang yichou wannian,"* The open door will hand down a good reputation for a hundred generations, but the Six-Four will leave a stink for ten thousand years.

"True," she said, recognizing the colloquial term *Six-Four*—shorthand for the Tiananmen incident, which had occurred on June fourth. Chinese liked to remember things by their numbers. "Do you think new leaders might change the situation?"

He lowered his voice, conjuring a bond between them. "It's a mistake to think it matters who's in charge. Of course the old leaders die. But then not much changes. The wolf just becomes a dog. Though as for the open door"—by this he meant China's new liberalism—"I am sure it will remain as it is. They'll never be able to close it." Under the table he placed his foot alongside hers, a gentle but insistent message. "You see," he said, and spread his hands disarmingly, "I care only for my personal success now. Completely selfish! But I'm educated. And—everyone agrees on this, Yulian—my heart is good. Therefore"—he leaned in and locked on her eyes—"will Yulian now go with me to some more peaceful place where friends can speak with their hearts at ease?"

Cigarette smoke, laughter, the throbbing bass swirled around her. Suddenly the Brilliant Coffee was a box of thunder, of unbearable noise. He really wants me, she thought with the familiar thrill. And then she hesitated.

He rubbed her foot with his. It was soft, he wore only a sock, when had he taken off his shoe? *"Yi bu zuo, er bu xiu,"* he whispered, Once a thing is begun, no one can stop it until it is finished.

He moved his foot away, not touching her now, only leaning close—but his entire body flamed with attention. Hers did too. She closed her eyes. Pretend, tonight. She felt a pull to the center of him, where surely lay entry to all China. *"Wei shenmo bu,"* she whispered finally, Why not.

He didn't speak as they pedaled side by side through the mud-rutted lanes that coiled away from the Brilliant Coffee—she remembered this the next morning as she rode her bicycle back in the misty, unfurling dawn to the Minzu Hotel. He had smiled at her once, radiantly, but said nothing. It was like a Chinese man not to speak, not now, not when it was about to happen. They all had this magnificent reserve. She knew how this wall of reserve would come to an end, too, and she had been right: even now, pedaling hard through the early half-light of Wangfujing Boulevard, her thighs cramped with desire when she remembered the way the door had closed behind them in his apartment and he had turned to her, reached for her, and all in one motion carried her down with him to the floor where in an instant the verbal, astute, urbane man he had been at the Brilliant Coffee vanished and in his place was a purely physical being, urgently male, frantic to enter her.

Later, when they were lying naked under sheets by the open window, he asked her whether, since she was based in Beijing, they could be friends. She didn't answer right away. This was the hard part for her. She loved it when they first touched her, and she would always cringe a little, pull back, savor the waves of shame and shyness and then, finally, surrender. That was the pleasure. But it always ended. The sex always ended and the talking came back, and with it the lines she could never seem to cross.

"Of course I couldn't visit you at your hotel." He lit a cigarette and exhaled a blue cloud toward the ceiling. "It would cause too much talk. You're *waiguoren,* an outside-country person. Not Chinese. But you could come here, at night."

Did he have to say all this? Though of course a lot of men talked too much, and unwisely, in the temporary state of total spread-legged candor which followed sex.

"Well?" he asked softly, fingers moving through her hair.

She guarded herself. "I know all about what you are saying."

He smiled. *"Mingbai jiu hao,"* he whispered back happily, I'm glad you understand.

She let his words trail off. In a few minutes he slept.

She moved away from him in the strange bed. And the next morning, when she rose in the half-light and tied on her antique Chinese stomach-protector and zipped up her black dress, and he whispered to her from the bed to write down where he could get in touch with her, she wrote just the characters for the phony name, Yulian, and a fictional Beijing number.

Sometimes, when she got up and dressed before dawn, the men didn't ask for her number. They would watch her go without a word. They seemed to know better than to say anything to her at all.

After a spotty and insubstantial sleep, Dr. Adam Spencer dragged his sluggish forty-eight-year-old body out of bed. It was only five A.M. but he was all out of sync and there was no way, his first night in China, he was going to be able to sleep anymore. So he shaved, tugged on his clothes, then pulled his son's photo from his wallet and looked at it for a minute. He was trying not to think about the fact that it was midafternoon back home in Nevada. And in California, where his son now lived. He replaced the photo and surveyed himself in the mirror. Bone tired, his blond hair straggly, but still pretty fit and not bad looking, in a middle-aged, soft-faced kind of way. He knew his reflection well, his plain gray eyes and his cheeks that seemed to have no bones under them and his round mouth, which had once been boyish; he had been used to himself for a long time.

He sat down in a scuffed armchair, flicked on a puddle of yellow lamplight, and paged through one of the many books by Teilhard de Chardin he had brought—this one a volume of the great man's letters from China—forced down a cup of hot, iron-tasting tea, and began to make notes in his habitual blue pocket notebook. After a time he switched off the light and wandered to the window to part the curtains. A faint gray dawn was rising over the city. Changan Boulevard, the Boulevard of Long Peace, was waking up: here came rumbling what looked like an Army truck, and there, half real in the mist, was a clopping mule-drawn cart.

And there—what was that?

He pressed his forehead to the glass. God, it was a Western woman on a bicycle! He squinted through the glass.

She wheeled quickly across the parking lot and disappeared alongside the building. In a moment she emerged on foot. He could see she was delicately built. She glanced furtively from one side to the other, and then darted inside.

Gone. He stared down at the parking lot, narrowed his eyes, wondering.

*　*　*

He was to meet his interpreter in the hotel restaurant at seven-thirty. He sat down and glanced through the mostly Chinese menu, flush with the thrill of finally being here. It had taken more than a year to make it happen. First studying everything published about China's northwestern deserts, reading all that was available in English and even scraping together the money to have some of the Chinese stuff translated. Retracing Pierre Teilhard de Chardin's desert expeditions of more than seventy years before. Reviewing the whole career of Father Teilhard, who had been an important paleontologist in his time and then, after his death, become famous for his books of transcendent Christian philosophy. Sifting clues out of his books, his published letters and diaries. All of it sparked by the secret Spencer's grandfather—in his own youth a well-known geologist, a friend of Teilhard's—had confided to him, the grandson, shortly before he died. Gradually seeing how the puzzle fit. Then writing the grant proposal. Getting leave from the university. Finding the interpreter.

He was startled by the sound of a chair scraping over the floor, and then: "You're Dr. Spencer?"

He looked up and swallowed. The red-haired woman.

She was dressed in blue jeans now, and a simple cropped T-shirt, but it was her. Unmistakably. The hair was tucked behind her ears and she had a pleasingly freckled, high-cheeked little face with moss-colored eyes.

"Good morning," she said, and stuck out her hand. "*Zaochen hao*. I'm Alice Mannegan."

"Adam Spencer." They shook. Her hand felt small and fine-boned. "Sorry, I'm a little surprised." He smiled apologetically. "Because I saw you this morning."

"Saw me?"

"Before dawn. That was you, wasn't it? Coming back to the hotel on a bicycle?"

She paused and looked at him. Something indecipherable ran across her face. "Yes. That was me."

"Well." He bit back any more questions. "Anyway."

"Anyway." She sat down, beckoned a waitress, and ordered food in rapid Chinese. She centered her plate and dark wood chopsticks on the tablecloth. "Your flight was okay?"

"It was fine. Thanks. It's great to be in China."

"Oh, yes—I love China." Her face lit; for a moment everything about her seemed to lock happily together. "I love it, the sense of the past, the civilization, the language. And it could hardly be any more different from"—she paused—"America."

"You don't like America."

She moved her shoulders.

"But you grew up there?"

"That doesn't mean I liked it. Anyway, welcome." She settled against the back of her chair. "Now tell me about this job."

"Okay. Right." He took out his notebook and set it open on the table, uncapped a cheap ballpoint. "Do you know the work of Teilhard de Chardin?"

"Teilhard de Chardin—yes, a little. The Jesuit. I think it was in college I read *The Phenomenon of Man*. Actually I haven't read him in years. Though he did live in China for a long time. I guess you know that."

"Yes." He made a note. "And I guess you know he was a famous paleontologist as well as a theologian. That's what got him exiled to China. The essays he wrote about evolution were a little too real for the Vatican. Their idea of the origin of man was Adam and Eve. Period."

"Well." Alice smiled slightly. "Teilhard knew too much to go along with that."

"Right. So they sent him off to China. Lucky for archaeology, I guess—because he found some of the first early-man sites in Asia." Spencer leaned back from the table in mock fear as the waitress downloaded a precariously balanced pyramid of steaming dishes. "You order all this?" His face fell open at the shock-ingly yellow eggs, the soup, and slick green piles of pickled vegetable.

"Don't worry. It's cheap. They just devalued the renminbi again." She scooped up fried pea sprouts and a tangle of tiny silvery fish, mounded them on her plate with white pillows of steamed bread. She felt good from the night before. Hungry. Alive. Exalted. Later she knew the feeling of being stuck would creep back, but for now—she flashed the American archaeologist a smile. "So, you were saying. Evolution."

Spencer stared. God, she could really pack it in for someone so tiny. "Yes. Teilhard did some great work here. He found some important Late Paleolithic sites, especially in the far northwest. Then in 1929 he started working with the group that uncovered Peking Man here, outside the city."

"Oh, yes," she said. "Peking Man."

"It was one of the most important *Homo erectus* finds in the history of archaeology, a whole hominid settlement. At a time when people were still questioning the theory of evolution, sud-denly here were these bones—obviously a human predecessor. Half man, half . . . something. And now we get to our re-search, Alice, because that's what I've come to China to look for—Peking Man. *Sinanthropus*."

"It's missing?"

"Don't you know? It disappeared during the Second World War. It's never been found."

She stopped chewing, eyebrows in a half lilt. "Really."

He nodded. "By 1941 China was dangerous. The Japanese had occupied Peking since '37 and were gradually swallowing up the rest of the country. So the foreigners crated up the bones—they were priceless, you know, a really comprehensive find—to send to the Museum of Natural History in New York." He put his chopsticks down, excited. "But just as the fossils were to be shipped out, hidden in the luggage of this American naval officer, the Japanese bombed Pearl Harbor. Suddenly America was in the war. Ships leaving Peking for the States were blockaded. The few U.S. troops here were quickly overwhelmed. The naval officer who was going to carry Peking Man to New York was hauled off to a prison camp down in Shanghai. Months went by. Finally he got his luggage back. But guess what? The bones had been removed."

She considered. "So the Japanese got it."

"Well, that's what the Americans thought. Not the Chinese! Some of them still think the Americans conspired to steal it. Of course"—he spread his hands—"that's silly."

Now she swallowed back an ache of sexual awareness, for the gesture brought washing over her and twining back around her the ivory arms and legs of Lu Ming. He had spread his hands that way, in the Brilliant Coffee. *You see, Yulian, I am completely selfish*— Not that Dr. Spencer, a white man, had the same effect on her. White men never had that effect on her. Though he was nice, this archaeologist. She liked him. "So." She pushed food around on her plate. "What do you think happened to Peking Man? And what does it have to do with Teilhard de Chardin?"

Conspiratorial pleasure flickered in his eyes. "I think Teilhard got the bones back in the last days of the war."

"You're kidding."

"And I think he hid them here in China."

"What!"

"It's true. Listen." He strained forward. "My grandfather was this famous geologist. Henry Bingham. Taught at Stanford, knew Teilhard well. Teilhard came to Stanford a couple of times, you know. Anyway, Teilhard told him he was getting Peking Man back. Swore him to secrecy."

"Your grandfather told you this?"

"Yes."

"And did he tell you what Teilhard did with Peking Man?"

"That he didn't know. He got only hints. But I've studied the whole picture—Teilhard's letters, diaries, books of philosophy—and I think the bones were hidden out in northwest China. Somewhere in the desert."

"Incredible." She laid her chopsticks on the table, pushed back her plate. A silence fell between them, one that was instantly filled by the dining room's clatter of dishes and its multilingual well of voices.

Then their waitress was there. *"Chibao-le?"* she barked, Are you finished?

"Eh." Alice glanced up, nodded. *"Suanzhang?"* she murmured.

"You speak great Chinese," he marveled, closing his notebook and slipping it into his pocket.

"That! I was just asking for the bill."

"No, you do." He turned serious. "There is one thing I've been wondering about you. May I ask—I've been thinking—ever since we talked on the phone—you're not any relation, are you? To Horace Mannegan? The congressman?"

She hesitated and he saw her face pinch in ever so slightly.

"So he is your father! I thought he might be. After all—the 'Alice Speech.' The firebombing. You know, *I have a little girl named Alice.* I mean, your name is Alice."

"Yes." She closed her eyes against the naked free-fall.

"So you're *the* Alice." He reached over and squeezed her arm. "Man. Rough on you. Wasn't it? Growing up with that. Those three little girls who were killed . . ." He shook his head sympathetically.

Oh, yes. Alice knew the deaths of those three girls. Knew their smiling school before-pictures, the ones in all the papers, soft brown eyes and shy expressions and plastic barrettes. Knew the TV-news images of their parents screaming.

It was the thing that seemed to have been frozen around her

forever. The warm evening, the crowd packed into the stadium to listen to her father's acceptance speech to Congress. She remembered huddling with her small hands covering her ears as the throng whooped and cheered his every word, their arms waving and punching the hot air. "My little girl sit next to a colored boy in school? Never!" She felt his powerful grip around her waist, the *whoosh* as she was lifted off the ground and waved like a ceremonial flag. "*This* is my little girl named Alice. The prettiest little girl in the world!" She remembered her panic, her torn, jumbled breathing that didn't let her form the words *Stop— please*—then the staccato burst of flashbulbs and it was over. She was dropped back down on the chair. Then the crowds streamed out, poured into the streets of the Fourth and Fifth wards, where the blacks lived. Hands that had applauded now brandished ax handles and Coke bottles filled with gasoline.

People always remembered her name after that. When the smoke cleared and the charred houses had been hosed down and the three girls were carried away in bags, her name had been found, scrawled in chalk on the soot-blackened sidewalks: Alice.

"Yes," she told him softly over her pounding heart, "I'm the same Alice. But I was only a small child then, and I prefer not to get into it. I mean, now you know. But let's just leave it there."

"No problem," he said, stabbed with embarrassment. "Look, I'm sorry. And hey. If I were you I'd spend my whole damn life in China too. Really. I understand."

"I doubt you do," she managed. "But thanks."

The waitress returned and left the check. Alice slid it across the table to Spencer. "One thing," she told him. "Nobody knows me as Alice Mannegan here. I use a Chinese name—Mo Ai-li. It's easier."

"You want me to call you that? Mo—"

"Mo Ai-li. No. You don't have to. Call me Alice." She pushed back from the table and stood up. "After all. You're a foreigner too."

*　*　*

Vice Director Han of the IVPP, Institute of Vertebrate Pale-ontology and Paleoanthropology, leaned his blocky frame back in his teakwood desk chair. His office was plain and functional but the furniture was dark old wood, solid, and good antique brush-paintings hung on the walls. Outside the windows roared the mighty flow of Xizhimenwai, the stream of trucks and carts and cars, people and bicycles, the wall of voices and horns and the mechanical clamor of a city under construction. The vice director surveyed the American Ph.D. Crude and washed out and covered with curly yellow hair. So outsidelike.

And with him this copper-headed interpreter, who went, in Chinese, by the professional name Mo Ai-li. Mo Loving and Upright. A good name, old fashioned; she had some taste, clearly. Of course she was still a foreigner, she had that manic aggressive look in her eyes that they all had. Though she was easier to look at, small and less—a fleeting purse of his lips—less flamboyantly shaped than most of the outside women.

"Vice Director Han," she was saying, translating closely be-hind the blond man's English. "We need permits. In 1923, in the Northwest, the French priest Pierre Teilhard de Chardin discov-ered the first buried Late Paleolithic site in East Asia. This is the site called Shuidonggou, in Ningxia Province. Teilhard de Char-din loved the northwestern deserts. He always longed to return there. Dr. Spencer says it is critical to begin searching at this site in northern Ningxia, and in the desert around it called"—she turned and asked the man for the name again—"called the Or-dos."

"Those areas are closed."

"We know. Thus it is we ask for permits."

They are more than closed, he thought, annoyed. They are full of missile bases, gleaming nuclear prongs concealed in caves

16

and aimed at Russia. And not only missile bases—forced labor camps. Aloud he said: "The Peking Man remains were excavated here, at Zhoukoudian, just outside the city. They were never in that part of China. Never sent there for exhibition. Never studied there." He coughed meaningfully.

She nodded. Then the two talked in their broken and bumped-up English. "Still,"—she returned to Chinese—"this scientist believes that the French priest may have recovered *Sinanthropus* at the end of the Japan War and sent it out there."

"May I ask why he believes this?"

"Because his grandfather was a friend of the priest. The priest confided in his grandfather that he had been befriended by a Colonel Akabori, an officer in the occupation force and an amateur paleontologist. Teilhard was anti-Japanese, like a lot of the French trapped in Peking during that period, but Akabori appears to have been offering him something—Peking Man."

Vice Director Han mulled this: Takeo Akabori, yes, a minor figure, in charge of handling Peking's foreigners of neutral nationalities, if his memory served him right. But an interest in paleontology? In Peking Man? This he did not recall.

Now the blond man was speaking.

"Dr. Spencer wants to stress the research importance of these fossils," said the female interpreter. "Peking Man was the most coherent group of *Homo erectus* fossils ever found in Asia. If it were somehow recovered it could be used to resolve the most important disagreement in the study of human origins—the debate between the regional evolution theory and the out-of-Africa theory. When the remains were last seen, they included one hundred and fifty-seven teeth. Pieces of forty different individuals. All that is needed is one that is completely intact. By taking tissue from such a tooth plug, the scientists could analyze the creature's DNA structure, and compare it with the DNA of modern Asians and modern Africans. This would be research of worldwide importance."

Worldwide importance? Han thought. *Ke bu shi ma.* If Peking Man were found, international interest would surely return to this once-preeminent *Homo erectus* site. As it was now, the new fossils they'd managed to unearth since 1941 were stuffed here and there, in dusty boxes, around Beijing. Unsorted, unlabeled, low priority. Recovery of Peking Man would change everything. But aloud, he parried, "You know, I have been searching back and forth the technical literature ever since I received Dr. Spencer's letter." He paused and glanced away from them, out the window to the busy boulevard below. "Forgive me. I am ignorant! I do not find any citations from Adam Spencer of the University of Nevada at Reno. No articles, no references, no footnotes . . ."

The interpreter rendered this hesitantly. Vice Director Han observed the man's discomfort when he put a reply to her. Eh, the childlike Americans, was there nothing they could conceal? It was obvious this man, making such careful notes in his *benzi,* was a minor figure from an inconsequential university.

She spoke. "Dr. Spencer does not contribute to the international journals. His work has only appeared in two journals: the *Journal of California and Great Basin Anthropology,* and *American Antiquity.* His specialty is archaic desert cultures. In the last year, though, he has concentrated all his research on the recovery of Peking Man."

Vice Director Han nodded, but thought, preposterous! They would never recover Peking Man. Though what enormous face such a miracle would confer on the nation! The entire world would be reminded that China was not only, of course, the oldest continuous culture on earth but also—quite possibly—man's point of origin. Ah, yes, the honor would be huge. But it would never happen. The bones had been missing too long.

He stroked his chin, staring out the window at the crowds on Xizhimenwai parting for a marching formation of green-clad, lockstep PLA soldiers, the kind of strong-arm show of force that had become so much more frequent in the capital since the Six-Four at Tiananmen Square. The soldiers stamped past and the milling crowd re-formed in their wake, the black-headed human tide of pedestrians and bicyclists that poured always through the streets.

He returned his attention to the room, reminding himself that there was another thing about Peking Man he should consider—that the Europeans had always wanted the fossils for themselves. Were not the museums of London, Paris, and Berlin filled with the treasures of China? A thrill of fear ran through Vice Director Han as he contemplated the chasm that had just split open in front of him. Peking Man was one of the country's great cultural prizes. If these foreigners found it, they might spirit it out. Was that not more or less how things had gone before? Vice Director Han studied the polished surface of his desk and thought back. At the time of Peking Man's disappearance it had been en route to the Museum of Natural History in New York, whence—wasn't it so?—it would almost certainly never have been returned to China.

He allowed a silence to take shape and then drag out until it was vaporous, almost a visible coil in the air between them. The American man perched and craned. With great interest the vice director watched him exhibiting his *waibiao*—his impatience with his pen and notebook, his bluntness, his superior Western certainty that everything would, eventually, be done his way. As if that were the right way to do it.

The vice director could grant the permits, of course, if it seemed expedient. Did it? Should he? The project would fail, certainly. Though there was one facet of this American hypothesis that was irresistible to him—its potential for ruling out the distasteful possibility that the Chinese race might be descended from Africans. It would all be worth it just for that. And if Peking Man *were* by some miracle found, and he prevented the foreigners from stealing it, the face he personally would gain would be endless. Ah, yes. Endless.

Through these thoughts he noted that the foreign woman retained herself implacably. At least she had control, unlike the yellow-haired man. Interesting.

Another possibility: If he allowed the expedition he could send along his father's second cousin, an archaeology professor from Huabei University. Then he could monitor things as closely as he liked.

And there was a final, even more delightful consideration— the Americans had money to spend.

"I will take this matter up with my colleagues," he told her, his Mandarin rich and educated but still trailing the liquid burr of the native *Beijing-ren*. "We will consider each aspect and discuss back and forth."

"Thank you. It's a great trouble." Unconsciously she, too, was now rolling and drawing out her *r*-sounds, unable as always to check this chameleon quality of her Chinese-speaking. She invariably absorbed and replayed the other speaker's accents.

"No trouble," he answered, hearing the local patina of her speech. Impressive. And she still sat cross-legged in a small calm. Where was her husband? Could she be unmarried? Strange. But he had heard enough. "So sorry, I have another appointment. Can you return next week? Maybe Tuesday? We'll discuss this again."

"Ah. Tuesday." She pressed her lips together.

"I will need time to consult others. But in the meantime you should visit the Zhoukoudian site, where Peking Man was found. Tell me the day you choose. I will arrange for you to pass the tourist barriers."

"Ah." Now she smiled. It was obvious she understood this hint of positive inclination. She turned to the American. There was the bubble of English again, then her "Thank you. And regarding the research—Dr. Spencer says he is sure both sides will benefit."

"Both sides benefit," he repeated, and hid a surge of contempt. This was a thin Western fantasy. Pathetic. One side always won. The other lost. Win, that was the thing, and get the others to pay. Oh, yes, he looked at the American man with satisfaction, you'll pay, vehicles and supplies and personnel at four times the rate we get normally, and it's still nothing to you, money drips from your hands like water.

He glanced over at the brief redheaded woman, contained and watchful. And you, he thought, you can talk, but you don't know so much and you are not Chinese. "May I say, Mo Ai-li, how pleasant it is to meet an outsider who really understands China. So many don't. Really. You are an expert."

She looked at him, for an instant, unprotected. First he saw the quick confusion—should she believe he was sincere? Certainly not, he wasn't—and behind that, in a frightened leap like a rabbit, snared quickly and then hushed behind her eyes before her control arose again and locked in around her, he saw her longing. It was only an instant, her eyes flicked away, but he saw it. This woman actually wanted to be Chinese!

"Thank you, Vice Director Han." She folded her freckled hands.

Through his well-crusted, many-lacquered shell, layered on through the childhood of world war, revolution, then the anti-rightist movements, the Great Famine, the Chaos, then finally the death of Mao, the gradual normalcy, through it all he felt a brief scratching flare of compassion for her dislocation. He noted this and pushed it aside. There would always be wildcat foreigners in China, running from their lives. There always had been, ever since the arrival of the first Jesuit missionaries five hundred years before. He had never understood it. But he was a busy man, with no time for reflection.

"Wish you good luck," he said brusquely, and ended the meeting.

After he heard the elevator door open for them, Vice Director Han pressed a small metal button, discreetly positioned on the side of his desk. Instantly his secretary appeared. She wore Western-style jeans, a glossy synthetic blouse, and a bright red false flower in her up-to-date, overpermed hair. "Sir?" She shut the door.

"First, get Commander Gao on the line. PLA, Beijing District Command." Commander Gao was his brother-in-law, but this relationship was not something he would mention to his secretary.

"Commander Gao? Oh. Yes, sir." She scribbled.

"I think we'll have to have these *waiguoren* followed."

She nodded, pen poised.

"Next, contact Professor Kong Zhen at Huabei University. Archaeology Department. Tell him to come up to Beijing in the next few days." Kong Zhen was the vice director's cousin.

"Yes."

"Last." He raised his eyes to meet hers. "Start a file on this interpreter, Mo Ai-li. I want to know her background, who she's worked for, what her habits are. We don't usually put translators under surveillance. But this one"—he stared out the window at the honking, squealing flood of traffic—"there's something strange about her. When you see two faces, beware of three knives. Isn't it so? She hides something beneath her surface. Yes. I'm sure of it."

2

ALICE AND ADAM slid into a vinyl booth in the coffee shop
of the Empire Hotel. They had spent the afternoon walking
around the Forbidden City, now acres of empty, windswept,
magnificent courtyards and silent palace chambers. The Great
Within. Then the two Americans had plunged back through the
massive gates into the congested, overpopulated present, walking
north through the chaotic, shouting shopping district of
Wangfujing. As they walked Alice explained that this had been
the Tartar City, the sector of the Manchus and the place where
the artisans and merchants and bureaucrats who had served the
court had lived and worked. She told how the intersections and
alleyways had often been named for the outdoor markets they'd
housed—here was the place where for centuries decorative lan-
terns were sold for a particular autumn festival, there was the
lane where a hundred years ago one purchased freshly caught
water-insects as feed for prized pet goldfish. Adam Spencer tried
to take all this in, but to him the city was a seething, homoge-
neous labyrinth of people walking, pedaling, driving, buying,
carrying, talking, eating. And if he raised his eyes from the

human herd, then as far as he could see there was nothing but clear white sunlight washing over the graded steppes of gray-tiled roofs.

"But behind those gates," she told him, pointing down one of the *hutong*s into the warren of stone walls, "the courtyard houses are still there. Very quiet. Very sane."

"Sane? Really?" To him, used to working alone in the desert, Beijing was an exhausting crush.

Then they pushed through the hissing doors of the Empire Hotel, and in that instant entered an abruptly different world: a three-story marble lobby with a waterfall and a massive glass-shard chandelier like a small planet hanging in the center. Uniformed staff members walked efficiently back and forth through the barely perceptible hum of air-conditioning.

They turned into the coffee shop, legs aching pleasantly. "A beer?"

"Great."

"Two Tsingtaos," he told the waitress. "This is bizarre," he said, staring at the waterfall. "It could be L.A."

She laughed. "Most of my clients love it here."

"You're kidding." He raised his eyebrows.

"They hate being away from home, hate what's foreign. They prefer to spend as much time as they can pretending they're *not* here."

"Unlike you," he observed.

She smiled.

"So where do you live? Not the Minzu."

"No, I'm based at a smaller guesthouse. It's one of the old ones, a compound, with courtyards. I like it a lot—even though the utilities are, shall we say, unreliable. But I travel. And when I'm working I move to the client's hotel, so I can enjoy the amenities."

"And keep the other place? Nice."

She shrugged. "It works."

He picked up the menu. "I bet you don't eat like this, though."

"Definitely not."

"Neither do I." He snapped the menu shut and gave her a good-natured challenge with his eyes. "During this job, I want you to make sure that every meal we eat is Chinese—absolutely local—the weirder the better. Okay?"

"You're on."

"Good." He opened his notebook and wrote it down, as if it were a contract point and he planned to hold her to it. "Tell me, Alice. What made you decide to learn Chinese?"

"I guess I always wanted to." She closed her eyes. As a child, long before she had known her fate lay in China, when all she'd known was she needed another world to which she could escape, she had made up a private language for her diary. For no one would she translate. This had been her first ticket out. Then she got to Rice University, and found Chinese, and it had been so much better. A door to an alternate self. This self was another Alice, not the childhood Alice: capable, free in the world, independent.

Their bottled beer came, trickling ice-sweat, and each took a long drink. "It's a relief to have a client like you," she admitted.

"Oh?"

"Most of my jobs—selling oilfield equipment. Distributing peanut butter. Bartering intermediate chemicals for finished compounds. Once in a while it's something fun. Last year a company that arranges religious tours to remote monasteries hired me to ride the route ahead of time and make sure all the rural buses were functioning. That wasn't bad. But I don't meet too many outside people over here who are like you, who are"—she searched for the word—"open minded. Most Westerners seem to look right through China. They don't even see what's in front of them." She shrugged, drinking her beer, and he grinned at her. She liked his grin. He was smart, he had a nice human quality despite his oddities. For one thing, he appeared to wear a clean version of the same outfit every day: jeans and a blue chambray shirt. He must have three, four, five sets of the same thing, she thought. Strange. Still, we could be friends. I need friends. I hardly know any outside people in Beijing these days.

Alice had once had a lot of expat friends, but they were all either gone, or married, or had children; nobody's life now matched hers. And they clung so to their Westernness, their imported newspapers, their Sunday touch-football games in the diplomatic compound, weekly trips to McDonald's. Alice had drifted away. She spent most of her time with Chinese now, trying to fit in.

"What about you," she said. "You have a family?"

"I'm divorced." He swallowed. It still sounded strange. Divorce was a dark bridge behind him, a bad dream, something he'd never expected. Though he should have expected it. He'd waited so long to get married—until he was almost forty—and then he'd chosen too quickly. Ellen was fifteen years younger and not really ready to settle. There was always something partial and half committed between them. But two years into their marriage she had given birth to Tyler and then, finally, Spencer had known what real love was. With Tyler there was nothing he would not give, no sand-and-grit playground on which he would not push a swing for hours, no Saturday cartoon he would not sit through. Ellen complained that he spoiled the child. Maybe he did. But he gave love, and got it back, in a form so unconditional that he could not even bear to go away—to a dig in the desert, say—without a worn piece of baby clothing that carried Tyler's smell. This was a rapture he'd never known with any other person.

And then Ellen had met another man and left him, moving back to northern California, taking the boy with her.

"I'm sorry," Alice said.

"Thanks." He drank. "I have a son, though: Tyler. Want to

see?" He dug out his current school picture, third grade, a tow-headed boy with a serious, freckle-faced gaze.

"Cute," she said. "Do you share custody?"

"I get half of each summer and school vacations."

"Oh." She nodded sympathetically, hearing the pain in his voice. "That's tough."

"Yeah." He looked at the picture for what seemed like a long time before putting it away. "You? You have kids?"

"Me? Oh, no." She picked at the label on her beer. Children were way down on the list of things she figured the universe was ever going to allow her to have. Like love. Start with love. "I'm not even married," she said.

"Oh," he answered, as if he didn't know, but of course he knew already, for he had seen her riding her bicycle back to the hotel in a short black dress, had seen her walk into the building at dawn, tugging her hem down over her thighs. Then at break-fast it was obvious. He had not written it in his book, it was a private observation, but he'd seen: she was single. Very. He'd been drawn to women like her when he was much younger, when excitement was the thing he wanted. When he had not yet learned to assess how twisted up a girl was inside. Not anymore. Not now. If it ever happened for him again it would be with a woman who could be trusted. But not now, not soon. All he wanted now was his son. And to get his career back on track. Peking Man.

Yet this interpreter was interesting. Likable—as long as he didn't get too close. "By the way, Alice. I brought you a book." He removed *The Phenomenon of Man* from his day pack and pushed it across the table. "Father Teilhard's best seller. Thought you might want to reread it."

"Hey. Thanks." She flipped through it, remembering the pic-ture of an expanding universe, the sense of Christian revelation, the coherent, unified vision of human growth. Whereas her own evolution had been stalled forever. "Are you interested in Teilhard's philosophy, then?"

"No. I find it a little hard to read. I'm interested in his life here in China—who he knew, where he went. Because somewhere here, he hid Peking Man."

She closed the book. "So tell me about his life, then. Here in Peking. He lived here on and off for . . ."

"Twenty-three years. Nineteen twenty-two to 1945. He went back to Europe and America a few times, but this is where he lived."

"He had a lot of friends?"

"Everybody knew him. The foreigners' community was a small one. And he was an explorer, a scientist—a real man of the world. Women found him fascinating. One woman in particular. Lucile Swan."

"Who was she?"

"An American in her thirties, a sculptor. She had come to Peking from New York after a bad divorce, and stayed on. Peking was a fantasy world then. Foreigners could have anything, live any way they wanted, cheaply. I think all she wanted to do was sculpt, and find a man to love. Couldn't have been easy for her in China."

"I think she sounds interesting."

"You do?" He drank from his bottle, and thought: Of course you do, she's right up your alley.

"Did she ever fall in love?"

"Yes—with Teilhard. Unfortunately, he was a priest. That kind of limited things." Spencer smiled.

"Did they . . ."

"Doubtful. I don't think so. I think they were so emotionally enmeshed it didn't matter. I haven't researched her too much— I'm pretty sure she had nothing to do with where he hid Peking Man. But if you're interested, you can read their correspondence. It was recently published, all twenty-three years of it."

"I think I'll start with this one." She glanced at the volume in her hand, Teilhard's masterpiece of theology. "Thank you, Dr. Spencer."

"Don't call me that."

"What, then?"

"I don't know—Adam? Spencer? But no 'Doctor.'"

"Okay." She liked the detached, friendly way he talked. He didn't seem interested in her as a woman any more than she was interested in him as a man. Which was not at all. Western men didn't get to her.

"You ready?" he said.

As they crossed the gleaming floor of the lobby he tapped her elbow. She took in the row of girls flaunting brief skirts and pouty, red-painted lips. They were giggling and whispering. One of them got up and intercepted a foreign man in a business suit, said something to him, and smiled prettily.

"Is that what I think it is?"

"Sure."

"What? You mean they're—"

"Hookers," Alice supplied.

"In China?" He was incredulous.

"Of course. Prostitution did disappear for a few decades, obviously, but now—now that we have the *kai fang,* the open door, it's back." She made her voice mischievous. "Commerce is booming everywhere in the Middle Kingdom, Adam. In all forms."

"But who's"—he looked around—"are they just independents, coming in here?"

"You mean who's running their business? The PLA."

"What!" Now his voice was a minor screech.

"That's right, the PLA." She was enjoying his reaction. "The Army owns this hotel. They control the girls and, of course, the profits. Or so everyone says."

"The Army? I can't believe it."

"The Army is business," she told him, suddenly sober. "*Very* serious business. Remember that. You don't ever want to cross them. Don't be fooled by all these big glitzy hotels. Regardless of all the new stuff you see around you—all the Big Macs and the Italian shoes and the Seiko watches—the Army's power in this country is still absolute."

She left Spencer at their hotel and stepped into a taxi. "Where go?" the driver bawled in bad English.

"Am I a miserable white ghost from the western sea, ignorant of civilized speech?" she asked sharply. "The American Express office, quickly. And don't take Changan. The traffic's a dammed-up river which threatens to overflow its banks."

"The honored foreigner speaks." He pulled out from the curb. "Ten thousand pardons."

"None needed," she murmured, knowing she had been short with him, feeling her stomach knot up as it always did when she went to check for mail and faxes from her father. She had to go, she hadn't gone in too long. Plus, this time of the month, he usually sent her money. She closed her eyes, hating herself for wanting the money and relying on it; at the same time so glad it was coming.

The driver swung onto Ximen and crawled north through the traffic. He leaned on his horn and swore constantly at the swarm of cars and bicycles in front of him. "Sons of turtles!"

"Too many cars." God, she thought, fourteen years ago there was barely a car on the street here. Just bicycles. And I was a wide-eyed graduate student, freshly arrived, ecstatic to have escaped America and finally be smack in the middle of the oldest, most complex, most intricately structured society on earth. Safely walled in by what was different. By the labyrinth. She leaned her head back on the overstuffed, antimacassared seat and watched the bustling free-market stalls, the parade of offices and restaurants and shops, the lit-up character signs more discreet than the visual cacophony of Hong Kong and Taipei, but still so earthily and ineluctably Chinese. The pyramids of cabbages stacked on the stone sidewalks. The post-Soviet dinginess of the low block buildings. The fetid smell of rotting garbage and untreated sewage. The remarkable light, crystalline white when the air pollution cleared, which always seemed to Alice at its most beautiful in the *hutong*s, where it bathed the traditional gray courtyard houses in its distinctive weightless glow.

"Wait for me," she told the driver when he ground to a halt. She dashed inside.

The American Express office was empty. Young Wu looked up from behind the counter and broke into a smile.

"Eh, Mo Ai-li, truly it's a long time we haven't met," he said, even though she'd come in only a few weeks ago. "You're well?"

"Not bad." She smiled back. "Any mail?"

"Oh, yes. I always keep it for you, special."

"Sure you do."

"Eh! Aren't we 'old friends'?"

She laughed. "Of course," she lied. She had been picking up mail from Young Wu for almost two years, but the catchphrase *old friend* meant more, so much more, and they both knew it: permanent loyalty, mutual obligation, the promise to deliver on almost any favor when asked. And to weigh carefully before asking.

"Anyway . . ." He grinned. He reached under the counter and brought out a thin sheaf of faxes and letters.

She paged through the faxes. Most were from the U.S.-China Chamber of Commerce, relaying inquiries about her services from prospective clients. These she put aside for later. Two letters. One was addressed to Bruce Kaplan care of Alice Mannegan, from his mother. Bruce was one of Alice's few local foreigner friends: a bookish, reclusive American who had lived in

Beijing for years. His mother knew he never went to collect his own mail, so she occasionally sent him letters, like this one, through Alice. She tucked the envelope in her purse.

Then, on the bottom, the letter from Horace. His precise handwriting.

"Mind if I sit down a moment?" she asked Wu.

"Take your ease." Wu pointed to a generic waiting-room couch along the far wall.

She tore the envelope open. Immediately the check tumbled out, $1,000 U.S., not enough really to live on but, in combination with what she earned, a cushion that kept her always comfortable. Even if she was an outside person and had to pay more for everything. She folded the check and put it in her wallet, her heart banging with relief and shame. Another month set, walled in, and she could go on pretending that this freelance life she had carved out actually made her financially secure—when in truth without her father's help she'd be, sometimes, downright scraping.

She unfolded the letter. It was brief. The usual. His life in Washington, gearing up for the election next year. He always got reelected. As usual, no reference to the money. He never mentioned enclosing it and she never acknowledged receiving it. Finally, at the end, something new:

I wish you'd put some thought into coming back. I think about it now because we're coming up on the anniversary of her passing again. Will you think about it, Alice?

Her passing. Alice's mother had died when she was a baby, too young for Alice to remember. It was a source of loss for Horace still, after all these years, but to Alice just an empty place. She thought she should feel more for it than she actually felt. Naturally her life would have been different if she'd had a mother—

but there was no use thinking about it. She folded her father's letter back into the envelope.

"Are you by any chance free now, Mo Ai-li?" Young Wu inquired from across the room. "I am closing in ten minutes and wondered if you would care to go and drink coffee with my lowly self."

"Oh." She looked up. "Oh, thanks, Young Wu, but no. I have to go back and meet my client."

"Another time," he said smoothly, concealing his disappointment. He had asked her before, always in a casual way, to go out with him and she had always refused. Interpreter Mo Ai-li was appealingly *piaoliang* for a foreigner: small, intelligent looking, with a face that was pretty in a neat, trim sort of way. It was also said of her that she liked Chinese *yang*. He had always wanted to learn for himself whether it was true or not. Even if she was a few years older.

"*Zai jian, zai jian,*" she said absently, stuffing the papers into her handbag. She rose and pushed through the revolving door.

"*Zai jian,*" he answered, watching her go, watching her carry her body with frank, hip-rolling confidence the way a Chinese woman never would. She climbed back in the taxi and it roared away.

Wu put all his supplies in order and checked the fax machine to make sure it had a fat roll of paper and was set to receive overnight. He glanced at the clock. Four fifty-five. Well. He might as well lock up. He was just removing the key from the drawer when the door hissed and a bespectacled, pinch-chested Chinese man strode in. The man took out a name card and slid it across the counter.

Wu didn't look at it. "I'm closing," he said, still arranging things in the drawer.

"Wu Litang," the man said.

Young Wu looked up sharply. Somehow this man knew his

real name, not his work name, not his school name, but the name his parents had given him at birth before his ancestors.

"Did you recognize the foreign ghost woman who was just in here?"

"No," Wu said automatically, and then glanced at the man's card. Ice stabbed through him, not at the name—which was unimportant and undoubtedly false—but at the *danwei:* PLA, Beijing District Command.

"You've never seen her before?"

"She could have come in before," Wu evaded. "I'm not too clear. The foreigners who come in here are numerous."

"Well, Wu Litang." The man placed a delicate emphasis on his true and private given name. "Listen well. The next time she receives mail, or faxes, you are to call me at this number at once. I'll examine them before she picks them up. And any mail for a certain other American person, an archaeologist." He leaned over and wrote out the American names on his card. "Is it clear?"

"Yes," Wu said, hating him for knowing his name and using it so rudely, hating him because he was PLA and the Six-Four at Tiananmen was so unforgivable.

"Remember," the man ordered, and walked out.

Discourteous bag of flatulence, Wu thought. As soon as he saw the man step into a waiting car and slam the door, he picked up the card and crumpled it into the wastebasket.

He would certainly inform Interpreter Mo of this the next time he saw her. Though, of course, there was no telling when that would be. Foreign clocks and calendars running as they did, differently. Inexplicably.

"This used to be called Morrison Street." Alice pointed down congested Wangfujing Boulevard. She opened her antique guidebook to the city, published sixty years before. "Something to do with a British newspaperman who lived here a hundred years ago. Now. According to the headings on Teilhard's letters, the Jesuit House was off Morrison in Tizi Hutong. Ladder Lane." She leafed through to the index. "Ah, here. In the upper part of what used to be the Tartar City. This way."

They shouldered north through the throng. Spencer felt tired and still a little jet-lagged; it seemed that an ocean of Mandarin sucked at him in waves. But he noticed that Alice strode calmly, at home in it. She jostled easily through the surging flood of people. She ignored the vendors promoting their sweet potatoes, steamed buns, tea, and Popsicles. She stepped around the drifts of garbage on the sidewalk. Barely glanced into the shop windows teeming with cloth, clocks, cooking pots, shoes, canes, clothing, and everything in between.

And then she stopped at a dusty storefront. "I can't believe it," she said. "Look." She took out her old guidebook. "*Chang-er Bing Jia,* Chang-er's Cake House. Chang-er's the girl in the moon, you see, or so say the Chinese." She leafed through the guidebook. "It's still here! See? 'In business continuously since the late Ming, an acclaimed purveyor of mooncake molds.' People here make mooncakes every year for the Moon Festival." She pushed past him and went inside.

He followed her. A tiny room, a low ceiling, every surface covered with the hand-chiseled wooden molds, each cut and carved to produce a scallop-edged cake the size of a hockey puck, imprinted in intricate relief with beasts and flowers and lucky characters.

"*You shi ma?*" said a young girl who had been sitting in the shadows by the counter.

"*Mei you,*" Alice answered automatically. She was moving slowly around the room, squinting, examining the molds.

"You like old stuff, don't you?" Adam asked her.

"I love it. Look at this one!" She touched one with a carving of a fairy in fluttering robes.

"Why don't you buy one?" He took a mold off the wall and studied it. "They're beautiful."

"Oh, no." She looked startled. "I never let myself buy things. I can't carry stuff like this around."

"It's a trade-off. If it expresses your inner . . ."

But she was already nodding to the girl, pushing wide the bell-jangling door, heading back out to the sidewalk. "Just a little break." She unfolded her map and scrutinized the grid packed with tiny characters.

He waited, thinking how odd she was, absorbing the shade and the comforting, cooling rustle of an acacia tree growing up from the sidewalk, until she put the map away and started walking again. Then Spencer registered something peripherally: a man who'd been leaning against a building some paces back straightened at the same moment and began walking, after them, dodging easily through the moving crowd, keeping a calibrated distance.

"I know it sounds insane," he told her. "But you know what? I think someone's following us."

She looked sharply up at him from the corner of her eye.

"Is this possible?" he asked.

She quickened her pace. "Of course it's possible. Just keep walking."

"Has it happened to you before?"

She shook her head. "It's usually diplomats and journalists they trail, not people like me. I almost always work for businessmen, and business they leave alone. But Adam? Follow me."

She stepped abruptly to the side, turned, and walked briskly through an open courtyard packed with stalls and food vendors and walking, standing, eating, shouting Chinese. He scrambled after. She feinted to the left, threaded through a momentary gap in the crush of people, slipped through a door in a stone wall, and led him through an indoor dining room. It was walled in white tile, with a black-and-white tile floor, loaded with tables, all full. "There," she said, and pointed to a half-lit corridor off the clanging kitchens.

They slipped into the little hall, sank into the shadows, and watched the door. Workers in blue coats and tight-fitted white caps bumped past them, trays high, steam billowing, their guttural Pekingese bouncing on the narrow walls. Just a few beats, and then there he was, the man, moving against the crowd outside the restaurant door. His eyes searched the crush of people. He glanced into the restaurant, hesitated, then slipped on, out of sight.

"Nice work, Bond." She winked at Spencer, stepped back into the light. "Come on, let's cut over and go up Dongsi Beidajie. He'll come back to Wangfujing to look for us. But we won't be there."

"You seem pretty good at this. People follow you a lot?"

She grinned. "Once or twice over the years. But writers get followed all the time—anybody associated with a paper or a news service, forget it. Somebody's always on them, listening to their phone, opening their mail. It's just standard paranoid PRC procedure. So there's kind of a running competition among journalists living in Beijing. You know—what you did yesterday to elude your tail."

"But this is just archaeology."

Her smile faded. "Right. Obviously something about what you're doing scares them. What, I don't know."

"Is it possible that they could, what, arrest us? I know that sounds crazy—"

"Not so crazy. In the fifties and sixties, even early seventies, some of the Westerners who'd stayed around after the revolution *were* arrested. There were Americans and Europeans who languished in prison for years. But nowadays it's the *kai fang*, the open door. You do something bad, they just deport you. And they don't let you come back."

"That would ruin my project!"

"Your project—what about my life? It would ruin everything for me! I live here, don't forget. But you have to break some serious laws for that to happen. And we're not planning to break any laws. Are we?" She looked hard at him. "Are we, Dr. Spencer?"

"No! No, of course not. And don't call me that."

"So long as you promise. I like you, I like your project. But I'm not getting deported for you."

He straightened and solemnly held up his right hand. "Very well. I, Adam Spencer, swear—"

"Okay, okay." She let her mouth curve up again. "Enough."

They moved over to Dongsi Beidajie, walked on, and found the Jesuit House up a terraced set of broad, shallow steps, cobbles overgrown with tufted grass. Formerly Ladder Lane. Now—Alice checked the book, and then her map: there, People's Northeast Small Lane Eight. She smiled. A lucky number in Chinese. Eight, *ba*. It sounded like *fa*, which meant "to get rich." Enormous good luck to get an address with an eight in it. "Look," she said, and stopped by a wall with a round gate, "the house is still here."

Through a crack in the gate they could see a stone courtyard with rooms opening onto it, peonies and locust trees in ceramic urns, bright cloth fluttering behind open windows, a single bicycle leaning. A breeze ruffled their hair and the tendril leaves of the trees above their heads, a soft wind, the longed-for kiss of the Beijing summer.

She knocked.

They stood in silence a minute. No one came out. Nothing but the moon gate of thick, ancient red wood, the stone walls, the eaves with their swooping Chinese tiles.

"This was the Jesuit residence?" she asked.

"Yes," he said while he wrote. "I've researched his life here. You wanna know? Okay. He got up every day; they said mass. He went to work at the Peking Union Medical College, where the China Geological Survey was housed—that's because both the college and the survey were run on Rockefeller money. At five o'clock every day he left the survey and went to Lucile's house. They talked, and dined, and spent the evening together."

Alice peeked through the closed gate. "You know where she lived?"

"No. In his letters to her he refers to her place as *Da Tian Shui Qing,* but I don't know if that's the name of the street or just what he called her house."

"Without seeing the characters I can't be sure, but it sounds like it might mean 'Great Heaven and Clear Water'—probably an old *hutong* name." She searched through her guidebook's index, frowned. "No. Not in here. So—they spent the evenings together?"

"Right. Talking, studying, reading. Weekends, they would go with other foreigners on excursions. Picnics in the Western Hills. Visits to temples. To the seaside."

"Then she was always with him." Alice's eyes softened.

"Yes." He was staring through the hole at the inside of the compound. "She was his muse. She listened to his ideas, retyped his manuscripts, translated things from French to English and back again."

"But weren't most of his books published much later?"

"True." He grinned, pleased with her intelligence. "The Jesuits didn't permit him to publish much during his lifetime—essays mostly—almost all his books came out after his death. Think how he felt."

"God, you're right. Like a failure."

"But at least he had her."

"And she accepted him."

"Right, she stuck by him. Even though she never got the thing she always wanted from him," Spencer added.

Of course, Alice thought, but she didn't say it: the total commitment of his heart, his mind, his body. Pierre could love

Lucile, could care about her and be close to her—as long as he never became her lover. Whereas she, Alice, entered the sexual heart of China all the time—but only the sexual heart. Which way mattered more?

She looked hard into the courtyard, into the rooms which boxed around it, each presenting a wall which was half windows. Small panes, old-fashioned wood trim. In one of those rooms he wrote *The Phenomenon of Man*. Connected the scientific and the divine.

She had reread the book late the night before. *Love alone is capable of uniting living beings in such a way as to complete and fulfil them, for it alone takes them and joins them by what is deepest in themselves. This is a fact of daily experience.* Your daily experience, Pierre, she thought, gazing into his house. Did you really love her? Did you enter her heart and mind? Or did the two of you always remain outside each other? She pounded on the gate again.

"Come on," Spencer sighed. "Nobody's here. Let's go."

Alice took the steaming teacup and extended it to Mrs. Meng with two hands, the old way. The aged lady's face creased with pleasure. She liked the old customs.

"Eh, Six Tranquillities Black! Where did you find it?"

"Hong Kong." Alice poured her own cup. "It's nothing, a trifle, but I know how you like it." She glanced at the large brick of tea wrapped in a torn page of the *South China Morning Post* which she had placed on Meng Shaowen's table. Another forgotten grace of old Peking, the constant affectionate gift-giving.

"It is I who should serve you, when you come to my home," the old lady protested happily. The room was dark, the slatted shutters closed against the July heat. Long shadows fell over all Meng Shaowen's accumulated treasures: the Qing dynasty em-

broideries in their dusty frames, the bed quilt which had come
from Meng's own mother, the luminous sparrow carved from
white jade, the photos of her son, Jian; and, on Meng's desk, the
ornate old European-style clock, ticking off the days and months
and years of life that still remained. Mrs. Meng shivered. Despite
the summer heat she pulled her sweater closer.

"You, serve me? No, Mother Meng. And haven't we known
each other too many years to talk polite?" Alice smiled at the old
lady, who was always the first person she called upon returning
from any trip, always the first person she went to visit. Yet at the
same moment Alice noticed how old Mrs. Meng suddenly
seemed. Was it last winter, or the winter before, that Meng
Shaowen's hair had gone so white and her fingers had twisted
into the tangled briars of arthritis? Or was it back when her
husband died? Was it then that Mrs. Meng's eyes, once snapping
sharp through long nights of debate over the Chinese classics of
literature and philosophy, had begun to rheum over?

The Chinese lady doubled forward in a raking cough. "Forgive me, girl child. Though it's the time of heat there's cold in
my lungs."

"Nothing to forgive."

Mrs. Meng reached out and brushed a stray hair from Alice's
forehead.

Alice clasped the old woman's hand.

"It's my sorrow, I never had a daughter."

The words hung. But you had a son, Alice thought. Jian. And
I almost married him. And if I had I'd be your daughter now.

"They have a daughter," Mrs. Meng said. "Jian and his wife."

"Yes. I know."

"Little Lihua! She's my heart and liver!" The old woman's
face wrinkled up in fondness. Then went serious. "Of course,
girl child, Jian's wife is not like you! She is Chinese. She is not
free with her mind like you foreigners. Jian once said he never

41

knew any other woman like you. He said he could talk to you about anything."

Alice knew this was probably true. Most Chinese were educated through rigorous rote training. To even read books one had to memorize four, five thousand characters. So to a Chinese intellectual, more used to deduction than questioning, rarely presented in conversation with the unexpected, a Western woman—a smart, open-minded, sassy woman—was a marvelous companion. But only a companion. There seemed to be in the Chinese men she had known, even in Jian, the only one she had actually loved, the same hesitation she had to admit she felt within herself. They were exhilarating companions. Fantastically exciting as companions. But marriage?

"Perhaps this road is better," Mrs. Meng said gently. "It would have been hard for you and Jian. You can never be Chinese."

"Of course not," she said instantly. Yet Alice had begun to feel, during the year she was with Jian, that she had a place she belonged in the Meng family. A clan, a mother. A Chinese mother who taught her all the old techniques she herself had used to keep house during the decades of privation: how to maximize the things that were rationed and stave off hunger by using the *hou men,* the back door, to obtain more. Wash clothes in a bucket. Cook with a handful of coal. Buy slowly, cautiously, use the windowsill as your refrigerator in the winter.

Mrs. Meng had recited the history of the Meng family, told the names of all the ancestral souls who now dwelt beyond the Yellow Springs. Alice would always listen closely, Jian beside her, bored. Like so many modern young intellectuals he was impatient with feudal superstitions. Though he, an astute student of history, at least respected the past.

Jian. The bright, narrow black eyes, the expressive hands. Now a professor at *Bei Da,* Beijing University. Jian, loving her in his narrow bed in his small room, whispering to her in his musical, beautifully modulated Mandarin, of her body, its strange-feeling skin, the exotic way she walked and talked, and of his studies: the majestic tide of Chinese civilization, revolutions, upheavals, the march of legends and dynasties. Then the Khans and the Ming and the Qing and the Republicans and then the Warlords and finally, as if in a last gasp of *Luanshi*, Chaos, before the Communists nailed things down strangling tight, the rampaging Japanese. He had taught her that China's power lay in its endurance, its *shoudeliao*.

Jian. So open minded about some things. He knew he was not her first man but he never asked her to explain. Then, after a year he asked her, awkward and limpid at once, if she would come with him to his superiors at the *danwei* and "talk about love." Marriage! She said she needed to think about it. She knew instantly, sinkingly, that Horace would ruin it. He would wage some kind of war that would force her and Jian apart. And that was exactly what happened.

And since then no man seemed to be what she wanted.

"Yes," she said haltingly to Mother Meng now, "I often think back and forth on it. If not for Horace, Jian and I would have married."

"It's a bad road for you. Your *baba* forbade you." Meng used the familiar, intimate word for *father* even though Alice always referred to her father only by his first name. "And the blood and the flesh can never be untied. Isn't it so? But, girl child"—Meng lowered her voice—"listen to me. How old are you now?"

"Thirty-six."

Mrs. Meng shook her head. "Eh. Too pitiable! How can one tell how old a foreigner is? So you can no longer bear children."

"But in America, Mother, lots of women—"

"Ai-li." Meng drew her closer. "Children are for young women with strong bodies and innocent hearts. As you get older you eat too much bitterness. There's a legend, you know. It's like this. When you die you approach the Yellow Springs. Old Woman Wang waits for you there with the wine of forgetfulness. You drink this wine, you forget the life you've just finished. You are pure for the next life. You are yourself. And while you're still young this self is true—because all the memories, the pain, the burdens, have not started to come back to you yet."

"What do you mean, come back to you? Doesn't the wine erase everything?"

"By the last dynasty, people were burying the dead with cups that had holes in them." A smile touched at Mrs. Meng's thin, corrugated mouth. "Old Woman Wang didn't mind if you brought your own cup."

Alice laughed.

"At the time of your death you can choose, do you understand me or not? Leave it behind, or carry it forward."

Alice nodded.

"Don't carry it forward. Ai-li. Listen to your old mother. Find a man. You mustn't live without the *yang*. It crosses the rule of nature."

Alice nodded. She'd heard this before. As if I can just do it, she thought. Just pluck a rare, intelligent man, with kindness and room in his heart, out of the air. I wait. I look. And in the meantime, do I live without the *yang*? No. I allow myself to have a little.

"A strong man," Mrs. Meng was advising. "Maybe a Chinese man. You are older now."

Alice moved into the old woman's embrace, rested her head on the narrow chest. She felt the frail arms go around her. How could she have survived without the old lady's love? "I'll try. I fear I won't succeed."

"*Narde hua,*" Nonsense. Mrs. Meng touched Alice's cheek. "But don't let too many more seasons pass," she whispered into the red hair.

* * *

Alice laid her things out ceremoniously on the desk in her hotel room. Her "four treasures": brush, ink, inkstone, and paper. Today for paper she had a small piece of *xuanzhi*, the expensive handmade sheets one could still buy in certain shops here in the capital. She dripped a little water into the inkstone and rubbed the ink stick in the puddle until she had the right viscosity. In this she twirled the brush.

She looked at the exquisite, rough-textured rice paper. On paper such as this one should write poetry. Living, moving ideograms, their various meanings touching infinite shades of possibility.

Instead Alice found herself drawing the name *Yulian* with the brush—the name she had been using lately at night. First the radical for the moon, then the ear radical which brought in the notion of happiness through the senses and made it into *yu*, fragrant. Then *lian*, lotus, with the flower radical on top and combining below the sound, *lian*, with the symbol for cart or car, originally connoting the name of a related flower in Chinese. Lotus. Fragrant Lotus.

She looked at it, blinking.

She'd used other names in the past. *Yinfei, Yuhuan*. None of them her real name.

None of this her true self. She folded the edge of the paper over so the two characters, *Yulian*, were covered. Out of sight.

She took a long, cleansing breath and began again.

"Aiya, tian luo di wang!" Professor Kong Zhen grumbled as he picked up the hand of cards that just been dealt onto the table,

fanned them out, and studied them. You've filled heaven with nets and all the earth with snares.

"*I'm* the one whose luck is odious," Vice Director Han complained, keeping just enough bile in his voice to mask the glee that bubbled up in him when he saw the winning cards he now held. "You're one hundred and eighty ahead at the moment, cousin."

"And in one turn of the head it's gone." Kong Zhen sighed, laying down his cards, knowing he would lose the pile of well-worn bills in front of him, knowing, too, that he was capable of playing far more cleverly, and winning—certainly he could win if he wanted to—but the vice director was his elder-born relative and, more important, a high official in the IVPP, the Institute. Although the IVPP had no say over his own *danwei*, Huabei University, it controlled all the research money for archaeology as well as most excavation permits. And Vice Director Han was a powerful man in the IVPP. It would not do to win against him. "Aiya, cousin," he said, pretending bitterness, "I wanted that one-eighty."

"So did I," the vice director said happily, and pocketed it. "More tea?" He poured.

"Yes. It's excellent." Kong Zhen settled back in his chair. He was a lizard-shaped man with a fondness for shiny, tightly belted Western slacks and all the accoutrements of the *kai fang:* portable phones, beepers, computers, faxes, knockoffs of foreign suits, and clean, lustrous white running shoes. He loved these things almost as much as he loved the archaeology of the Late Paleolithic—but not quite.

He savored the lichee tea now, the hot Beijing night, the comfortable antique furniture and paintings in the vice director's study. He knew that the vice director had invited him to the capital so they could discuss his joining an American archaeological expedition, but he did not yet know why. What was so special about this particular expedition that it had to be monitored—and by a relative of the vice director, no less? But he did not ask. The Chinese approach was to talk, to socialize, to play cards, to cement the sense of a relationship, before undertaking anything. This took time. And who of consequence did not have time? Kong Zhen sipped his tea, content with the dinner and the round of cards. Elder cousin would say what had to be said in due time.

"Younger born," said the vice director at length. "There's this delicate matter of the expedition I have asked you to accompany."

"Yes," his cousin answered, face calm, senses alert.

"My colleagues and I may grant permits for the foreigners, but they will have to travel across military installations. And there are also"—he paused—"reform camps in the area."

Kong Zhen raised an eyebrow.

"Yes, I know. It's most unusual to let foreigners in. But what they seek is unusual as well."

"And what is that?" asked Kong Zhen.

"Peking Man." The vice director cleared his throat, drank from his cup. "They believe they can recover Peking Man."

Professor Kong let out a snort of surprise.

"It's so." The vice director smiled.

"But—in the Northwest?"

"They have evidence that the French priest got it back from the Japanese and hid it out there. Younger cousin. I need you to go with them. And I need you to select a colleague from your department to go too—a *Homo erectus* specialist. I know that's not been your concentration."

"I know a good man," Kong Zhen said, thinking of one of his fellow professors, the thoughtful Lin Shiyang.

"Do you? Then arrange it. And bring him back with you to Beijing in the next few days. We'll discuss all the facets of this thing."

"Of course," Kong Zhen answered.

"Cousin. Let me put the eye on the dragon. Why do I need you there, watching every step they take? Eh?"

Kong Zhen raised his eyes to meet the other's and waited. He knew the vice director wished to answer his own question.

"To stop them smuggling Peking Man out to America."

Kong gasped. "You believe they would?"

"Merely consider history! Where were the fossils when they were last seen in 1941?"

Professor Kong hesitated. "The war—the Americans were preparing to ship them to New York—"

"Just so," said the vice director. "The way of things is as clear as water. But please, *ni renwei zenmoyang*. Do you think it possible? Have they any chance of finding Peking Man again?"

A sad, indulgent smile flitted over Kong Zhen's face. He shook his head slowly. "Find Peking Man? After so many years? Oh, no. I'm sorry to say it's impossible. It would be like searching for a stone which has dropped into the ocean."

The village of Zhoukoudian nestled in a leaf-shaded bowl in the southwestern suburbs of the capital. Alice wanted to stop and get something to drink before continuing on to the Peking Man site. It was still and humid, with a hot, high-summer noon silence lying over the valley. She was thirsty.

"In the Northwest it's desert." Adam squashed his face into a concerned frown. "You'll have to carry a water bottle out there."

"Okay. I'll buy one. I just hate to carry extra stuff."

"But you must." He drew his shoulders up to his ears to emphasize. "Got to carry water. You're much too valuable to what I have to do for us to take any chances."

Alice smiled. So unconscious, so open about the fact that to him she was only a project asset, no more. At least he wasn't like her other male clients, who usually started signaling, after a while, that they were attracted to her. Not to her, exactly, for they hardly knew her. No, her businessmen clients were excited by her because they were in a foreign country, and she was the only person they could talk to, and there was a certain magic in that. A kind of casting off and floating free. But this soft-faced late-forties American scientist was not going to put her through that. She could already tell.

The driver stopped alongside a low one-room mud-walled hut with a window full of food and cigarettes, drinks, matches, and dubbed Hong Kong videos. Spencer lumbered out and followed her in, ducking his head. "You are valuable to this expedition," he repeated, eyes widening at the tight walls packed to the ceiling with boxes and coolers and racks.

"I'm glad you think so," she said. "Speaking of which—I'd appreciate it if you could pay me the first installment of my fee before we leave Beijing. My bank is here, you see. Can you do that?"

"Yes." He hesitated and his face clouded. Reflexively he reached for his notebook, opened it as if to write. "I think I can," he said, without writing.

She straightened up from the cooler she'd been scanning and looked at him steadily. "What do you mean, you think you can?"

"Just that I don't have the funds in hand yet—not today, I mean. But the money ought to come through before we're ready to leave Beijing. No problem. That's going to be a few more days anyway, isn't it?"

"Of course—we have to get permits. . . ."

"Right."

"So you mean you have someone in the States wiring you money or something?" Alice stopped and turned to the tiny, weather-beaten old woman in black clothes who had padded out from the back room and was standing expectantly by the counter. She smiled politely and fell into clear, unaccented Mandarin.

"Elder sister, greetings. Forgive me. Trouble you to wait a moment."

The gray-headed woman nodded, little oblongs of jade gleaming in her ears.

Alice turned back to Spencer. "So you're expecting a wire? Is that it?"

"No." He clutched his book. "Actually I'm still waiting to hear. I applied for a National Science Foundation grant for this project. I haven't heard. I should have heard by now. But I haven't."

She swallowed. "You came over here and hired me without funds?"

"No—no, well, not exactly. This grant is a sure thing, Alice. Peking Man is very, very big in the world of archaeology. Very important. The NSF Board met last week. Just hang on a few more days. So what are these in here—Cokes? I can't believe it." He pulled one out and a puff of frosty smoke came with it. He peered at the bottle. "Canned in Singapore. You want one?"

"Yes," she said, distracted. "And get one for the driver too. Are you sure about this, Dr. Spencer?"

"Of course. And I told you not to call me that." He dug some renminbi out of his pocket and handed a few bills to the old lady. "Jesus," he whispered. "Look at her feet."

"They're bound," Alice answered in English.

"My God." To him the little feet seemed hardly more than stumps, just three or four inches long, wrapped in black cloth shoes. Revulsion brought his abdomen shrinking back against his spine. "What did they have to do to turn her foot into that?"

"A lot. Though I personally find it fascinating." She bent to the old lady, who was counting out Spencer's change. *"Xie xie."*

"And look." Spencer's eyes flitted over the tiny cement cubicle behind the counter, with bed and washstand. "She must live back there."

"Of course."

"Doesn't it bother you?" He was ducking back out through the door after her. "I mean seeing this kind of life?"

"No. Why should it?" She turned her clear eyes on him, thinking how simple he was. "But it would bother me if you couldn't pay me."

"Don't worry." He popped open his can and took a long drink. "I can pay you."

They parked at the mouth of the canyon in the parking lot and gave their names to the single attendant, who confirmed that they could go past the fence and enter the cave. Using a series of metal rungs secured into the rock they climbed fifty feet or so up the canyon wall to the cut-out cave where Peking Man had been found. Below them, on the floor of the neglected gorge, disjointed Chinese tourists stepped over candy wrappers and cigarette butts, and gaped at the foreigners scaling the cliff above their heads.

"That was some climb," she said, damp with sweat, huddling in the cave mouth and peering back down the rungs they'd come up. "But the view . . ." She paused, drinking it in. Below, the leafy deep-green canyon, and beyond that the valley floor, with distant peasants moving in the fields. The scrolling clouds, the repeating green hills, the far-off roof of a temple. Vistas in China were so inexorably Chinese; they made so much that was in Chinese art seem inevitable. "So how did they find this site?" she asked him.

"It was like this. The local people were working a quarry, and they kept turning up fossils. Enough product found its way into the black market in Peking that the scientific community started noticing it. They tracked the influx to this valley." Spencer lay on his back, working himself inch by inch ever deeper into the narrow cleft. The French priest, the Canadians, the Germans and Chinese, who had scraped this out with trowels so many decades before, all of them were long dead. Maybe now it would be his turn, he thought hopefully, running his flashlight beam over the scarred dirt ceiling.

"So they just started digging and found Peking Man? Just like that?"

"No, it took years. They dug and dug through the late twenties, excavated huge sections of the canyon floor, you know, methodically, in a grid. They found a lot of stuff that was tantalizing but minor. Extinct animals. Pieces of bone and teeth that looked human. Or sort of human. They dug out a few sections of the canyon wall, like this one.

"And then in 1929 they decided to start closing down the site. They hadn't found anything significant. It was time to move out. Most of the workers were already gone. It was the last day. One of the Chinese scientists climbs up in this cave to take a few final measurements. He hauls himself up and lies down and runs his hands over the ceiling like I'm doing now—no reason, you know, it's an impulse, a crazy thing to do—but he feels something that doesn't belong there, a bump, feels almost like part of a brainpan, but that's impossible, a skull, how could there be a skull just protruding from the ceiling? And so he shouts for the others, the men that are left, and they all climb up and start digging. Imagine!"

She smiled at him; he had come alive for once, telling it. "You love archaeology, don't you?"

"Yes. The long thread of human life, you know, it makes me feel connected." He clicked the flashlight off, closed his eyes, and ran his hands over the cave ceiling.

"Find anything?"

"No." He spread his hands as wide as he could over the rocky dirt, moved in slow arcs, covering it in sections, methodically, feeling everything. He let out a tiny laugh. "Just the past."

*   *   *

After a time they climbed down from the cave and made their way through the hot, cricket-buzzing trees to the top of the hill, where a small museum stood. It was a forgotten-looking brick building. They stepped inside to a dusty silence and an ancient *fuwuyuan* at the desk by the door.

"Okay." Spencer's voice rang in the empty rooms. "When Teilhard got Peking Man back, he hid it somewhere. We have to think the way he thought. Take your time. Look at his pictures. Read the text. We have to know him, if we're going to pull this off. Really know him."

They stopped at a clay bust of Peking Man. The steeply ridged forehead, the crashing, shallow chin, the matted hair. The eyes, which managed to capture a look at once cunning and subrational.

Alice bent over the label. "By Lucile Swan!"

"Yes. She was a talented artist. And she could give form to Teilhard's visions." He paused, examining the sculpture. "It's not surprising. She was practically inside him."

But not really, Alice reminded herself. She couldn't have all of him. So close—but no farther. Because he was already taken, in a way.

They stopped in front of the huge, grainy 1929 excavation photos. The dig, which covered much of the canyon floor in addition to the openings higher up the rock walls, was shown all in black-and-white, marked off in squares and full of European and Chinese men leaning on shovels. Teilhard was easy to pick out. He was taller than everyone else, falcon faced, with hooded eyes frozen in a glance at the camera.

"You notice he wears plain clothes?" Spencer said. "He never dressed like a priest, not once he got to China."

"Is that Lucile?"

"That's her."

She peered at the photo. Lucile Swan was strong looking, small, and buxom; she stood half behind Pierre Teilhard de Chardin of the Society of Jesus. Lucile looked frankly into the camera, her gaze intelligent. She had old-fashioned braids twined around her heart-shaped face, but in her eyes was a world of experience. Alice smiled. This was a woman who stood easily among the men. "How long did she stay in Peking?"

He thought. "She hung on through the war, by hiding in the French Legation. Then she got out, went home. She died in New York—let me see—in '65."

There was something about Lucile's position in the picture, behind the priest, which formed a scraping stone of sadness in Alice's middle. The fate of the thing was all there to see, Pierre with a shovel and eyes piercing the camera, Lucile behind him, self-contained. She loved him, she couldn't live without him, she couldn't fully have him. Oh, yes. Alice understood.

She stared into Lucile's face. "I want to look at this for a while," she whispered.

Spencer nodded and drifted away. She contemplated the frozen pointillist images until they became gray shades of meaninglessness, with only Teilhard's sharp gaze still there, boring through her. Did you love her? she thought intently, memorizing his jutting face. Or did you use her for what you wanted and discard the rest?

When the picture was taken Lucile, wearing the demure dress of a European peasant, had been the same age Alice was now. Why did pictures of women in history make them look so much older than they were? Or did Alice now look this old? Alice glanced down at her own blue jeans. Face it, she thought, I'm thirty-six. And Lucile was just like me. Adrift in China. Lonely, for years. Then in love again, finally, but with a man already committed to the Church. Stuck outside herself, outside love. Empathy flooded Alice's modern heart.

Some minutes had passed when Spencer coughed discreetly. She walked over to where he stood near the museum's entrance and he handed her a book from the display shelf.

"It's the book I told you about," he said. "Their correspondence."

She looked down. *The Letters of Teilhard de Chardin and Lucile Swan*. She felt a smile tugging at her face.

"I'll buy it for you."

"No, I'll buy it." She smiled: solidarity.

"*Si-shi ba kuai,*" the old man said in a thin voice. His spotted hands trembled as he accepted the money and counted out the change. "Are you foreign guests interested in the French priest?" he asked, glancing up through small round glasses of hammered gold. His blood-cracked eyes, almost completely shrouded over, still radiated intelligence.

"Very interested, Elder Uncle," Alice answered. "This outside person is an archaeologist. He is researching Peking Man."

"Can I help you in some humble way? I worked for the survey as a boy."

"What!" Alice translated for Spencer.

"Yes." He inclined his snow-white, sparsely fringed head toward the blown-up excavation photographs. "At first I was an apprentice, hauling rocks. But the head of the survey, Dr. Black, trained me. I continued working there until—until the situation grew unstable."

Alice saw him stop, move his papery mouth in a soundless swallow. He had used the cautious euphemism *bu wen*, unstable, but she knew something of the war and the famine and the chaos behind the word; she knew how many terrible years there had been. She stayed silent a moment, to show him respect, and then cleared her throat. "Do you remember much about the priest? Or his American friend, Lucile Swan?"

"Eh, Miss Swan. Of course." His voice was thin. "They were very close."

"Did she mention—perhaps—near the end of the war, might she or Teilhard have said anything about Peking Man?"

"Eh, no, no, that was lost much earlier, near the beginning of the world war."

"Yes, I know, but—well. I suppose they said nothing."

He shook his head.

Alice quickly translated the exchange for Spencer.

"What sort of road did her life take?" the old man was asking.

"Ah." She delivered the answer as if she had known it for years, when in fact she had heard it the day before from Dr. Spencer. "Miss Swan returned to the United States. She died in New York in 1965."

"Eh. It is hard for my heart to hear it."

"Yes."

"Well. May I see your name card?"

She took one out and handed it to him. "We've troubled you too much."

" 'Mo Ai-li,' " he read. " 'Interpreter.' I am Mr. Zhang. The pleasure's all on my side. *Shuoqilai,* " he said, By the way. "I knew the widow who took over Miss Swan's house when she left. Of course, she has long since gone away from the world. I do not know what has become of the place."

"Really?" She felt a racing in her chest. "Lucile's house?"

"Do you wish to go there? I will give you the address." He uncapped a pen and began writing.

"We did go to the old Jesuit House, where Father Teilhard lived," Alice told him. "But it was locked up."

"Eh, but I can take you to that place too," the man said, lowering his voice a notch. "It was owned for a long time after the Europeans left by the Chinese Antiquities Association. I know the gentleman who occupies it now. Tomorrow night? Seven? I will meet you there. But better we do not talk anymore, not here." He blinked at her.

"As you say." She hadn't been aware of anyone else around, but she knew that, in China, eyes and ears were everywhere.

He finished writing. "Here." He pushed the paper with Lucile's address across the table.

"Deeply indebted."

He made his face blank and waved them away.

3

THEY HAD BEEN walking for more than an hour up Wang-fujing through the crush of Chinese that spilled over the sidewalk and crowded into the street itself, leaving barely enough room for the trucks and cars and bicycles and buses to force their way through. Still the man was following them. Spencer aimed a quick look over his shoulder, keeping full stride. "He's there, all right."

"I don't know if we can lose him this time." Damn, she thought. They're paying too much attention to us, and for what? Because this American is looking for some bones that have been missing for fifty-odd years? "We're supposed to meet Mr. Zhang at the Jesuit House at seven." She checked her watch. "There's not time for a detour."

"Screw it, then, let the guy follow us. I don't care."

"Yes, but I care," she said, controlling her impatience. "And Mr. Zhang will care. Believe me."

"Why?" He took one of his hands from its habitual resting place in his pocket and put it to his head, pushing back his sparse hair.

"Arrest, interrogation, the threat of losing his housing registration—any of those ring a bell? And there's the whole prison camp system too. Don't forget."

"Prison camps? Come on. Isn't the Cultural Revolution over?"

"Don't kid yourself. The government hasn't changed that much."

"You're actually saying Mr. Zhang could be arrested, for talking to us?"

"I'm saying you never know, here."

"My God." He stared at her. "Well. We shouldn't put Mr. Zhang at risk. That wouldn't be right."

"And what about me?" She stopped dead on the sidewalk and challenged him with her eyes. "I don't want to have to leave China. I told you that before! This is my home." China, home: it was at least one thing about herself, one thing she was willing to say, which was profoundly true.

"But why would you have to leave China?" His voice grew still with bewilderment. "We haven't done anything wrong. And we won't either."

She sighed. "I know—"

"Alice," Spencer interjected. "Look! He's leaving."

She craned over the crowd and saw the man talking on a cell phone; then, snapping it shut, he turned and evaporated into the crowd.

"I'll be damned." Dr. Spencer chewed his lip.

She turned back to him. "Look, Adam. I'm having second thoughts about all this. There are people following us, you haven't got the money to pay me—"

"I'll get the money, don't worry about that. As far as their following us—I don't know what that's all about. But I know one thing. You've been stuck doing basically the same thing for a long time. Right? And this is the most interesting job you've had in years. Right?"

"Well . . ." She had to agree. "Right."

"So this is one of those times when life is just handing you something, telling you what to do, which way to go. So enjoy it. It'll be fun. I guarantee. I can't guarantee we'll find the goddamn thing, but it'll be interesting. Then if we do find it—if we do—the payoff's huge."

"Huge how? What?"

"Attention galore. A moment on the world stage."

She considered. "Is that why you want it?"

His face changed. "No. Not really. It's more for myself, my son—my dreams, you know. I'm forty-eight, I've been teaching for a long time. I need a second wind."

"And finding Peking Man will give you that?"

"God, yes," he said. "It'll change my life."

She shrugged, knowing all too well how easy it was to long for a different life, how hard it was to find one's way there.

"But, Alice . . ." He frowned. "We don't even have permits. Is there any chance we won't *get* permits?"

"Of course there's a chance."

"How much?"

"I don't know. I get the feeling what we're asking for is not easy for the vice director to give. Couldn't you see it in his composure, the way he sat? I don't know why. Sure, it's a closed area we want to go to, but China is full of closed areas and foreigners can usually apply to visit them when important research is involved."

"Should we"—he searched his mind—"should we bribe him?"

"Not openly, never, oh no. Most un-Chinese. But if things look like they're not going well, a gift could be considered."

"How do we assess that?"

"We don't. We wait. He'll make a move. When he does we think as the Chinese think, and make the correct move in response." She studied Spencer. Was the correct move for her this job, with this pudgy-faced, aging blond American? She didn't know yet. But she did know he was right—she was in a rut. And the project *was* interesting. They turned onto Ladder Lane. Tizi Hutong. "Ah, look," she said. "Mr. Zhang."

The old man came toward them, shaking his own hands in the old way. "Welcome you to see where the French priest lived. Regrettably my friend had to leave, but he left the gate open for us."

They stepped over the raised sill and into a quiet courtyard framed by curving tile roofs and a square of inward-facing, half-glassed rooms. "The old Chinese name for such a house is *si-he yuan*," Alice explained to Spencer. "That means 'four-box court-yard.' A *si-he yuan* gave people privacy and a sense of their own inner world. In old China—"

"I don't really care about old China," Adam said. "Where was Teilhard's room?"

Alice bit back her words. He was desperate to find his one precious relic of ancient man, yet seemed indifferent to the recent past. It was a pity. Here on the back streets of Beijing the past was never far away. Close your eyes and you could just see the long-gowned gentlemen browsing bookstalls; the hawkers crying out in slushy Pekingese the names of their medicines and toys and candied crab-apples and roasted ears of corn; the ricksha pullers jockeying for position in the mud ruts, close up to the streaming, jostling pedestrians; and all around them silk banners snapping in the wind from gateposts, declaiming family news of weddings, the new year, births and funerals. She turned to Mr. Zhang. "Do you know which room the priest occupied?"

"Yes. In the back court. Follow me."

As they walked, his old steps shuffling quietly beside her, he asked, "Have you read the priest's books?"

"Yes, elder brother. But many years have flown and I am just starting to read them again. I find his idea of the spiral of growth—that total forward movement—so interesting now.

Somehow, when I was a student, it didn't ring deeply to me. Now it does."

"Ke bu shi ma," he agreed. "I, too, have sometimes gained hope for the future from his essays." He paused, perhaps wondering whether to say more. "Sometimes in the bad years I would come here to this house and stand in the priest's room. Do you know why I did this? Because here he formulated his ideas. Here he wrote at night—while by day he sifted the dirt at Zhoukoudian. Eh, foreign miss, you cannot imagine the excitement in those days at Zhoukoudian. After the ape-man was discovered."

"I think I can," she said in a low voice, glancing over at Adam Spencer, who walked beside her, his eyes round and wide with anticipation, his hands clutching his book and pen. "Here," she told Adam when the old man stopped and pointed to a half-open door. "Teilhard's room."

She stood back and let Spencer push his way inside. He flipped on a dim yellow bulb. "There's nothing here," he said, voice strangled with disappointment.

The room was bare. No furniture, no cupboards, nothing.

"It was an office for thirty or forty years after the Jesuits left," Mr. Zhang explained. "Since then it has not been used."

"Did Teilhard leave anything?" Spencer asked. "Papers, books?"

Alice translated and Mr. Zhang shook his head. "Nothing. But I tell you, if you stand just so"—he turned his frail, graceful body toward the windows—"you can still sense the essence of the man! Go on," he urged Alice. "Translate. Tell the foreign scientist to try."

Alice looked dubiously at Adam Spencer, who was pacing the room like a frustrated animal, holding his notebook, scanning the bare walls continuously as if they might suddenly yield something if he looked at them long enough.

"Sorry, Mr. Zhang. I don't think the American scientist is

interested in Teilhard's essence. You're sure there are no records, pictures, anything?"

"None."

"Nothing remains," she translated for Spencer, inside thinking: But everything is here, isn't it? Because this is where his vision was born. Dimly she knew there was something important in all this for her. "Sorry, Adam," she said.

"It's okay," he sighed. "Let's go."

Adam Spencer lay on his bed, studying the direct-dial instruction card, in eight languages, which had been placed on his nightstand. Outside line, international operator, country code . . . His eyes moved down to the rate listing and he swallowed uncomfortably. Expensive.

But he had to call. His longing for his son had grown so overwhelming that it seemed, these last few days, he was almost choking on it. It was a longing fraught with dread and apprehension, one that had started the day he and Ellen had told Tyler they were separating. He still remembered the child's frozen, color-drained face, looking up from his handheld electronic game. And then the long horrible moment in which Tyler, his heart split apart, did not know whose arms to rush into. Adam and Ellen swore they wouldn't make the boy choose between them. But they had, almost immediately, because she moved back to California. And Tyler had gone with her.

Adam swallowed hard, picked up the phone, and jabbed out the code for collect, then pressed a 510 area code, the San Francisco area, the East Bay. He listened to it ring.

Ellen answered, and the operator asked her in sawing Asian English if she would accept charges. She paused—and then she agreed. "Adam, my God, did you have to call collect?"

"Yes." He swallowed. "Sorry. I'll pay you back when I get home. Is Tyler there?" He rushed on, wanting to avoid her.

"Yes. Wait—" She covered the phone, muffled talking.

His precious boy came on. "Hi, Dad."

Adam's chest soared. He felt himself smiling. "Hi, guy."

"Where are you?"

"China."

"Weird."

"How's school?" Adam said.

"Fine."

"What'd you do today?"

"Nothing."

"Nothing?"

"I forget."

"Hmm. Tyler, guess what? Daddy's going to find these bones of an ancient hominid, ancestor of man, you know? They used to be in sort of a museum but they've been missing for a long time."

"Missing? Did somebody take them?"

"Yeah. But Daddy's going to find them. You'll see. It'll—"

"Dad? Sorry. I have to go. Mom says homework."

Adam opened his mouth to protest but there was nothing he could say. After all, he'd called collect. "I love you, Tyler," he got out, the words like cotton in his mouth.

"I love you too."

There was the far-off click, the deadening of the sound, and then his son was gone. Gone, gone. Adam held the receiver in front of him, looking at it, the heat pressing behind his eyes, and then put it back on its cradle.

"We're in luck," Alice told him in the lobby after breakfast. "While we were eating Vice Director Han called. He left word that he'd call back at two this afternoon. I told you he'd make a move."

"Great. So we'll be here waiting at two."

"What about the money? Have you heard anything?"

His hands shoved into his pockets. "No. But don't worry. This grant is a sure thing. According to my grandfather, Teilhard was clearly negotiating to get Peking Man back. No doubt. Plus, I have an *in*. Two guys I went to graduate school with are on the NSF Review Committee."

"And they have influence?"

"Influence! One of them chairs the committee. He's in the National Academy of Sciences—teaches at Princeton. The other one teaches at Berkeley. He happens to be head of the Leakey Foundation Review Board. They both publish constantly, give papers at all the international conferences—you know."

"And these are guys *you* went to graduate school with?"

He heard the dubious note in her voice and colored ever so slightly. "Right. We all got our Ph.D.'s at Columbia together. Look, Alice, they chose big-time academia. I chose—"

"The University of Nevada at Reno."

"—No, the desert. I went to UNR because it's smack in the middle of the Great Basin, the American outback, the place where everything—the wind, the rocks, and the sand—makes me feel alive." But not complete. He hadn't felt complete, even there, until he had Tyler. And now Tyler had been all but taken away from him. He fought down the familiar panic—his boy, growing older day by day, far away. At least he still had the desert. "I love it there. Can you understand that?"

She smiled up at him suddenly, his haphazard face, his gray eyes in their baggy pouches. "I'm not one to talk, am I? I live in China."

"No," he said, looking at her thoughtfully. "You're not."

"So when do you think you'll hear? About the grant?"

"Don't worry. Any day. They have the fax number at the hotel."

"Inside," the old woman said, kicking at the door. "This is where Wang Ma put the west-ocean barbarian woman's things. It's not a bit convenient! This closet has been needed many times! But Wang Ma is a superstitious old bone; she wouldn't let us remove them. She says then the woman's ghost would be ill at ease. Huh!" She shook her blunt, iron head. "Am I a credulous lump of meat from the countryside to believe such things?" She ambled away muttering.

Spencer knelt and examined the ancient, rusted-over lock. "Hasn't been opened in a long time."

She looked around the back of the *si-he yuan* on Dengshikou Hutong—the address that old Mr. Zhang at the Zhoukoudian museum had given them. The house seemed to have stayed not only intact but largely unchanged after Lucile's time. From what Alice had gleaned, this was because the widow of someone important had lived here in seclusion until her death. Now, her servants were being permitted to remain. Unusual. Alice yanked the lock once, then took a fist-sized rock. "Stand back," she said, and brought the rock down in a decisive swing. One good smash: the lock gave out a grating squeak and fell apart.

"Not bad!" Spencer punched her arm in congratulations, then jittered the door open. Inside the small, dust-choked space were Chinese wooden trunks, stacked high in the narrow gloom.

They lifted the trunks out into the sun. The first one contained sculpting tools; the second, big irregular blocks of ancient desiccated clay.

"Why'd she keep this?" Spencer wondered.

"She must have thought she was coming back." Alice reached in and put her hands on the clay, thinking in a blaze of envy and admiration what it must be like to have an art. The way Lucile did. Alice pressed her fingers against the dry cake of clay, wondering.

"Here's another trunk," he said. "Look. Cooking stuff." They pawed through kettles and woks and mortar stones and cake molds and vegetable cutters in the fanciful shapes of phoenixes and dragons, but nothing remotely related to Teilhard or Peking Man. Three cases of books, all in English. Novels, dictionaries, books of poetry and philosophy. Two trunks of clothing. "Hey, maybe this could fit you," he joked, holding a floral print dress up to her. "No. You're too skinny."

"Thanks a lot."

"Just stating the facts. What's this, now?" He pried open the last trunk. It was packed with small household goods: vases, table clocks, cloisonné ware, and all the treasures of the study: brush holders, inkstones, cases for chops and the small sticky pads of crimson ink that went with them.

"That's it," he said when he had cleared everything out and was staring at the bottom of the trunk, half dazed. He twisted behind and peered into the empty, dust-billowing closet as if surely there were something else within.

"Hold on." Alice had pulled the clothing half out onto the packed earth and was searching through pockets and inner folds. She was a woman and she hid things this way all the time, in the pockets of put-away clothing: her passport, her money, extra pieces of jewelry. Why not Lucile? "Ah!" she said. "See?"

"What is it?"

"It's a letter." With great care she pulled out the brittle, brown-mottled envelope, pressed back the flap, and drew out the folded paper. "It's in Chinese. It's—" She read. "It's not to Lucile at all. It's to Pierre Teilhard de Chardin, the address on Tizi Hutong."

"Tell me!"

There was a strained silence as she read through it. She looked up, green eyes big. "It's from a Mongol. He's talking about the situation in the Northwest. He's saying don't worry, the Communists won't get control out there, just like the Japanese never did, because the local warlord, some man named Ma Huang-gui, is so powerful. Seems the warlord executes everyone who looks at him cross-eyed—'execute ten to terrify a thousand' is the phrase." She paused, read further. "It's composed point by point, as if he's answering questions." She looked up, finishing it. "It says the region's stable, safe from civil war, safe from Communists."

Spencer's lips worked for a minute and no sound came out.

"You think he's answering questions that Teilhard wrote to him?" she asked.

"God." He exhaled in a giant push, staring ahead into nothing. "Are you kidding? Of course. He wanted a safe place to put Peking Man. It was a time of war."

"There's one other thing—in the margin. It's a drawing." She showed it to him: a monkey's face, simply but beautifully drawn, with huge staring eyes and, streaming out all around its head, a halo that looked like a crown, or the sun itself. In another way, the face of a monkey was also suggested by the little nose. "What is it?"

"Don't know," he said. "Never seen anything like it."

She squinted. "Looks like ancient art."

"Like a petroglyph, but—certainly nothing like it has been found in the Americas. Or Europe. What do those say?" He pointed to a few characters scrawled in the margin.

She tilted the page. "It says, 'This is what it looks like.' 'It'? What's 'it'?"

"I don't know. The drawing, I guess. This letter seems to be only one piece of some ongoing correspondence. Any return address?"

She examined both sides of the page, turned the envelope over. "No."

"A date?"

"March 1945."

"God." He sank into a squat.

"It does fit right in, doesn't it?" She eased the letter back into its envelope.

He looked around the empty courtyard. "Look, Alice. Ordinarily I wouldn't do this. Wouldn't take anything, disturb anything. But let me ask you a question. Do you think the people in this house have any idea this letter is here?"

"No."

"Do you think they'd care if they knew it was?"

She hesitated only a fraction. "No."

He was silent.

"You're asking if we should take the letter?"

"Yes. Listen. No one would ever find out. This stuff has been locked up here for years. It's forgotten." He stared at her, hard.

A chill ran over her. Someone had definitely been following them, although they hadn't glimpsed the man today. How much can they watch me? she wondered. Can they know everything that's in my mind? Can they know what I do in my private life? It seemed inconceivable and yet the government always knew more than one expected. Alice looked around quickly. Nothing seemed out of place. Gray stone courtyard walls. Potted camellias. Twittering birds.

"Okay," she said in a moment of firmness, handed him the letter, and watched him slip it into his notebook. "Let's move everything back."

"Good afternoon, Vice Director Han. Yes, of course we were here. We received your message. Thank you." She locked eyes with Spencer and nodded. She continued on in Chinese, trading good wishes with the vice director and chatting about what she and the American had done, their visit to the Zhoukoudian site—playing out the courteous line that was essential to any Chinese exchange, establishing the sense of connection, of relationship. She followed patiently along with the vice director. She knew he had to be the one to bring up business.

Finally he coughed as a mood break. "Oh, now that you mention the ape-man site, I have had the chance to discuss the matter of Dr. Spencer with several of my co-workers. They are considering his requests. I hope to be able to let you know soon."

She held back disappointment. He was going to stall again. "Yes, that is what we hope as well."

"You know, it is difficult. The scope of our work includes so many responsibilities. And our institute has limited staff. We do the best we can. Unfortunately we must spend much of our time editing scientific articles and arranging for their publication. You see, it's so critical in China for scientists to publish, and to contribute to their fields internationally. It is the only way we can grow."

"Yes, I see. You're quite right," Alice said carefully. "Of course the research we propose could be of great importance to both countries."

"Perhaps. In any case, the pleasure has been mine to converse with you. Please convey to Dr. Spencer my sincere hope that his project will be reviewed soon."

"Yes, Vice Director Han." She paused.

"Is there anything else?"

"May I trouble you to hold for a moment?" She covered the mouthpiece firmly. "Offer him coauthorship," she urged in English.

"What?" Spencer's face contracted.

"Suppose you find this thing. Would it be okay if Chinese archaeologists shared authorship on your paper?"

He bit at his lip.

"Seems to be the hint he's dropping."

He paused.

"Come on, Adam. A collaboration would only enhance your credibility."

"True." He raised his brows, studied her. "You think we need to offer this?"

"I do."

"Well . . . okay."

She returned to Chinese. "Please forgive me, Vice Director, for making you wait. Yes, Dr. Spencer understands your problem. It is probably of limited interest to your staff, but if his own insignificant project should engage anyone's attention, he would welcome a colleague on your side. Otherwise he would not presume."

The vice director's voice was neutral. Only the alacrity of his answer betrayed his satisfaction. "Eh, is it so? Well, I will mention it and see if any of our scientists are so inclined. Pardon me, Interpreter Mo, I have taken too much of your time. I know you are busy."

"Not at all. Don't be polite."

"Good-bye."

"Good-bye," she repeated, and hung up the phone. "Okay," she said to Adam, "he's interested. Now you should host a dinner."

"I'm listening."

"Invite him and the colleagues of his choice to a restaurant as your guests. Strictly social. No negotiation. But an essential stage of Chinese business relations."

"All right—if you say. Will you call him back?"

"Of course." Alice was thinking of a certain restaurant in Beihai Park which served food in the imperial style—scaled-down versions of the meals eaten in the Manchu court throughout the Qing dynasty. "I'll call him back—but not today. Tomorrow. We don't want to look too eager."

* * *

"Yi jin." Alice pointed to the shredded lamb in the street-side stall. One pound.

The rotund Chinese in the stained white apron emitted a rude monosyllable of agreement, ladled up the raw, ruby-colored meat, weighed it out, and dropped it with an ear-splitting sizzle on the huge meter-wide griddle in front of him. With one hand he added deft scoops of vinegar, soy sauce, and bean sauce. With the other he moved the quick-cooking meat around in rapid staccato swipes.

"It smells great," Spencer said. "But how much did you order?"

"One pound."

Spencer's eyes widened.

She shrugged, watching the cook's assistant pile hot *xiao bing,* sesame buns, on the plates. Meanwhile the cook was adding handfuls of green onion and cilantro to the lamb, and then, before the vegetables could wilt, whisking the whole thing off the griddle and mounding it on the two plates. *"Xia yige!"* the cook shouted, Next!

They crossed the dirty tile floor and squeezed into an empty spot on the jammed trestle table. "Venerable brother, excuse us," Alice said politely to the man next to them.

"Eh!" he grunted, turned away angrily, and spat on the floor.

She ignored him. They sat down.

"There are so many people here," Adam said, staring at the tightly packed, boisterous little room. As with all Chinese eating spots, the light was overpoweringly bright, the noise riotous. "Everyplace is so crowded."

"Oh, this is nothing," she said lightly. "Shanghai's much more crowded than this."

"More crowded than *this?*" Following her, he split the *xiao*

73

bing open and stuffed in the steaming shredded lamb, then added a squirt of hot sauce from the common bottle on the table. "But the strange thing is, I haven't seen any street people, any beggars. Have I missed something? Are there street people here?"

"There are a few beggars. Though you don't see homeless people, people living outdoors like you see in America. But there's something else, that actually runs into millions of people. The floating population."

He paused, *bing* half up to his mouth. "Floating population."

"Right. People without housing registrations. A housing registration is the key to life in China. Without it you can't get an apartment, get free medical care, work in the system, or buy food that's on ration."

"And why is it millions of people can't get housing registrations?"

"It's not that they can't get them. They can. They just don't want to live where their housing registration is, in some poverty-stricken remote village or wherever, so they leave and go someplace else. Someplace where they're not registered. They join the floating population."

"So then where do they live?"

"On the margins. Some of them get rich. But most of them— well—crash somewhere, if you know what I mean. Stay with friends, or relatives. Patch something together."

He bit into his *bing*. "Alice, you were right. This is great. And for street food! Oh. Here. I almost forgot." He dug into his pocket and handed her a small, two-inch-square newspaper clipping.

Lucile Swan, 75, died May 2, 1965, at her home in New York. Noted artist and lifelong confidante of the Catholic mystic Pierre Teilhard de Chardin. The cause was heart failure. . . .

"Her obituary," Alice smiled. "Where did you get it?"

"When I first started researching all this I went back and poked around a little bit in New York. That's where Teilhard died too. But they didn't see that much of each other in those last years, even though they both lived in New York."

"There was a lot of bitterness—she was resentful and jealous," Alice said. "I can tell from their letters, the book we bought at Zhoukoudian. It's fascinating."

"Really?" He ate thoughtfully.

"Oh, yes. I can really relate to her life. What I wouldn't have given to have had somebody like her, so smart, so aware, for a mother."

"What was your mother like?" He added more hot sauce.

"Died when I was a baby. Never had one."

He looked up, penetrating. "That's too bad. God. Some life. At least you have your dad."

"Who?"

"Your dad."

"Oh, you mean Horace." She smiled wryly. "I never call him Dad."

"You don't?" He stared for a second. "Hey. Look. I've been meaning to apologize for bringing all that up, the first day we met, at breakfast. You know, the Alice Speech. I know it made you uncomfortable. I feel bad about it. I won't mention your father at all if you like."

"I don't really care that much," she said, staring at the obituary. "I hate everything he stands for. Basically, I don't have anything to do with him."

"Ah." He examined her face. "That simple?"

"That simple."

"Well. Anyway." He nodded at the newspaper clipping. "I got to wondering about Lucile's death, so I looked up the records. This is all I found." He saw how Alice was looking at it. "Why don't you keep it?" he said kindly. "It's not like I need it for the research."

"Really? Are you sure? I'd like to have this."

"Keep it." He resumed eating. Just then the Chinese couple on their left got up to leave, and the man pushed against Alice so hard, she almost fell into Spencer's lap. Instead of apologizing he muttered, *"Waiguoren,"* Foreigner, and stalked off.

Spencer stared after him. "The Chinese don't like us too much, huh?"

"Not a bit," she said. "We're barbarians. Ghosts. Even the lowest laborer feels superior to the most educated, most successful foreigner. You'll see."

"That must be hard for you, being an American."

She tore into her third *bing*. "I'm not what you'd really call an American," she said between bites. "And believe it or not, that attitude is actually one of the things about the place I find appealing." She could feel his stare, but there was no use explaining. He'd never understand the safe, settled feeling it gave her to be a foreigner in China, an outside person, barely tolerated. The way the geometry of her world seemed righted here, all weights and balances, all retributions, called into play.

He put down his *bing* and pushed his plate away. "Best lamb I've had in years. But I can't finish it."

She eyed his food. "Really? You're not going to eat any more?"

"No."

She pulled it over and started in.

"Alice. How do you do it?"

"I don't know. I just do."

"But you're so—so slim!"

"Yeah. I keep eating and eating, and I don't get fat. Sometimes I even think I'm *trying*—to pack something in around me. And then other times I realize that actually, I'm not even hungry. But I just keep eating anyway."

*   *   *

Alice sat on the bed naked except for the antique red silk stomach-protector, two strings tied around her neck, two around her waist. It was no more than a silk trapezoid with four strings. As an undergarment its purpose had never been clear to Alice, for it covered only the belly and left the breasts and the genitals bare. She had always assumed its function had been to conserve *qi*, the vital energy traditionally thought to be centered around the navel—but she wasn't sure. In any case she felt good in it, and it suited her, since she never wore a bra. She loved the way she felt in it, especially when she went out at night.

She opened the book of Teilhard and Lucile's letters to a passage she had marked the night before, this a letter Teilhard had written to Lucile: *Sometimes, I think I would like to vanish before you* into *some thing which would be bigger than myself,— your real yourself, Lucile,—your real life,* your *God. And then I should be yours, completely.*

Her real self, Alice thought, her real life. Somehow Lucile had accomplished a thing Alice had only imagined: gotten her true core coupled with Teilhard. Even if they'd never fully committed to each other.

She put the book down and opened *The Phenomenon of Man. To connect the two energies, of the body and the soul, in a coherent manner* . . . Had Pierre and Lucile achieved that? Maybe. Though Lucile's letters and diary entries—also included in the book—made it clear she was dissatisfied. *The live, physical, real you, all of you. I want you so terribly and I'm trying so hard to understand.* . . .

She rolled over on her stomach and dropped the books to the floor. She figured she, Alice, could connect the body and the soul—definitely, she could, if she just found the right man. A

Chinese man, maybe. Though would there ever be one who'd accept her?

Of all the men she'd known, only Jian had come close. He'd understood her; he'd taken the time. But in the end he didn't love her enough to fight for her. His separateness, his Chineseness, had won.

And who had she known who'd truly accepted her? Who'd been truly, seamlessly unconditional?

Only Horace.

God. She groaned and covered her eyes. He never understood her, it was true, but he was loyal and he never wavered. It was a kind of love. Punishing maybe, unfair, controlling, but love nevertheless.

Like the day she graduated from Rice University.

He had flown in early. As a senior member of the Texas delegation to the U.S. House of Representatives, Horace didn't get back home to Houston much. But she knew he would come to her graduation from anywhere. From Boston. From Bahrain.

She could still see the dorm room, the books and typewriter and stereo packed in their boxes, the posters down, the bare-box walls bereft. Outside, the sweat-bath Houston summer was already rising from the ground in waves. Then he got off the elevator. She could hear the special tap of his walk. She felt the ripple of recognition, the thrill that followed him as he strode down the hall.

He stepped in the door, saw her. His face brightened with joy. "Too long, darling." He put his arms around her and squeezed. "So good to see you."

"You too." She smiled. He was someone who'd always known her. At school she'd been mostly on her own.

"I'm proud of you, Alice." He stood back and admired her.

"Thanks. Hard to believe it's over." She looked balefully around the room. "And still so much to pack!"

"Go on, continue. I'll watch." He sat on her plastic desk-chair in his gray tropical suit and wine-colored tie. He was a small man, exact, articulate. When he was onstage he grew to evangelical stature—but now, in repose, it was easy to see why he was the perfect elected official, conservative, smiling, devoted to the business and progress of the South. "Congratulations. And graduating cum laude too!"

"Oh, Horace." She'd gone back to pulling folded clothes out of her bureau drawers and stacking them in their cardboard box.

"Really, sweetheart, I mean it. You've done a great job."

She let out a modest laugh.

"And now you can come to work."

She looked up sharply. Had he said come to work?

"You see, I've talked it over with Roger." Happiness played around her father's mouth, so proud and pleased was he with the prize he had to offer. "You know Roger oversees all my staff needs. And he's already terminated someone so that the assistant-director position in the head office in Washington is open. For you." He beamed.

"Horace." She stared, stricken, the words all mashed up in her throat. "I can't work for you."

"Now, honey, I know what you're thinking. Working for Daddy!"

My God, she thought.

"But you won't report to me, or Roger. We have it all worked out—"

"No," she interrupted. "It's impossible. I can't be around your life, your people. The things you stand for." If there was one thing she knew by then, by age twenty-two, it was that she had to get far away and stay away. Here in his world she was trapped in an intolerable corner, which seemed to grow tighter and tighter each year. And now no place in America felt right.

How clearly she remembered the night she'd first realized it.

She'd been only eleven then, exactly half her age on that day of college graduation. It was a regular dinner at the home of

Janie Boudreau, her best friend from school. Alice was a frequent guest. She knew the Boudreaus felt sorry for her—there was no mother in Alice's big house, only Horace and a housekeeper.

On this night Janie's older cousin was there, visiting from Dallas. "So you're *the* Alice, aren't you?" He looked at her hard, through narrowed eyes.

"What do you mean?"

"Well—you're Horace Mannegan's girl, aren't you?"

"Yes." She glanced quickly at her friend. Janie's eyes slid away.

"I knew it! You're the one who didn't want to go to school with colored kids, right?"

"No," Alice insisted. It hadn't been her idea! Not her, never.

"Yeah—come on. I remember. You didn't want to go to a mixed school! Then your father made that speech, then the riots got started, and that's how those girls got killed."

"It wasn't me," she pleaded. "I never said—"

"Of course it was you! You're Alice Mannegan. Alice Mannegan! Right, Aunt Dee? Huh?"

"Yes, Jackson," Janie's mother had said in a quietly stern voice. "But Alice is Janie's friend. Let's talk about something else. Come. Who wants dessert?"

By that point, though, a messy silence had squashed down over the table. Everyone avoided everyone else's eyes. The meal scraped to a nauseated conclusion.

It was only the first time, the first of many. After that night she'd known she was doomed. And she was. She grew up in the center of it, everyone's lightning rod for pity, loathing, fascination, the whole freight train of emotions that followed the charging tension between the races.

Now, packing up her dorm room at Rice, she looked at her father, stunned. What he was suggesting was horrible, unthinkable. And as usual he didn't even see it.

"I can't work for you! Sorry, but it's out of the question.

Everyplace I went I'd be the 'Alice' from the 'Alice Speech'!
Especially in Washington. I'd never get away from it."

"Alice!" He got up, disturbed, and circled his chair a couple of
times. "That speech was years ago! And we were only trying to
restore a little bit of what was so good about America, what this
great country has lost—"

"Like slavery?" she said bitterly.

"Please," he said mildly, as if she referred to something that
was simply a bygone fashion and not a searing fount of human
shame. "All I did was make a speech. It's not as if *I* went out and
burned the Fourth Ward down."

What? Her mouth fell open.

Just then a giggling group of girls stopped outside the open
door.

"It isn't—"

"I told you, her father's Horace Mannegan!"

"Alice, is that your daddy?"

"No," she said sullenly. "It's Horace."

"See! I told you, it's him."

"You go in!"

"You!"

"Mr. Mannegan, sir, may I have your autograph?" The girl
had long honey-colored limbs, short blond hair, and a string of
pearls over her pale green silk blouse. The hand that thrust the
pen and paper toward him had perfectly manicured pink nails.

"Yes, of course, dear." Horace smiled benignly, uncapped his
gold corporate-looking pen, and signed. "We'll be counting on
your support in the next election."

"Oh, yes! Yes, sir! My parents—we always vote for you, sir!"

"Good. Don't ever give up on this great country of ours."

"No, sir!"

"Here. Anyone else?" He signed autographs for all of them.

"Thank you, sir! Bye, Alice!"

"Bye," she said, hating them.

Horace turned back to her the instant they were gone and she saw his composed, boardroom mask drop away and leave, in its place, a father's hurt and confusion. "I always assumed you would come to work for me."

Alice closed her eyes.

"I need you, Alice. I . . . depend on you."

"I know," she said. He depended on her to be the family in his life. When she was young, and living with him, she was the one who'd made sure he ate right, who told him it was time to stop working and go to bed. No one else ever told him he needed rest, or he was drinking too much, or he ought to cancel a meeting or an airplane trip because he was sick. She did. And he showered her with most everything she wanted in return. Everything except the freedom to be what she wanted to be—whatever that was. She had to break away. Whether he liked it or not. She had to.

Tell him. "Horace, I'm going to China."

"Where?"

"China."

"China! Why?"

"Please, Horace! You are aware, aren't you, that for the last four years I've been earning a degree in Chinese?"

"Yes, but—"

"And that I visited there last summer? And loved it?"

"Yes, but—you don't mean you really want to live over there? In *China?*"

He had gone silent, and she had started to cry herself, because after all she was leaving him. And it hurt him. Despite all her tangled emotions she didn't want to cause him pain like this, him, her own—she could barely form the word in her mind—father. But she knew she had to go. And finally he had said all right, if it was what she wanted, he would go along with it.

And he had. He had bombarded her with love, and sent her regular checks every month, for the past fourteen years. The only time he had gone to war with her was over Jian. And he'd won. She hadn't fallen in love since.

Ah. Alice lay back on the bed, feeling the knotted silk strings under her backbone, the scratchy chenille bedspread against her bare skin. Love. The love of her father. Love of her mother, which she'd never known. And grown-up love, or what passed for it, in whose arms she could always briefly forget before moving on.

She shifted on the bed. Mother Meng was right. She was getting too old now. Soon, she was going to have to make some kind of change.

Her eyes wandered to the dark crack of the Beijing night barely showing along the edge of the curtain. She reached down and fingered the soft embroidered silk of the stomach-protector.

Should she go out?

A few hours later, at the shift change down in the hotel lobby, Second Night Clerk Huang told First Morning Clerk Shen that the foreigner Mo Ai-li had left on her bicycle just before midnight.

"Ah, then I'll watch for her return."

"Around dawn."

"Yes, around dawn." First Morning Clerk Shen smiled to himself. That was the time Mo Ai-li always came back. Her face would be soft and her *yin* would be satisfied—for a while. *Aiya,* the outside people! So strange and secretive about their coupling. So entertaining to watch.

*   *   *

"I'm sorry we could not accept your invitation for dinner," Vice Director Han said as he ushered them into his office. "You understand, we are so busy."

"Yes," Alice said politely, "we understand." She glanced quickly at Adam. She had explained to him that this refusal was not a good sign.

"Nevertheless I am trying to make some arrangements for Dr. Spencer to do his research in the Northwest. Why did I ask you here today? I want you to meet two of our scientists." He pressed the button on the side of his desk and his secretary put her head into the room. "Show them in."

She nodded and opened the door wider for two Chinese men.

"Professor Kong Zhen of Huabei University." Vice Director Han indicated one of them.

"Interpreter Mo Ai-li," Alice responded, and handed the man her name card. He looked to her like one of those too-thin Chinese men who seemed vaguely unkempt in Western clothes and really belonged in the loose robes of a feudal Chinese gentleman. Instead he wore Western suit pants with a cell phone clipped to his belt. His face was long, narrow, and flat. "And this is Dr. Adam Spencer, from America," she said.

"Spencer Boshi," Professor Kong said to Adam. He smiled, showing less-than-perfect teeth. "I confess I'm relieved," he told Alice. "At least there's one of you who can talk!"

Typical, Alice thought. Not speak Chinese, just talk.

"And this is my colleague," Dr. Kong said. "Dr. Lin."

The other man stepped forward. He was the opposite of Kong, a hulking man with a broad face, small intelligent eyes, and a full, eggplant-colored Asian mouth. He was tall for a Chinese, over six feet, but he gave the impression that he placed his limbs about himself with deliberate care. "Professor Lin," he said to her in the soft, sibilant Chinese of the Yangtze Valley, and indicated himself.

"Interpreter Mo." They exchanged cards.

"It is my happiness to meet you," he said carefully, studying her.

"And mine," she answered, following him in *keqi hua*, Polite speech.

"The idea of the American archaeologist is most interesting to me. In our country, we had almost given up hope of recovering Peking Man."

"Do you study the ape-man, then?" she asked.

"All my life."

"Really." Like Jian, she thought: fascinated by the past.

"It's been my life's dream to find Peking Man. Without it, the fossils we have for our research are very limited."

"I see." She looked up, aware of the others. It was inappropriate to conduct a private conversation in a Chinese business meeting. *"Duibuqi,"* she murmured. They all sat down.

"Dr. Kong and Dr. Lin have some interest in your research," Vice Director Han announced. "As they have luckily consented to accompany your expedition, they can help you with the many arrangements you would naturally be unable to make on your own." He cleared his throat. "This means I do not have to allocate so much time to assisting you, do you understand me or not? It removes a difficult problem for me. Under these circumstances it has been decided that I can grant the permits."

Alice translated everything for Spencer in a neutral, professional tone, smiling at the American when she put the words into English: "I can grant the permits." They went through the arrangements, the date they would depart Beijing, the plan for these two archaeologists to return and make preparations at their home in the city of Zhengzhou, Henan Province, then come north on a separate line and join their train at the halfway point. Through her Dr. Spencer explained, all over again, why he believed Father Teilhard had gotten Peking Man back from the Japanese and hidden it in the Northwest.

As she did her job, her mind humming in its two languages,

she tried to keep her eyes off Dr. Lin. But she couldn't help seeing how he turned her name card over and over in his hands, large hairless hands with smooth, fine-textured pale-amber skin, studying her name in Chinese characters and then in English letters before glancing at her once, briefly, and then carefully sliding her card into his pocket.

"Fax for Dr. Spencer," said the short Chinese woman in the green hotel uniform, and thrust the folded paper at him.

"Yes—thank you. . . ." He stared at it—amazing, it was here—then looked up. She was already off down the hall, her short, curved legs pumping. A young man was holding the elevator for her. She jumped inside and Spencer heard their quick, giggly Mandarin bubble up and then click off when the doors whooshed together.

He closed the door to his room, heart racing with excitement. Open it!

He'd known they would back him, James Hargrove and Fenton Wills. Old friends. They'd been kind to him all these years, even though their stars had soared straight into the stratosphere and his—his had gone nowhere. Just teaching at the University of Nevada. Publishing the occasional minor paper. An unimpressive academic life which would contribute to Tyler's inevitable realization—someday, when the boy was much older—that his father had been a failure. He had not succeeded in staying married to Tyler's mother, and as if that weren't bad enough, he hadn't done much with his career either. Adam felt he had to turn things around. He had to be at least as good as his own father, who, though cool and preoccupied, had been a humanities professor of some note at a small campus in Sacramento. He, Adam, couldn't even seem to measure up to that slim standard. These days he was never quoted, never cited, never invited to present work at conferences. Whereas James and Fenton quickly became the people *running* the conferences. Still they'd always taken his calls. Always had lunch with him when he passed through town. Maybe they knew what he knew, that he was just waiting for the right idea, the right opportunity—and then he would make his mark. Then he would break out.

Open it.

He turned it over in his hand, visualizing what it was going to say: Dear Dr. Spencer, the National Science Foundation is pleased to inform you . . .

He swallowed and pressed the single page open. He read it. Looked out the window for a minute, heart pounding.

He read it again.

And again.

We regret we are unable to fund . . .

How could they?

Heavy limbed, underwater, he stood and crossed the room to the wooden desk, opened one of the Teilhard books, and slipped the fax between its pages.

How could they? How could they turn him down? This was Peking Man, for God's sake. And he *knew*, he had what his grandfather had told him, Henry Bingham. . . .

Not only that. Now he and Alice had found the letter, the letter to Teilhard from the Northwest, hidden in Lucile's clothes. It was solid evidence. It proved everything.

This rejection in no way reflects on the quality of your project. We receive far more proposals than our funds allow us to support.

His heart seemed to be trying to hammer its way out of his chest. He walked heavily to the bed and stretched out. He lay there, motionless, staring at the ceiling.

How the hell was he going to pull this off now?

4

ALICE HADN'T BEEN able to find Spencer—he wasn't in his room, or if he was, he didn't answer the door—so she wrote the address of the restaurant out in Chinese and slipped a note under the door suggesting he show it to a cabdriver and meet her there.

Now she sat at their table in a side room, off the middle courtyard. The clean, tiny room was exquisite with the beauty of old China. High ceilings were crossed with intricately painted beams. The floors were antique tile. Doors and windows, open now to the breeze, were framed with scrolling woodwork and fitted with etched panes of glass: each pane depicting mythical beasts, or figures from legends, or scenes from famous Chinese novels. Outside she could see waiters bearing dishes to and from the many private dining rooms which ringed the courtyard. The summer night sounds of clinking dishes, laughter, and conversations swelled all around.

She liked coming to this Sichuan restaurant because it was housed in an historic old mansion, the former home of the warlord Yuan Shikai. He had controlled Peking for only a brief time—between the fall of the Qing dynasty and the establishment of the ill-fated Republic—but he had certainly lived well, Alice thought. The mansion was right in the heart of the city, only a few blocks from Tiananmen, but like all old Chinese *si-he yuan* it was a timeless island of peace and removal. All the rooms faced inward, to the trees or ponds or rockeries in the yards. They were kept clean and perfect, even though the streets outside might be filthy. Often when she was in old Chinese houses, Alice reflected on the way in which the colloquial term foreigners had once used for the Forbidden City—the Great Within—so perfectly summarized the domestic sensibility of feudal China. Actually she knew that in old Chinese the Great Within, the *Danei*, referred to the part of the Forbidden City which housed the administration for eunuchs. The *Danei*. But foreigners found the metaphor so apt, so completely aligned with their image of the Chinese mind, that they adopted it to refer to the Forbidden City as a whole. Still today it rang true to Alice—and she could never look at the high-walled, mysterious palace complex without thinking of the words. The Great Within.

"There you are," said Spencer, stepping over the wooden doorsill. "Sorry."

"No problem," she answered. "Here." She began serving him the spicy dried tofu, shredded jellyfish, fried peanuts, and hot pickled cabbage that had been waiting on the table. Until he arrived she had not wanted to touch these *leng-pan*, cold dishes, but now she took some for her own plate and started eating.

He sank into his seat.

She looked up, chewing, and realized he was just staring at the table. "Something wrong?"

"I didn't get the money," he blurted.

She finished chewing, put her chopsticks down. She took her napkin up off her lap and dabbed at her mouth, replaced it. "What did you say?"

"I didn't get the grant. They turned me down."

She sat silent for a minute, then picked up the teapot. "Here." She poured. "Better drink some tea."

He looked at the cup as if he'd never seen anything like it before, and finally picked it up and drank from it. Then he smiled the soft, lopsided smile of someone who knows all about being hurt, who's been hurt before and who knows this won't be the last time either.

"So what are you going to do?"

"I'm going ahead."

"Be serious."

"I am serious. I can't go back now. This is my chance to make something of myself."

She drew her brows together, trying to sort out this logic.

"I just have to figure out where to get the money."

"It's going to be more than you think. You have to pay for these two extra guys now. And the vice director is sure to pile on a lot of fees and charges."

"He is?"

She shrugged. "I'm sure he wouldn't have granted the permits unless he thought it'd be profitable."

"Hmm." He ran his hands through his pale hair and looked at his plate. "This any good?"

"Very. Try some."

He tasted the jellyfish. "Hey, you're right. Alice, listen. I have a great project here. If I find Peking Man, it'll transform the field. It'll answer some huge questions. I can't let the whole thing go just because the people back in Washington don't understand it—can I?"

"I guess not."

"Right."

"Teilhard wouldn't."

"What?" He looked at her.

"Teilhard wouldn't let this go. Think about it. He had this vision of evolution—he *saw* it, saw the whole design, the spiral of life from the most primitive to the highest levels of development. He saw it, and he got the fossils to prove it. But his Jesuit order said no, no way. *Littera scripta manet*, Holy doctrine. So they exiled him to China. They forbade him to publish. But did he stop studying it and writing about it? No!"

"And he wrote books, and put them away, and then after he died they were read by millions of people."

"Exactly."

He thought about this. "So what was it, after all, that the Church objected to so much? What made them exile him?"

"Original sin. The Fall. His vision of man's development didn't jibe with the Adam-and-Eve myth—the idea that all humans are born soiled, sinners, and need to be redeemed. The Jesuits ordered Teilhard to sign a statement explicitly endorsing original sin. He refused. So they sent him to China."

"It sounds so insane," Spencer said. "The idea that we're born with guilt."

"I don't know," she said, uncomfortably aware of her own burden of shame. "Maybe some people still believe it."

"Well, *he* saw the truth—and he had the courage to be himself. I've got to have the same courage, Alice. I have to go ahead."

"But you don't have the money."

"Look." He leaned across the table. "I think I can scrape up enough for the out-of-pocket. I'm not sure, but I think I can. What I want to ask you is this. Would you consider deferring your fee? It's not like I wouldn't pay you. I would pay you"—he swallowed—"I would pay you just as soon as I could."

She looked at the table, dismayed. I should back out, she thought. It's his problem. Not mine.

"Listen," he rushed on. "Don't answer me right now. Okay? Think about it. Please. Take your time."

She found herself remembering the things Teilhard had written—the carefully composed thoughts in his books and the more spontaneous lines in his letters to Lucile: *I don't believe fundamentally in anything but in the awakening of spirit, hope, and freedom.* And for some reason she saw, flitting across her mind, the profoundly reflective face of the Chinese archaeologist, Dr. Lin. His eyes, aware. His hands holding her name card, turning it over and over.

"Okay," she said. "I'll think about it."

A waiter stepped over the doorsill and placed three dishes on the table. *"Gan bian niu rou si,"* he declaimed. *"Yu xiang qiezi. Siji dou."*

"Dry-cooked shredded beef," Alice said quietly. "Eggplant in garlic sauce. Four-season beans."

"I can't do this without you, you know."

She sighed. "I know."

"Here. I want to give you this. I copied it." He opened his notebook and removed a small square of paper with the pictograph traced on it, the disembodied monkey-head that looked like a sun. "I don't know what it means yet, but—keep it with you. Ask people about it. Maybe you'll run into someone who's seen it before."

"Okay," she said, sliding it into her jeans pocket. "But I don't know if I'll be going with you. I mean, if you can't pay me . . ."

"I know." He raised his hands to stop her going further. "I know. Just think about it. All right?"

They went together to the Bank of China counter in the hotel.

"Dr. Spencer wishes to draw cash advances on all these credit cards." She handed the three cards across the shiny new marble counter.

"In what amount?" The clerk had one hand on a computer keypad, the other on an abacus.

"How much?" she asked him in English.

"To the limit," he whispered back.

He watched her convey this in Chinese. It seemed effortless for her, all the strange singing syllables.

She leaned close to him again. "Altogether, she says there's eighty-two hundred dollars available."

"What? I thought I had more. Ask her if she's sure."

The woman shrugged, touched something on her keyboard, and the computer spit out a little slip of white paper. She passed it across the counter.

"Shit," Spencer said softly, studying his balance.

The woman let out a stream of Mandarin.

"You want all the eighty-two hundred?" Alice translated.

He chewed his lip.

Alice raised her eyebrows, waiting.

"What about you?" he said. "Are you coming with me?"

"I don't know yet." She closed her face off, not wanting to commit either way. The truth was, she found herself wanting to go. Lucile had taken chances. So had Teilhard. *Breaking some respected boundaries means a torrent of new life,—then I feel safer and stronger. . . .* "I haven't decided," she said.

"Okay," he said, "keep thinking. Tell her"—he nodded toward the clerk—"tell her I want all of it."

She took a bus up to the quiet, leafy neighborhood where Bruce Kaplan lived and knocked on the round wooden gate. His old *Ayi,* gap toothed and steel haired, exchanged pleasantries with Alice as she led her over a succession of doorsills, under the clicking boughs of ailanthus, past wood-and-glass-walled *si-he* courtyard rooms that Alice knew had been closed and curtained for many years, back to the inner court. When she saw Bruce she ignored the Chinese conventions she knew he now followed—

the protracted interchange of dispositions—and in a rush poured out the story of Adam Spencer and Peking Man. "I don't know, Bruce. Should I go?"

"Bruce." He tried to form the English word with his mouth, smiled his moonlike smile, and lapsed into Chinese. "The world calls me Guan Bai now, you know. And I find I am no longer able to speak English—even with you. It dries up in my mouth."

"Chinese, then. Eh, I forgot. But hasn't my memory long been pitiable? This letter from your mother." Alice reached into her purse and withdrew the letter she'd picked up at the American Express office. "Do you still read English or not? I could translate."

"Just leave it here." He lifted a hand toward a teakwood table, on which his *Ayi* had just placed a pot of tea.

Alice examined him compassionately. Bruce Kaplan—Guan Bai—lived in another world. Whenever Alice visited him she always found him seated in this same spot, under this plum tree; only the leaves changed with the seasons, and his clothing changed from the lumpish, thickly padded robes of winter to the thin, loose silks of summer. Now his hand played over the book he'd been reading, *Mengzi,* the Confucian masterpiece of Mencius. Written more than two thousand years ago. She checked the characters on the book's cover. Archaic. Of course.

Bruce was far down the road, farther than she'd realized.

"What are the opinions of your other friends?" he asked her.

"Those I know in Beijing now are few."

"Is it so? What about Tom and Maureen, the journalists? And that German diplomat—Otto, wasn't it?"

She shrugged.

"They've moved away?"

"No, they're here. Things change." She felt she could not really explain to Bruce, who led the secluded life of a Chinese scholar, how her friends had grown up. How their concerns were different: the hardships of bringing up children in China, the struggle to find good *Ayi*s, the schools, the apartments, the price of imported milk. And like a barb in the center of it all the fact that she herself was single, and over thirty; an almost unmentionable creature in China. The expatriates, like the Chinese, seemed almost not to know what to make of her now. In the States, not marrying might have been acceptable. Here it was an embarrassment. She couldn't deal with her old friends. She stopped calling them.

"It would be interesting for you to see northwestern China," Guan Bai offered.

"That's so."

He poured tea out of the ancient brown Yixing pot. A real one. "And what about this American archaeologist? Is he interesting?"

"Yes. Hapless in a way—but interesting."

"Not someone with whom you could be close."

"No."

"Why? Because he's American?"

"Partly. You know I am *not* an American, not anymore, not really."

"I used to think that of myself," he said wistfully. "Now I'm not so sure. But the archaeologist—he's not someone you could be interested in."

She shook her head. "No. Definitely—no. But"—she brightened—"I *have* been reading these last few days about a mesmerizing love affair that took place here, in Beijing, sixty years ago."

He hoisted his brows, amused.

"Between two people who agreed never to become lovers. The French priest Teilhard de Chardin and the American sculptress Lucile Swan."

"Ah, the philosopher. He lived here in the city, didn't he?"

"Yes. Loved this woman. Really loved her. And she loved him. So she gave up the physical part, buying into this idea that they'd reach something higher. She went with him, you know?" God, Alice thought as she said it, what commitment.

"And did they reach something higher through this love? Or was it only his way of asking for her on his terms?"

Alice smiled, enjoying his intelligence. *"Wo bu zhidao,"* I don't know.

"Was she happy about it?"

"Oh, no," Alice said promptly. "She wasn't."

"Would you be happy in that arrangement?"

"Of course not." She bristled. "I'd go crazy."

He lifted his tiny brown sand-textured cup and looked at it lovingly. "I see. Yet I wonder whether Lucile Swan wouldn't go crazy trying to live life the way you do. Ai-li, many are the years we've been friends. It is curious, is it not? The myriad eddies and whirlpools in the river along the way."

She waited at Mrs. Meng's door, clutching half a Yunnan ham wrapped in brown paper.

No answer. She pressed her ear to the door. Voices within. She tapped once more. This time, footsteps. Laughter. A male voice gaining.

Fumbling, the doorknob, creaking open.

Jian.

His long oval face froze, the color running out of it.

Ah, she thought helplessly, it's you.

In the next instant she saw how he'd aged in the couple of years since she'd last seen him. His skin showed the soon-to-crackle veneer of Chinese middle age and his eyes revealed a tired urbanity—the story of pain he'd endured and then given along to others.

He must hate me, she thought.

But hate was not his first feeling. "Ai-li," he whispered.

"Jian."

"Hao chang shijian," Long time. A grin tugged at his rice-grain-shaped face. "Still beautiful."

She felt the pull to him, the pull they had always felt together. But she could also feel the other anchor, the one that dropped straight down into her private well of failure and regret.

He met her gaze, and she felt him remembering everything. His eyes hardened. "Yes. But what are you doing here?"

"I came to see your mother."

"My mother?" His composure faltered.

"I visit her often."

He looked at Meng Shaowen for confirmation. Then back, suspicious, angry. "How dare you come here?"

"Jian, please, I'm sorry it didn't work out. But—I loved you."

"Don't use such words," he said softly, repulsed now by her use of the word *ai*, love. Americans always used that word so freely. At first, with Alice, he had found such liberty exciting. Now he knew better.

Alice felt lost in him, staring at him, remembering what had happened nine years before.

She had written that she was in love with a Chinese intellectual, talking about marriage. Horace replied at once, by cable, instructing her to meet him in Hong Kong three days later. The ticket was prepaid, the room reserved. He had not booked one of the fantastically expensive hotels—not the Peninsula, not the Mandarin—but the Holiday Inn, Kowloon. Just to remind her who filled her rice bowl.

So she had flown to Hong Kong, checked in, taken the elevator up to her room. She changed her blouse, adjusted her jeans, and studied herself in the mirror. Why did she look so girlish and frightened? She should be strong, assured. She was a grown woman. Her father had no right to tell her what to do.

But he was going to try—that was obvious. He hadn't come

all the way over here to say, "Congratulations, honey: I'm happy for you." Alice steeled herself.

Jian had offered to come with her. She had said no. "First I have to see him alone. When he's used to the idea, when he accepts it, then we'll meet him together."

"What could he find so difficult to accept?" Jian had asked her, eyes narrow, not understanding.

"You're Chinese!"

He shook his head. "But I am the one who should be worried about this. *I* am the one who should hope for *you* to be accepted. I am Chinese. You are—I'm sorry to say it—a Westerner."

She sighed. "My father sees things differently."

"And you?" The faintest edge seeped into his voice.

"What?"

"Do you see things as your father does? Does his mind live within yours?"

"No! No, no, no."

"Yet you don't want me to come with you."

"No," she said heavily. "I don't. I have to face him by myself."

He had looked at her for a long time, and then had finally nodded his agreement. And she was here, without Jian. The way she'd wanted it to be.

I don't have to listen to my father, she thought now in Hong Kong, gazing into the hotel mirror. If he tries to turn me against Jian I'll just leave, just turn around and walk out and let him go back to America. . . .

She walked into the hotel restaurant, heart quickening. There he was, Horace, rising to his feet in slacks and an open sport jacket. He looked older. She put her arms around him, tentative at first. Then she felt the flash of warmth and gladness—through all the trepidation it was still good to see him—and hugged him a little harder.

He hugged her back. "Thanks for coming, Alice."

"You came the longest way."

"Well, I had to talk to you. This is a *very* big decision."

They took their chairs and she blinked, trying to adjust to the buzzing brightness of the Hong Kong restaurant. It looked so alien to her, everything from the packets of sugar in the metal holder to the ketchup bottles and the garish yellow light globes overhead. And Horace. He sat in his loafers like an affluent tourist, legs crossed, American. Am I from him? she thought. Am I really? She sighed. "I know marriage is a big decision."

Then the waitress was there, and Alice asked for coffee in passable Cantonese, pinning the tones—so different from those in Mandarin—a little too tightly to sound truly colloquial.

He listened. "That's Chinese?"

"Cantonese," she said. "A different dialect than the one I speak—"

He waved the concept away with a patronizing smile. "They're all the same. All sound the same."

She stared. "They're not, I assure you."

He glanced at the ceiling, pulled his mouth to one side in a so-what expression. "Listen, sweetheart. I came over here because I was so shocked when I got your letter. You're a grown-up woman. You also happen to be beautiful, intelligent, and worldly—but there's a lot you don't know about life. Obviously. So we need to talk about this marriage."

"There's nothing to talk about," she said, swallowing back the pounding in her throat. "Jian is a wonderful man. He's the kind of person any father would want his daughter to marry! He's getting his Ph.D. in history—Chinese history. He comes from a brilliant family. And our children would have dual citizenship, when they grew up they could choose—"

"Children!" Horace's voice shook. "Children!"

"Of course, children. I'm twenty-seven, Horace."

"That's still young! Not that I don't want grandchildren. Of course I do! Nothing would make me happier. But not like this!"

"You mean not Chinese. Right?" She spit her words out, the anger starting. "Is that what you mean?"

"People should stick to their own kind!" he shot back.

"Their *own kind?*"

"Yes. Race, creed, and color." He slapped his palm on the table. "Their own kind."

Conversations around them halted. People were staring.

Alice narrowed her eyes. "That is the worst kind of shallow, thoughtless prejudice—"

"No! It's common sense. To marry a fellow like this—it's like getting a tattoo. It's exciting. At first it looks great. But you have to live with the damn thing for the rest of your life!"

She lifted her lip in a show of disbelief. "You are comparing Jian to a tattoo?"

"Alice! You know what I'm saying." He leaned forward. "You want me to be blunt? Very well. Don't marry this man. If you do you'll ruin your life."

The nerve! As if she had to ruin her own life. He'd already done it for her.

"I mean it, Alice."

"Listen. It's my life, not yours. Anyway, who says this would be such a mistake? You? Your racist cronies? What about me? Doesn't it matter at all what I want?"

"And what exactly do you want?"

She marshaled herself. "I want to settle down. I want to marry Jian. He's a good man. We could be happy together. I could have someone, finally. I could have a family."

"You do have a family! Me."

"Horace—"

"And you're my little girl, and I love you—why else would I fly all around the world to stop you making a mistake like this? Unless I loved you? Why else, Alice? Come on."

Mad as she was, something about what he said and the way he said it tugged at her. Of course she wanted his approval, of course; she wanted it terribly. She hated the idea of having to choose between a husband and a father. So if not approval, at least neutrality. . . .

He sensed her wavering and pushed on. "We're a family, Alice. I look out for you. I'm the only person you've ever known who's cared for you, consistently. That's why you could never marry a man without my blessing. Right? Because I'm part of you and you're part of me."

"I'm not part of you. I have my own life."

He made a dismissive gesture. "You can't even finance your own life! Speaking of which, can this man support you? I doubt it. How much money does he make?"

Now her eyes burned. "It doesn't matter how much money he makes."

"Well. It's not as if *I* can keep sending you money forever."

"Why do you have to make it about money!"

"I don't," he said instantly. "I just want my little girl to be happy. Be happy and find the right man. And you will, Alice. If you'll just come back to the States and look."

"*This* is where I live. *This* is where I want to find a man."

"I thought you already had. Find a man! Find a man! Maybe you don't even love this man—what's his name?—Jian?"

"I do love him! I told you that."

"No, you didn't."

"Well, I do."

"I'm not convinced." He looked at her hard.

"How dare you!" She felt herself flaring, anger and discomfort all mixed up because in that unerring way of his he'd gone right to her weak point. Did she truly love Jian? She did, of course she did. He was the best, most appropriate Chinese man she'd ever met. But at her core she still didn't feel they were completely connected. How could Horace know? It wasn't something she even acknowledged to herself, consciously. "Don't tell me what I feel."

"Then you tell me. What do you feel?"

"I feel that I love him and I want to marry him!" Inside, she knew it was not a clear certainty. It was messy, ambivalent, a hot-wire confusion of needs, desires, and ideals for the future. Do I love Jian? she thought desperately. Have I ever loved anyone?

"Alice." He was asking for her attention.

She looked up. Tears stood in his eyes. When was the last time Horace had cried? Ages. Years.

"I just want you to be happy," he was saying, quietly now, with feeling.

"Then don't interfere! Let me marry him."

"Are you in love with him?"

"Yes, I told you—"

"No. Are you?"

"Horace—"

"Are you?"

She groaned and covered her eyes.

"I think that's an answer."

"Stop it!" She was crying now. "It's wrong for you to do this. You can't force me!"

"Force you?" He looked at her hard, fully in control. "Of course I wouldn't force you. I would never force you."

"But you—"

"Oh, no, sweetheart. I had to say what I've said, but you are a grown woman. You'll have to choose for yourself. Here. When I got your letter I took all these out of the safe deposit." He removed a folder from his briefcase and reached into it.

Her eyes grew wide.

As she watched he slapped down her birth certificate, photos of herself as a child, alone, with Horace, as a baby with her mother.

"Take these, if you marry him. Leave this Mannegan family, this family of you and me. You want to be Chinese? Go ahead. Be Chinese. But you won't be my daughter any longer."

She still remembered how, without anger now, without sharpness, but with infinite sadness and his eyes still brimming, he had clicked the briefcase shut, risen, and walked from the restaurant. As if it were not some personal, vengeful choice of his own but inescapable natural forces which drove him to do what he did.

Now, standing in the doorway of the Meng apartment, she suddenly remembered what she was holding. She thrust the grease-spotted, paper-wrapped ham into the Chinese man's arms. "Jian," her voice came cracking out, "if I could say how sorry I—"

"Zenmole?" What is it? sang a pleasant female voice from the cooking area at the rear of the apartment. A woman in her twenties with a plump, tight-porcelain face sauntered out, baby riding her hip. Alice stared, feeling something die inside her. She knew about Jian's wife, of course she knew, but she hadn't seen Jian face to face since his marriage and she'd never seen the bride. Now here she was. With their baby. *"Shui-a?"* the young woman asked, glancing to Mother Meng, Who is this?

"A family friend," the old lady murmured.

"Jian?" the wife asked.

"Shi," he clipped. It's so.

Alice saw the young woman look openly at her, innocent of their whole situation. There must be a million things about him you don't know, Alice thought in a brief, violent burst of satisfaction.

"Ta jiu yao likai-le," Jian added crossly, She's about to leave.

Alice threw a desperate glance to Meng Shaowen. Mother Meng? she begged with her eyes. Must I go?

Mrs. Meng nodded once, a bowing of grass in front of wind. Jian was married to someone else now. Alice did not belong.

Jian stepped close to Alice. "Alice." He spoke in English, English she'd taught him during their year together. "You should not have come here. There's no more to say about what happened. I understand now. You could not commit to me."

"Neither could you, to me."

"Shenmo?" What?

"It wasn't all me. It was you too. Wasn't it? You didn't love me *quan xin, quan yi.* If you had you would have said: Forget your father. Marry me anyway. And I would have. But you didn't."

He tightened his mouth, unwilling to respond.

I knew it, she thought, and the hurt blazed over her. Hurt and all its ripples of revelation. "Jian. You couldn't bring your true self to me any more than I could bring mine to you."

"Naturally. You're American. You're white."

"Oh, come on, Jian—"

"Guoqu-de shi jiu rang ta guoqu-ba," he retorted, reverting to Chinese. Let the past go.

She felt her cheeks reddening.

"Jian?" the wife queried.

"Anyway," he went on, ignoring his wife. "I have responsibilities to my ancestors. Now"—he motioned with his eyes to his Chinese baby, in his wife's arms—*"wo zuodao-le."* He evaluated her one final time, as if to commit her to memory.

In some basal pit of herself Alice wanted to reach for him. She sensed he felt it too. If it were not for the tangle of the present day all around them, if what was inside them could have been free, they might have crumpled into each other's arms. As it was he shook his head and spoke to her softly, sternly, in English: "Now don't ever come here again."

Gently, he shut the door.

* * *

She lay in bed the next morning. The rush-hour mob of bicycles and cars and trucks on Changan subsided from a roar to a rumble. Spencer came to her door once, knocked. She couldn't deal with him then; just couldn't rise to it. She called out for him to come back later.

Seeing Jian again. Thinking about what she'd had with him, about almost being able to connect with her true heart. Lucile had found another self with Pierre, a self higher than man-woman love. Had she fulfilled her true heart? *The worst failing of our minds is that we fail to see the really big problems simply because the forms in which they arise are right under our eyes.*

And Adam Spencer was right. She was stalled. Years now she'd been working as a low-level translator when she should have been so much more—a scholar, a sinologist, an intelligent woman taking the four treasures—the brush, the ink, the ink-stone, the paper—and turning them into a lifetime of insight and erudition.

She heard a movement outside the door. It was Spencer again. "Alice! I have to buy the train tickets. Are you coming with me or not?"

"Wait a minute!" She limped into the bathroom, threw cold water on her face. Examined herself, the water running from her cheekbones. Not young any longer. The years were starting to pull her face downward, she could already see where the lines and the sags were starting to form.

Thirty-six, she thought, touching her cheek. But I'm smart, really smart, and I have heart. I could love again. If I could only get the chance.

"Alice?" Spencer's voice was muffled by the door.

She toweled off. With the canyons of scratchy cotton cloth pressed against her face she suddenly pictured the man she had met in the vice director's office the day before. Dr. Lin. The man who had seemed to take in everything, and who had held her name card for such a long time, so attentively. She locked eyes with herself in the mirror. *The forms in which they arise are right under our eyes.*

"Alice."

She walked out of the bathroom. "All right! Dr. Spencer? Can you hear me? I'll come with you."

5

THE TRAIN STOOD gasping in Beijing Zhan. They pushed aboard with the Chinese and all their boxes, suitcases, bundles, and bags full of fruit, melon seeds, and steaming, fragrant *baozi*.

She glanced around the second-class hard sleeper. It would be a rough two days and nights, sleeping on flat, narrow berths stacked three up to the ceiling. Though it was better than sitting up all night on a wooden bench, in "hard seat."

"Berth forty-three," he said, handing her a stub.

A middle bunk, just above his. A couple of slots facing them on the right, empty. Those were for their Chinese colleagues, Dr. Kong and Dr. Lin, who were scheduled to board at Baotou.

"Where's your luggage?"

"This is it." She tossed the black Rollaboard on her berth. Her point of honor: never more than one carry-on bag, plus a purse. And of course, she had to make it smaller than regulation size, which then catapulted her into an agonized stratosphere of wardrobe planning. Pants, shirts, and socks that all matched, all the colors and weights and textures in line and interchangeable. One baseball cap, weighing nothing. Tiny vials of shampoo and cleanser and moisturizer and makeup and toothpaste, all rationed out day by day. The collapsing hairbrush, the minitoothbrush. The clothes with labels snipped out. Her one concession: the black dress, for going out. The antique Chinese stomach-protector.

"That's really all you have?"

"All I need."

"You're incredible."

"I notice you don't carry too much either. You always wear the same thing."

He laughed. "That's lifestyle engineering. Just think of the hours I've saved in my life wearing only jeans and work shirts. Days, by now. Weeks."

"Never thought of it that way."

He rolled his shoulders modestly. "So tell me about our destination—Yinchuan. Have you been there?"

"Actually no. I've never been to the Northwest." Most of Alice's jobs had been in commerce, and most of the commerce buzzed around China's eastern cities. Guangzhou, initially, after things started to open up in the mid-seventies, and then Beijing and Tianjin and Nanjing and, of course, the jewel in the trading crown, Shanghai. But the Northwest, no. She shivered with anticipation, a touch of fear, because she'd heard it was a different China out there, in the desert. A place where the rules varied. Be alert, she reminded herself.

"Well, I'm excited about seeing the Chinese deserts," he said. "The Gobi, the Taklamakan, the Tengger, the Ordos. Even their names sound like music. They're interesting archaeologically too—especially the Tengger and the Ordos, where we're headed."

"Because Peking Man is out there?"

"Not just that. Because they're said to be full of prehistoric sites, and totally undisturbed. *Pristine* is the word we use. It's not like America, where everything's been looted and picked over.

Out where we're going, ancient people left stuff behind and it's still sitting there just the way they left it."

"How can that be?"

He beamed. "Chinese grave robbers only went after tombs from historical times—tombs with treasure. They had no interest in Neolithic and Paleolithic sites."

"Lucky for us." She visualized the little drawing from the letter, the sun head with the face of a monkey. It had a primitive, archetypal look.

"It's odd that nobody's surveyed out there since Teilhard." Spencer settled back. "Nobody's even looked for sites. Do you know how far it's going to be, to Yinchuan?"

"About two days." Though she hadn't been there she had read about Yinchuan, the closest town to the Shuidonggou site, where they were going to stay. It was an oasis city. It sat near the top of the Yellow River's horseshoe curve, on the Ningxia–Inner Mongolia border. It was the edge of the genetic Chinese world, the place where the Chinese and the Uighurs, Muslims, and Mongols started mixing. The region of the three great north-central deserts, too, the Ordos and the Tengger and the Gobi. All cut by a majestic mountain range called the Helan Shan.

Outside, she watched the Beijing suburbs thin. City of history, six hundred, seven hundred years. Teilhard had lived there, had left Peking on a day like this for the Northwest, had ridden a train on this very line. *What I like most in China is the geometry of the walls, the curve of the roofs, the multiple-storeyed towers, the poetry of the old trees teeming with crows, and the desolate outline of the mountains.*

She watched the trees in a blur, and the villages in their momentary clumps—the few buildings, the crossroads—between stretches of fields. She watched this changing terrain for a long time before the hills appeared, green walls sloping steeply up away from the train. Every few minutes a break in the landscape, a cleavage, would reveal the triumphant, snaking form of the

Great Wall in the distance, marching along the crest of the hill above them. Shudderingly beautiful. Built on death and heartbreak. Like so much in China.

These hills, and the stone line of the Wall, disintegrated into the advancing dark. Then it was a shrouded nighttime world roaring by, the ghostly hills cradling north China against the hydraulic train-whistle scream.

Eventually she crawled under her thin blanket and slept. By the time she opened her eyes on her hard pallet the next morning the hills had flattened out; all the green land had vanished and they were rattling across the yellow rock-strewn desert. It seemed to stretch to the limit of the earth. Nothing but boulders and steppes forming low, tired plateaus tufted with struggling gray-green grass.

"Teilhard took this train," she said.

"That's right. In 1923, on his way to find Shuidonggou, his first big site. Shuidonggou's in the Ordos Desert—that's where we're going to start."

"Because you're thinking, he hid this crate of fossils out there in 1945. How? He shipped it to someone?"

"Or he carried it there himself. There is this one month, April of forty-five, when he's unaccounted for. He wasn't in Peking, but there's no record of where he went."

"How could he have traveled out here during the war?"

Spencer lifted his hands. "I don't know. Maybe he just found a way. But I know one thing, from his letters. He loved it out here. Shuidonggou was a place that gave him hope."

Her eyes locked in. "You know—I think you're right. I remember a line I read last night in one of the books. He wrote from somewhere—Ethiopia, I think—that he felt homesick for Mongolia. For Mongolia! I thought it was odd."

"But if you think about what happened to him out here it makes sense. He stumbled on a site of ancient man. The locals dropped everything they were doing and pitched in to help him. It was the proof he was looking for."

"Though it didn't help—with Rome, I mean."

"No. It didn't."

They settled back, Spencer making notes, Alice watching the morning bustle that had taken over their crowded railroad car. It was overflowing now with bodies and luggage and had become a noisy, hurtling village—a Mandarin wall of shouting, laughing, and singing. Old men coughed and hacked and spat at the floor, none too accurately. Spencer winced at the sounds, but Alice was used to it. And she knew, when she got up, to step carefully over the splintered sunflower-seed shells, gnawed watermelon rinds, and sodden black tea leaves.

By noon the pebbly sea outside had given way to grasslands. Baotou was scheduled for twelve-fifteen.

Now on the horizon Alice could make out the huddle of sand-colored buildings.

"Our colleagues." Spencer closed his notebook.

"Yes." She peered ahead, trying to make sense of the far-off skyline. The two men from Zhengzhou would be there, just ahead, in that town, waiting on the platform. Right now. That tall, contained man, Dr. Lin. And Dr. Kong.

They shot into the squat, sun-baked town, clanked into the station, squealed to a stop.

All around the train was a hissing cloud, the surge of people, shouts and cries, and suddenly there they were, Dr. Kong and Dr. Lin. They bumped their big suitcases down the aisle, smiling. "Hello again," they said. "Hello."

"Hello."

"Hi."

Alice and Spencer stood up. Alice spoke. "Was your journey pleasant?"

"You trouble yourself too much to inquire," Dr. Lin said, using the kind of honorific Chinese one didn't hear so often these

days, except on Taiwan. Mainland people were more *suibian,*
follow convenience, casual. Not him.

"It is of your journey that one should speak," he continued.
"You are the foreign guests." He ran his hand through his shock
of black hair, then turned and settled his suitcase up into the
storage net above the window.

Her gaze settled on his back.

He seemed to feel it, glanced behind. "Truly spoken, it's an
amazing thing. You can really talk."

"Your praise is unjustified," she answered. It was a proper
answer, but she tempered it with a smile. She knew her Chinese
was good. Mainly, of course, it was because she had a good ear.
She had always loved music. All her life, even when she was
small, she'd been aware that she heard music the way most other
people did not—*really* heard it. And when she got older and
studied Chinese, she found that the other students didn't listen
the way that she did. They thought they did, but they didn't.
And because she *heard* Chinese, the way that she had always
heard music, she quickly picked up the small lilts and angles of
Mandarin speech. So what was exceptional about her Chinese
was her accent, not her vocabulary. It took years of hard work to
build a Chinese vocabulary, and hard work was not Alice's
strong point. Smart but ever so slightly lazy, that was Alice. To
Dr. Lin now she demurred politely: "There are lots of foreigners
around who can speak better than I."

"Really? I hardly know whether to believe you or not. Still,
you are the first foreigner I've ever spoken with, so"—for the
first time he allowed a hint of a smile onto his composed face—
"my research is not complete."

"Not yet."

"Not yet," she heard him answer, but she couldn't tell if he
was agreeing or merely echoing, the way Chinese often did.
"You've really never met another foreigner?"

"Oh, yes, I have met other foreigners. I'm originally from Shanghai, you know. I moved to Zhengzhou as an adult."

"Yes, I hear that in your accent," Alice said, for he had the *s*-laden pronunciation of someone from the Yangtze River delta.

"As a child in Shanghai, I sometimes met foreigners. But you are the first one I've met who can talk." And the first one, he thought, who seems aware and civilized. He studied her peculiar skin, pale but covered with freckles, and her sharp but not entirely unpleasant nose. He was careful not to look directly at her body. Peripherally he registered it, though: spare and compact, wider across the shoulders than a Chinese woman, but narrower through the hips and legs. How strange, he thought, the way Western women wear clothes that show every curve and line of their bodies, leaving nothing for a man to imagine. . . .

"Then I'm honored to meet you," she was saying.

Dr. Kong had stabbed out a number on his phone and was talking rapidly to someone in a slurred, provincial accent. Dr. Lin stood for a minute, nodding politely to her and to Spencer, and finally fitted himself onto the berth opposite Alice. He lay on his side, head propped on his hand, and kept his serious gaze on her. "If you permit me to ask, Interpreter Mo. How does an outside woman come to learn Chinese? Your parents were perhaps missionaries?"

She laughed. "No—far from it."

"Your father is a diplomat, then?"

"My father is a United States congressman," she said, and instantly regretted it.

"A congressman," he repeated.

She sighed. This would be repugnant to him. In China, everyone scorned the bratty children of the ruling elite. Why had she told him?

"A difficult road," he answered.

"Shi zheiyangde." That's how it is.

Professor Lin's eyes lit on the book she still clasped in her hand. *"Ni kan shenmo?"* What are you reading?

"The letters of Pierre Teilhard de Chardin." She showed him the book. "Do you read English?"

"No. Eh, the French priest." He turned the book over, regarding Teilhard's solemn picture on the back cover, the spiritual blue eyes, the black-and-white priest's collar. "So Teilhard is famous in the West for his discoveries."

"Not at all. Hardly known for that. Famous for books he wrote about religion."

"Religion?" He stared at her.

"His church"—she had to search a moment for the word for *Catholics*—"the *tianzhujiao* didn't accept evolution. Teilhard wrote books describing evolution itself as an act of God. Reconciling science and religion. These books are quite famous."

"I see," he said. "But is it not strange to have to prove these things? Because man has evolved since the ancient times. That is the fact."

"Now this is known," Alice agreed. "But in the time of the French priest, a lot of Western people still believed in their old creation myth—that the world began with a man and woman in Paradise, and they sinned, and because of that the world is tainted and none of us is pure."

"Oh, yes, I have heard this religious idea from the West." He narrowed his eyes. "Do you believe it?"

"Of course not." She grinned. "Who of intelligence believes such a thing? The world did not suddenly appear four or five thousand years ago. So much in archaeology goes back so much farther! It seems like every year they find something older—isn't it so? *Homo sapiens* has been here a hundred thousand, maybe two hundred thousand years. And before that—*Homo erectus.*" Her eyes were bright with interest.

He smiled. "I'd always heard Western people had no interest in the past."

"Not me, Dr. Lin. I love history. I love everything old."

"Me too," he said softly.

Then suddenly Spencer was there, speaking, pointing outside to the heat-shimmering rocky tundra. "Tell him it looks just like Nevada."

She translated this.

Lin drew his brows together.

"Did you tell him I'm from Reno?" Spencer asked. "It's amazing how much it looks like home. The geology and topography—I could be in Nevada!"

Alice put this in Chinese.

"Come on," Spencer said. "What were you and Dr. Lin talking about?"

"Oh. Chinese-Western attitudes on evolution."

"Okay. He got the briefing. He knows what we want, the intact teeth, the DNA sample, to find out who modern humans are descended from. So ask him. Ask him if he believes *Homo erectus* came from Africa or evolved in China."

"Dr. Lin. Dr. Spencer wonders if you think Peking Man evolved separately here in China, or if *Homo erectus* evolved everywhere out of Africa."

Lin opened his small black eyes wide. "Separately in China. Naturally. This is well known."

She conveyed this to Spencer.

"What?" the American pressed. "How is it known?"

Lin lifted his big shoulders in a shrug. "It is borne out by the fossils—Acheulean tools are found with *Homo erectus* in Africa and Europe, but never in China. Asian *Homo erectus* must be a separate species. Of course, this is logical. China is the seat of civilization. It's the place where all ancient life took hold. Also, it hardly seems possible that modern Chinese could be descended from Africans. The races are too—too different."

Dr. Spencer opened his mouth, then closed it again. He gave Alice a look that said: Aren't they silly. She could tell Dr. Lin, eyes crinkling with humor as he leafed through the book of Teilhard's letters, was thinking the same thing about them.

Late that night, just before she slipped into the deep, disassociated well of sleep, a shaft of light crossed the car and she caught a glimpse of Dr. Lin's face in the opposite berth. His eyes were open and he was watching her.

The lush oasis fringe around Yinchuan appeared as a sudden block of emerald, backed right up to the rocky brown desert. One moment there were mountains bare as flesh undulating to the horizon, the next the train was flashing through grove after grove of oleaster trees, their leaves rustling green and silver in the wind. Canal trenches jumped out of the Yellow River, itself a muddy silt ribbon in the distance, and sprinted in all directions. They vanished into fields of eggplant, tomatoes, and peppers. And miles of rice: the seductive carpet of deep green so rarely seen in north China.

In 1923, she knew, the rail line had ended at Baotou—where Lin and Kong had boarded the train. There Teilhard and his fellow priest, Émile Licent, had paid silver Mex dollars for mules, and ridden across the desert to this city, Yinchuan. The name Yinchuan was incomprehensible to Alice. Yinchuan meant Silver River, and nowhere was the river anything but a slow, plodding brown. She noticed as the train clattered through town that the city walls Teilhard had mentioned in his letters were gone. Instead there was a string of masonry buildings, and the billowing smokestacks of factories. Here and there Alice could see a few of the original gates and watchtowers, still standing up, shocked and ancient.

They fell exhausted into the lobby of the Number One Guest-house, spilling on the limestone floor with their bags and their gear and their dust-streaked clothes. They were given their rooms: Alice and Adam in one building, Kong and Lin in another.

"Why?" Adam wanted to know.

It was the way it always was, she explained: Chinese and foreigners separated.

She shut herself in her room and immediately and obsessively unpacked, the way she always did upon arrival in a new hotel room. Her clothes formed neat rows in the wooden drawer, the antique silk stomach-protector and black dress hidden at the bottom. She dug from her pocket the small folded drawing of the monkey sun head and the obituary of Lucile Swan, and placed them on the bureau. Then she drew the heavy Pompeiian-red velvet curtains, filled the bathtub, stripped, and climbed in.

Ah, she thought. Light from the overhead bulb broke up on the water's surface, clinking and distorting the pale line of her naked body underneath. She soaked until she felt clean, delivered, all true and restored again. For a time.

She closed her eyes.

She must have dozed, because when she jolted back the water had grown cold and still. She splashed to her feet, shook the drops from her hair, rubbed hard at herself with the towel.

Awake again, alive.

Tea.

Suddenly she wanted to get out, walk, see Yinchuan. Was it really different from the China she knew? So far it seemed like any backwater town, and this hotel—with its barely functional toilets and old-fashioned velvet curtains—was just another provincial establishment.

Dressed, she stepped into the hall. She saw that Spencer's door was closed. He'd said something about reviewing Teilhard's maps from the 1923 Shuidonggou expedition. She listened at the

door, heard nothing, and went out, crossing the courtyard between the buildings, to emerge finally from the front door of the
Number One complex. There Dr. Kong and Dr. Lin were sitting
on the steps. *"Zenmoyang?"* she said politely, and sat beside
them.

"I must compliment you," Kong remarked. "Your Chinese is
very standard."

"Guojiang, " she demurred, and then pointed to a small black
machine wrapped in its cord on the cement step. "What's that?"

"My fax." Dr. Kong raised his narrow hands in despair. "I
need a line for it, and the hotel cannot spare one. Is it not
unthinkable? A hotel in this modern age without extra phone
lines . . ." He shook his head.

"He loves that fax." Dr. Lin laughed. "He got it on a trip to
Japan last year. Now he takes it everywhere."

"No extra lines. Really, I had no idea this place would be so
tu."

Alice smiled. *Tu,* hick or rustic, carried a veiled insult. Most
urban Chinese looked down on rural Chinese. "It is pretty *tu* out
here," she conceded.

"Regrettable," sniffed Kong, and picked up the machine. "In
Zhengzhou this would never happen."

"Nor in Beijing," Alice said. "But does not progress have its
price? Every time I go out it seems I see some lovely old neighborhood torn down, and in its place a new concrete building."

"Yes," Kong said, "but *they* are beautiful. They are modern.
Life in those narrow alleys in Beijing is—is"—he searched for
the word—"unhygienic." He thought about his visit to the vice
director's Beijing home, just a few days before, in just such a
hutong. True, his cousin's courtyard house retained a certain feudal charm. But the smoke from the cook shed! The dogs running
free! And worst of all, the primitive bathroom, no more than a
tiled trough on the floor through which water gurgled. "You see,

Interpreter Mo, we Chinese are most anxious to leave those primitive conditions and move into modern housing."

"Not me," she said. "I like the *hutong* houses better." She glanced at Dr. Lin.

"I feel the same way," Lin said, speaking to Kong but smiling at Alice. "I like the old courtyard homes."

"When they disappear a part of old China will be gone forever."

"Exactly."

Kong rolled his eyes. "The past is the past. Anyway. I'm going to the Bureau of Cultural Relics. They'll have an extra phone line for me."

"The Bureau of Cultural Relics?" Alice asked.

"The office in charge of archaeology for all of Ningxia. They run the historical museums too." Kong hoisted his fax machine. *"Zai jian."*

"And what are you going to do?" Lin asked her as Kong walked out the gate.

"I thought I'd look around the town."

"I noticed a place around the corner that rents bicycles," he said carefully. "Would the foreign woman want to get a bicycle and sightsee with me?"

"Yes, I would, but if you continue to call me 'the foreign woman' I might have to curse your ancestors for eight generations."

He laughed. " 'Interpreter Mo,' then?"

"That's at least a little better." She knew she could not ask him to call her 'Alice' or 'Ai-li'; given names were only for intimate use in China. Mostly, people addressed each other by title. She didn't mind. There was a certain security in it. One always knew where one was, in the group. *Is this my group?* she thought for the thousandth time. China. The Chinese.

"Better wait here," Lin advised. "I'll go rent the bicycles. If the old man sees you are a foreigner he'll want a huge deposit from you—a hundred yuan, say, or your passport."

"Oh." While he went around the corner she studied the old Chinese Muslim women behind their yogurt stands. They sat in their wide cotton trousers behind the rickety little tables, waving flies away from crude paper-covered crocks of yogurt. As she watched them she felt her heart pounding pleasantly. Did Lin feel the same flutter of affinity she did? Of course he does, she thought, he must. If experience had taught her anything it was that when she felt it, the other person felt it too.

Riding up Sun Yat-sen Boulevard, the main street and biggest commercial center for nearly a thousand miles of desert, Alice saw an endless stream of functional, Eastern-Bloc cement buildings. Everywhere were majestic signs in Chinese characters and Mongolian script, announcing the Number Three Light Industrial Store, the Municipal Committee for Liaison with the Minority Peoples Subheadquarters, the Hua Feng Institute for the Training of Herbal Medicine, and the Number Eight People's Clinic.

The streets were not crowded—at least not by Beijing or Shanghai standards. They passed a few carts, an occasional car. There were no streetlights and pedestrians ambled in all random directions, hardly seeming to notice the distinction between street and sidewalk.

They paused at the West Gate Tower, which now kept only a silent, symbolic watch over the streets. She recalled one of Teilhard's letters; he had written about standing at this West Gate of the city in 1923, looking down the long dirt road to Tibet. Tartary, he had called this place. A bygone word now. Tartary. She looked at Lin from the corner of her eye. Maybe the kind of word he would like.

"Shall we turn?" he asked.

"Sure."

They swung to the left. The road out of town was just a continuation of Serve-the-Nation Boulevard, a two-lane blacktop lined with noodle stalls and barbershops. As they pedaled west on Serve-the-Nation this crumbled into animal pens and occasional dispensaries for hardware or vegetables, and finally into farmland. They were alone. No one was following them. "Let's stop and have a rest," Lin called over his shoulder.

They steered off the road where a small hill sloped up to a grove of willows, dropped their bikes, and sat in the grass. Off in the distance the fields marched in squares, marked off by brown-ribboned canals, punctuated here and there by the sand-colored houses made of earth. Lin pulled an orange out of his pocket and gouged at the peel with a small knife. He gazed out at the landscape and nodded as if satisfied.

"You seem to like it here."

He handed her a section, cradled in his broad palm. "You can say I have an interest in this area. I tried to get a permit to visit here in seventy-four."

"You mean you wanted to be sent here to do your work in the countryside?" She knew that educated city youth had been forcibly reassigned to rural areas then. The Cultural Revolution. She thought back. Sixty-six to seventy-six: she had been so young then, a child playing along the damp, oppressive Houston bayous, alone and jealous and full of rage at a world which seemed all wrong to her and dreaming about someplace where she would belong, really belong, and meanwhile here in China hundreds of millions of souls were flying apart. The blood in that decade drained out onto the earth faster than it could be dammed up. Later, when she came to understand the language, and began working here, she heard the stories gushing bitterly from everyone. The horror of it finally settled on her. "Why did you want to be sent here?"

"I wanted to try and visit my wife."

A wife! But of course, he was a mature man, older than she. "So—she was the one sent here?"

"That's how it was."

"And why do you say 'try to visit'? If you were both sent here, couldn't you just be assigned to the same place?"

He didn't answer right away, but made a great show of peeling the orange.

"This was a Cultural Revolution thing, right?" she persisted.

"It was during the Chaos, yes."

Alice kicked herself. She couldn't shake the habit of using the phrase *wenhua da geming,* cultural revolution. Stupid. Naive. Many Chinese didn't reply with that phrase, cultural revolution. To them it was something so much larger and more engulfing. They often called it the Chaos.

"Dr. Lin, I guess you're not talking about her just being sent downcountry." His hand shook and the point of the knife made a jagged tear in the orange's delicate membrane. A drop of juice welled up and dripped down the side. "Of course not," he said, and now an edge was in his voice.

"So you mean . . ." She didn't want to say the word, in case she was wrong.

"Laogai," he said, and dug hard at the orange with the knife. Just the one word was enough, *laogai.* Literally it meant "reform prison," but everyone knew it was a shadow world of hard labor, and lots of people disappeared into it and never came out. She saw the tight irritated press of his mouth. This happened to her a lot. She spoke pretty well, and so people thought she would float easily into the oblique nuances favored by Chinese intellectuals. For them, it was all about allusion: more beautiful than definition. But she never seemed to talk that way. Language fluency was only language fluency. It didn't make her Chinese.

"Look, I'm sorry." She didn't know if she meant about his wife, or her west-ocean-person rudeness.

"Mei guanxi," he said, It doesn't matter. But of course it did.

* * *

"Call to America," she told the *fuwuyuan* at the front desk. "Houston, Texas." Horace still paid for an apartment in Houston and she checked her voice mail there from time to time. Jobs, she usually got through her referrals from the U.S.-China Chamber of Commerce. But sometimes people called her apartment.

She penciled in the form the clerk gave her and headed back to her room to wait for the connection to go through. She'd been surprised to learn that her international call had to go through Beijing—it had been years since she'd been in a hotel of any size that didn't have international direct dial. She picked up the book of Pierre and Lucile's letters and tried not to watch the phone.

A few thousand kilometers away, in Beijing, Fourth Apprentice International Operator Yu Lihua noticed a blinking red light on her board, one she hadn't seen before. She called her supervisor over.

"It means the call's to be recorded," Supervisor Ling said. The older woman covered her surprise. She glanced at a sheet of little-used codes, tacked to the wall. "Ah," she said, "it's PLA."

Yu Lihua just looked at her.

"Are your ears clogged? Has your brain run out through your mouth? You know the sequence. Tape it! They'll pick up the tape next shift." She turned and walked away.

Finally Alice's room phone stabbed out with its twin bursts. She snatched it up. On the line another phone was ringing, far away. She visualized her studio apartment in the Heights, upper right unit in a pleasingly outdated white clapboard, once a family home in Houston's boomtown cowboy days, when jalopies were roaring down dirt roads and Hank Williams was blaring from jukeboxes, now walled off and turned to apartments for four single people. She was old for such a life, she knew. She was stuck in the past, with the same rough Mexican table she'd had since her days at Rice, same bookcases. No more ferns, no ponytail palms, no artful bonsai. Was never there long enough to take care of them. My life is my art, she liked to lie when people asked her. She waited now through her outgoing message and then beeped for her calls.

"Alice, how are you, dear? It's Roger."

As if she would not know the parched voice of her father's top aide anywhere.

"Call in, please, Alice. There are some things we need to talk—What?—Wait a minute. . . ."

Some whispered voices in the background. Urgent tones, disagreement. Someone's hand muffling the mouthpiece. She pressed closer to the receiver, concentrating. "Give me that," she heard distinctly, her father's polished corporate voice.

A fumbling noise, then Horace.

"Alice, darling, please call as soon as possible. Something's come up. Nothing to worry about. But call as soon as you can—"

There was a sharp breath, a silence. Horace, groping for words? Impossible.

"—Okay sweetheart. Good-bye."

The message beeped off.

She stared at the phone. Nothing to worry about? He never left messages for her like this. It was always Roger, crisp as the Chinese word for a dry stick snapping, *gancui*, checking off what needed to be conveyed to her as if he were discharging his to-do list. Or else Horace would call her message machine himself, to tell her he missed her or he loved her or she was the most wonderful girl in the world—or to ask her when she was coming home to visit him—but he was always warm, eloquent, and fully in command.

This message had sounded downright nervous. Very un-Horace.

Something had to have happened.

She scrabbled for her wallet and her sunglasses, glancing at her watch and calculating the time difference. Eight-thirty in the morning in Washington. Good. He might be in the office.

Still, she had to go out to an anonymous public phone hall. She couldn't call him from her room. China was too full of listening ears and prying eyes—and Horace was an important man in America.

On this afternoon the public phone hall three streets over from Sun Yat-sen Boulevard was crowded with Chinese, Mongols, Muslims. Black-eyed stares lapped at her as she walked lightly across the stone floor and to the end of the booking line. She pulled her baseball cap low over her eyes. Her eyes narrowed as she saw that the people around her were different, not what she was used to, not wholly Chinese. There was an insolent, almost truculent air in the place that one rarely saw with an all-Chinese crowd. Finally she got her ticket number and slipped over to wait against the wall. The ceiling was high, vaulted stone, and it turned the noise of the crowd into a bouncing roar.

"Qi shi ba hao!" a voice sang over the din, and Alice threaded back to the counter to be directed to a phone booth. As she eased down onto the polished wooden stool in the wood-paneled cubicle, she fought down apprehension. She stared at the black metal phone, the beautiful old rotary kind she hadn't seen in the United States in forever. Why would Horace sound so agitated?

She eased up the receiver. *"Wei!"*

"Meiguo dianhua! Deng yixia!" the operator screamed, Phone call to the U.S., hang on.

The faint stew of indiscernible languages, the trans-Pacific phone lines, and then the far-off ring of an American phone. Horace's private line, the small phone on his desk, next to the framed pictures of herself and her mother—young, fresh faced.

She was already so much older than her mother was then. A second ring. Was he at his desk?

"Mannegan," he answered crisply.

"Horace, it's me." She'd intended to be the concerned, bustling caretaker. She'd also intended to remain Alice, separate, safe on the other side of the world. But as usual, the minute she heard her father's voice she felt the rush of belonging. He was the one person in the world to whom she was permanently connected. "How are you?" she asked.

"Alice! So good to hear your voice. I'm fine, sweetheart."

"I was a little worried about you. Nothing's wrong, is there? With you?"

"With me? Oh, no. Everything's all right."

"It was such a weird message. You sounded—" Her voice caught and she closed her eyes. For a moment she was a girl again, a girl on her own in the world, with no one but Horace. Horace, who took care of her with all his power, his clout, his strength.

"Wait a moment, darling." He put her on hold; clearing out his office, probably. He came back on. "Now, my favorite girl, that's better. Don't worry, everything's terrific. Where are you?"

"China, Horace. Of course."

"And what are you doing right now?"

"Working for an archaeologist. He's looking for some proof about the origins of man."

"That sounds interesting."

"It is," she said, and felt herself smile, the echo of Pierre and Lucile coming to her mind, the ghost of the Peking Man skull. "But I was worried, Horace. The message you and Roger left—"

"Oh, that was nothing," he assured her. "I'm perfectly strong."

"Did something happen?"

"Nothing, really. An anomalous number on my blood test."

"What blood test?" Her stomach dropped.

His voice was casual. "I had an elevated PSA level, that's all."

"What's that?"

He paused. "Prostate."

"But what does it mean?"

"Nothing much. An infection. Don't worry! You're not getting rid of me that easily."

"Oh, Horace." She kept a chuckle in her voice but inside she felt she might collapse, she was so washed with relief. The stasis she had built around herself was teeteringly fragile, and Horace's continuing presence in her life—from a distance—was one of its building blocks. But he was okay. He was.

"Call me in ten days or so when the antibiotic's finished, if you like."

"Okay—"

"Or better yet, come home and visit. You haven't come in two years. Please, darling. I'd love to see you."

"I don't know, Horace. I'll try. But please take care of yourself—"

He cut in, his voice different, businesslike. "My meeting's here now. Got to go."

"Bye, Horace—"

But the line had gone dead.

She sat staring at it before she replaced it in its heavy black cradle. Then it rang again.

She jumped. *"Wei?"*

"Shuo-wan-le ma?" the operator screamed, Are you finished?

"Wan-le," she answered, fighting back her apprehension, I'm finished. She tumbled the phone back down.

In Beijing, International Operator Yu finished filling out the little onionskin form with its six layers of carbon. She filed one copy in her logbook and carried the rest to her supervisor. "This call was to an official government office," she told the older woman. "It came up on our highest-level track."

"Well done, Fourth Apprentice Yu." Supervisor Ling did not conceal her excitement. Phone numbers that sorted to top diplomatic status were always reported. And this call originated from the people they'd already been asked to record—by the Army, no less. By the PLA. Supervisor Ling set aside the stack of paperwork she'd been sorting through, and lifted her tea mug for a long lukewarm drink. She clicked the ceramic lid back on the cup decisively.

"Try to get through to District Commander Gao of the PLA," she ordered the apprentice. She watched the girl hurry to an empty desk and dial.

"It's ringing," Apprentice Yu reported, head twisted over her shoulder.

Supervisor Ling laid a hand over the receiver, ready to pick it up. She felt flushed, important, her heartbeat steady and strong. Things like this never happened on her shift.

6

"OKAY," SAID DR. SPENCER. "Here's what we're going to do."

They sat facing him in his room.

Spencer waved at the pile of books, manuscripts, and essays on his desk. He might just have brought along every single thing Pierre Teilhard de Chardin had ever published.

"All right. Nineteen twenty-three. He and Émile Licent took the train as far as Baotou, then rode mules. When they arrived here in Yinchuan they stayed with a Dutch missionary, Abel Oort. Interesting man; Catholic, but knew a great deal about Buddhism and Lamaism. He and Teilhard seem to have had a philosophical meeting of minds. Then the two Frenchmen stocked up on supplies and rode out of the city on April twenty-sixth."

Kong and Lin listened attentively.

Spencer studied his notebook. "Heading northwest, they found the Border River and followed it. This was the edge of Mongolia. And here is the important clue: the Mongol family. When they stumbled on the site alongside the river—the site we now call Shuidonggou—there happened to be a family of Mongols living nearby. The Mongols helped them, and Teilhard in particular struck up a close relationship with the family. He said he felt free there, with them."

"He felt free—why, exactly?" Lin asked.

"Because there he could be his true self," Alice said. "Imagine. Him traveling along the river on mules, stopping, sitting by the water to eat. Then glancing up to see a stone tool protruding from the cliff! He must have seen it all—the site, the first proof of ancient man in Asia—and yet he knew the Church would only laugh at him. All others might see the truth, but it was to the Church he'd made his lifetime vows. And they would say it proved nothing."

He stared at her. Eh, how her face shone with feeling and fascination. She seemed to want so badly to make him see. Like Meiyan used to do. She'd have had some point, some insight, and would come near to tears, explaining it to him. As if nothing on earth mattered more than that he should know. So long since he'd thought of that. "I see," he said to Alice now.

"The Mongols were different," she finished. "They were wild about the find. Totally into it. They dropped everything to help the priests dig. Sorry," she said, turning back to Spencer. "Go on."

"Okay," Adam continued. "They found the skeleton of a man, bone ornaments, crude stone tools. Crates and crates of stuff. And the Mongols, of course—they believed in him. That's why I know he brought Peking Man back out here. Teilhard scholars never made much of his relationship with them, but I think it was central for him. Birth of hope. Acceptance."

"Who were they?" Kong asked.

"He never mentions a name. They must have been living there in 1923. Now . . ." Spencer shrugged. "Way I see it, we go out to the site and start looking. Maybe their descendants will be there. Or somebody who knows where they went."

"Because," clarified Kong, "you believe this Akabori actually returned Peking Man to the priest in 1945, and then the priest carried it out here? And contacted the Mongols?"

"That's . . . one scenario."

"Hmm," Kong said. He crossed one narrow leg over the other and wagged a running shoe rhythmically in the air.

"And just to refresh your memory . . ." Spencer pulled out a photocopied list and passed copies around. "Alice, would you . . ."

She began reading aloud from her list in Chinese, while Lin and Kong took notes. "Six facial fragments, fourteen cranial pieces and six partial skullcaps, fifteen jaws, one hundred and fifty-seven teeth, four arm pieces, eight leg pieces, one collarbone—parts of forty different hominids, in all. These were the contents of the crate when it was last seen."

They all stared at the list.

"There's one other thing," said Spencer. "Alice and I found this letter in Beijing, in some boxes left by Lucile Swan. You both know the name, Lucile Swan?"

"Yes—the American," said Dr. Lin. "The woman friend of the priest."

"Right. It was among her effects, but it actually appears to be a letter written to Teilhard." Spencer handed it to the Chinese scientists. "Whoever wrote it is talking about the warlord out here, Ma Huang-gui, saying he kept out the Japanese and he'll keep out the Communists too. See? As if he's reassuring Teilhard that it's a safe place to hide Peking Man. It all fits. Except that little drawing—I don't know what *that* is."

"That's the Helan Shan petroglyph," Kong said promptly.

"What?" Spencer's eyes popped. "You know it?"

"Of course. It's a rock art design found only in the Helan Shan Mountains around Eren Obo—that's a village over the border in what's now Inner Mongolia. They're quite controversial, these petroglyphs. Nobody knows whether they are from a thousand years ago or twenty thousand years ago. And no one knows what they signify. Or what culture created them." Kong's thin, high-cheeked face was lit with knowledge and pleasure. "Here!" He reached for one of Spencer's maps, uncapped his ballpoint, and drew a circle around a section of the Helan Shan mountains. "This is where they're found. No place else."

"Only here?" Spencer's grin pulled slowly at his mouth. "This is great. We've got to check this out. I've never seen any design like this in the Americas, a sun with the face of a monkey."

"Isn't it so. Moreover, monkeys were never native to this part of north China. Never."

That stopped Spencer cold. "Then the image must date from after trade was established."

"Yet the patina on the rocks suggest these petroglyphs are much, much older," Kong countered. "We don't know. We only know that this motif—we call it the monkey sun god—is unique to the Helan Shan."

"And it was sketched in this letter, written to Father Teilhard in 1945. What does that tell us?"

Dr. Kong touched his fingertips together. "Let me think back and forth. Certainly by 1945 nothing would have been published about this rock art. At that time the monkey sun god would only have been known to local people."

"*Suoyi,*" Alice said, "whoever wrote this letter lived in or near the Helan Shan Mountains."

Spencer picked up the map Dr. Kong had drawn on. "So worst case—I mean, suppose we don't find what we're looking for here? We could go on to"—he squinted—"Eren Obo." He propped open his notebook and wrote swiftly, beaming. "You're something, Dr. Kong. How'd you know about this petroglyph?"

"How could I not know? Late Paleolithic hunter-gatherers are my specialty."

"Late Paleolithic . . ." Spencer glanced from Kong to Lin. "I'd assumed both of you were *Homo erectus* specialists."

"Dr. Lin is an expert on *Homo erectus*," Dr. Kong clarified, pointing to the other Chinese. "Early-Middle Paleolithic."

Dr. Lin nodded.

"And I study nomadic foragers in the Late Paleolithic," he finished. "Also the Neolithic, the transition to agriculture."

"Ah. Like me," Spencer said.

Kong nodded.

"Then why were you selected to come, Dr. Kong?" Alice asked.

"Oh! Because I am the vice director's cousin."

Aha, Alice thought. Of course.

"The vice director depends on me to take care of you. And, of course, to watch you."

Alice jumped on his candor like a small animal. "Do you know anything about those men who were following us in Beijing?"

He shook his head. "I don't know who they were. But it was ordered, I know that. They are watching you. Surely you realize they watch foreigners."

"Yes—sometimes—" Alice said.

"It's because you're looking for Peking Man. Please understand, this is considered most important."

"Of course it is," Spencer agreed. "And thanks for being honest. I appreciate it. I think you're all right, Dr. Kong. I like you."

"*Bici.*" Kong smiled. It's mutual.

An hour later they were bouncing out of Yinchuan in a cheap rented jeep, an old machine that had seen many better years. It had gray splotches of primer everywhere, rudely patched tires, and one door that wouldn't shut. The driver grinned at Alice crazily when she addressed him in Chinese and asked if he thought the jeep would make it. He had a mouthful of silver teeth and lentil-shaped freckles splashed over his jutting cheekbones. "I have my tools!" he explained, waving a thin, muscled arm at a single screwdriver and a plastic jug filled with water. "It's no problem!"

"*Those* are your tools? That's it? You have a spare tire?"

"Foreign woman, don't worry. I can drive to the shores of the four seas and back."

"What's he saying about the jeep?" Spencer asked nervously.

"He says it runs great."

And it did attain surprising speeds as they roared out of the city, out of the oasis with its lush fields and into the desert. The dirt and rocks became a carpet, rolling gently away toward the horizon, where the wall of the Helan Shan could faintly be seen. No one followed them. Alice could see miles of empty road behind. Scotch broom and sagebrush and other scrubby plants Alice could not name grew in patches. The terrain was so like the Mojave that Alice expected to see a green-and-white sign at any moment, announcing Barstow or Needles. But the road was unadorned and the desert was empty under the brilliant azure sky. Alice held on hard to the window frame as they slammed over potholes and rattled in and out of ruts.

"Dr. Kong." Spencer leaned over the seat. "Is it true as I've heard—the archaeological sites out here are undisturbed?"

"Oh, yes! Untouched." Kong smiled, though his bony frame was bouncing cruelly against the hard seat. "Man has been here continuously for eons. We just have not had the resources to study the place. Only a few of the major cultures have even been identified!"

"God," Adam groaned next to her. "Alice, there's nothing like this in the West. It's a gold mine."

"Want to change your project?" she joked.

"No! Peking Man's the thing. That's what we're after."

"But it's heaven for Dr. Kong," she said, glancing at the rapt Chinese professor.

Lin was watching her. "Dr. Kong loves the Neolithic," he said.

"And you, Dr. Lin? You love *Homo erectus*?"

"I do," he said, and excitement touched his mouth and eyes. "I've studied *Sinanthropus* all my life—from pictures, you understand, and from the bits and pieces we have found at other sites around China. It's not much. A skull fragment here and a tooth there. Of course, we keep digging at Zhoukoudian, but during the fifty years since Peking Man disappeared we have found almost nothing. Nothing like the original cache of fossils."

"Yet you've learned a lot about the *yuanren*."

"Yes—his tools, what he ate, how he hunted, how he used fire. Where he found shelter."

"Did they have language? Imagination?"

He laughed out loud. "Of course, we don't know this. But, truly spoken, we could learn so much more if we could locate Peking Man. That is why I had to come on this expedition. If there is any chance at all to find it—even so little as one blade in a field of grass—it is worth going to the ends of the world."

Ah, she thought, such longing. "Wouldn't it be wonderful if we succeeded?"

"*Ke bu shi ma,*" he said in the soft voice of a man who has learned not to allow himself to hope, Isn't it so.

Presently the jeep left the road and bounced through a grove of oleaster trees. The trees stopped at a barren, skidding slope of bare dirt. At its bottom, slow and brown with the sun shattered all over it, crawled the Yellow River.

The jeep coughed to a stop in the trees. Red-cheeked children ran shrieking up the bank, and a gaggle of older women appeared with a watermelon, a cleaver, and a piece of bright cloth. In a moment they had rigged up a little table and awning and were selling slices for thirty *fen* apiece. Other passengers rolled down into the grove to wait with them: a truckful of armed People's Liberation Army soldiers, a man driving goats, and a stunted little pickup truck overflowing with a family of Mongols. Alice stared at the ancient patriarch, tiny round glasses of hammered gold on his nose and a few wisps of white straggling from his chin.

"Good morning, Elder uncle," she said politely.

"The foreigner talks! The foreigner talks!" The children punched each other and giggled. The old man's eyes were almost lost in folds of skin; his papery mouth trembled.

Then she studied the soldiers, wood faced, sitting in two rows in their flatbed truck. Each gripped the worn stock of an automatic rifle.

"What are soldiers doing out here?" Spencer whispered.

She swallowed. "Remember what they've been saying. This is a military area."

"So's Nevada," he said sourly.

He was right, of course. She noticed the other passengers had edged away from the soldiers and turned their backs to them. An unpleasant silence ballooned over the group, broken only by the slight slapping of the waves and the hum of the barge's little motor as it bellied up to the shore and loaded everyone on.

They crossed the river in silence and drove off the barge on the other side. "The PLA's not too popular out here, is it?" Spencer asked. She translated softly. Kong and Lin looked at each other but didn't answer.

The road was now dirt, rutted and unpaved, and they drove west on it through landscape which had subtly changed. Instead of rocky, pebbly desert there stretched away all around them a carpet of yellow earth—loess, Spencer called it, the dust and silt carried and spread by the Yellow River over geologic time. This blanket of loess was not flat, but billowed and rolled in every direction, making hills and hollows and soft eroded canyons, all the same dun color. Loess. Left by the river. Carved out of this

earth, every so often, were little settlements of houses, with sun-
flowers and hollyhocks blooming by their doors. But as they
drove through these settlements the people Alice glimpsed didn't
look as she expected. They had neither the flat, scornful faces of
the Mongols nor the mixed, half-Turkic faces of the Muslims.
They weren't tall the way northern Chinese were either. The
people she saw were small, with wiry, curved legs and compact,
corded bodies. They looked like the people in China's southern
provinces. Puzzling.

"Have these villages been here long?" Alice asked Dr. Kong
as they rattled through one.

"Not long," he answered.

"Like . . . a few generations?" she pushed.

He shifted in his seat, adjusting his cell phone on his belt,
looking away. "The people you see out here were resettled. East
China and South China are very crowded. Here, the population
is small. So people moved here."

She heard the careful diction of Chinese evasion and glanced
imprudently at Lin. He darkened his eyes in the universal signal:
Don't ask about this. She turned, mind racing, and fixed an
innocent look out the window. So! These villagers must have
been inmates of the *laogai*, released from the camps but not
allowed to leave the area. Of course. She could see they were
poor people with hardscrabble lives, hanging washing over rocks
and pulling carts down dirt tracks. They had all been prisoners,
and now were doomed to a lifetime in this yellow dust. Was Lin's
wife one?

It was almost noon when they finally topped a rise and headed
down a long slope to the Shuidonggou site. At the bottom of the
little dirt valley lay a winding, glittering creek lined with rustling
acacia trees. Behind the creek rose a canyon wall, and along the
top of the canyon limped what was left of the Great Wall.

In the center of the canyon face, halfway up, a huge boxlike
hole had been excavated.

"This is it," Kong whispered. He jumped out of the jeep and scrambled eagerly up the yellow-earth wall.

They all followed. "This is one of the few archaeological sites in China that's really been excavated," Adam told Alice. "Like Zhoukoudian."

Lin pried a tiny piece of stone out of the dirt wall. "See? This type of rock is native to this area. It could have occurred here naturally. But this one"—he worked another one loose—"had to have been brought here by someone. That's how we can tell humans lived here. And look." He brushed off the bits of dirt. "See these scrape marks and chips? It was worked by someone's hands."

"Incredible," Alice breathed. "What kind of culture lived here?"

"This is a Late Paleolithic site," Dr. Lin said. "So, of course, I do not know as much as Dr. Kong." He glanced at the other Chinese professor, on his knees, excitedly picking bits of rock from the dirt wall. "But I know a little. We should find microliths everywhere. You see, stonework was quite advanced here, and they trimmed pieces like this into scrapers and blades. Hunting was crucial—until about eight thousand years ago, when they started domesticating steppe animals and growing crops. Then their tool making changed." He smiled down at her. "Do you find it interesting?"

"Interesting!" She examined the stone he had handed her. "It's almost beyond words. How old do you think this is?"

He peered at it. "Maybe ten, twelve thousand years."

"I've never held anything so old," she breathed.

"Look!" Spencer cried suddenly.

He had picked up a tiny circle of something white, and laid it on his palm; it had a perfect hole drilled through its middle. A bead. "See?" Spencer said. "Only a human with a tool could have made this. It's ostrich shell. That makes it easy to date—

ostriches have been extinct here since the end of the Pleistocene. Beautiful, isn't it?"

Alice translated, skipping over the words *ostrich* and *Pleistocene*, and saying instead, "a big bird that has been extinct here for a long time." She stared awestruck at the tiny thing. Someone made that at least ten thousand years ago, she thought. Ten thousand years—the time unit of commitment in the Chinese mind. I will love you for ten thousand years. May you live for ten thousand years. *Wansui.*

"What?" said Dr. Kong, looking up from the spot where he was working.

Spencer held out the bead.

"Let me see," said Kong, reaching for it, and somehow in the fumble the thing dropped to their feet, glanced off someone's shoe, and bounced out of the cutaway toward the valley floor below.

Alice saw Lin's face, stricken, follow the tiny, threading arc the bead made for a split second against the air. White, almost the same color as the earth below, it would be hell to find.

"Oh, shit," Adam mumbled. "Sorry."

"The fault is mine." Kong sighed.

"No, really. God."

"It doesn't matter," Kong said. He turned to the wall and returned to prizing out chips and rock bits. "There is more here to find."

"No"—Lin shook his head—"it was perfect. I'm going to look for it." He turned and climbed back down the handholds in the wall.

Adam sighed. "I feel terrible."

"It's okay," she said, knowing it wasn't, not really.

"Listen, Alice. Let's start looking for the Mongol family. They're the thing we should concentrate on."

She closed her eyes and visualized the empty rock-and-earth expanse of this little valley the way they had seen it, driving in.

There had been no signs of habitation. None. "Did you see anything from the jeep?"

"No, I didn't. But let's just start walking."

She explained to Dr. Kong, and they followed Lin back down the wall. Kong was absorbed in the microliths embedded in the loess walls, Lin in pacing back and forth by the stream, head down, scanning the soft earth. Alice and Adam left them and hiked upstream.

"Teilhard never says exactly where they lived."

"What if they're gone?" she asked.

"They might be."

"What if even their house is gone?"

"That's unlikely. The climate here preserves things, which is why Teilhard found so much at Shuidonggou in the first place. We'll find them. We just have to cover the whole area."

So they walked, in the pulsating yellow sun, through the silty dirt. The crumbling canyon walls rose around them. Ravines and washes tumbled down from the crest above, where the ridgeline was still topped with the eroded backbone of the Great Wall.

Spencer said they should explore each ravine in turn. So they climbed as high in each one as they could, struggling up the grade, slipping in the quick, fine earth. Sometimes they got close enough to catch a glimpse of the worn-down Wall above them, sometimes they hit a jumble of rocks or an impossibly narrow cleft or some other formation that told them no house could possibly have been built any higher up. Then they would turn around. They stopped talking. There was no sound except their sand-sucking footsteps, the drone of wind, and the scratching of Adam's pen in his notebook as he mapped the system of canyons.

"Keep going," Spencer insisted when her disappointment started to show. She did. Even three hours later, when his shirt was sweat blotched and his nose starting to show pink, he kept saying it. "Let's do the next one."

"The house could be anywhere. In any direction."

"We'll find it," he said stubbornly.

It was like this, dragging, empty handed, that Dr. Lin Shiyang spotted them moving around the lip of a wash, at the turn of the canyon a mile or so up. *"Tamen zai ner,"* he said with relief, and pointed them out to Kong with his chin. A small movement, economical. He was hot and tired too.

"Na hao. Women zou-ba." Kong sighed, and walked away to collect the driver from his patch of shade.

When the Americans walked up Lin could see they'd found nothing. Their eyes sagged with failure.

"It should have been right here," Spencer said, the rust-headed woman putting his words into melodious Chinese. "Right by the site. But it's okay. Tomorrow, we'll keep looking."

He nodded and looked down at the woman. *"Zenmoyang?"* he asked her—How did it go?

She shook her head. Nothing.

"Tai zao-le," he said sympathetically.

Alice sighed in acknowledgment. All she wanted at this moment was to get back to Yinchuan and have a bath. She was coated with dust and grit. Her mouth was dry and aching with thirst, but she had finished off her water bottle as they hiked back down the last canyon.

Lin saw her glance at her bottle, empty, saw the flush in her freckled cheeks. He held out his own, still a third full. *"Gei,"* he said quietly.

"Oh, no," she said. *"Na zenmo xing."*

"Gei," he said again.

She took it, drank gratefully, and handed it back to him. "Thank you."

He nodded and reattached it to his belt.

"What did you get?" Spencer was saying in English to Dr. Kong, nodding his head at Kong's sack bulging with microliths.

Kong smiled broadly and opened the bag for Spencer, who inspected the contents and gave him a thumbs-up. "Good work."

The driver, who stood next to Lin, cleared his throat and glanced pointedly at the sun's angle above their heads. The light had grown long and yellow, the shimmering heat almost unbearable.

"Yes," Lin said. "We should go."

"Dr. Spencer," she said, taking a few steps toward him, "the driver says we should hit the road."

"Oh? Okay. Hey, congratulations, Dr. Kong. Great stuff." He twirled the bag closed and handed it back to the Chinese, smiled tiredly at her. "Let's go."

"God, Adam," she said in English, "look at your neck! Don't you feel it? It's bright red!"

"It is?" He reached back and touched it, winced.

"You have to be more careful. Sunburn is no joke." As she spoke she reached out and unfolded his shirt collar, positioning it gently so it covered his neck. She smoothed out the denim. "Really. Be careful."

Lin felt his stomach drop, watching them. Don't stare, he ordered himself. Turn away. The way she touched the American man! So familiar, so intimate. So there was something between them. When he and Kong had been briefed it had been made clear that these two foreigners did not know each other until a week ago, when the man hired the woman as his interpreter. Both, they'd been informed, were unmarried. He'd heard stories about Americans, just as all Chinese had. Their restlessness, their high sexual interest. These two had worked together only one week. Could they already be *qing ren?*

"You ready, Dr. Lin?" Now her face was turned to him, those khaki eyes wide open, pleasant, expectant.

"Eh," he said. "Ready." Remarkable.

"Zou-ba," she said, watching Lin climb into the rear seat.

She stepped into the back and sat next to Lin. He showed her a millisecond of mild surprise, and then faced front again. She adjusted in her seat for Spencer, who climbed in the back on her other side. Kong got in front with the driver.

They bounced up the dirt road, twisting and turning through the long series of canyons. It would take an hour and a half to get to the ferry crossing. She let the first hour go by without a word.

As they passed through the resettled villages, she saw that Lin scanned out the window constantly.

He thinks his wife might still be out there, Alice realized. He thinks he might actually see her.

So she waited until they came almost to the river before she spoke to him. By then, she knew, they were out of the *laogai* zone and the only people they would see would be the Mongols, and the Muslims, driving their camels and their sheep and their two-wheeled carts.

"Dr. Lin," she ventured. "Find anything today?"

He turned to her with his mouth bent in the smallest smile. Instead of speaking, he opened his clenched palm and extended it.

There, all but invisible in the brown landscape of hollows and calluses, gleamed the tiny ostrich-shell bead.

Sun Gong, third assistant Party vice manager for Ningxia Province, was back in his office after a week's leave, glancing through a sheaf of faxes on his desk. One from Beijing caught his eye. It was his prudent habit to always look carefully at faxes from Beijing.

Vice Manager Sun squinted at the letterhead: Institute of Vertebrate Paleontology and Paleoanthropology. Curious. The IVPP was the national research institute handling anthropology and archaeology. They gave out excavation permits and oversaw Ningxia's provincial Bureau of Cultural Relics. What was odd was that they were communicating with the Party office—with him, Sun Gong. Normally their directives went straight to the Bureau of Cultural Relics.

He scanned through the fax. Alerting him to the presence of an American archaeologist and his female assistant . . . attempting to recover Peking Man, the single most important batch of fossils lost by China during the world war . . . calls placed to highest-level U.S. Government offices. . . . Peking Man! Sun's eyebrows went up. One of China's great lost treasures. He read on: Two Chinese scientists accompanying, from Huabei University . . . permits granted to cross Xi Xia Missile Range . . . please coordinate with regional PLA command. They are providing security. Cordially. Vice Director Han.

Security! Sun's fingers trembled as he pulled a crumpled pack of Flying Horse cigarettes from his shirt pocket, shook one loose, and lit it. The words seemed clear enough, but what lay behind them? Did Vice Director Han imply that if they found the precious Peking Man remains—though surely that was impossible, for the Japanese had spirited the bones away fifty years before—the Americans might try to smuggle the fossils out of the country? The very idea made Sun Gong bridle in righteous fury.

Or was it possible—could it be—did they suspect espionage?

Yes, he thought, pulling hard on the strong cigarette and feeling his heart race, yes, it was possible. Anything was possible. The archaeologists were going to cross a missile range, after all. Highly sensitive. State secrets.

For years, Sun Gong had been looking for a way to prove himself to the bosses above his head. It was not easy, out here in the provinces, where nothing ever happened.

He snatched up the phone and jabbed out a number. Miles away, at the PLA command post, he heard the insistent ring.

"*Wei?*"

"Give me Lieutenant Shan."

"Lieutenant Shan! Who's calling?"

He raised his face and blew a perfect smoke ring, which

floated lazily toward the ceiling. "His cousin," he answered, satisfied, for a moment, with his lot in life. "Ningxia Province Party Vice Manager Sun Gong."

Back at the Number One, she stopped at the front desk after dinner. "Phone call to Beijing." She took a form and filled it out.

The *fuwuyuan* took the slip, bored. *"Hao-de,"* she said. *"Deng yixia."*

On her way back to her room Alice thought through what to say. Mother Meng, I'm sorry for the scene I caused, showing up like that with Jian and his wife there, at your apartment. Next time before I visit you I'll call first—

The phone in her room was jangling. Next to it she saw the clipping, the yellowed newsprint, the obituary of Lucile Swan. She snatched at the receiver. *"Wei!"*

"Beijing dianhua!" the operator screamed.

Suddenly there was a male voice on the other end. *"Wei! Wei!"*

A male voice? But this was Meng Shaowen's apartment.

"Wei," she said tentatively, *"Duibuqi."* Sorry. "I must have punched wrong. I'm seeking the home of Meng Shaowen."

"Who is this?" The voice tensed.

"Jian?" she whispered. Of all the bad luck—

"Mo Ai-li," he said flatly, recognizing her.

"Jian, please. Is she there? I need to talk to her."

"You can't."

"Please, Jian—"

"Do you understand me or not!" he cried in a swift, miserable spurt. "She's gone away!"

"What?" *Gone away* was the Chinese euphemism for dead, but he couldn't mean she was dead, he couldn't possibly—

"Ta zou-le," he repeated, She's gone away.

147

"But what are you talking about!" she cried.

"It was her lungs—an embolism, they think. The neighbors took her to the hospital but"—now she heard his voice cracking —"it was too late."

"But I just saw her Saturday! She was fine!"

"It happened that night. Later."

"I don't believe it!" Behind the words her heart was screaming and thrashing in her chest. "Are you sure?"

"Ai-li," he said softly. "Of course I'm sure."

"But, Jian, it's impossible."

"Ai-li, please," he said. There was a strained silence, as if he was trying to decide whether to comfort her, which was danger-ous, for it might let some of the love back in between them, or whether to cut her off quickly and decisively. *"Eh,"* he said gruffly. "How do you think I feel? She's my mother. But now she's gone. Gone to the Yellow Springs. You'll see her in another life. Isn't it so?"

He waited for her to answer but she couldn't, she could only stand frozen with the tears burning and forcing and finally seep-ing out of her eyes. She pressed the phone against her forehead. How could he expect her to answer?

"Eh, Mo Ai-li, *bie ku,*" Don't cry. "I'm sorry if I was rough with you the other day. I never expected to see you here. And my wife—my baby . . ."

"I know," she gulped through her tears.

"I wish you good luck in your life," he said. "Really." He paused and she didn't answer. He waited a little more and finally cleared his throat. "Good-bye, Ai-li," he whispered softly, and hung up the phone.

7

"ALL RIGHT," SHE CALLED through the door. "I'm coming." She splashed a little more cold water on her face, then checked the mirror. Anybody could tell she'd been crying.

"What's wrong?" Spencer said instantly.

"Nothing."

"Come on. Don't be so Chinese. Something happen?"

"I just learned a friend in Beijing died."

"Oh." He studied her. "Close friend?"

"Yes."

"Hey. Sorry. Was it sudden?"

"Yes. Well, no. She was old. She had lung problems."

"That's too bad." His baggy gray eyes were kind. "Still want to go out on our mission this evening?"

"Yes," she said firmly, and wiped her face with the backs of her hands. "Yes. Let's go."

"Good. That's what Teilhard would have said, you know. He didn't let stuff keep him down. Okay. The Dutch missionary, Abel Oort. During the days that Teilhard and Licent stayed with him here in Yinchuan, they posted one letter—luckily." Spencer pulled one of the paperback editions of Teilhard's letters from his day pack, and opened it to a marked page. "Here. The heading is Gansu Street, Yinchuan." He showed it to her.

"So." She read quickly through the letter's text; it revealed nothing. "Let's start there, then. Gansu Street."

They set out in the evening light on Sun Yat-sen Boulevard, alone, their Chinese colleagues busy sorting microliths in the hotel. Through her grief she noticed that the air was soft and warm, that the boulevard was throbbing with carts, crowds, full-laden mules, and camels. Itinerant Mongols lined the sidewalk, their goods spread on hand-loomed wool blankets. Yes, she thought, pausing sadly to stare at knives and inlaid daggers, kitchenware carved from wood, and bundles of camel-hair stuffing for quilts, Mother Meng is gone. But I'm still here, living. They walked alongside the mosque and stared at it, walking past. On its mosaic steps a kneeling tile-setter pounded, his pinging hammer a high-pitched heartbeat over the crowd. Snatches of Mandarin, Mongolian, and other dialects swirled up and were gone.

Gansu Street, which marked the border between the Muslim quarter and the old Chinese neighborhood, was only partially cobbled now; it had probably been nothing but a dirt lane when Teilhard came here in 1923. Yet almost at its end the two Americans came upon a weathered stone building, sagging in disrepair, that had the triple-arched doorways and the soaring facade of a Western-style church. To one side of the entrance, there was a small metal plaque. HAPPY FORTUNE CONSULTING SERVICES.

"Welcome to the new China," Alice said. Something like a smile stretched her mouth, piercing her pain for a moment.

Spencer knocked, then pushed the handle. It was unlocked. Inside they stepped through the darkened, gritty-floored nave and into the church itself, with high vaulted ceilings where sparrows beat at the air. No pews. No altar. Empty.

"Wonder where Happy Fortune Consulting Services is?" Her voice bounced unpleasantly around the hall.

They stepped back into the nave and ventured up a narrow stone stairway. At the top there was a small office, its desk cluttered with papers as well as a modern phone and fax machine.

"We strike out again." Spencer stared at the empty chair.

Alice leaned over the pile of faxes. "Looks like his name is Guo Wenxiang. I'll leave a note." She picked up a pen and paper and sketched out the quick characters:

Esteemed Mr. Guo—

I am an American named Mo Ai-li, visiting at the Number One Guesthouse. I want to ask you a few questions on behalf of my employer. Thank you for contacting me there in Room 542.

Outside the church, Yinchuan was just slipping into the day's last mysterious margin of light. Alice and Spencer fell into the moving crowd and walked on.

Lin Shiyang left the hotel, having been vague about his errand to Kong Zhen. He murmured a few words about something he needed, something at the light industrial store—one of the small requirements of travel. Kong had nodded absently, immersed in his fine pebbly mountain of artifacts.

"I'll see you later, then," Lin told him, and left.

From the Number One he walked quickly east, toward the drum tower, along one of the main arteries of the old town. Behind the gray blocks of commercial-looking buildings life descended abruptly into narrow streets lined with close-fitted apartment houses and small, back-street establishments like market stalls, barbershops, cafés. Into one of these, a corner ground-floor room in a nondescript structure, Lin stepped.

"*Xi fan,*" he told the man behind the counter as he sat at one of the three tiny tables, Rice gruel, the simplest of Chinese comfort foods. A stumpy lady in her sixties bent over at the table next to him, slurping *xi fan.* He had seen her eating it and ordered the same. She was not a person of his educational class; on the contrary she appeared to be a simpleminded, *tu* woman. But she would serve his purpose.

"It's good, elder sister, is it not?" he had said politely when his came and he started spooning it down.

"Eh?" She looked up. "*Hao chi,*" Delicious.

He ate for a minute.

"You're not from around here," she observed.

"You're right."

"I knew! You have a southern accent. Shanghai?"

"Eh, sister, your intelligence surpasses me. You're right. I lived there as a boy."

She laughed, finished her bowl, put it down.

He cleared his throat. "*Wo xiang qing wen yixia.* Do you know—do you happen to know—were all the camps in this area closed or are any still open? I am talking of the women's camps."

"Eh, younger brother, it's not always good to speak so boldly."

"I know," he said. He was careful to look away from her now. One never knew who might be watching.

"But you have a good face, an open face. I'll tell you to the limit of my knowing. All of them were closed, the last ones more than five years ago."

"Thank you," he said softly, and finished his porridge, not speaking to her or glancing at her again. As he left he did not notice a man observing him, a man who stood in a doorway on the other side of the road staring distractedly, now, at the ground. A man who at this moment was swiftly recataloguing in his mind every movement Dr. Lin had made, his route here from the hotel, his time inside the little café. In which a conversation seemed to have taken place, but too far away for the man to hear.

Dr. Lin turned the corner to walk back toward the Number One.

The man stepped into the street and followed him.

The four of them plodded the steep, rock-rubbled canyons for a few days more and found nothing. The third night Spencer walked into her room with a bottle of Russian vodka. "Do you mind?" he said, his face squished over to one side by his lopsided grin. "I really hate to drink alone."

"No. No—it's fine," she answered. She'd been sitting alone, staring out the window, replaying Meng Shaowen's death in her mind. Now the sight of Spencer's soft, lived-in face and his worn American jeans was a welcome relief. I need a friend, she thought. "Come in."

"Thanks." He strolled past her, dropped into one of the two armchairs, and twisted the cap off the bottle. "You feeling better about your friend's death?"

"Actually no," she said. "I'm not feeling better."

He shook his head, uncovered the ceramic tea mugs, and gurgled vodka into them. "Here." He handed her one. "My sympathies."

They clicked teacups and drank.

"Grief is a killer, isn't it?" he said. "Brings you right up to the truth."

Truth. Sometimes she wasn't sure what the word even meant. What had Teilhard written? *Truth lies in seeing that everything gives way in the direction, and under the influence, of beauty and goodness. That is the inner face of evolution. . . .*

"Like me," Spencer was saying. "I have this son. Tyler. Be-

153

fore his mother and I split I used to take him everywhere with me—when I wasn't working, I mean. We'd go out to one of the rock ranches and dig agates, cheer at the ball games, drive around the desert to the old mining ghost towns. I used to put him to sleep every night. Now he doesn't even live in the same state as me. He's growing up and I'm not even getting to see it." Spencer's eyes clouded, pinched; he looked away from her.

"I'm sorry," she said quietly.

"Yeah. Well."

"Maybe one day you'll get married again. Then he can live with you."

"Married?" He let out a short, empty laugh. "Impossible. I'd have to have sex again first."

"Frightening, isn't it?" She laughed, working hard not to show her discomfort.

He took a sip of vodka and closed his eyes for a second. "Look, Alice, maybe we could just talk about this. We're on this trip together, I'm a single man, you're a single woman. But believe me, I'm not coming after you. I can't deal with any of that stuff at the moment. The only person I care about is Tyler. So. You can relax." He glanced at her.

"Thanks. I appreciate it. Male clients are one of my occupational hazards. They're always coming on to me."

"I won't. Don't worry."

"And I feel the same way about you. I mean," she said delicately, "I'm not interested."

"Friends, then."

"Friends."

He held out his cup and she tapped hers against it. He was glad they had gotten it out on the table, glad he had not mentioned the real reason he would never approach her, which was that she seemed far too various. He would never let himself trust a woman like her, not at this point in his life. Permanence, that was what he wanted now. Loyalty. "Can I ask you a question, though?"

She nodded.

"There *is* something different about you—I can't quite place it." He studied her. "It's almost like you're off the board somehow. Like you're not playing on the same field. You know?"

"No. I don't."

"I remember the first time I saw you—at five in the morning, you were coming back to the hotel on a bicycle. Wearing some little black dress. So I figured you probably had a boyfriend in Beijing—what, a Chinese guy?" He stopped, saw the click in her eyes, and understood. "So that's it, then. You only like Chinese guys. That's it, isn't it?"

"Full marks, Dr. Spencer." She smiled, drained off her cup and held it out for a refill.

He poured for both of them. "So, I was right."

"Hardly a state secret. I love Chinese men."

"Really? What is it about them?"

She thought. "They incite a certain race memory in me."

"Very funny."

"Not a joke."

"Seriously. What is it? It has something to do with your father, right?"

"No!" she answered, a few notches higher.

"Okay!" He put his hands up. "Okay. Sorry. I said I wouldn't mention him, I know. So why, then?"

"Well. They're beautiful, for one thing. Chinese men and women both—haven't you noticed? Edgar Snow once wrote that the Chinese were arguably the most intelligent yet *certainly,* without a doubt, the best-looking people on earth. It's true."

"So they're beautiful, that's one thing." He licked his index finger and tagged the air.

"Yes. And another thing. Their skin is different. Smooth. Almost hairless. Not like barbarians."

"Number two, smooth skin." He marked the air again. "Wait a minute. Aren't you a barbarian?"

"Not really. Inside I'm half Chinese. Okay: another thing. You have sex with one of them, you have sex with China. Know what I mean? You're not on the outside anymore."

"Does it last?"

"Only for a minute. Now the most important thing. Chinese men are reserved. Much more reserved than Western men."

"Reserved?"

"That's right."

He knit his yellow brows at her.

Like Jian, she thought. Jian, who had been able to communicate to her with a single hard look in some public place—on the street, or in a roomful of his friends—what he planned to do to her the minute they were alone. Jian, who had been with her for weeks before finally reaching out and touching her neck, her hair; who had taken over her body with agonizing slowness, over a period of many more weeks, showing her finally when he went to bed with her that physical sex was only one more link in the chain that bound them.

"Reserved?" Spencer asked. "Okay, reserved." He licked his finger and made a final mark in the air. "Interesting. So your boyfriend in Beijing—the man you saw the night before we met—he's like that? Reserved?"

"Well . . ." Alice hesitated. Lu Ming, of course, had only been reserved on the surface. He had woven his net around her with words, looks, the touch of his foot under the table. But when he had gotten her alone, he—like most of the men she picked up—had driven right into her. No reserve. Not like Jian. Jian had understood sex the way that she, all her life, had understood music, and then later, language. He was aware of it: the thousand ways of touching, breathing, smelling, the rhythmic exchange of physical innuendoes. The theme and variations. She sometimes realized—faintly, as if from a distance—that she was going from one to another in search of a man like him. A man with all his subtlety, his intelligence, but a man—unlike Jian—who was willing to accept and love her true self. Though what was her true self? The vodka was like a bubble now, pushing against the top of her brain. She laughed. "I suppose I'm holding out for the true Chinese man—the type who waits until he has a woman's heart. When a man like that delivers, watch out."

"But it's just love that does that, isn't it?" Spencer asked, syllables starting to get mushed. "You can be English or Eskimo or anything. It's when you truly love someone that happens."

She closed her eyes and leaned her head back over the top of the chair.

"Don't you want love?" he pressed on. He carried his cup to the spot where his mouth was supposed to be, slopped a few drops over the side. "Don't you want to get married, settle down? What about kids? Don't you want to have kids?"

"Yes," she said. "Absolutely."

"I bet your dad wants you to have kids."

"You mean Horace. Of course he wants grandchildren, but only if they're Anglo-Saxon. That's Horace."

"You never call him Dad?"

"Horace. Look—he's my father. But I don't call him Dad, or Daddy. Dads take care of their kids, and help them, and let them be whatever they want to be. They *let* them grow up. We're not a family that way, Horace and I. We're—" She stopped, stuck, not sure how to say what in fact they were. A diagram. A pattern formed by a famous politician and his daughter. Locked together. The man loving the daughter deeply, but too overpowering to know how to let her live. And the daughter needing his love, but unable to bear it.

Was this the price of Alice's life? And why did her price seem to be so much higher than everyone else's? She thought of what Teilhard had written about evolution: *Every synthesis costs some-thing. . . . Something is finally burned in the course of every syn-*

thesis in order to pay for that synthesis. Well, she had paid, certainly. Paid and burned. Why didn't things change? "I really do want love," she said nakedly to Adam now. "I do. I'm just waiting for it."

"You and Lucile," he said, meaning it as a joke, not meaning to hurt her, but cutting through her with the words nonetheless. Because Lucile had succumbed to self-deception. Lucile had told herself Pierre would leave his order for her, and had ended up waiting all her life in vain. As she wrote in her diary: *I suppose a lot of the things I have been living on were built by my own imagination—that is not his fault. . . .*

Lucile, alone in the bitter sea, with only a priest at her side. But Alice's life was going to be different.

"To love," she said resolutely to Spencer, and they drank.

That night, small and shiny with sweat, the vodka worn off, she lay in bed thinking about it. She was thirty-six. Old. But there was still time to change, wasn't there? And now Mother Meng was dead. Alice sighed and twisted to one side in the sheets, staring through the window.

The street outside was empty now, it was past midnight. Quiet had settled like snow, and the only sound she heard was the far-off approach of the cricket vendor. This was a sound she loved, a sound of old China: the surging waves of cricket song, and under it the sad creak of the vendor's bicycle wheels. The man approached and then seemed to pause under her window.

The chorus of crickets. It always carried her back to Houston, Texas, to running along the top of Buffalo Bayou in the dusk, the trees, the path, the bayou banks blurring to something else. Black stick or cottonmouth snake? Jump over it. Do the others hate you? Show them. You want to change yourself? Leap. Just leap.

She concentrated on the sound of crickets, and the smell of the cigarette the cricket man was smoking. She slid out of bed and to the window: yes, there it was, the leaning bicycle, the hundreds of tiny woven cages. The man was staring, shave headed, white capped, off down the deserted street. No, this was not Houston, it was bleach-dry Ningxia. And outside there was only the oasis night, the dim boxy shapes of concrete buildings, the spires of the mosque.

She gave up finally, dressed in the dark, and slipped out of Building Three. The hotel courtyard was silent except for the small slapping of fish in the pond. She padded down the covered walkway and found a spot on the little bridge that curved over the dark water. To one side was a decrepit gazebo; to the other beds of hollyhocks, bunched between intersecting stone paths. Everything had been laid out in the spirit of formal Chinese gardens, the kind that were popular back East, in towns like Suzhou and Hangzhou and Shanghai, where the affluent men of the Ming and Qing had had the time and money to create them. Here in the Number One the gardeners had made do with a pond, some aging carp, and an arched bridge cast from concrete. They had managed to raise big deciduous trees, not often seen here in Ningxia, but most of these were clumped against the two-story hotel buildings. It was a pleasant spot, if out of place. Sitting here, it didn't feel like Yinchuan, an oasis at the intersection of two deserts. A flowering patch of farmland at the foot of the Helan Shan range.

Teilhard had loved the Helan Shan, had written rapturous letters about the ways in which their purple peaks rose up to God. In the shadow of those mountains he had found his proof, Paleolithic proof. But it didn't help. Man was doomed in the Garden, they told him.

A waste, she thought, staring at the trees waving and whispering by the wall of Building Two.

There was a movement in the trees, near the door to the building: a person, perhaps, or an animal, or just a rippling bush.

The motion detached and wove through the plots of hollyhock. Something white glimmered about its upper half—a shirt, maybe, pale and detached in the darkness.

A man. She squinted.

He came toward her. Only when he was almost upon her could she see it was Dr. Lin.

"Shuibu-zhao?" he whispered, Can't sleep? and squatted beside her. A carp broke the water and slid under again. Dr. Lin folded his arms over his knees.

"How did you know I was here?"

"Meiyou zhidao." I didn't.

Then there was quiet for a stretch, in the temporarily unreal night world of the Number One courtyard. They sat so close, their legs were almost touching. She knew he spoke no English at all, so her thoughts, her mind, her senses, slid entirely into Chinese. "Dr. Lin. Do you ever wish you were somebody else?"

"Trouble you to repeat?"

"Do you wish your life had been different?"

He made a chuckle, but it was a hollow sound. "Of course, but I don't think of it that way. We Chinese can't think that way. It's different here. I don't know if you can understand."

"I think I can," she countered. "I have worked here a long time. I have listened to many people's tales."

"So you have," he said, looking briefly into her face. Privately he thought: She knows a lot. But whether or not she knew about the insides of a man after the Chaos, the barren soul, the fields sown with salt—he could not tell.

"I know it was bad," she said in a softer voice, respectful, knowing something terrible must have happened with his wife.

He nodded.

She sighed, aware that he saw her as an outsider. They all did, at first. If he got to know her, he would see that she was more Chinese than American. Wasn't she? Sometimes, when she looked back on the thick, damp air of Houston, she wondered if she had ever really lived there at all, if it had been anything other than a strange dream of before. Not that Dr. Lin would have understood this. Not that she felt ready to say it.

He let a beat of quiet fall before he continued. *"Hao chang shijian han xin ru ku,"* It's such a long time we've been drinking from the bitter cup. He sighed and rubbed his eyes with his large, hairless hands. "But this is our circumstance. These are our times. And the road behind cannot be changed."

"What of the road ahead?"

He smiled. "What of it?"

"Can you change it?"

He considered silently. His road was made up of everything he was and everything he had endured, so it was deeply paved already. All he had allowed himself to feel and all he had walled off from his feeling. Like his wife, led away one day, one look back, over her shoulder, and then a universe of nothing ever after. Years of nothing. He would, of course, not say such a thing to an outside woman, whom he barely knew, in the middle of the night. Instead he said: "I don't think the road can change."

"I used to agree with that," she said slowly. "Lately I feel different." She thought of herself in bed earlier that evening, reading *The Phenomenon of Man*. *In fact I doubt whether there is a more decisive moment for a thinking being than when the scales fall from his eyes and he . . . realises that a universal will to live converges and is hominised in him . . . the axis and leading shoot of evolution.* She breathed in fully, deeply. He had a spicy, wonderful Chinese smell, Lin Shiyang.

"Perhaps you are right. Eh, Mo Ai-li, I can't believe I'm talking to you in the middle of the night like this. You're a strange woman. Are other outside women like you?"

She laughed. "No."

"May I ask, are you married?"

"No," she said, and then added, "not yet."

He looked into her face but she couldn't read him in the dark.

"You were married," she said boldly.

"Yes."

"Are you still?" Her heart beat faster. Had he put his wife aside, that's what she wanted to know, had he *huaqing jiexian,* drawn a clear line between them, as so many Chinese had been coerced into doing in those years?

"Eh, yes. I suppose I am still married." He looked at her through the dark. "Xiao Mo, I've said too much to you."

"No," she insisted. "Not too much."

But the slight cramp of pain crossed him again. "It's been a long time since I talked to anyone of my wife, and now here I am dropping my guard and clearing my heart. So you know my wife was sent to Ningxia. Zhang Meiyan was her name."

So that was her name, Meiyan, it meant "beautiful swallow." How could she be named Beautiful Swallow in an era when most girls had been named Benefit China or Serve Truth? Old-fashioned parents, maybe, why hadn't she changed it—

You're jealous, she stopped herself.

"Yes, Zhang Meiyan," Lin said again. He had so few chances to even say her name anymore. And yet he never forgot her. Meiyan.

"So you don't know what happened to her?"

He shook his head.

"Kelian," she said with feeling.

"Of course, she may be dead."

May be dead? Alice thought. Kind of an understatement. "How long since you've heard?"

"Over twenty years," he said, finding that he wanted to sit here, wanted to talk to Mo Ai-li. There was something about her that pulled at him, something at once female and unearthly. "It's a long time. So I do not know her fate."

I think you do, Alice thought.

He closed his eyes, remembering. "I was told to forget her. Do you understand me or not? We were never actually divorced. But I was told to remain in Zhengzhou. It was later, after the Chaos ended, that I came to Huabei University. It's a good life there, teaching. I don't want to lose it."

"But?"

"*Yin hun bu san,*" The ghost refuses to leave. "And I need to know what happened to her. So now—now that I am in Ningxia anyway . . ."

"You'll try to find out."

Lin turned to her. "Don't speak of this to the others."

"*Ni fang-xin ba,*" she said. She wished she could lean over, just a few inches, and rest her shoulder against his. She wished she could sit here with him all night. "*Fang xin hao-le,*" she said again, and touched his smooth forearm briefly with the cool flat of her palm. It was a casual gesture in the West, a gesture almost purely conversational, but here in China it burned with physical presumption.

Dr. Lin withdrew his arm and got to his feet in a quick stumble. "Eh. Well."

She stood up sadly.

"At breakfast. See you."

"See you."

He was already walking away.

She went in to breakfast the next morning and sat with her back to the dining-hall door. She could barely sit still on her seat, waiting for Lin to arrive.

Finally she heard the two sets of footsteps, the brisk tread of Kong and the listing walk of Lin.

The screen door clicked open, banged shut.

"*Zao,*" said Dr. Kong.

"Zao," she returned, Morning, and she slid her smile over both of them.

"We've been talking about the site," Kong said. "So far there's been no sign of the Mongols at Shuidonggou."

"That's true," said Spencer, looking dejected.

"Then what about going to Eren Obo next?" Lin put in. He leaned intently toward the American. "The rock art drawing in that letter to Teilhard definitely comes from around Eren Obo. To find Peking Man again, Dr. Spencer—it would change everything in our field. It would bring our *Homo erectus* studies back to life." Lin paused. He did not say aloud his private reason for wanting to find Peking Man so badly, that it would be the highest tribute to Meiyan—or to her—memory, if she no longer lived. *"Wo henbude,"* he said, I want this so powerfully. He looked from one to the other. "If there is even the smallest chance your theory is correct, we must try everything. We must go everywhere."

Passion! Alice thought. She put his words in English.

"Of course," Spencer agreed. "I'm with you on that. But let's give Shuidonggou a little longer. We haven't covered the whole area yet."

"True," Kong said. "It will take days to get the visas anyway. Crossing the Helan Shan and taking you to Eren Obo will require very special permission. So Dr. Lin and I should not go with you today. We should go to the bureau and work on it."

Spencer looked worried. "Do we have to go back to Beijing for these visas, to Vice Director Han?"

Kong and Lin exchanged tactful glances. "Why don't we seek this permit locally," Kong said.

"All right," Adam said, understanding. "If you say so."

As she translated this Alice locked eyes briefly with Dr. Lin. He didn't smile at her exactly. What he did do was incline his head ever so slightly, and place his gaze fleetingly on her as if to say: Yes, I was there last night. I remember.

* * *

Driving out of the city, thinking about Mother Meng, she noticed an unusual sign.

YIN YANG XIANSHENG, Yin-yang master.

What was that?

"Driver." She leaned over the seat. "Trouble you with a question. What does a yin-yang master do?"

"Eh, that's from feudal times. Like wind-and-water masters?"

She nodded. *Feng shui,* of course, Geomancy.

"None left now," the driver barked, all pride and satisfaction in the bustling new world.

"What are you talking about?" Spencer demanded.

"Nothing." Alice cracked her own little book open and scribbled the names of the cross streets. Drum Tower Road. Wool Market Lane.

Spencer peered out the back window for a minute, then faced front again. "You won't believe this."

"What?"

He pointed his gaze to the rear. "Someone's following us."

The car kept an implacable distance behind them, mirroring their speed, locked in to their every turn. "Do you see that?" she asked the driver, who nodded, shrugged. They stayed on the West Road, kept a steady speed through the checkerboard fields. Past the place Alice and Lin had stopped the day they rented bicycles, past the end of any kind of city, into the farmland with its interlocking trellis of canals. They passed the edge of the oasis, the point where the moisture dropped, suddenly, and the green earth reverted to yellow. Watching in the rearview mirror they saw the car slow when it reached this natural borderline; slow, then turn around and roar away in the opposite direction, back to the city. "Thank God for turf," Alice said.

"Maybe Teilhard is watching over us," Adam joked.

"Maybe." She laughed.

"You're reading his stuff, aren't you?"

"Yes—just about every night."

"Learning anything?"

She thought. "That as a human being I'm not necessarily static, but . . . evolving. That I'm supposed to grow and develop, just like the physical world, the planet, the universe."

"No." Spencer rolled his eyes. "I meant about what he did in his life—something that would tell us where he put Peking Man."

"Oh! I don't know. I only know he was in love with Lucile, and she with him. Did you read that book of their letters?"

"Some of it."

"They connected on every level—mental, philosophical, emotional. But she couldn't have him, not all of him. He was promised to God. Though he loved her." And that's the one thing I've missed, Alice thought to herself. Someone who loves me. Though since Jian I've had plenty of physical satisfaction. Nothing else. "Lucile fought against it, and finally agreed. She went along with him on his spiritual journey."

"And?" Spencer prompted.

"And Teilhard adored her for it. He knew what a sacrifice it was for her." *And thank you, so much, for forgetting as you do, for me, what you might, naturally, expect, but what, for higher reasons, I cannot give you. I love you so much the more for this "renoncement." And there is nothing I will not do for you, in order to repay you.* "From that point on," Alice said, "he confided everything in her."

"So you think he told her where he put it."

"Exactly."

"Interesting," said Adam. He worked his blue book out of his pocket and wrote it down. "You're probably right. But how do we pursue it? Lucile's been dead for a long time."

The sun was straight and blue over their heads when they

pulled into Shuidonggou and started walking. First they traversed the ridge, following along beside the corroded, hip-high huddle of the Great Wall. There was little left of the Wall out here, yet it still marched in a crumbling, orderly line, disappearing over the far-off mountain passes. On one side, for millennia, China. On the other, Mongolia. On the Chinese side the desert was scruffy bits of grass and craggy, eroded buttes. On the Mongolian side it became a shifting ocean of white sand. Dunes that went on for miles. Over everything a bowl of hot, deepest blue.

She rationed her water more carefully today, knowing the heat and the thirst by now, knowing how to manage them. Still the sweat trickled down her spine, itching her as she scrambled down a ravine after him, kicking and scuffing against rocks and pebbles, brief clouds of fine dust rising wherever their shoes exploded in the soft sand. Spencer rubbed his putty face. "What do you think of our Chinese friends?"

"They're okay," she said cautiously.

"Kong's a good guy," Spencer went on. "Lin, I can't read. He likes you, though."

"What do you mean?"

"Oh, I see him looking at you. Can't you tell? He likes you."

"I hadn't noticed," she lied.

They kept on through the hot canyons. Nothing. Dead ends. They would climb each wash to the narrow brush-tangled limit. Then they would hike back down to the main canyon and mark another one off on their map. Then turn west again. Always west. They kept it orderly. Adam sketched each little canyon in his book, listed its identifying features. But no Mongols, no houses, no sheep pens, no gardens, nothing. Just desert.

It was quiet too. Every so often on the wind they heard the far-off honk of camels, but they never saw them. They had seen some from the jeep, though, driving in: the camels moved across the desert in clumps of two or three, heads high in their slow rolling walk or heads down, nosing in the rocks and dirt. She supposed they were grazing, though there seemed little for them to eat. Still, the Number One Guesthouse had served a peculiar vegetable every night, one which looked for all the world like clumps of wet black hair. And that was the Chinese word it was called by: *fa-cai,* hair vegetable. One of the older Muslims around the guesthouse had told her it grew in a fine low-hugging net across the desert floor. He described the tool they used to harvest it, something like a wide, curved-tooth fork, and indeed she had seen this mysterious item displayed in Yinchuan's hardware stores. She thought of it now, laboring in the sand behind Dr. Spencer, how one would drag it across the dirt and pull up clumps of hair. Perhaps the camels were eating *fa-cai.*

And the Mongols who'd lived here when Teilhard had come, what did they eat? But of course they'd have kept sheep, and some goats, and peppers and eggplants must have struggled up in their gardens. She knew that the Yellow River yielded only one thing out here, a flat, bony carp: so the Mongols had probably had commerce with the people who lived closer to the river, trading mutton for fish. And then when their camels had grown old and sick and outlived their usefulness, they ate those too. God, the sand was hot, it burned right through her shoes. She had been served camel hump, in Yinchuan. It had been a tough, rubbery membrane of a meat, cloaked in a brown bean sauce that did nothing to hide the taste of old, mean animal. And the sauce hadn't really disguised the look of the meat, either, she thought: it was the same dun color that was everywhere here, the color of the river, the roads and houses, the color of the loess, the color of—

Spencer stopped so suddenly, she walked into his back. "Oh, my good God in heaven," he whispered.

In front of them shimmered the homestead.

8

THE WALLS OF packed loess had looked like a natural desert outcropping until they were right upon them. Yet these were certainly structures built by man. They were too symmetrical for nature. The two Americans stared open mouthed at the rambling house, the storage sheds, the animal pens, and beyond all that the arid patch that once had been a garden. Nothing but dust now. Empty, abandoned.

Spencer froze for a long moment, rearranging his hope, his optimism, his faith, in a way that would accommodate the vast disappointment in front of him. "I guess this was it."

Definitely, she thought. This was it. She sat heavily on the ground.

"They've been gone a long time," he whispered.

Yes, she thought. It looked like decades since this place was alive with the racket of dogs and horses, men working, children calling out, the smoke curling up, and the slapping sound of grain in the baskets.

And it wasn't even the physical homestead Spencer was hoping for. It was the Mongols themselves. They were the ones who might have known. Because Teilhard had to have told somebody—the Mongols. Lucile. Both.

But none of them is here. She scanned the place. Nothing but old yellow walls and sheep pens.

Spencer stood in silence. "Okay," he said finally. "Let's look around."

Hours later Alice was back in her room, trying to read, when she heard a knock. "You are Mo Ai-li?" said the wiry man in the ill-fitting green suit.

"I am," Alice said.

He produced a card.

She read it aloud. "Guo Wenxiang, Happy Fortune Consulting." Damn, why hadn't he just called? She was exhausted from the afternoon, going over the homestead, sighting down every inch of it in the broiling sun and finding nothing, nothing. She dug out a business card and handed it to him.

"Mo Ai-li, Interpreter," he read, strolling past her.

"I'm so sorry, my employer is not in right now." And Lin and Kong were still out at the Bureau of Cultural Relics. She'd have to talk to this guy alone.

She left the door open, pointed to a chair, and poured tea. "It's put you to too much trouble to come over here. I thought you might telephone."

He smiled a car-salesman smile, which dragged his sharp extruding cheekbones almost up to his eyebrows. Pomade glimmered on his sculpted head. "Ah, no, it wouldn't do. One must call on a new friend in person. Don't you think? Tell me, Miss Mo. How do you find Yinchuan?"

"Interesting."

He looked disconcerted. "Interesting? Well . . ."

"I like history."

"Ah, yes, history. Have you been to the Xi Xia tombs?"

"Not yet. We're working. We've been busy." She had heard about the tombs, of course. For a few improbable centuries Yinchuan had actually been the capital of northwest China under the Xi Xia, or western Xia, dynasty, until Genghis Khan had roared in and toppled everything. Now the tombs of the last Xi Xia emperors still lay out in the desert, eroding in the wind, and Yinchuan had slid into obscurity.

"I'll take you," he proposed. "Whenever you have time. What about this evening, if you're not working? Or maybe tomorrow."

"Mr. Guo, I wouldn't want to trouble you—"

"No trouble."

"No, really, Mr. Guo. Please. Listen to me. I want to ask you about the building your office is in—"

He raised a nicotine-stained finger. "Not one more word about business, until you read this! It's all prepared." He whipped out a four-page document densely printed with Chinese characters.

She read the title. "Contract for Consulting Services." Oh, damn, she thought, and started plowing through it. Reading Chinese was never effortless, even after all this time. She still went character by character. There were always ideograms she couldn't recognize.

The client therefore and in confident mind agrees to pay a retainer of 5,000 yuan for services rendered in the first three months. . . . She put it down. "Mr. Guo. Among friends, one should put one's heart in one's mouth and say what one thinks. Tell me. Have you ever had an outside person for a client before?"

"No, but I have many important clients. I know someone whose second cousin is fourth Party vice-chair for Ningxia Province, and I have connections within the police. So, you can see"—he leaned back in his chair and smiled his chatty smile— "I know where all the back doors are."

"I understand. Well. We outside people don't use contracts.

They are unnecessary between real friends." She handed it back disdainfully.

"I quite agree." He stuffed it in his pocket.

"Good. As the words go, the actions will follow. I require one service, a simple one. It concerns the building your office is in."

"Ah, the building—I can arrange for you to buy it! You know it was the Number One Jesus Church at one time, architecture very distinctive. First class. Total price two point three million yuan. That's just a trifle, you know, when one talks of such a fine building."

"Mr. Guo—"

"I know, it's not legal for outside people to have more than a forty-nine percent ownership in real estate, but that can be handled, I can set up a false proxy company for the other fifty-one points, I would be the director, maybe a cousin as trustee, everything in the family, but it would all be controlled by you, of course—"

I'll bet. "Mr. Guo, *duibuqi,* it is entirely my fault, but you misunderstand."

"If you are worried about recovering your U.S. dollars upon resale, put your heart at rest, we can put the funds through a textile mill and then give you quality cotton, the best, good resale value, and you'll pay only a third of the price, do you see? I can get the quota fixed, special for you. Export's no problem. Guaranteed. I have contacts in the Textile Ministry in Beijing."

"No."

"No? But Miss Mo."

"I don't want to buy the building. I want information. That's all."

"Information?" His smile evaporated, eyes narrowed, calculating.

Alice weighed her options rapidly. She didn't know enough about this Guo Wenxiang to reveal everything to him, but she could probably start him off with research on Abel Oort, the

Dutch missionary. If he proved resourceful, they could all decide what to do with him and how much to tell him. "Mr. Guo." She cleared her throat. "In the nineteen twenties that church was operated by a Dutchman. Abel Oort. I want to know what happened to him, if he died in Yinchuan where he is buried, if he left anything, any letters, any diaries—especially, I want to know if there is anyone still alive who remembers him."

Guo sat silent for a moment before he spoke. "You are his relative?"

She sighed. *Stretch it.* "My employer is a friend of the family."

"Ah, a family matter." His smile returned.

"Yes."

"Eh, well, since we are good friends and this is a family matter, I will see what I can do. But I remind you, many years have flown."

"I know."

"You're sure you're not interested in getting into the Shanghai stock market? I can arrange—"

"No. But you must name your fee for the service I require."

He looked crestfallen. "So sorry, Miss Mo, between good friends like ourselves, how can I face you when I mention the price? Expenses are very high these days. Inflation's a river, out of control."

"Yes, I know." She kept her face patient and polite. God, she hated this. "What would be fair?"

"I will need at least a thousand yuan, up front."

Outrageous! Three months' salary for the average Chinese. "Mr. Guo," she said, touching her forehead as if she had just remembered something, "in fact I do have another small problem. I brought U.S. dollars with me on this trip, and stupidly forgot to exchange them in Beijing. I'm afraid I don't have such a large amount of renminbi." This was disingenuous, as they both knew, for any local bank—to say nothing of black market currency privateers, a few of whom still lurked in every city—would gladly convert U.S. dollars.

His eyes gleamed with delight. "I believe I could help you with that problem."

"Tai hao," Wonderful.

"Shall we say, eighty U.S. dollars for the whole job?"

"Thirty."

"Forty."

"Hao-le," Done. She counted out the American bills.

"Thank you. I'll return in a few days with the information. May I say, Miss Mo—oh, no, no, don't see me out, I'm quite all right—may I say with what exquisite subtlety and scholarship you speak. Since you're an outside person, it's most unexpected."

With effort she said, *"Nali,"* nonsense, and shut the door.

Lin Shiyang was walking behind Alice on the way to the dining hall that night, and he stared down at her striding along the tiled courtyard path in front of him. He was taken by her dark red hair, its gloss, the alive way it moved around her head. And she had a way of pushing back a strand of hair that was bothering her, a way of twirling it around her finger and then tossing it aside. Meiyan used to do that, exactly the same way. Yet how different this woman was from Meiyan! He had never seen hair like Ai-li's, except in pictures. And he had never seen a woman smile the way she did. He forgot all that was strange about her face when she smiled. Because then, pleasure just burst out from somewhere inside her. He liked that. It was uncontrolled, it was un-Chinese, but he liked it.

* * *

At the public phone hall Alice called her father's office on Capitol Hill. He wasn't there, of course—she hadn't expected him to be. But Roger was, and a secretary went to pull him from a meeting. Alice waited.

A thousand miles away in Beijing, Supervisor Ling saw a light on her board; she pressed a button and activated the preset wiretap authorized by the PLA. She pushed another button; this would inform Commander Gao's office.

In Yinchuan, Alice gripped the phone. "Roger. Be straight with me. What's wrong with Horace?"

"I don't know if I should—"

"Come on, Roger, I'm in frigging Mongolia." Almost.

He sighed. "He had his routine physical. The bloodwork showed an elevated PSA. Prostate-specific antigen. It was, uh, rather sharply elevated. That can mean various things. It can mean the prostate is infected, in which case it's a simple course of antibiotics. Or . . ."

"Or?"

"Or else it means prostate cancer."

"Oh, my God." She swallowed. "How bad is it?"

"They don't know yet. It might be quite far along—or it might be the kind that advances very slowly. But, Alice, often the cause of the elevated reading is merely infection. So right now they have him on an antibiotic."

"Oh." Relief flooded her. Her father, her only family, her sole living ancestor—despite all he did that was barely forgivable. "So everything's fine."

"Well, dear—we don't know yet."

"But he's on the antibiotic."

"Yes."

"Then he'll be okay."

Silence.

"Roger?"

"Yes?"

"I'll call in a few days."

"Do that. And, Alice—naturally—not a word to anyone, hmm?"

"Roger, please." She glanced through the glass booth-window at the unruly swarm of waiting Mongols. "If you could see where I'm calling from, you wouldn't waste your breath."

"Heh, heh." He emitted his humorless cackle and hung up.

It'll be okay, she told herself on the way out of the phone hall. It won't be cancer. Horace will go on like he always has. Horace has always been there, he'll never leave me. She held her breath. And I'll never be free of him either.

She boxed it up in her mind, and within minutes managed to hide it away as she walked, fast and hard, away down the baking, dust-shimmering Yinchuan street.

She pulled her one pair of black underpants up slowly and then tied on the antique stomach-protector. Outside, the streets were vibrant with life, the evening warm and soft. The long, pleasantly yellow light, which she knew would linger till nearly eleven, streamed over the city.

She had drawn the sheer undercurtains and now watched herself in the mirror. The phoenix, its wings a riot of color, spread beautifully across her, its small, graceful head raised in an attitude of love. The female principle, enfolding. The phoenix which sought the dragon, the sign of the male.

She sighed at her reflection. Her hair was a neat, burnished wedge. Her makeup, invisible, the way she liked it. Nothing showing but copper lip gloss. She looked good.

But why look for a stranger?

She ran her hands through her hair, adjusting it.

Why not Lin?

She examined her high Irish cheekbones, her gold-flecked

eyes, her freckles. Did Lin find her appealing? Did his thoughts drift to her? Was he thinking about her now?

She turned from the mirror. The only thing she knew for sure was that he was a man she couldn't toy with. A closeness with Lin would not be for one night, for pleasure; it would pull in her real self. Only, what was her real self? Again the question hung over her.

This, she thought in a prepatterned flood of resignation, the makeup and the silk stomach-protector and a night out, looking. This is me. And if Lin knew who I really was, he wouldn't have the least interest in me. He'd be repulsed.

She sighed and turned to her clothes. The black dress—no. Not in Yinchuan. Here in this *tu* provincial town she was conspicuous enough. It would be better to wear jeans. Her second pair of jeans, which were pleasingly tight. And a black T-shirt.

She tucked away her room key and money, renminbi. Checked her look one more time. Now. Where should she go?

There were bars in Yinchuan, only not the kind she wanted. She'd slipped into one a few evenings before, a karaoke bar, just to check it out. She'd known immediately she wouldn't come back. It was full of Mongols, high flat faces staring sullenly into space, none of them willing to get up onstage and sing along with the blaring Madonna songs. She had heard other foreign women say that Mongol men were fabulously virile, but she had also heard that they all wore daggers at their belts, and though they approached women confidently, they tended to be dangerously possessive once the deed was done. It was a little too *tu* for her.

Anyway, maybe it was time to move forward. She should try to meet the type of man she could be herself with—not be Yulian. The very idea that her real life and her sexual life could come together seemed strange, yet ever since she met Lin she'd been thinking about it. To be all of herself, together, to feel as Lucile felt when she wrote in a private note: *I am so happy and feel so completely yours.*

177

Yes, Alice thought. Tonight would be different. She would try the local college.

She took a pedicab to Xibei University. Normally she avoided pedicabs, there being something feudal and horrible about being pulled around in a cart by a sweating, brown, sinewy man. On this evening, though, Alice did not want to be observed. She pressed herself all the way to the back of the cracked leather seat, and the ancient awning made her all but invisible to those who passed by.

She got off at the campus, a forest of low concrete buildings. She had watched through the awning cracks as best she could while they crossed the city, and had not seen anyone tailing them. She glanced around quickly as the man pedaled away. Nothing unusual. She walked onto the campus.

Like most Chinese universities it was mainly a clump of buildings, with none of the academic-village atmosphere for which Western institutions strived. In China, of course, colleges did not have to please students. Violent competition raged for the privilege of attending at all. Once in, the lucky few took what they got. Because unless one had a key to the back door through family connections, it was the only way up and out.

And that's how it's been here for thousands of years, she thought, it's just a new version of the imperial examination system. And today's students, these pinch-chested, pimply-faced kids, here because they won the top scores on the national exams, were the new incarnations of the Ming and Qing mandarins.

But they're all too young for me, she thought bitterly, too young and too awkward. Weren't there any older men around—any professors?

She watched the girls and boys on foot, back and forth, carrying their books.

Somebody like Dr. Lin.

She parked herself on a bench and waited.

It was almost an hour before a man near her own age walked

up and sat next to her. He was not like the men in the bars. He was faintly disheveled, with a high, sparsely fringed forehead and a bulging briefcase.

He looked at her sideways. *"Dong Zhongwen-ma?"* he asked softly, Do you understand Chinese?

"Dong," she said simply, I do.

His eyes widened and a kindly chuckle bubbled up. "I never thought I'd sit here on a bench on this campus with an outside woman who was able to talk. I'm surnamed Wang." His grin was controlled, intelligent; it made his middle-aged face seem pleasantly companionable. "How are you called?"

"Yulian," she answered, Fragrant Lotus. She noted his slight confusion.

"But what are you surnamed?"

"Bai," she lied. Usually the men in the bars didn't ask for a surname. In China, to allow someone to call you by your given name was in itself an act of intimacy. When she introduced herself in these encounters with the name Fragrant Lotus, no surname, it was like honey in her mouth, and the men in the bars always understood. Their usual response was a sly smile. However, this was Yinchuan. The provinces.

"My wife was surnamed Bai," this man Wang said slowly.

Oh, no. "Is she—"

"She died in the Cultural Revolution."

"I'm sorry."

He shrugged. "Years pass like water."

"Did you have children?"

"One daughter. She was raised by my parents in Shanghai. That was after I was assigned here."

"And you remained here after the Cultural Revolution ended?"

"Yes. That's how it was." His look revealed his clear surprise that she appeared to know all about the Chaos, the forced reassignment of workers, the tearing up of families.

"It's a bitter road," she said softly.

"Yes. But now it's not bad. The university is a good *danwei*. You know what they say. A brave man bows to circumstances as grass does before wind."

"So now you're a teacher?"

"Administration."

She thought it over for a minute, and then laid her freckled hand over his smooth brown one in sympathy.

He stared at it.

She did not remove it.

"Yulian," he said slowly, wonderingly, "would you like to return to my place for tea?" He looked at her, everything in his face certain she would say no.

"I would." She smiled.

"Zou-ba," he said with an amazed crack in his voice, Then let's go. He stood with his briefcase.

They walked in silence. He lived behind the university, in an expressionless block of high-rises. They climbed up six flights of gray concrete, lined with a plain metal rail, to his apartment. Yet once he opened the door they were in another world, for like the carefully maintained interiors of so many private spaces in China, it was spotlessly clean and pleasingly fitted out. A scroll painting and a Xinjiang carpet of surprising quality dominated the room, and brilliantly colored cloths were spread over the table and the bed. In the window above the sink hung an ornate wooden cage with a twittering brown lark.

Wang put down his briefcase and turned to her, his eyes soft. "Do you like flowers?" he said. He drew a red peony from a porcelain jar on the table and cupped it in both hands.

"Yes," she said.

"I do too." He touched the flower to his cheek, then to hers. Just for an instant. She closed her eyes at its softness. She felt his fingers gently seeking hers.

They stood for a moment, their hands joined, and then she turned her back to him and began to remove her T-shirt. She liked to do it that way. From behind they would see nothing except the red silk strings. Then she would turn around, and watch their faces when they saw the phoenix spread across her middle—nude above, nude below—

This time, though, in Mr. Wang's gracious little room, she stopped, with her T-shirt almost to her armpits. This was not her. Not really her. She dropped her shirt.

"Yulian," Wang said.

All she could think about was Dr. Lin, Lin Shiyang, the tall man from Zhengzhou who seemed to be watching her all the time.

He stepped close to her. *"Shenmo?"* he whispered, What is it?

She put her hands up to her face. "I can't."

He touched her arm. "Yulian."

I feel so completely yours. She could almost hear Lucile's voice, speaking to Pierre, the man she loved. Lucile had found real love in Chinese rooms like this. Even though she agonized over the one thing Pierre Teilhard de Chardin could not give her, and this thing ballooned in importance until it all but obsessed her. Still she returned his love. Why couldn't Alice make that commitment? Even half that commitment?

"I'm sorry," she said to Wang. "It's not your fault."

"So you will come another day?"

"Yes. Of course." Though she knew she would not.

"I will call you, then." He fetched a paper and pen from the table and held them out to her. She scrawled the name, Yulian, and a nonsense phone number.

"Remember where I live," he said. "Come anytime."

She walked heavily to the bottom floor and back into the fading light. Beating in her ear like a faint night insect was the drab awareness of life. Her life. She was still alive and Mother Meng was dead. If only she could connect with Mother Meng one more time, talk to her . . . maybe she should go see the yin-yang master. Maybe, through him, she could reach the old lady again. Because Mother Meng had said to find a man. And it was impossible.

On Shanxi Avenue, in front of the university, she found another pedicab. "Number One Guesthouse," she said.

"Eh," he agreed, glancing back at her. He noticed the tight press of her mouth, and the way she sat with her fist pressed against her forehead. He pulled out into the street, straining against the pedals, picking up speed.

He saw a man jump into a pedicab and follow them, never deviating, never veering away, staying behind them no matter how many twists and unexpected turns he added to the route as he pulled the foreign woman across town. When they stopped, he meant to tell her. But when he turned and he saw her strange, freckled, tofu-colored face streaked with tears, he said nothing. He accepted her money, let out another monosyllable, and pedaled away.

She squeezed onto the polished stool in the booth at the public phone hall. The signal came from the operator and she picked it up. Come on Horace, she thought, be home. Please be home. She swallowed. Eleven in the evening in Washington. *Come on.*

The burping disturbance to the ring, and then his recorded voice mail. She listened to his greeting: calm, smooth, business-like. When the tone sounded and the inert void of the recorder came on, she spoke in a thin, childish voice, made tight by worry: "It's just me. Wondering how you are.

"Bye," she said, and reluctantly hung up.

* * *

Lieutenant Shan, Army commander for the Ningxia–Inner Mongolia region, snapped the report he'd been given back down on his desk. "So the oily-mouth from the Golden Country only stayed inside the man's apartment ten minutes, eh? Ten minutes! What could they do! Are the west-ocean ghosts not strange!"

His men looked at each other.

"Did you find out anything about her yet? The other American's a scientist, what about her? She's a scientist too?"

"No, sir. We don't know."

"No? You dog bones! You have to be clever. Now, listen. If she calls that number in Washington again I want her very closely watched. Is she stupid? No! She's a crafty barbarian."

"Yes, Honorable Sir!" the line of men barked.

"Move! *Diu neh loh moh,*" Do your mothers.

The men did not flinch at this Cantonese obscenity their commanding officer from the South was so fond of throwing around. They were used to it.

"Report back to me!"

They hurried out.

"See this?" said Dr. Lin, and handed it to her, a polished bone, familiar, twin knobs at its end. "It's a human femur."

She gasped and her fingers came out, then stopped. "Can I really touch it?"

He laughed. "Of course. *Gei.*"

She took it and almost seemed to stop breathing as she held it, studied it, felt it. "Can you tell how old it is?"

"Not here, not now. In the lab we could, since it's organic material. But when you have this kind of site you can't date things in the field. The shifting sand mixes the ages together. You see." He glanced, to illustrate, at the chalky, fine-grained dunes of the Ordos that rolled away in front of them. They had climbed to the ridge after lunch and stepped over the Wall, and now sat, sifting through sand with their fingers. Almost immediately he had found this bone. It was just a few inches down. He had been rolling his hand through the sand, and had suddenly drawn it out, smiling, ecstatic with the discovery. When he turned to her he saw her staring, not at the bone but at his face. Quickly she'd looked away. There'd been something so unguarded in her eyes, so open—those strange agate eyes, the like of which he had never seen before on a woman.

"Just think," she said softly. "It was part of a person in Stone Age times—someone who lived, hunted, grew food. Yet he or she must have thought. Must have spoken somehow." She touched the bone wonderingly.

"You surprise me so," he said. "You are a Westerner—yet you are drawn to what is old."

"You said that before. Let it go. It's just a prejudice. When I see something this old—when I hold it—I feel the connection of the past and future. It gives me hope, though I am only one small being. Do you understand my words?" *To write the true natural history of the world, we should need to be able to follow it from* within. *It would thus appear no longer as an interlocking succession of structural types replacing one another, but as an ascension of inner sap spreading out in a forest of consolidated instincts.*

"I'm not sure if I understand you or not," he said quietly. "But I want to, very much."

She lowered her eyes. They both returned to shifting sand.

Lin focused on the sand trailing from his fingers. It was so hot. The other part of the Ordos, the rocky dirt cut by canyons and shallow steppes, fell away behind them at the bottom of the ridge. This was the dune region of the Ordos, the subdesert called Maowushu. Sand rolled away over the pattern of hills in front of him, rose and fell until it ran into the blinding sky. Lin stared off to the horizon as far as he could. It was hard to believe he was here, at last, in the place he had dreamed of coming for so many years to look for Meiyan. She seemed gone, vanished. And now he sat here talking to another woman. He was not a man who was completely free to engage with a woman, yet this woman—this outside woman . . . He looked at her. There was something about her. When he was with her he felt happy, excited; when he was apart from her he found himself wanting to be with her again.

But she was a Westerner. What did such a woman take, what did she give? He had heard Western women were superficial, that they were interested in diversion, not love. That they could not be trusted. Was it true with Mo Ai-li? As he considered this he watched his hands, and her hands. With a jolt he saw that they were playing with the sand, in unison, a dangerous physical harmony between them. Did she notice?

Ah. She did. Because suddenly she looked up at him, reddening. "We'd better go back."

He couldn't stop himself from smiling as he got to his feet. "All right. *Zou-ba.*"

"Mr. Tang," Alice said, reading the name of the yin-yang master off of his card, "I have come to you about the death of someone I love." She glanced around his cluttered reception room. In addition to the stacks of well-thumbed almanacs there was, on every shelf and counter, a bizarre jumble of paper objects meant to serve the dead in the underworld. Small reproductions of horses, grain carts, wine pitchers, rice bowls, stacks of play money, paper clothing and linens, miniature chests and beds and tables, and even tiny models of servants and concubines and family members, all cleverly fashioned and folded and printed in a riot of garish paper colors.

"Mo Ai-li, Interpreter," he read from her card. "This is most uncommon. No *waiguoren* has ever come to me before. Even among Chinese, only the old ones still come. You are perhaps researching feudal culture?"

"No. I require your services, that's all."

He raised his scanty white eyebrows and laid her card carefully on his desk, then focused his lidded, rheumy black eyes. "Please explain."

"A woman has just died who was like a mother to me, though she was Chinese and not my real mother. I fear she has not been properly mourned."

"What of her children?"

"One son. He does not follow the old ways."

"Husband?"

"Died a few years ago."

"Eh! A bitterness. But this is a Chinese family. Not your own."

"It's so. . . ."

"You are not Chinese," he reminded her.

"Yes," she said heavily. "I know."

"Yet you wish to observe the rituals. What about your own ancestors? Do you serve them?"

Alice thought of Horace. This was her Fall—just being born with the Mannegan name. "Yes," she evaded. "I have ancestors." But I need new ones, she thought.

"If you are sure you wish to proceed . . ." He lifted his shoulders in the classic Chinese attitude of disavowal. "A few questions. At the time of the woman's death, was an auspicious object placed in her mouth—a pearl, or a coin? Were mirrors placed about her body?"

"I was not present."

He paused, cleared his throat. "Was notice of her death given to the local gods? Was a geomancer engaged to determine the proper siting of her grave?"

"I'm sorry, Master Tang, I don't know, but I believe none of this was done. She lived in the city—in Beijing. They don't do these things there anymore." She didn't want to say aloud what they both also knew: that when people died in the big cities now their bodies were disposed of quickly, quietly, through routine cremation.

"The date of her death, please?"

"July fourteenth." Alice closed her eyes and pictured Meng and Jian. "Her son—he loved her. But I don't think he will worship her spirit." I could, she thought. I could be the worthy spirit child of Meng Shaowen.

And Lucile Swan too.

Why not? The practice of filial piety was one of the many things about old China she'd always found appealing. She had just never had the right kind of parent. Now, though . . . She cleared her throat. "Is it possible—may I make this woman my ancestor?"

Avoiding her eyes, Master Tang tented his gnarled fingers and regarded them. "It is sometimes done. But only by Chinese. And always when the departed one is childless. You say she has a son?"

"Yes."

"One must consider him."

She saw Jian in her mind with the open-faced wife, the perfect baby. "He will never follow the rituals."

He pondered. *"Xing.* I will prepare her *ling-pai,* the spirit tablet. We will meet again in seven days for the rituals of *ci-ling* and *an-zhu,* which will call her spirit back to the tablet and then enshrine it in your home. This makes her your ancestor and a part of your family forever. You understand the responsibilities?"

"I do."

"You'll make regular offerings? You'll honor her every year on Qing-Ming?"

"I will."

"Good. I will come to your room one week from today. In the meantime, you must go to the temple and complete the *bao-miao* ritual. This will announce her death to the neighborhood gods. Yet you can't—you say she lived in Beijing. . . ." He stopped and considered the problem.

"Master Tang, I know nothing, I am an outside person of low intelligence, but may I humbly suggest we use a local temple to the Goddess of Mercy, Guanyin?"

"It will suffice, I suppose." He prepared his inkstone, took up a brush, and with perfect form, despite the swollen joints of his long fingers, wrote a few characters. "The temple address," he said, and pushed it across the desk. "Now. So I can prepare the *ling-pai*, your friend's name?"

"Meng Shaowen."

"Which Meng?"

"Mengzi-de Meng," she clarified, and he wrote the characters down.

"There is one more matter, Mo Ai-li. You must choose some spirit objects to send on to Meng Shaowen. Things that would have meaning to her and ease her life beyond the Yellow Springs. These objects are to be burned in the next seven days, preferably at the intersection of two streets. This is *jiao-hun*, Calling back the soul. Well?"

She stared helplessly around her at the welter of paper symbols crowding the room.

"I see you do not know. Most people select spirit money, food vessels, wine cups—such things as these."

"Ah," Alice said. She rose and circled the room, scanning the miniature world of flawless, loudly colored paper replicas. For Meng she chose kitchen goods, a tiny chest for wardrobe, and a paper Victrola. Then there was Lucile. The women were connected now in her mind. Every prayer, every ritual, would be for both of them. For Lucile she selected a tiny bed, a pile of paper linens, and a little paper man. He was meant to be wearing old-fashioned Chinese robes, but it could have been the raiment of a priest. It could have been Teilhard.

"These things," she said, and handed them to Master Tang.

The Temple to Guanyin, Goddess of Mercy, was on the edge of the old Chinese quarter. It was a Qing-era building with elaborate red-and-blue frescoes painted along the curving eaves, ornate but run down. Inside Alice found no one except a novice monk, a boy no older than fifteen with a saffron robe and a close-shaven black fuzz covering his head.

"Wo lai bao-miao," she said to him tentatively, I've come for the ritual of reporting a death at the temple.

He looked at her blankly.

"My friend has died," she explained.

He removed a packet of incense wrapped in red paper from a pile of supplies on a side table, and handed it to her. *"Si mao san,"* he said absently, Forty-three cents.

She counted out the coins.

He waved her toward the altar, a bank of Buddhas rising up behind a sweet-faced, larger-than-life statue of the Goddess of Mercy, Guanyin.

She lit the incense, stuck it into one of the sand-filled bowls, and bowed three times. "Meng Shaowen," she whispered, "on July fourteenth of this year, you drifted away from this world and went to the Yellow Springs. There you met Old Woman Wang, who gave you the wine of forgetfulness to drink. In this way you could go on to your next life with your sins, your memories, wiped away. . . ." Another start, Alice thought. It was what she needed too.

She stood silent, staring up at the statue. Guanyin had a beautiful face, shaped like an almond, narrow black eyes, and a rosebud mouth. She stood with her hands outstretched, her colored robes swirling gracefully around her.

It occurred to Alice, for the first time, that Guanyin looked exactly like the Virgin Mary.

Strange she'd never noticed.

A note from Guo Wenxiang was slipped beneath her door at the Number One:

Mo Ai-li, I am happy to inform you that I have obtained some information about the Dutch missionary Abel Oort.

He died in Yinchuan in 1934. Tomorrow evening, if you are free, I will take you and Dr. Spencer to his grave.

She wrote the English translation beneath the spidery characters and slid the note under Spencer's door.

Back inside, her door locked, she removed all her clothes and stood in front of the mirror. Too boyish, that was her problem. A spare, narrow-hipped frame that rose from slim, wiry legs. Not much of a waist. Her breasts swelled out only slightly. Well shaped, though, she thought, twisting her body to put one of them into silhouette. And she had a reasonably good-looking bottom. She turned and looked at it over her shoulder. Her *pigu,* as the Chinese called it. Round and white and no droop. Not yet. She faced front again. Her eyes trailed down her pale belly past her legs to her feet, knotty and curiously strong looking. Too long for her small body, not soft and white as they should have been, but at least they were not all wide and splayed out.

Feet were important to Chinese men, or at least they had once been. Alice, as yet another way of achieving separation with herself, had often imagined herself with bound feet. Three inches long, that had been the ideal, and the helpless woman with soft pleading and submissiveness in her eyes would sway above them in that lotus-foot gait. *Take me*. Alice had read that the most profound sexual act in old China was when a woman actually allowed a man to remove her foot bandages and do things with her deformed foot. She knew that many women were married to men all their lives, bore them many sons, and never let them do it.

Often Alice had imagined it: the soft-eyed woman finally saying yes, the yards and yards of white bandage spiraling into a heap on the floor, the tiny wrinkled hoof, bare, the smaller toes bent under, sometimes fallen off. The strange smell of decayed flesh mixed with sweet talcum. The foot, pitiable, longed for, lifted at last in the man's ivory hands.

"Horace," she said, glancing at her watch in the dim flickering public phone stall—it was four forty-five in the morning where he was, "—why didn't you tell me there was a problem?"

"There is no problem," came back the sleepy, insistent voice.

"But Roger told me there was a chance it might be—" She stopped, not wanting to say the word, *cancer*. "He said it might be something serious."

"Did he? Well, it's not, though I love hearing from you. Alice darling, you haven't called me so much in years! Not since your first week at college."

"I got a little scared when I heard your message, Horace. And then when I talked to you and Roger. You can understand that." She pressed her lips together, holding back the words and the thoughts. To be any kind of person she needed, desperately, to stay away from him. With him, she was Alice Mannegan. The Alice from the Alice Speech. Prejudice and revulsion clung to her like a smell. And it was her own personal curse that she lacked the authority to tell him so, bluntly. She just couldn't. He was too powerful, too in control. All she could do was stay away.

And yet Horace was all she had. She was in so many ways his issue: the auburn hair, the small frame, the high intelligence. There was a confused stream of familial commitment between them that—despite everything—still survived and still had love in it. It was an alliance Alice couldn't imagine living without.

And she knew Horace couldn't imagine it either. "Come back, sweetheart. Please. Come back and visit me."

"I can't right now. Soon maybe, but not now. I'm on a job."

"I miss you so much."

"I know. Me too. Horace, come on. Tell me what's going on."

He coughed. He had stopped smoking years ago, at her urging, but he still coughed, especially in the morning. "I'm just on the antibiotic, sweetheart. Really. It's okay."

"Are you taking care of yourself? Are you getting enough sleep?"

"Are you coming home?"

She sighed. "Horace . . ."

"Seriously," he continued. "It's a big country, America. There's lots of room. You could come back. You don't have to be anywhere near your old dad."

"Oh, Horace," she said, instantly moving the conversation away from the word *Dad,* as she always did.

"You could come back and live somewhere else," he insisted.

"It's not that. It's just that this is my life—working—you know." She didn't want to say what she felt, what she knew to be true: that he had ruined America for her, that she could no longer be there, that for better or worse she was entwined here in China. Though what would her life be like after—if—Horace was gone? She tried briefly to imagine a world without him. His dominance, his paternalism, vanished. Would she be free, then? Could she be herself, could she love someone?

These thoughts, first shafts of light in darkness, made her wince; she quickly closed them off. No, she thought, taking a deep, jagged breath. Losing Horace would be awful.

Her father was still talking, a stubborn edge to his voice. "Well, then, just come and visit."

"I'll try."

"Okay."

"Horace, be sure you get enough sleep, and vitamins, and everything."

"Of course, my darling."

Please don't die, she thought desperately, hanging up. Don't leave me.

All through the next day she was able to think of nothing but Horace, and the possibility that he was seriously ill. By the time they got back to Yinchuan in the afternoon she had decided to call Roger. That was it. Get hold of Roger, and just demand that he tell her the whole truth. How sick was Horace? What exactly had the doctors said? She lined all this up in her mind as she walked up Sun Yat-sen.

At the public phone hall they kept her waiting. Forty-five minutes, then an hour. It was outrageous. She had never waited this long before in a public phone hall, anywhere.

She plodded back to the counter again.

"*Qingwen,*" she said politely to the *fuwuyuan*. "I've been waiting such a long time—"

"Destination?"

"United States. Washington, D.C."

"Oh, yes," the woman said. A sudden light flooded her eyes. "Calls to Washington take a long time."

No, they don't, Alice thought, but she returned to her seat.

"Yi bai wushi hao!"

Finally. Her number. She walked quickly to the booth, slid inside.

The phone rang.

Jesus, about time. *"Wei!"* she said.

"Phone call to America?"

"Yes."

"Wait a moment." The line went dead.

What? thought Alice—

Now a man was tapping sharply on the booth window. Sharp faced, authoritative, narrow eyes, and a crisp PLA uniform. With a brusque wave of the hand he ordered her out.

She stood up too quickly, caught the belt loop of her jeans on the edge of the tray that held the telephone. She heard a small ripping sound, felt her body restrained for an instant. A moment of confusion swirled around her. "What the hell?" she said to herself, reverting to English. Then she saw the snag. "Oh, it's this thing." She leaned over and unhooked it.

But the soldier had heard her English words. "Western cow," he muttered in Mandarin. "Supposed to be an archaeologist! But she makes phone calls to sensitive numbers—top diplomatic status—"

He thinks I don't understand him! she thought. He thinks I don't speak Chinese.

"Lai," the soldier said gruffly, and motioned toward the door.

She knew instantly that it was to her advantage to play dumb. So she answered in English. "Okay, okay. What's the problem?"

All conversation in the high-ceilinged hall had stopped. The Mongols all stood silent, staring at them.

Now the soldier took her arm and attempted to pull her away from the booth.

She planted her feet, resisting.

He responded by signaling aggressively, exaggerating it, using his hands.

"All right, all right. Take it easy." She had to cooperate, she knew that. Keep calm, she told herself. Use only English. It'll be okay. She let him prod her outside.

A van waited there, in the hot glassy light. People rushed by, all careful to look away from the soldier and the foreigner.

The rear doors of the van lay open.

"Shang che," he ordered softly, Get in, and gave her a gentle push.

She looked inside to see two rows of soldiers, seated. In one motion they brought their rifles up, *click,* pointing straight to the ceiling.

"Okay," she shook out. "Cool down."

She climbed into the van like a remote movie image of herself, a bad dream, a sheet of water over everything. It can't really be. But it is. Somebody bolted the van doors from outside and the motor turned over, howled to life.

She grabbed for something to stay steady on her feet as the van lurched into the street.

The soldier on the end moved down to make room for her. He pounded on the seat and made wild eye motions, as if communicating with a gorilla.

A searing Chinese reply came automatically to her throat— *Idiot! Do you also look at the sky through a bamboo tube and measure the sea with a conch shell?*—but she bit it down. She nodded in silence, then sank onto the bench.

"Waiguoren," she heard one of them murmur in amazement. Foreigner.

"Hao chou-a," another one swore in the soft accent of Shanghai, What a stinking mess.

"Ta yiju hua ye tingbudong," She doesn't understand a word. Don't let on you understand.

Her eyes were barely adjusted to the dark, her heart still battering; but she could see around her. There were eight of them. PLA greens. Recruits. Kids—no more than nineteen, twenty. Driving somewhere, bouncing over the city streets, at lurching, slamming speeds. She wrapped her arms around her torso and squeezed down the trembling as hard as she could. *Jing tian dong di,* Terror startles the heavens and rattles all the earth.

9

IT WAS TIME for Adam Spencer to admit there was nothing at Shuidonggou. He knew what he was doing: he was a former Leakey Fellow, a full professor, a published scholar of the archaic cultures of western America. But this time he'd been wrong.

Because there was nothing here.

He took his book from his patch pocket and wrote rapidly. One, where did Teilhard put *Sinanthropus?*

He sighed. He felt lately that this question was strangling him.

Two, he wrote. Whom did he tell about it?

The Mongols, the Mongols, it should have been the Mongols. He sighed and rubbed his chin. It was itchy all the time now, dusty and sticky like the rest of him in this desert sun. There was no wind yet. It would come up later, in the afternoon, as it did every day.

Where did he put it? What clue had they not yet followed?

There was Eren Obo, of course, Spencer thought; the village at the foot of the Helan Shan range. He wrote it down. They could go out there and find the petroglyphs. Though how many monkey sun gods were carved into boulders in the Helan Shan? Dozens? Hundreds?

And could they really obtain permission to cross the missile range, and the mountains, to get to Eren Obo in the first place? According to Kong and Lin it was a godforsaken spot in the most remote western part of Inner Mongolia. Closed to outsiders, because of the military. Closed even to Chinese.

Alice had told him that Kong and Lin were working on it. He had to rely on her; he couldn't understand a frigging word they said without her. Though he felt he caught the essence of the Chinese men. Kong was a walking flurry, all faxes and phone calls and excited conversations. Lin was quiet, removed.

And Alice. Such a strange woman. Smart as a whip. Would obviously have had some kind of hugely successful career if only she weren't so held down by her life.

But she was doing a great job. Tonight, for instance, that Mr. Guo she'd hired was supposed to take them to Abel Oort's grave.

Though it didn't look like Peking Man was here at Shuidonggou. They'd already found the one thing they'd known to look for—the Mongol homestead—and it was as dead as skittering leaves.

Still, they had the petroglyph. The monkey sun god. Had that been what was in Teilhard's thoughts, his secret mind? Spencer continued to write. As usual, the act of forming the words, the scratching sound of the ballpoint on the page, made things clearer for him. Eren Obo. That was the next place. They had to get visas for Eren Obo.

"Can't you whores get anybody who speaks English?" growled the man everyone addressed as Lieutenant Shan. "What am I supposed to do with this foreigner? Eh! Little Wang! Drag your lazy legs back to the base and get pockface Wu! He graduated high school." Shan took another pull on his fat, strong-smelling Chinese cigarette. As he smoked on the other side of the rough wooden table she could see little distinction between his breathing in and breathing out, so that when he talked smoke leaked and eddied constantly around his tobacco-stained teeth.

"Wu studied Russian in high school, not English. Sir!" The little man named Wang stood at terrified attention, trying not to look at Alice, with her unnaturally red hair and her green eyes. Eyes of a ghost. Eyes of a demon.

"You whores have twisted everything up!" the lieutenant barked. "Why did you bring her in here! I only told you to watch her! Now look what you've done. We can't detain an American like this!"

"But, sir, she resisted—"

"Shut up," Shan said darkly. "Why didn't we get a background report on these people from Beijing? Where's my briefing? We don't know anything except that they're Americans and they're doing something with archaeology. All right, so they're both archaeologists. And now they've got two of our Chinese archaeologists from Henan hooked up with them. That's not enough! We should know everything Beijing knows before we even make a move! And now"—his voice shook with anger—"you've dragged one of them in!"

"Sir—"

"Do your mother's smelly delta," the lieutenant snapped, switching to Cantonese.

Alice's eyes widened. She didn't know much Cantonese, but every Chinese speaker who'd ever passed through Canton or Hong Kong had heard this phrase. It was the stock obscenity of the streetwise Cantonese-speaking male. The Cantonese were known for their earthiness, and this was one of their favorite knee-jerk vulgarities. She had already deduced that this lieutenant was southern—he spoke Mandarin with an accent—but this crudeness was still a surprise, for he was a man of considerable military rank. Clearly, he didn't know she understood him. It was obvious he thought she was an archaeologist, not an interpreter. She had to keep this illusion going.

She forced out normal-sounding words in English. "Look, I don't know what the problem is." She looked around nervously. Where were they? Some Army office, a cement block building on the outskirts of the city. *Please don't take away my life in China.* "I'm just a tourist."

"If I may, sir," said a man she had heard called Zhao. He was a squat man with a broad face. His uniform was smartly cut, the belt around his thick waist real leather. He looked higher in rank than the others, though not as high as Lieutenant Shan, whose uniform was of the finest, softest tropical wool and whose pockets, collar, and shoulder seams were expertly detailed. "We've got the trace on the last call. It was to a private residence in Washington. Of course, there is nothing unlawful—"

"Do your mother," Shan hissed.

God, she thought, tracing my call. Is it about Horace?

But the lieutenant continued: "You should have let her talk on the phone. We were taping. Don't any of you whores have brains? How can we know now whether she was going to make arrangements with her government to remove Peking Man? How can we even know how close they are to finding it!"

Jesus, she thought, it's the expedition.

Shan was jabbing his brown finger at a sheaf of densely charactered pages in front of him. "The penalties for smuggling antiquities out of China are very—oh, *very* severe. We might have had a case that could turn into some true political currency. No. Oh, no. You dog bones have to bring her in before she even gets on the phone. *Zao-le,* Now it's all exposed!"

Take Peking Man out of the country? she thought. They can't be serious.

Shan, disgusted, was lighting another cigarette.

The men stood silent, watching him. Finally the one called

Zhao spoke: "Sir, permit this lower man to speak, but what is exposed? She cannot understand a word we say."

"You brought her here, didn't you? Does she think this is a tourist diversion? Look at her!"

They all shifted their gaze to her, not daring to speak.

"Look at her," Shan said, and suddenly his voice was slow, almost thoughtful. "Do you suppose her hair is red down below?"

"I personally wouldn't want to find out," Zhao said primly.

"Actually, she's not bad," Shan said. Smoke curled around his mouth.

Oh, God, not this, she thought desperately. It took all her self-control not to scrunch up, cross her legs, or do something else that showed she understood.

"You know, their women do it with everybody," Zhao remarked. "That's what I've heard."

They all looked raptly at him, then at her.

Stop, she thought miserably. Out loud she spoke English: "I wish I'd brought my passport today. Sorry. I left it at the hotel. But I'm an American, you see—here—I have an idea. Give me a pencil and paper." And she made writing motions with her hands.

"See that!" said the emaciated underling named Wang. "She wants to write something."

Shan looked at him witheringly. "Wang, you little whore, I don't know why I continue to expect intelligence from you. One can't get ivory from a dog's mouth, can one? Do your mother! Get her some paper and stop up your mouth!"

Little Wang yanked open the table drawer and shoved paper and a leaky-looking fountain pen in front of her.

"Thanks," she said, careful to stay in English, laboring to keep her voice steady. Quickly she sketched a creditable outline of the United States. Should she put a mark on Houston, Texas, her hometown? Hell, no. No mark. She pushed the paper back toward them.

"What fun," Shan said dryly. "The little oily mouth gives us a geography lesson. Zhao, Wang, listen. I'd like to lock this little west-ocean slut up and teach her a lesson, lock the other American up, too, but they haven't done anything yet and it would bring too much bitterness down on my head. We're all supposed to be friends with them now, can it be believed? The imperialist fucks. Eh? Who would have thought now I'd have one of their whores in my office and I'd have to play polite! Enough, I'm wasting too much time." He turned to Alice and stretched his mouth in a phony smile. "Mistake!" he shouted in English, the word barely comprehensible. He raised his palms. "Sorry! Mistake!"

She drew her brows together. Had he said "mistake"? Was he backing down? "Oh," she said in English. "Okay. No problem."

He glared at his men. "All right, you whores. Take this baggage back to downtown Yinchuan and let her off. Courteously. And then keep an eye on all of them. If they find the bones, I want to know it. Good and fast! Understood?"

"Sir!" Sharp salutes from Zhao and Wang.

"Diu neh loh moh," Do your mothers. Shan waved them out.

When she finally stepped down from the back of the van on the back street behind the Number One, her knees were like water and she wasn't sure where she was, what had just happened, or even what language she was thinking in. She tried to start walking. The pillared entrance to the guesthouse blurred in front of her.

Then there was a hand under her arm. "Xiao Mo."

She looked up. Dr. Lin.

"Are you all right?" He steadied her, eyes wide. "What happened?"

"I got picked up by the PLA."

"*What!*" His composure fractured. "*Zenmo keneng!*" Could this be? Meiyan had been picked up by the PLA too. But Meiyan was gone and this woman was alive, she was here, in front of him, unhurt. And they had taken her—questioned her—what? He felt the hammering of fear. Out of concern for her he made his voice soft. "Tell me all that happened."

"I went to the phone hall to call my father. My father's office"—she looked half destroyed—"ah—perhaps you remember, it is a high government office. A soldier took me from the booth and into a van, but you see, he thought I couldn't talk, and I let him think so. They drove me to some building, out of town, I think, and a man everyone called Lieutenant Shan talked. He was—very rude."

Lin tensed. "Rude how, exactly?"

"Just . . ." She paused. "Crude."

"What?"

"He was Cantonese. I've heard talk like that on the street before, in Hong Kong. You know."

"Of course," Lin said, exhaling hard. "But for him to speak that way in front of you—it's unimaginable! You're an outsider. Especially a man of authority—"

"Oh, no!" Alice cried. "He thought I couldn't understand! He was complaining about not getting a briefing. He doesn't know much about what we're doing, just that it's about archaeology and Peking Man. He didn't know I was an interpreter. He thought I was another archaeologist. He'd never have talked that way if he thought I spoke Chinese."

Comprehension dawned in his chest as he looked down at her. "So they spoke freely in front of you?"

She rolled her eyes. "God, yes. Completely."

A sense of wonder started up in him, side by side with his fear.

"You are brave! It takes courage to do such a thing." So she has more than intelligence, he thought, looking down at her—she has inner strength. "Now tell me. What did you learn?" He was still holding her arm. "Why did they take you in?"

"You won't believe this."

His eyes notched into a more brilliant, deeper black.

"They think if we find Peking Man, we're going to smuggle it out. They think that's why I called Washington."

"But that's—that's . . ."

"Insane?" she suggested.

He closed his eyes, shook his head slowly. "At least we know now, the four of us. We must be careful. Though"—he paused—"I am sorry beyond words for this. It should never have happened."

"I'm all right," she insisted. "Really, I am."

"And ingenious too," he said softly. "Do you know, Xiao Mo, that today you were successful at *jia chi bu dian*? To pretend to be stupid when one is smart. It is one of the classic ancient strategies."

"It is?"

"Yes. And a difficult hand to play. I salute you."

"And I you," she returned.

He felt her open intelligence all the way through him. Again like Meiyan. Meiyan who had never returned, whose fate was unknown, who was still his wife. Meiyan was always there between him and anyone else. Would it be so with this outsider Mo Ai-li? Her hands were the pale color of nephrite, speckled, jittery. Her face a triangle, constructed differently from all faces he had known. Her hair.

"Dr. Lin?"

"You make me think of the legend of Mu-lan," he told her. "She's a famous Chinese heroine. She was very brave, like you."

"Yes. Mu-lan." Mo Ai-li smiled up at him. "I know the story. But I must disagree. I am not like her. In order to go to war, and express her duty to her father, Mu-lan posed as a man. I'd never do that."

The yawning rush of *yin* came from her and he felt his face warming. He looked down and saw that he was still holding her arm. He let it go. "No," he had to agree, "I think you would not."

Lin went directly to Kong Zhen. "The PLA picked up the female interpreter!" he shouted, as soon as he had closed Kong's door behind him. "They questioned her, they were rude to her—is it not unthinkable!"

All color drained from Kong's face. "Did they let her go? Is she all right?"

"Yes. All right. But it's a disgrace!"

"Speak calmly. What happened?"

"A soldier approached her at the phone hall. She was calling her father—you see, he's an official in the U.S. Government—and the soldier ordered her off the phone and into his truck. They took her somewhere, she doesn't know where. None of them knew she could speak, so they talked in front of her—"

"Oh!" Kong said. "Very good."

"She said their language was crude. The leader argued with his men—he hadn't wanted her brought in. They said they thought the Americans might smuggle out Peking Man if they found it. Then they apologized to her and let her go."

"*Aiya,*" Kong sighed.

"This cannot happen," Lin said firmly.

"I know, I know. Ten thousand years of stink! All right, Shiyang, don't worry. I'll take care of it."

*   *   *

"Elder cousin," said Kong Zhen into the phone barely an hour later. He had gotten a call through to Vice Director Han as quickly as he could. "We have had a small problem. The Army detained one of the Americans—the female. They frightened her." He paused, listening to the flood of indignation on the other end. "Yes. I know you never intended it. Yes. Yes, they let her go. But this sort of thing cannot be permitted. Consider the potential for *guoji yinxiang*," International repercussions. "Elder cousin." Kong took a deep breath. "I truly believe these particular outside people will not smuggle out Peking Man. The possibility is as remote as a needle at the bottom of the sea. Yes, I know this is only my humble opinion. Yes. I know you must be careful. But, elder cousin"—he swallowed—"my lowly suggestion is this: You should remove the surveillance."

"Here is buried Abel Oort," said Guo Wenxiang, kicking lightly at the small, moss-eaten headstone in the weeds.

Alice watched Spencer drop to a squat and lay his hands on the pocked, lichen-molded surface. She had told him right away about being picked up by the PLA. He'd been pissed. Good and pissed off like a friend should be. Then she told him the rest, that they thought he meant to steal Peking Man if he found it, and she saw him frightened, pale for the first time. He had turned around and walked away from her, and closed the door of his room. An hour later he emerged, in control of himself again, and said he was ready to go and meet Guo at the graveyard.

Now Guo and Alice stood watching Spencer bent over the gravestone, writing in his notebook. "I understand you ran into some trouble today," Guo said.

She froze.

"It's so, isn't it? I told you my connections were top level."

She swallowed. "Yes," she said. "You did."

"You must move carefully." He threw each syllable at her emphatically. "There seems to be suspicion that your group will smuggle national artifacts out of the country. Now, Interpreter Mo. If I am to be your consultant, you should explain your business in China." He waited.

Tell him. "Dr. Spencer is an archaeologist. He has an idea he may be able to recover the remains of Peking Man."

Guo's eyebrows flew up in abhorrence. "He would take Peking Man out of China?"

"No, no. That's crazy."

"Are you certain?"

"Certain."

"Really. Do you know the true face of this man?"

She looked at the middle-aged American in the weeds. "No," she said honestly. "But I know that's not what he's after. It doesn't fit—not in the world he comes from. He's a scholar. He wants academic success. Were he to smuggle an artifact, he'd lose unimaginable face. It would ruin his career." To her it all seemed so clear that she was sure Guo Wenxiang must perfectly understand it. An American would change his expression, say, Ah yes, I see, you are right. But Guo was Chinese. He stonewalled, staring across the graves and weeds, as if she had said nothing of import.

Then he answered: "Of course, the PLA is basically business, do you understand me or not? The business of holding the plate of sand together. This is China." He stopped and lit a cigarette, sucked hard, and blew out smoke. "Also, Mo Ai-li. The place Dr. Spencer is talking about in Inner Mongolia is even more sensitive than here. Don't do anything that might be wrongly interpreted."

"You mean near Eren Obo?"

"Yes. That's Alashan County. It's a military area—most classified. Missiles. Mo Ai-li, be more careful. Think back and forth."

She nodded, pushing down anxiety.

"If there are things you want to know, come to me," Guo advised.

"Perhaps you're right." She closed her eyes. The advanced Chinese, the command of colloquialisms, the slang: at a certain point, when you got close to things that were *neibu*, Inside their damned private bubble, it was all worthless. "There is something"—she sighed—"a most delicate matter."

"No problem."

"And no one is to know of it."

"You will trust me," he said. It was a cold observation, a twist of the knife that said, Face it, you'll trust me, you have no choice. He sucked on his cigarette. *"Shenmo shi?"* What is it?

"A colleague of mine is searching for his wife. She may be dead. Her name is Zhang Meiyan."

"Zhang Meiyan?"

"Yes. Originally from Zhengzhou, but interned here in the *laogai*. Early seventies, I think."

Guo blew a smoke ring. "Interned where? Which camp?"

"I don't know. But I believe there were a lot of camps on the Nei Meng side, over the Helan Shan, in the desert—"

"I know that," Guo cut her off. His tone said: I know because I live here and I lick crumbs out of the gutter for my living, but it's something *you* are not supposed to know. He studied her strange green eyes.

She stared back.

"Did he hear from the wife after she was sent away?" As Guo spoke his lips came apart around the cigarette, revealing small, pointed teeth.

"I don't think so. Not for a long time, at least."

"Boundless is the bitter sea." Guo exhaled one last blue cloud, then ground the butt under his shoe. "Well. The women's camps were all closed. In 1980, all the women still alive were released. Some were given housing registrations in villages on the Ningxia side. Others were assigned in Inner Mongolia, across the mountains. What's the husband's name?"

"Lin Shiyang."

"And the wife, again?"

"Zhang Meiyan."

"All right."

"See what you can find."

He nodded.

She felt the sick tug inside her that told her she shouldn't be doing this, she had no right to invade Lin's life in this way. It was wrong. Ah, but maybe in a way it wasn't wrong. He wanted to find his wife, didn't he? She could help. Help him find her; or if she was gone, help him forget her. Everyone can change, she thought. Even him. *The axis and leading shoot of evolution.*

Spencer had covered the yard and was walking back toward them. "Nothing here."

She glanced at Guo. "It's too bad you couldn't find anyone who remembered the Dutch priest, only this grave. It's a dry end."

She lowered her voice. "Better luck with the Chinese archaeologist's wife."

"Look," Spencer said. "I think we're going to need some more help. Ask Mr. Guo if he'll do another assignment. Get him together with Kong and Lin for a briefing. See what he can find out about the Mongol family."

When they got back Alice sat in her room, looking at the paper spirit-objects she'd bought from Master Tang. The bed, the wedding chest, the upright paper man. These were the things she would burn and send to the women on the other side. A barb of discomfort went through her.

What was she doing?

* * *

Guo Wenxiang went to the apartment of his friend Hu Bin, a fellow Sichuanese who, like him, enjoyed undocumented status here in the oasis city. Both came from mountain villages where there'd been no money to be made, no future to be had. Both were men who were young and strong, who had to get out.

In China that meant leaving organized society and floating, living by the wind and one's wits. People who belonged to the floating population had no assigned apartment, no *danwei*, no iron rice bowl. But Guo didn't really need those things, not at this point in his life anyway. He was a man approaching his prime during capitalism's fin de siècle. There were plenty of things he could do.

"Old Hu," he called, rapping at the door. "Old Hu!"

"Lower the noise," Hu Bin grumbled, opening up.

Guo pushed into Hu's room, a congenial concrete-walled space with large windows open to the desert breeze. Everywhere were local oil paintings, landscapes, city scenes, desert roads, all framed by rough, handmade wood. Hu liked paintings. He traded any service he could come up with for works by Yinchuan artists.

"I have a job." Guo grinned. "Americans."

"Americans! You'll line your pockets."

"It's so! With *dollars*." Guo tried to say the English word and they both laughed. Guo listened to Voice of America and the BBC. His ambition was to learn English. That would be the ticket, to learn English. Unfortunately he had little formal schooling, and it was rough going.

"What's the job?" Hu asked.

"Search for some Mongols who used to live out to the northwest in Hetao County, across the river—that's in the foothills of the Helan Shan."

"It can be done. What else?"

"Find out what happened to a woman who disappeared here in the *laogai*."

Hu Bin sucked in his cheeks, his wide, poetic mouth puckering into a circle. "You must watch over your shoulder, making inquiries like that. The people who know those things cannot be crossed."

"I know," Guo said dismissively. He paused, looking at his friend, assessing mood, warmth, receptivity. Just launch the question, he thought. "Hu, my good friend. Can I stay here for a few days?"

It was July twenty-third. Alice seemed to recall that this was the day of the Great Heat by the Chinese lunar calendar. She stood nervously at the intersection of two lanes behind the hotel. Nearby there loomed a Ming dynasty fortress tower. She supposed this had once been some critical defensive cog in the old city walls; now it sat useless in a grassy, neglected lot.

Do I have to do this here, she thought desperately, out in the middle of an intersection? Couldn't I do it in my room, behind closed doors? Though, of course, that would bring the fire alarms and the hysterical, shouting staff. Kong and Lin and Spencer would be crowding into her room with questions. Maybe outside was better after all. And this was how Master Tang had told her to do it. At the intersection of two streets.

She took out the paper replicas, the tiny figure of a man. She settled him in the dust at her feet. He had a heroic air. Teilhard. Lucile. Mother Meng. Help me. She arranged the bed, the chest, the linens, around the man.

"*Jiao-hun,*" she murmured, trying to sound formal to herself and also to the spirits of the dead. "I call back your soul."

She knelt quickly, struck a rickety match from the cardboard Double Happiness box, and lit the miniature bridal chest.

"Waiguoren!" a boy chirped, Foreigner! An army of other boys thundered up behind him, stumbled together, and froze.

She sighed. How strange she must look to them—a five-foot-three chestnut-headed blue-jeaned creature, in a squat on the sidewalk lighting matches.

Ignore them. She trained her eyes doggedly at the ground.

The flame ate eagerly to the edge of the elaborate little box-for-hopes, and fell panting on the folded pile of paper linens. The little man was still a few inches off, at the end. The last thing. The most important thing she had to send.

Mother Meng, may you never want for anything in the place of spirits. Lucile, you too.

The flame lit onto the paper bed, pulsated up its sideposts. The man would be next.

"Eh, foreign lady guest, are you ill? Are you lost?" It was the strident voice of an officious older woman, the kind who dominated every Chinese neighborhood.

"Woman Liang, how can you expect a foreigner to talk?"

Alice fanned the flame along the bed, her mind divided now, half of her trying to envision, and hold, this ballooning reverence for the dead, and half of her nervously following the Chinese babble around her.

"Woman Liang, he's right. They can't any of them talk." This was another voice, a man, careless. She made no sign of hearing.

For a minute they watched in silence; now finally the man figure caught. Tiny breaths of smoke circled upward and dissipated to nothing.

Mother Meng. Lucile. Please be my ancestors.

"Aiya, burning spirit-objects, my great-aunt used to do that!" one of the boys hooted. He was instantly hushed. The small crowd murmured disapproval, embarrassed like most modern Chinese about older customs, loath to even admit that such customs had once existed. These days it seemed to Alice that the masses had their eyes on only one direction, forward.

The pyre was down to ashes now. She rose in a single movement and ground them out under her shoe. Then a sideways kick
brushed them away.

A coolness swept over her, the suck of air when a door closes.
Good-bye for now, Mother Meng. Good-bye, Lucile. She brushed
her pants clean.

"Zou-ba," one of the boys hissed, and the pack of them moved
off.

"Eh, she's crazy," came the voice of the neighborhood
woman, smaller now, retreating in the darkness down the alley.

"The west-ocean people—huh!" another one said.

Only one man was left. He watched her from under a low
forehead and a thicket of hair. He stared at her fixedly. They
stood alone on the street.

She couldn't resist speaking to him.

"What is it," she said in friendly Chinese with a solid urban
east coast accent, "—you don't approve of the doings of ghosts
and gods? Is it not a clear and deep way for releasing sorrow?
And haven't you heard it said?" She leaned a few inches closer to
him and softened her voice. *"Ai mo da yu xin si."* Nothing gives
so much cause for sorrow as the death of one's heart.

He flushed. "Deeply excuse me. I never would have thought
you could . . ."

"Talk."

"Yes." He gazed openly. "Talk."

She felt her mouth part into a smile. She felt powerful, she felt
like Mu-lan. Hadn't Dr. Lin compared her to Mu-lan? Lin
Shiyang. Thinking about him brought a wave of happiness. A
tiny breeze eddied the ashes at her feet. "May your road be level
and peaceful," she said to the man, turned, and walked away.

* * *

Dr. Lin Shiyang left his room, where he had claimed to be suffering from fever, and where he had stayed until the others left in the jeep, and walked out of the Number One and around the corner to the bicycle rental. The old man looked up at him pleasantly. "The gentleman will ride today?"

Lin nodded.

"I kept this one for you specially," the old man lied, presenting a wreck of a wine-red three-speed. "Three people tried to rent it this morning. But I felt you might come."

"Old uncle"—Lin smiled knowingly—"you shouldn't have gone to so much trouble."

"It was nothing—for you." The man swiftly pocketed the five-yuan rental fee. Five yuan! A scholar from the eastern cities—rich, obviously, money flying from his fingers.

"I thank you," Lin said formally, and took the bike. Poor old uncle, he should have been dozing in some teahouse and here he was scratching a living in small change. "May I depend on your discretion?" he asked the old man carefully, and handed him another one-yuan note.

The man took the note, shrugged, and looked away. "I never remember anyone."

Lin walked the bike away from the stall and carefully swung one leg over the seat. He steered onto Sun Yat-sen, turned left, and pedaled toward the drum tower. That was where the West Road began. Over the past week, from time to time, he had asked directions to the outlying villages of people chosen at random along the street. Never too much of any one person. He didn't want anyone remembering him. This was an art many Chinese of his generation had perfected: absorbing as much as possible, while escaping the notice of others entirely.

And the Americans, how much did they notice? It was an interesting question to him, one he had pondered at some length. The main thing about the two Americans was the way they constantly emanated. Talking, exclaiming, explaining. Especially explaining. They seemed obsessed with making themselves understood. On the other hand they seemed to take in rather little.

Of course, until now he had never actually had dealings with an American. They were what he'd expected, although Spencer and Mo Ai-li were different from each other, maddeningly individual. This in itself he found confusing. In his own world each one had his thoughts and dreams, his private life—but in a group endeavor, especially one which involved outsiders, this would be concealed in favor of a united front. Factions and disagreements hidden. Truths evaded.

He would never do what the woman interpreter had done that night they had met in the courtyard, for instance—ask him straight out if he wished his life had been different. Remarkable! And yet this forthrightness was what excited him. She kept saying outrageous things—first about the Chaos, then about his wife being sentenced to the *laogai*, and then asking him rudely whether he had put aside his wife and taken someone else. Surely she had some idea how shattering it was when a man was forced to denounce his mate on government orders. Yet that night she had baldly demanded to know if he had done this, as if she was asking no more than what he had eaten at his last meal. Each time she had come at him this way, he had been momentarily numbed by disbelief, then pinpricked by excitement. Mental. And yes, sexual. Even though he was forty-six years old and the women he met who stirred him this way now were few. He shook his head slowly. The drum tower. Left turn.

Perhaps she will be my wound story, he thought. He'd had a peculiar aversion to Wound Literature, though this popular fiction movement of the late seventies and eighties had captivated many of his friends and colleagues. They had eagerly devoured every unbearably sad novel and short story collection that came along, each man reliving his own Cultural Revolution tragedy in the reading. Lin hadn't been able to do so. To open these books, read them, and close them again would be to put Meiyan behind him. And he preferred to hold on to her.

Even though he knew—a part of him knew—that this was wrong. It prevented him from loving again. His closest friends, even his mother, who had adored Meiyan and longed for the grandchild he and Meiyan never gave her, had advised him, finally, to stop. "You are bottled up in the past like a turtle in a jar, my son. The years are passing: the sun and moon fly back and forth. Don't continue on this way."

"But there's always a chance, isn't there? Some people return from the *laogai*. Like Little Yan's uncle. Remember? The family had given him up for lost? And then they found him again, his teeth gone, his health ruined, but alive, he was alive. . . ."

But that had been years ago. He knew of no one who had been gone as long as Meiyan had been gone, gone without letters or messages, and come back.

And now a surprise, Mo Ai-li, Little Mo—not so little, clearly a woman past thirty who should have been married long since. There was no doubt he felt drawn to her. And she seemed to feel the same way. At least she prodded him with her questions, stared at him when she thought he didn't see, even sat next to him in the vehicle and at meals. None of this had escaped Kong's notice. Kong had even joked to him one day that he must let him know whether Western women were really different, as was said. *"Bie shuo-le,"* Lin had replied curtly, Don't talk like that, but his answer only made Kong laugh and he regretted, later, having responded at all.

Yet she *was* different. She didn't retreat, didn't defer, didn't laugh behind her hand like a Chinese woman—in spite of her reasonable grasp of the language and her constant, often ridiculous attempts to follow Chinese manners. Despite all that she spoke to him with a bold intelligence. She might, he thought, be a woman with whom he could talk of the many things he considered in private: linguistics twisting back three thousand years to the scapulimancy of the Shang dynasty; the magical jumble of stories and legends that remained from the dawn of Chinese history; the faint picture—which he often reviewed in his mind—of *Homo erectus* roaming this land half a million years ago. Then north China had been fertile, wet, a green jungle, not the arid ocean of alluvial silt it was today. There *Sinanthropus* had not made his own shelter, but had taken refuge where he could, in caves and under outcroppings and in groves by the side of the river. . . .

It had been Meiyan's field, too, *Homo erectus*. He pedaled harder, thinking of the afternoon they got married in Gao Yeh's room in Zhengzhou. They had got the go-ahead from the *danwei*, months after requesting permission from the university Party boss to "talk about love." It had been winter. The other students crowded in, padded blue jackets and stuffed-up trouser legs jostling for space. Gao Yeh shouting, drunk, how lovely their life together was going to be, and singing the children's song:

> As the sun rose over the mountain
> A student came riding along.
> He sat on a dapple-gray pony
> And sang a scrap of song.
>
> To the home of his bride he was going
> And he hoped that she wouldn't be out.
> He saw as he pushed the door open
> The girl he was thinking about.
>
> Her cheeks were as pink as a rosebud.
> Her teeth were as white as a pearl.
> Her lips were as red as a cherry.
> Most truly a beautiful girl!

How strange he could remember that, he thought now, pedaling past the patchwork of open fields, the wind off the Helan Shan whistling by. He remembered, too, the laughter that had exploded at the nursery rhyme's end, everyone nodding, yes, yes, wasn't it so, and the bowls of hard candy going around and around the room—Happiness Candy, the politically correct substitute for the then-forbidden wedding banquet. Nineteen seventy-one. Meiyan had worn a blue cotton suit like everyone else, except that it was her sharply ironed best. He remembered how her milk-white oval face had radiated joy.

Then after they were married, there was the single memory that had become a well-marked door in his mind: lying in bed with her afterward in the small room on Renmin Road in Zhengzhou, the sheets crumpled on the floor, talking about Lantian man, the *Homo erectus* find in south China to which she had devoted her study. Playing with the *Homo erectus* tooth she wore on a cord around her neck, never took off, not even when her entire naked length was smothered beneath him. She had stolen it from the vault where the Lantian County fossils were kept. Strange. Had she been caught stealing and wearing such an important cultural relic she'd have earned herself a PLA bullet in the head. Yet this had never been discovered and she had been sent to prison for a political misstep in a scholarly essay, a trifle, chicken feathers and garlic skins.

How she had loved that piece of bone. Davidson Black, the Canadian doctor who headed the group Teilhard had worked for in Peking, had worn a *Homo erectus* tooth around his neck, and Meiyan would do the same. Nothing Lin could say could convince her to bury it somewhere until the Chaos ended and she could safely reclaim it again. No, she would wear it. And just before he entered her, when he had her gasping and pulling his hips frantically down to her, he liked to pick the tooth up off her sweat-glistening chest with his lips and take it in his mouth and play with it, a gesture she found unbearably intimate, and a way of making her wait another few moments. . . .

Ah, a millennium ago—he'd been so young then. West Road,

Tibet Road. He soared down the hill, away from the heart of the city, through the flat oasis suburbs.

It was in 1973 that her article had been submitted. Why hadn't she just lied in the article? Why did she have to be so heroic? A resounding silence had followed. Fear crept in and ate at all their thoughts and words until it smothered everything. Finally they heard she was going to be arrested. So many others they knew had already been taken. They had offended someone else, or had a "bad" job before liberation, or had owned land, or their parents had owned land before them. All someone had to say was that you were *fan geming,* Counterrevolutionary, just those two words, then the death grip at your throat.

"Eating bitterness won't kill me," she had said, sitting beside him on the bed, affecting bravery. "And I should have expected it. How often have you heard it said? When a rat scurries across the street, kill it! Kill it!" She'd smiled slightly at this overused maxim of the Chaos. All he could think of were the nights when she was writing the article, the hot July nights without air, the heat-muffled shouts and traffic sounds rising from Renmin Road. He had told her: Invent something about class struggle among the ancient hominids. Make something up. He himself had done it. Everyone did it.

But she refused. Ah, Meiyan. So faithful to something higher. She had been a better person than he. He had lied easily in his scholarly papers. It had seemed easy and obvious to him—of course, lie, why get arrested? He had made up whatever drivel about class and capitalism seemed necessary to stay out of trouble. Had told himself it didn't dilute his basic work. Not Meiyan. She would not do it. So the people struggled against her.

After she was taken Lin learned, through the human net that spreads news like a fire through tinder grass and can never be quite contained, that she was sent out to Inner Mongolia. Camp Fourteen, it was whispered: a cluster of loess huts in a flat yellow plain—across the Helan Shan Mountains from the city of Yinchuan.

He'd had one brief smuggled message from her. Then nothing.

The years dragged by. Things started to get better. Chairman Mao died, the nation pinned all its hate on the Gang of Four, and the era of Wound Literature began. He held himself apart from it, buried himself in his obsession with the ancient human ancestor, clung to Meiyan in his mind. How could he live with himself otherwise? He'd only survived because he'd been willing to lie. Then came the open door with the 1980s, a rush of money and relaxed thinking and new culture from the outside. He started teaching at the university; he published work on *Homo erectus*. All his colleagues pretended he had never been married. Some of them did not know. Some knew, of course—Kong knew, he had once made a reference to it, not unkindly. But Lin never talked about it.

During these years Lin had not been completely without women. Now, decades later, riding his bicycle out from Yinchuan, he recalled them. There had been Ping, the reedy woman mathematics professor with the terse little mouth, who had lost her husband; she had discreetly been his special friend for some years until, finally, she said she could endure his impermeability no longer. Ping and then Lan-zhen, the shy, bespectacled graduate student who had sat mesmerized through his every class until finally he'd approached her. She'd come to him gratefully, completely open, mad about him, so much younger than he, yet through a year of physical intimacy he never let himself love her, never opened his door, never forgot he was married to Meiyan. He saw how deeply Lan-zhen was hurt by this. She wanted desperately to hold first place in his heart. They finally parted, after defeat and resentment had destroyed her love. Her pain brought him even more shame. But he did not know how to stop loving his wife, even though she was gone. And Lan-zhen simply was not like Meiyan. Neither was Ping. Though Little Mo was, wasn't she? She had the courage and the mental alacrity— do not think like that, he admonished himself. She is an outside person. A joint-venture colleague. American!

He left the main road behind now as he had been directed and pedaled off on a dirt track to the north. He crested a hill, broke through the pass, and there was little Laishan Village spread out in the yellow dust below him. He knew, in his first snatch of breath and his first glimpse of the jumbled settlement, that Meiyan was not there. Her energy, her intelligence—these things were simply missing from the landscape. This realization was like a powerful voice in his ear, and it nearly made him falter off the path. He was not used to instincts. Lin Shiyang was an educated man, from a modern city; he would never willingly concern himself with forebodings and premonitions. Yet this instinct was so powerful, he almost felt he could trust it. Meiyan was not present.

As any careful man would do, though, having come so far, he locked up his bike and removed the precious photograph from his pocket. Meiyan, 1972. Young eyes shining with intelligence, black hair pulled back. The children's song bounced around in his brain.

> Her cheeks were as pink as a rosebud.
> Her teeth were as white as a pearl. . . .

He shook his head. Too many years had flown. What did she look like now? Nothing like this, certainly. If she was alive.

But the picture was all he had.

He approached the first of the dozens he would speak to that day, an older man with a wiry body and gently bowed legs, hurrying now down the dirt-packed lane with a bundle of dirty sheep's wool.

"Elder uncle, forgive me—"

"Eh?" The man bolted back in alarm.

"No, don't fear, uncle, just a question, forgive me. Have you seen this woman?" Lin thrust forward the small square picture with its ghostlike, girlish smile.

The old man narrowed his eyes and fired a single glance at the photo. "No!" He walked away.

10

THE SECOND-TO-LAST night in Yinchuan they ate dinner at the Number One. Alice noticed that when the plate was turned in Lin's direction he selected a charred, wrinkled chili pepper with his chopsticks and bit into it, eyes closed. With his other hand he dragged his teacup to his mouth, forehead squeezed in pain and gratitude.

"I don't think you're supposed to eat it," she ventured.

He swallowed. "I like it." He gasped. "I want it. It's just that I can't bear it." He turned his gaze to her, letting all the weight of it fall on her. Eh, he thought, seeing her strain toward him and aware of the same stirring within himself, something's between us. *Shi bu shi?* But they were in public. He dared do no more than look at her a certain way.

Of course, he could touch her now. He only had to move his leg a few inches under the table. Then he would know, and she would know, and it would be done. But what if he was wrong? Such a misstep would be disastrous. She was an outsider.

He picked up another hot pepper with his chopsticks, and placed it on her plate. "You know," he said to her softly, "it's like life." Then he paused, and turned away to his left, where Dr. Kong was speaking to him.

Lin stepped out into the street, Meiyan's photo in his pocket. He had left the hotel quietly when the group broke up after dinner. He was sure none of the others noticed. He paused for a moment, feeling the vast reassurance of a city around him, the swell of people, the tide of ongoing life. Pedestrians passed him, unconcerned. Animals, carts, children.

He opened his city map and thought through the places he'd covered. The new town—the industrial section on the other side of the train station. The old Chinese quarter. The old downtown. Tonight he would walk the Muslim quarter. He wondered what it would be like. The Muslims, the *huimin,* they were not like other Chinese. This was what he had always heard. An idea that had hardened in his mind. What was the word Interpreter Mo had used? *Prejudice.*

As he walked he thought about Mo Ai-li. The PLA had picked her up, then released her. That meant certainly they were watching him too. Should he change his plan? Stop looking for his wife?

No. All of the last twenty-two years had led him to this point. He had to find Meiyan. Besides, what could they do to him? He'd already lost everything.

Everything of then. This is now. Again he thought of Mo Ai-li. No. To Meiyan he'd made vows, he'd made promises. This was the least he could do for her now. He'd follow it to the end.

He touched his long fingers lightly to the photograph in his pocket and kept walking.

* * *

Master Tang arrived at Alice's room at the appointed hour. The seven-day interval was finished and she had completed the rituals as he'd instructed her. Now from a small velvet cloth he unwrapped the wooden *ling-pai,* the spirit tablet.

She read the characters carved into it:

Meng Shaowen
Passed over July 14
Beloved by her descendant, the host of this house.

"It's completed?" Alice asked.

"Eh," Master Tang reproved her, "obviously you are not highly literate! I suspected you might not be. Did you not notice that the dot is missing on the character *zhu,* host?"

"Oh, yes, of course." She felt herself flush. "I cannot face you."

"It doesn't matter," he grumped. "Anyway, this is what the *cheng-zhu* ritual is all about, do you understand me or not? The tablet does not come to life until we paint the eye on the dragon. The dot on the character *zhu* must be completed. Now. Usually to do this we choose the most literary member of the family. This person is the *dian-zhu,* the Inscriber of the tablet. But in this case—"

"You do it, Master Tang," she said swiftly.

"It will not do." He sighed. "The yin-yang master as the *dian-zhu*—oh no, it is unlucky. You must be the one to do it, Interpreter Mo."

"I'm not worthy."

He did not disagree. "Anyway, you must. In ink or in blood. You choose."

"In blood."

He bowed his head, removed a ceremonial pin from a silk box in his inner sleeve, and handed it to her.

He intoned a prayer while she stabbed her index finger. "Oh, shit," she breathed, as too much blood bubbled out.

"Just complete the character," he said softly.

Thank God I know where the dot goes, she thought, bending over the tablet, it would be so humiliating to have to ask him. The blood was dripping now. Quick. Right above the top horizontal stroke—there—she stood up. It was messy, but in the right place.

"Thus we send the spirit on its journey," Tang said softly. "The *ling-pai* is its earthly home. Now: the ritual of *an-zhu*, in which we place the *ling-pai* on the altar and reincorporate it into the family. Now you will become part of Madam Meng's line. See that you serve her ghost well. In return she will always guide you."

Alice waited.

"*Koutou,*" he said, Kowtow.

"What?"

"*Koutou!*" More sharply.

Alice fell to her knees in front of the altar and knocked her forehead against the grimy carpet. Each time, she felt jolted a little farther off the track she'd been trapped on for so long. Could she really change ancestors so easily? Could she drop the scaffolding of Horace—or at least relax it?

When he was gone it would all change. She shivered with fear: this thought again, this possibility, Horace dying. Yet it might happen soon. She pictured herself in a world without him, a world where she had only her own heart and mind to follow. A world open and blank with possibility; terrifying, almost. She thumped her forehead on the carpet. All of you in the land of the dead, she prayed, help me. Let me become myself. And, Horace. When you go I want your love, I want to keep it to remember. But please go on and leave me in peace.

She paused in midreverence, half shocked at herself. She could feel Master Tang watching her. She looked up at him.

"You may rise now," he said. "You are the daughter of Meng Shaowen."

And Lucile, she added in her mind. And Horace. Then she thought: This is crazy. Even Chinese don't do this anymore. Not educated Chinese. To them this was like the earth being flat. Like curing illness with leeches.

The discomfort billowed up inside her and she wanted to get the whole thing over with. Quickly she counted out the sum to which they had agreed.

He pocketed the money. "Good health. Long life."

"*Bici,*" she whispered, The same to you.

Guo Wenxiang slipped into an unmarked doorway in a back alley of the Chinese quarter, and knocked softly. He'd walked here casually, making many unnecessary turns, twisting and changing his route, entering buildings where he knew no one and standing in dark hallways, then leaving again quietly by other doors.

He was sure there was no one behind him. But in China there almost always was. He knew this well.

So as Guo knocked now, he glanced nervously around. The man who lived in this apartment had been a guard years ago at Camp Fourteen, the women's camp on the other side of the mountains. Camp Fourteen had been a cluster of ocher huts on the flat, silty plain that spread out below the purple wall of the Helan Shan. By all accounts evil attended it. There were women who died of illness and malnourishment. Other women lost their health, and whatever remained of their humanity. It was said of this man, this former guard, that he had seen everything, and knew everything, but that it angered him when people asked him about it. *Hua you shuo huilai,* it was also said that after a few cups of wine his mouth loosened and his memories flowed. Guo held a bottle of Red Crane sorghum spirits tightly against his chest, waiting.

When the door was opened four men stood there, none of them the man he was looking for. Something was not right. He took a step back. "I'm sorry," he said. "I'm seeking the Honorable Chen. Perhaps he is not at home."

"Eh, but he is. He awaits you."

Guo pivoted to dart away, but a powerful hand clamped his wrist, and then another. "Don't go," one of the men said cruelly, pulling him in and latching the door behind him.

A cold fatalism settled over Guo. He knew better than to show fear. And meanwhile he had his wits, and should he not deploy every power he had? Sometimes, the legends told, a man could prevail at times like this through words alone. Guo marshaled himself, sharpening his intelligence. He was prepared to speak—

But they were already advancing toward him.

Spencer and Kong were bent over a table in the back room of the Bureau of Cultural Relics, examining the mountain of microliths Kong had collected near the Shuidonggou site. Sorting them, grading them, packing them. Cobbles, flakes, hammerstones, points, and scrapers. From the Neolithic, pottery shards and beads.

"You see this?" Spencer examined a powerfully shaped stone scraper. "Beautiful. Late Paleolithic. Twenty-five, thirty thousand years." He placed it in one of the piles.

A secretary burst in with a sheaf of fax papers. *"Datongle."*

"Haode." Kong took the papers. He scanned them at once, then turned his smile on Spencer. *"Qianzheng!"* He indicated the pages. "Visa! Visa!" He managed to get the word in English.

"Oh! Oh, my God! The visas for Eren Obo?" Spencer took the pages and grinned at them.

"Tai hao-le!"

"And what's this?" Spencer pointed to the rest of the pile of fax pages. "Is this the literature search from your graduate student?"

But Kong only went off in a stream of Mandarin. Nevertheless his hand holding the pages aloft told Spencer they were practically the first scholars out here, the first since Teilhard. There'd been no surveys on archaic hunter-gatherer sites out here, no organized attempts to locate and date and describe and excavate anything besides Shuidonggou. No coherent picture at all of the nomadic foragers, or their transition to the Neolithic with its advent of settled life and agriculture. Nothing published—just the stuff on Shuidonggou itself.

Because, Christ, Spencer thought, they haven't even looked! They don't even know *where* to look. But I know. I know from the years of surveying back home. I know exactly where ancient people lived in this kind of terrain. Winters they lived in the alluvial fans, the creek margins—then in the summer they might have gone up in the mountains. Just like in the American West. Only, in America you're lucky if you find a handful of intact sites in your whole career. . . .

"Yanjiu jihui bu shao," Kong exclaimed happily, tossing down the fax. His cellular phone rang and he pulled it off his belt and clicked it on. *"Wei! Wei!"*

Spencer sat, listening to Kong's rapid Chinese, allowing his mind to drift. The opportunities in archaic desert cultures here were unbelievable, Christ yes, but he had to keep his mind on the real prize. Peking Man! Peking Man was the find that would make his career, that would get him noticed all over the world. He'd be back in at the conferences. He'd do papers, be quoted. And even though the agonizing reality was that he was now going to miss most of his son's Halloween costumes and campfires and summer fireflies in jars, at least—when the boy had grown into a thinking adult—he would know his father had done something. He would know his father had brought back the first forebear, the man from the dawn of time. That would count for Tyler, someday. It had to.

He glanced at Kong, working the phone now, drumming his long fingers on the fax paper. Kong caught his eyes and grinned. It was amazing how he and Kong communicated, considering they couldn't speak.

"*Hao! Hao!*" Kong shouted, and hung up. He folded the phone and clicked it back on his belt.

Adam pulled a piece of paper from his pocket, unfolded it. "Dr. Kong," he said, "last night I wrote this letter to my son. Do you think I could use their fax machine before we go? Fax?" He pointed to the fax pages on the table.

"*Keyi,*" Kong said kindly, and pointed to the fax machine in the outer room.

"Dr. Lin?" She knocked again, harder. Was he there? It was late afternoon, they were leaving for Eren Obo the next day, she hadn't seen him in hours. "Dr. Lin?"

Stirring sounds, then the faint sibilance of feet, and the door clicked open. "Xiao Mo." His eyes went wider. He'd been sleeping.

"Oh, I'm sorry," she said.

"It's nothing." He yawned, straightened his shirt.

"I wanted to talk with you." She held her breath. He could tell her to come back later if he wanted.

He looked down at her strange light eyes, her rumpled clothing, her dusty athletic shoes. His own clothes were haphazard. He'd got up and covered himself in a hurry. "Come in."

She pushed past him into the cluttered room, still warm with the smells of sleep, and he saw her gaze move about. "I suppose I shouldn't come here like this, just knocking on your door. . . ."

"No, you're welcome," he said, meaning it. "You're always welcome."

"But I wanted to say something to you." She turned back toward him. She opened her mouth, then closed it. Could she just say it?

"Please." He indicated the two armchairs, the low table in between. "You'll have tea?"

"Yes." She let her breath go in relief. "Thanks."

He stepped behind her and closed the door. She felt a thrill. They were alone.

"Iron Goddess of Mercy okay?" he asked, taking a small packet from the tea caddy.

"Oh yes, please."

"It's strong."

"I know."

So she liked it that way too. He smiled, uncorked the thermos, and poured steaming water over the leaves, then put the cups on the table and lowered himself into the chair opposite her. "What's happened?"

"Nothing. It's not that anything's happened."

He waited.

"Dr. Lin. Frankly speaking. I don't know how to ask you this. I think perhaps it's impolite to ask you. But I find that I need to know."

He made his voice quiet. "Whatever it is, Xiao Mo, put your heart at rest. It's okay." He picked up her cup from the table and handed it to her. *"Gei."* Then he took up his own cup, welcoming as he always did the black, bracing taste of bitter metal.

She sighed. "Dr. Lin. Are you—all this time, all these little things you say—are you trying to tell me something?"

Aiya—was she going to say it, just like that?

"Are you interested in me?" she blurted.

"Of course," he evaded. "You are our interpreter—"

"Dr. Lin!" she pleaded. "You know what I mean."

"What do you mean?" he asked softly.

"Are you interested in me!" she hammered. "The way a man is in a woman!"

There, she had done it, remarkable, broken all the rules of discretion and subtlety with which a new relationship ought to be forged. It was rash, ill thought out, un-Chinese. Oh. But exciting.

Nevertheless he was still Chinese, and had to turn it around. "Are you?" he said. "In me?"

She stared at him, aroused, exasperated. The American in her wanted to scream, but the Chinese thing to do was deflect. She closed her eyes. "Dr. Lin. Didn't you ever have a dream, and in this dream you saw someone, let's say someone you didn't know very well, but in the dream you cared powerfully for them, maybe you even felt love, and when you awakened you knew immediately that this acquaintance was far more important than you had realized? Well? Have you?"

She opened her eyes and saw him looking at her, that hard look again.

"Yes," he said finally.

"Do I need to explain more?" she asked softly.

He shook his head, and felt his heart burst into bloom. So she did want him! Couldn't he be sure now? She did. Sometimes it had seemed so clear—the way she was looking at him, talking to him. *Zai shuo,* he'd told himself so many times, she was a foreign woman. An outside woman. What did he know about such creatures? And what if he moved to couple with her and he was wrong and he grievously offended her—what bitterness might rain down on him then?

"What about Dr. Spencer?" he asked with difficulty. "The way I've seen you touch him, I thought perhaps—"

"No!" she cried. "There is nothing between us. That's just being American. We are more *suibian* in America. It's a friendly thing. Please. Believe me."

He smiled in relief. "Then what do you say I shall do?"

She thought. "Go with me now? Let's walk around the city."

He stood and held out his hand. They stepped over a warm, messy pile of undershirts, socks, and trousers on their way out.

They followed Sun Yat-sen to Shanxi Avenue, which cut across the center of the city. She watched him. Would he tell her about himself now? It was odd that she didn't know. Most Chinese, once they got comfortable with her, immediately and at considerable length spun out their life stories. Especially they detailed all that they had suffered during the Chaos.

Not that it had always been that way. In the seventies, she'd heard, everyone was furtive and afraid. Eyes down. But by the time she first came to China in the early eighties Mao had died and it had all erupted, everyone talking at her, talking, telling her their terrible stories. At the time it had seemed to her like a strange, sudden, ad-hoc form of Chinese opera, this verborrhea, so extravagantly histrionic. So like the squealingly choreographed dramas, played to audiences who knew the story already, knew it intimately, could then appreciate it as they laughed, applauded, gossiped, ate, and spat. The *Luanshi,* the Chaos.

"Did you have a bad time in the Chaos?" she asked softly. They had come to a park, and walked now under the trees.

"You can't imagine it," he said tightly.

"I believe you're wrong about that," she answered, which made him look at her. Inside, she thought: You should tell me, because I know all about holding and hiding. I could help you.

"Eh, Xiao Mo, I'm sorry." He stared at their scuffling feet. "If it was I who suffered, I could talk about it. I know, most people have told it all, they told it years ago and now it's a boiling river that has finally run out of them and left them in peace. But it was not I who was hurt. My wife would express only the truth—and she was the one who was taken. Not me. Do you understand me or not?"

"You mean you feel guilty. Because you survived. And it was Meiyan, and you don't like to talk about Meiyan."

"Yes. Especially—" he stopped.

Especially to me, she thought willfully, because you have feelings for me. Say it.

"Especially to you," he said, looking at her.

A group of rough-cotton-clad men brushed by them, talking boisterously in Mongolian. After several solid blocks of cement low-rises they were passing a temple, with its ornate red pillars and curving golden roofs. Rustling acacias stretched out in front of them along the sidewalk.

"Will you talk about her now?" she whispered.

"If it is what you want."

Ask him. Just ask him.

"Do you still love her?"

He stopped and looked down at her. "Yes. I've never stopped."

She looked frozen back up into his face.

"Eh, Xiao Mo." He sighed. "It's true that she has been gone for more than twenty years. But I never got any definite answer . . . so in my heart, and according to the law, I am still married. I was never willing to denounce her. Do you understand me or not?"

"Of course I do," she said. "But Dr. Lin, that was years ago. You have heard nothing for so long, isn't it so? Don't you think—"

"I think she is my *airen*," he said simply, stubbornly, with an edge in his voice.

She felt stung. *Airen*, Loved one, the word that meant a wife, or a husband—for life. Caution, she thought.

"And it's a strange thing," he continued. "In some way my feeling for her is even greater now than when we were together in life."

Alice felt numb. Teilhard had written about that to Lucile:

Sometimes I think that this very privation I must impose you makes me ten times more devoted to you. "It's a . . . level of commitment," Alice said, not sure how to respond.

"Yes," he said, looking at her strangely, "very Chinese—commitment."

"Not just Chinese," she corrected him. "All people feel this way." She knew he probably thought Western women were loose, casual, *suibian*. As she'd been up until recently—up until now, as a matter of fact. But she was through with that. She was going to start a new life.

"I don't know if all people are the same," he said. "I am Chinese. I made the commitment to my wife and I have held to it. Though lately"—he looked at her—"I begin to wonder."

Oh, this man could change, Alice thought with a streak of hope. He could. She laid her hand briefly, sympathetically, on his arm. It was the same American gesture that had made him jump like a frightened animal in the middle of the night, in the garden at the Number One. This time—though they were in public, in daylight, in a crowd—he responded by touching her hand lightly with one finger.

"My life has also been hard," Alice ventured.

He looked down, his face open.

"I mean my father. He's an elected official, very famous, I think I told you, but I am so ashamed of his beliefs. He is a racist. He thinks whites are superior to all the other races in the world."

"You mean blacks."

"I mean everyone."

"Including Chinese?"

"Yes."

Lin snorted in disbelief.

"Of course I don't agree with such things."

"No."

"But I am his daughter. It follows me everywhere."

"Terrible."

She saw the sympathy in his face and felt that she did not have to explain the Alice Speech, the thirty-year march of civil rights, the terrible immorality of racism in America. Because the immoralities in China had been equal—maybe greater—though different. And there were certainly leaders in China whose children struggled under shame the same way she did.

"So that is the thing in you I can feel," Lin said softly. "Some bitterness. Is it your father?"

"Horace," she corrected him. "Yes. And perhaps my mother too—I never had one. She died when I was a baby."

"*Zhen bu rongyi,*" he said, with genuine sympathy. She felt him wanting to touch her.

"Let's sit a moment," he said. They had come to a grassy area of stone benches flanked by beds of hollyhocks. In front of them rose the ancient, pagoda-style drum tower.

A northern-type opera was being performed at the foot of the tower on a makeshift wooden stage. A few old men carrying wooden birdcages had gathered to watch the actors shriek and strike their poses through the story. She rather liked the sound of opera. She liked it the way she liked the sound of a baseball game on the radio—which in fact, she hated, just as much as she actually hated Chinese opera if she had to sit down and watch it. But both Chinese opera and baseball, as background noise, gave her a secure and filled-up feeling. She had a childhood memory of Horace listening to baseball on the radio.

Now she and Lin sat on the stone bench while the female impersonators in their brilliant face paint flourished their fake gilt-crusted fingernails, and the old men swung their birdcages and cracked sunflower-seed shells between their teeth and laughed their bubbly phlegm laughs, and a boy in mended clothes beside the stage beat on the big brass gong.

Suddenly Lin reached over, took her hand in his, and squeezed it. Then he let go of her hand, and returned his hand to his lap.

She looked. He was immobile, but his whole frame blazed with alertness. She loved this quality in Chinese men, this physical hyperawareness, this restraint. It was like a guide wire, anchored in her softest heart.

"Truly surprising to find the two of you here," said a voice, and they looked up. Guo Wenxiang.

"What happened?" Alice gasped. There were ugly bruises on the side of Guo's face, blurring out all around his sunglasses.

"I asked too many questions about history," he said, eyes traveling briefly to Lin.

For a moment she thought he was going to say something about her asking him to look for Meiyan, but he did not.

"Can we do anything for you?" Lin asked, voice low.

"No. Part of my job. Isn't it so?"

"Do you want to say who they were?" Lin asked.

Guo laughed, long and thin. "I'm not even sure." Then he turned, and wove away from them into the crowd.

Alice and Lin exchanged brief glances. "My God, Lin," she breathed. "Is that going to happen to us next?"

"Oh, no." He touched her knee. "They wouldn't dare! You are not one of us. You're an outsider. This is international cooperation. Really, Mo Ai-li, you are safe."

How I wish it, she thought, looking up at him.

11

FIRST THEY HAD to cross the Helan Shan. Through most of its length, running north-south parallel to the local flow of the Yellow River, it was a towering escarpment—completely impassable. Its limestone walls rose from four thousand to thirteen thousand feet in less than a mile. So they had to drive around to the south end, where the range crumbled down to brown peaks of dirt and rock and was cut by passes. They rattled up the burning asphalt road. The jeep engine groaned down a gear. Alice laid her head on the seat and watched the gray specter of the Helan Shan's crest, the wall of rock Teilhard had loved, a million years in the making.

Through the pass itself there was a brief shady forest of cedar and pine. This was not the highest zone: in the upper elevations, to the north, Alice could see the deep green belt of spruce. Higher still, above the tree line, rose the glaciated peaks of bare stone.

This long, thin range divided the two deserts Teilhard had written about, the Tengger and the Ordos. It was the Tengger that spread out in front of them now, as they roared down the

Mongolian slope. The road was less steep on this side, winding a little more gently down through the oak brush and rock piles. It settled finally into a long, rocky alluvial apron that landed in a sea of stabilized dunes, shadowed with a thin, patchy cover of brush.

Near the bottom they passed a few dwellings, simple earth boxes with holes cut for their doors and windows. Roofs of mud and straw, held by a jutting row of rafters. These were the only signs of human habitation.

The last half hour into Eren Obo was on a dusty, unpaved road cut with deep ruts and potholes. And then Eren Obo itself: a desert town frozen in time.

To Alice, Eren Obo was another Tonopah, Nevada—the way Tonopah had looked to her when, years before, she'd first driven out west from Texas. Just the sight, now, of these low sand-colored buildings, this contained little grid backed right up to a tributary range of brown desert mountains and the blazing blue sky, brought back the memory of being a college student, on the highway, in an open car, pretending she was flying away from her life as she drove west.

But this was Mongolia. The streets were full of dark, chisel-faced men, laughing over their complicated board games on the sidewalk, piloting pickups through the unpaved streets.

"This is the hotel?" Spencer asked. It was a two-story stucco building with glass doors, linoleum in the lobby. And no other guests besides themselves.

A *fuwuyuan* took them up to their plain white-walled rooms, each with a narrow bed and toilet dry as bone. And a powdery sink—also never used. There appeared to be no running water. So why had they installed the plumbing? Alice switched the plaintive faucet on and off. There was a TV, though—naturally! She flicked it on. Only one channel, a horse-oriented sporting event in Mongolian.

"Will you be comfortable?" came a voice in Chinese.

She turned. Lin in the doorway. "And where is your room?" she asked.

"Duimian," Across the hall.

"Amazing. We are near each other."

He inclined his head.

"Do you like that?" she asked boldly.

"Lin Boshi!" They heard from downstairs. Kong's voice.

"You should come, bring Dr. Spencer," Lin said. "The forestry man's downstairs."

"Xing."

On the first floor they found a kind-faced, rough-and-ready Mongol in loose clothes. "I am called Kuyuk," he said in heavily accented Chinese. "Is it true you're looking for the ape-man?"

They walked into a side room off the lobby and eased into upholstered chairs around a low wooden table. "This is what I was told," Kuyuk continued. "But ape-man fossils have never been found here. Never! I am therefore not sure how to help you."

"We're not looking for a new ape-man site," Spencer explained. "We're looking for the original cache of Peking Man bones—the artifacts from 1929."

Alice's translation caught up, and Kuyuk's sun- and wind-burned face with its towering cheekbones creased in bewilderment. "Peking Man! But why here? We are so remote."

"We think there's a chance it was hidden near here at the end of the war. We need to determine first if anybody is alive who might know whether a tall, thin Frenchman visited the town in the spring of 1945. Here is his picture." Spencer produced an old photograph and passed it around. Kuyuk studied it seriously, as if Father Teilhard were someone he might have seen recently on the desert-dirt streets.

"We have evidence he was corresponding with someone here at that time. That someone sent him a drawing of your local rock art. Here." Spencer pulled out a sketch of the monkey sun god and showed it to the Mongol. "What if the French priest hid Peking Man near Eren Obo? Somewhere near"—he pointed to the drawing—"one of these? As a forestry manager you know the land. You know where these petroglyphs are. We need you to help us pin down the places he might have put it."

The man stared into space for a moment, rubbing his brown hands, then said: "Yes, of course—I have seen this rock art up in the Helan Shan. But you will have to talk with our Leader. Anyway tonight, at six o'clock, we hold a dinner for you. The Leader will attend. The Leader knows more about past events than anyone else. See you at six."

A silence fell after Kuyuk walked out. "Who's the Leader?" Alice asked.

"Ah!" Kong smiled. "They used to call the man who controls Alashan Banner the Prince. Now he is simply the Leader." In the last few days Kong had become more relaxed. He had stopped clipping his cell phone to his belt, since they were out of range. There were no lines for his fax. He had changed his suit pants for khakis and his white athletic shoes were streaked with dust.

"Whoever he is," Spencer said, "let's hope he kept good records."

The Leader waited at the banquet table in the small outbuilding that passed as the guesthouse dining room. Kuyuk sat on his left. A young woman with high, narrow eyes and a wide, composed slash of a mouth was to his right. Other Mongols lounged against the walls.

"Sit!" the Leader barked. He spoke Chinese with an accent. He was in his mid-fifties, vigorous, the black hair racing straight back from his bronzed forehead. He half rose from the round table set with plates and teacups and tiny wine cups. "Tea!" he called. One of the men from the wall sprang up and poured.

"You know Kuyuk," he said, and then indicated the woman on his left. "Ssanang. My daughter. Eh, it's a long time since an outsider came to Eren Obo. The last one was a soil-conservation man from Australia. Let me see—five years ago. Welcome. Trouble you to explain your work."

Spencer fell right into his theory. The Leader listened carefully as the American told how Teilhard got the bones back late in the war. Everyone at the table looked at the drawing of the petroglyph. "So you see, we have to think like Teilhard," Spencer concluded.

"Cigarette?" the Leader asked. He held out a pack of the smelly local brand.

"Uh"—Spencer drew back—"no thanks."

The pack went around the table. Kuyuk and Kong helped themselves. The woman Ssanang declined. Alice stole a glance at Lin. No. He didn't take one.

The Leader leaned to Kuyuk, accepted a light. All around, the Leader's men took out smokes and lit up. The discreet *fffft* of matches, the pull of indrawn breath circled them, then the cigarette smell rolled overhead.

"Now," said the Leader, exhaling a pale cloud, "you say we must think like the Frenchman. First?"

"First"—Spencer grinned—"he loved it here—the countryside, the Helan Shan. Okay. I figure to Teilhard, the Helan Shan might have been a perfect place. It was a landmark, a mountain range. It had unique rock art, a motif that was found no place else in the world. Something to guide scientists to the spot later. But more! He sensed beauty here. I mean divine beauty. He said in his letters that here he felt close to God."

The Leader listened closely to her translation, approval replacing the neutral glaze on his face. "It's so! Any man with a heart would feel that in the Helan Shan!"

"Yet it was remote," Spencer pointed out. "He could hide

something and know it would never be disturbed. There'd be a marker—the petroglyph. And a dry, favorable climate.

"Other types of terrain around this village, I think Teilhard would have passed over. He wouldn't have hidden anything in the desert floor, for instance. The sand shifts too much. He might never find it again. And the alluvial fans are no good either—flash flooding. So if he got Peking Man back, if in fact he came out here with it in 1945—I say he took it up to the mountains. Near some rock art." Spencer sat back.

"Interesting." The Leader stubbed out his cigarette. The doors flung open at the end of the room and three garishly made-up Mongol girls twirled in with platters above their heads. With a flourish they set down steaming platters of sculpture: sautéed eggplant and hair vegetable, arranged in small mountains and canyons to look like the desert's wide open spaces, with a Great Wall of crenelated Spam down the middle of each plate. "Please," said the Leader happily, and he helped himself.

Alice stared. So different from Chinese manners! In China the host would serve others first, would not eat until the guests began. She bit into the eggplant; it was simple, but fresh and perfectly cooked. The Spam she pushed discreetly to the side. This was just the first course, she knew. She loved banquets. They always included a stupefying parade of food, endless dishes, five times as much as anyone could eat. In America, where food was plentiful, such a display would be impolite. In Asia it was de rigueur. She ate happily.

"To your visit," the Leader cried, and raised his tiny cup.

They all drank. She had to hold in a yell, the alcohol was so strong. It burned all the way to her stomach.

"That's some moonshine," Spencer sputtered. "So." He wiped his mouth. "What do you think about my idea?"

"Most interesting." The Leader reached into his shirt and withdrew an envelope.

"What's that?"

"Please have a look." He handed it over.

Spencer opened it and gently extracted a frayed, folded paper. Then he almost tipped over his chair.

Alice craned over. Teilhard's signature! She could not really read French, or speak it, *Je sais me faire comprendre, c'est tout,* she would answer when someone asked her, but this was clearly a note of thanks. She swallowed. Even with her patched-together French she could see the phrasing was not current, but reflected the flowery style of a bygone time.

"See the date," Spencer breathed.

She swallowed, nodded. May 1945.

"This is the man, then?" The Leader made a small gesture to the men by the walls, and one sprang up and refilled their wine cups.

"Jesus—yes—it's him!" Spencer thrust the note over to Kong and Lin. They erupted into Chinese.

Spencer pressed open his notebook and wrote excitedly, then leaned forward. "Where'd you get this?"

"From my father."

"You mean—"

"Your Frenchman came here in 1945. He saw my father, stayed for many days. He talked of his love for this Banner. Do you know its name? Alashan. And it was as you said. The priest told my father he had been happier here in Alashan than any-where on earth."

Spencer, Lin, Kong, and Alice exchanged glances.

"But so sorry, according to my father he said nothing about any fossils. The subject of Peking Man was never raised. In fact, my father said the visit lacked any obvious purpose."

"Yet that could be consistent," Kong said slowly.

They all stared at him.

Kong puffed on his cigarette. "Suppose the Frenchman did bring the Peking Man bones? Would he take the Leader into his confidence? Maybe not. It might have seemed too risky."

NICOLE MONES

The three girls swept back into the room with the main
courses: shredded lamb with chili peppers; deep-fried carp,
hauled overland from the Yellow River; creamy scrambled eggs,
and high piles of tomato and eggplant stir-fry, all with huge
tureens of white rice.

"Still," said Alice, "he would tell someone where he put it—
wouldn't he? Someone?" She translated her words into English
for Spencer.

"True," Lin put in. "He was growing old. He wouldn't have
wanted the secret to die with him."

Ssanang, the Leader's daughter, cleared her throat and spoke
for the first time. "I agree." Her gaze was direct and candid. It
affected none of the womanish retreat a Chinese woman would
use. "Perhaps there is someone here the French priest contacted—someone with whom he cleared his heart."

"The Mongol family," Lin said.

"Shenmo?" Ssanang asked.

"Shuode shi di yici lai," I'm talking about the first time he
came here. And Lin explained how Teilhard had come to
Shuidonggou in 1923 and befriended the family of Mongols there.
"We did find their homestead," he concluded sadly. "But it was
long abandoned."

"Of that family, from Shuidonggou, we would know nothing," the Leader apologized. "It is out of our Banner. You should
seek the help of someone on that side of the border."

"We have," Alice told him. She thought about Guo Wenxiang.
Would he yet learn anything? Would he even be able to get in
touch with them up here?

Food was served around, and in the silence of their temporary
impasse they fell to eating. "Is your father still living, then?"
Spencer asked the Leader.

"Yes."

Everyone felt the sudden increase in voltage. "Can we meet
with him?"

246

"Oh, no, the Leader doesn't see anyone anymore, especially outsiders. He spends his time in contemplation."

"I thought you were the Leader. . . ." Spencer glanced around the table, confused.

The man shook his head. "No. His son. But I attend to all the Banner's affairs. And I assure you, he has told Ssanang and me everything. He remembers these events with great clarity." He snapped his fingers for more wine, which was instantly poured by one of his men.

Dr. Lin stood. "Health, long life." They all drained their cups.

Alice put her empty cup down with exaggerated slowness, afraid she would somehow miss the table and send the tiny thing crashing to the floor. Her mind was a whirl. There. The cup met the tablecloth with a hard bump. God, the stuff was strong. She looked at her plate. Had she eaten all that?

"Will you have more?" Kuyuk asked, following her gaze and reaching for the nearest platter, which still held a gelatinous mass of hair vegetable and green, glisteny peppers.

"No," she said, feeling the word come out of her throat like a bubble and float to the top of her head. "No—I couldn't possibly—"

"The lamb, then!" the Leader cried. "Bring the lamb!"

"What did he say?" Spencer whispered.

"He said, the lamb." Alice closed her eyes, feeling full now, finally. God, could they really bring more food?

Of course they could, in China.

The Leader had his cup up in the air again. His grinning face seemed to swim at her. "To the friends of the Frenchman!" he called, and upended his cup.

She translated, then drank again. Before, it had seemed like fire going down; now she barely felt it. Just a warm liquid line running from her tongue to her stomach.

"Mo Ai-li," said Kuyuk, leaning toward her. He looked almost sober, although he had drunk every round. "Tell me how you learned to speak."

"In school," she said, and with the two abrupt words a kaleidoscope of her years at Rice rolled over her, pulled into flaccid Edvard Munch shapes by the alcohol: beginning Chinese, intermediate, advanced . . . the two hundred and fourteen radicals, streaming down the page in the front of her notebook, the nine thousand characters she had committed to memory, writing each a thousand times, then another thousand times, then more. . . .

Her teacher had been a soft-spoken little gentleman of Manchurian ancestry who wore old slippers in the classroom and always buttoned a sweater vest over his trim shirt and tie, even in the summer months. He had a lined, dark-bronze face and a fastidious way of clearing his throat before he spoke. "See how each character combines the radicals, the component symbols of its basic nature—man, wood, fire, water, rain, the sun, the moon—to form an ideogram for each thing known to man. Thus each time you sit down to write, you review, by inference, the nature of the world itself. It is an unending labyrinth, timeless and secure. Yet never static. For," he told her, "each phrase can be interpreted in different ways—especially in spoken Chinese. Never one meaning, always many. Not like English. And our idioms—the best ones are not literal, no, not at all, instead they are oblique, they make reference to legends, stories, famous dramas, and books. They do not offer specific information, do you understand me or not? They produce a state of mind! Ah, so few of you outside people grasp the pleasure of speaking a truly civilized language—never base, never obvious and therefore clunky and painful, as English is. . . ."

But Alice had understood. Chinese was a huge maze-world: stable yet evasive. Nothing was permanently what it seemed. *Yes* meant maybe and *no* meant maybe and so did everything in between—other Westerners saw this as Chinese prevarication but to Alice it was simply the natural mutation of things. Natural *and* welcome—because here in China the self could always be reinvented. She, too, could become someone else. Eventually. Or so she'd told herself all these years.

"Your Frenchman," said the Leader. He threw a loose, lubricated wave at the letter, which was propped now at an odd angle against a soy sauce bottle next to the wine.

"Teilhard, my good friend!" called Spencer. "Turn my life around!"

Alice did not translate anymore. No one seemed to care.

"The Frenchman," the Leader repeated, but in a different voice, an insistent voice which commanded their attention. Silence settled. He continued: "The Frenchman went to the lamasery during his visit. To the *baisi*. It is recorded. This is a sacred place, high up a canyon."

They stared.

"What?" Alice managed.

"Kuyuk will take you there tomorrow."

But just then the doors flew open and the girls in the shiny red lipstick bore in the lamb, still whole except for the head, slow-roasted out in the open air to a dark crackly caramel. The smell was round, pitched, monumental. The men who'd been lounging around the edge bolted from their seats now, and with instant, sinuous grace produced long and copiously decorated daggers from within their clothes. They fell on the meat in a circle. Slices dropped into their hands and were carried to plates.

She whispered to Spencer what the Leader had said about Teilhard visiting a lamasery. He leaned over, intent on her English, eyes fixed in a glassy stare at the steaming meat in front of him. Then his face broke open in an unfettered smile.

"This is it," he whispered, writing the three words in his notebook as he said them to her. She watched him underline them.

He's drunk, she thought, but he might be right. We might actually find the damn thing.

"I have a toast," Spencer announced, pushing away from the table and standing with exaggerated care. He held his wine cup in front of him. Then he dipped two fingers in the wine and tossed the drops on the floor. "To the earth!" he cried. He dipped again and flicked drops into the air. "To the sky!" The third time, he wet his fingers and drew them across his own forehead. "To the ancestors!" he finished.

There was a stunned silence, broken by a thundering cheer as the Mongols leapt to their feet and drank. "The American!" they called, hoisting their cups. "The American!"

The Leader drank, beaming. "How do you know this toast of ours?"

"Books!" Spencer cried happily. He raised his cup and drank. "History, letters, memoirs of foreigners who have come here."

"Impressive," Alice grinned, toasting him.

They all fell to eating lamb, which was lean and long-cooked and fell apart perfectly in their mouths. When she pushed her plate back she was aware of Lin's gaze and risked a glance at him. He was watching her quite openly, as if there was nothing to hide. He smiled, a smile that seemed magically to target only her.

She smiled back.

"Now!" called the Leader with a hearty clap, and one of the knife men was back in a spinning instant to the table.

On the Leader's signal the man used a quick pirouette of his hand to disengage the glistening suet oblong of the lamb's tail. He deftly cut off a long, paper-thin slice, and bore it to Alice on his open brown palm.

"All Mongols must do this." The Leader laughed.

"Oh, I can't," she said, affecting retreat. It was an accepted ploy in Chinese manners. Women could excuse themselves from any excess by saying, simply, that they could not. As if they were physically unable. This invoked the female frailty that Chinese society, despite the fact that it no longer actually bound the feet of pampered girls, still found endlessly compelling.

Lin smiled at her Chinese decorum and looked away. Whether his smile was one of affection or amused superiority, she could not tell.

"Then to the American scientist," insisted the Leader.

The brown man, his planar face creased by a smile, carried the lamb fat to Spencer.

"To be a man, you must." The Leader smiled.

"All right!" Spencer slapped the table with his palm.

"You should take it all in one gulp," Alice whispered in Spencer's ear, repeating what the knife wielder was declaiming in Chinese. "Don't stop. This is a manhood thing. Don't look back."

He nodded, an intimate glance to her, they were confederates, the Americans.

The Mongol pushed the tip of his middle finger right up against Adam Spencer's pale Caucasian lip. He tilted the blond head back with his other hand, as if in baptism, and then the white slab, with a sickening fat sluicing sound, disappeared down Spencer's mouth. The American contorted a long instant. Then he swallowed hard, grinned broadly.

The room roared with approval.

"The scientist! The friend of the Frenchman!" the Leader cried. "He's as one of the Mongols!"

Alice made it back to her room, across the open courtyard, then the stone-floored empty lobby, then the stairs. Come on, up. Up. Next loomed the linoleum hallway, and her door, then suddenly there was her tufted bedspread, which flew up and slammed her in the face.

Where was she? Eren Obo, the Mongolian desert.

She groaned and turned over. Was that someone knocking on the door? Again. A knocking sound. Yes. "Come in," she said. Now that she was down she couldn't get up.

"Xiao Mo?"

"Oh—Lin . . ." She struggled to a sitting position.

"No, no." He held up his hand. "It's quite all right."

She sank back gratefully, closed her eyes. At least she was still fully dressed. She opened one eye to see him looking at her.

"You're all right?"

"Yes." She propped her head on the pillow, aware that she was floating, and he was standing over her. "Dr. Lin," she said. "Do you not think it remarkable that we met like this?"

"You know, Mo Ai-li, what's remarkable is that we came to this place and Dr. Spencer was right: they do know something about Teilhard. He did come here. It makes me think there is hope, where before I had no hope. It makes me think things can change. I thank you for this. You and Dr. Spencer."

"Don't thank me." She rolled her eyes. "It's not like my life is much of an example."

"No, no. You've exerted yourself against the fates. You told me about your father. In our world, Mo Ai-li—our Chinese world—we just endure these things."

"So you do," she said, looking at him. *Accept my world,* she begged in her mind. My world where I am walled in, where Horace may soon be leaving me. Oh, was Horace going to die? Was he desperately ill right now? "But I get so frightened sometimes," she admitted.

"I know. Fear is only fear, though."

"And somehow you live without it."

"No," he corrected her. "You live *with* it." He smiled down at her. "Good-night, Mo Ai-li."

* * *

Alone in the hall outside her room, Dr. Lin paused. Could he do this, with this woman? Could he keep advancing toward her? She was so intelligent. He could talk to her, really talk to her. But she was a Westerner. Later she might grow bored, turn to some other man. Lose interest in him. The idea made him sick, even though he had not yet possessed her. He stared down the dimly lit hall, which ended in a square window framing the desert night.

No, he thought finally. She was not like that. Other Western women might follow convenience, but not Mo Ai-li. He could see her character in her face, her words, her actions. She would be a woman he could trust.

It was more than an hour next morning in the jeep, climbing steadily up into the arid, rubble-pile mountains, before they finally turned up a deep, cutting canyon. The ravine was covered with pebbles, the walls so narrow they scraped the jeep. As they climbed they saw smaller tributary washes twist down to join them. Then the canyon opened out to an enclosed plateau and Alice caught her first sight of the *baisi* temple complex. It was built in pagoda style, its vermilion-and-gilt colors howling against the brown cliffs. The repeating, supplicating roofs under the endless blue desert sky.

They got out of the car. Alice breathed deeply the good baking smell of hot sun on rocks. Then over the dry silence she heard a long, mournful note, calling like a boat horn.

A young man in plain terra-cotta robes, barefoot, shave headed, walked out into the light from the courtyard wall. He turned and spoke through the doorway behind him. The horn sound ceased. Another monk emerged, carrying a long metal instrument.

Kuyuk spoke to the lamas, who turned and led the way into

the inner courts. One by one they all stepped over the bottom beams of a succession of great round gates, until they came to the central cell of the compound, where loess-brick rooms surrounded the bare yard.

The lamas said something to Kuyuk in Mongolian and he turned to the group, disappointment on his face. "I don't know what we'll be able to learn. These monks have only been here a few years. Records—there are none. The whole place burned in the Chaos and was rebuilt."

That's the fresh paint, she thought. "No older monks remain?"

"None left living."

"The petroglyph, then," prompted Spencer. "Ask if they've ever seen one in the hills around here."

She took the paper from her pocket and gave it to Kuyuk. He talked to the monks and passed it back to her. "They say they have seen these before. They are carved on rocks here and there in the mountains. Some of these places are well known to the local people. But they have never seen one around here."

A silence. Finally Lin spoke up. "May we have a look around the area, then?"

Kuyuk conferred. "They ask only that we do not disturb the land, for it is sacred. Also he cautions that it is the time of wind."

Wind, yes: she had noticed the wind yesterday, at this same time, and then when the afternoon came to an end it had sunk low and died. Now that afternoon was upon them again the wind was back, a stinging fine-grained roar that whistled and slammed at them outside the high, protective walls.

They filed out of the complex and trudged up a narrow path that switchbacked steadily higher up the dirt flanks toward the sky. This was one of the side canyons, but one that looked like it went all the way up. They all tied on handkerchiefs, scarves, anything against the screaming wall of air that fought at them.

They stopped at a rise. Spencer heaved a look back at the sweep below. "Think like Teilhard!" he said.

"Anzhao Teilhard-de silu xiang!" She breathed heavily, looking downward. How marvelously and lucidly arranged is the geology here, she thought. The pattern of rock and shadow marching, like ripples in silk, down to the sea of dunes, then all the way out to the edge of the sky.

Lin was thinking the same thing. "The priest would have loved it here."

She put this in English, prompting Spencer to quote the man. " '*The earth's crust changes ceaselessly under our feet*'—what's next?"

" '*While the heavens sweep us along in a cyclone of stars,* ' " she finished. Spencer laughed.

They kept climbing against the onslaught of wind. They scanned the rocks, boulders, cliff faces on all sides, but there were no petroglyphs. Nothing but the sun and the wind and the walls of stone.

"A cave," Dr. Lin said finally.

"What?" Spencer stopped.

"Teilhard would have looked for a cave."

"Goddamn, yes, Dr. Lin, that's exactly right." Spencer had been gleaming all day with the renewal of hope he'd been given last night at the banquet, grinning, writing in his book like a madman. Now, answering Lin, he seemed to ratchet up one notch more.

"The Helan Shan is full of caves," Kuyuk put in.

At that the wind roared louder, sending small rocks and pebbles dancing across the path. They huddled their heads down and climbed again, but this time studying the walls, each cleft and shadow and overhang, for signs of a cave as well as for the rock art.

They panted around a corner and saw, abruptly, the lamasery

far below them, a box-walled labyrinth. They stood in silence a moment. *Think like Teilhard.*

"Look at that," Kong called, and pointed upward. It was a rock cairn, all the rocks piled on over many years by many pairs of hands, by travelers passing along the crest above where the five of them stood right now, the travelers stopping at the temple perhaps, or saying a solitary prayer, or adding a rock. From the top of the pile prayer flags, cloth long faded but still faint with Mongolian letters, crackled stiff and straight out in the wind.

"We need a cave." Alice sighed. "We need the monkey sun god."

"Let's climb higher," Kuyuk said, muffled.

And later, after winding much higher and not talking, heads down in the wind, suddenly Kong's voice was snatched out of him and tossed around: "I see one."

"What!" They all cried and shouted, but then, following Kong's slim pointed finger, they froze, all seeing the abrupt black cleft in the hillside, the dark opening that was deeper somehow, blacker, than the mere shadow it should have been.

They scrambled to it, rocks and sand raining down away from their shoes.

"Careful," Dr. Kong said from the ledge above her. He extended his fine-boned hand.

"Caves are dangerous," Kuyuk barked. He seemed to have suddenly remembered he was responsible for two academics from Zhengzhou and two Americans, actual foreign guests. "It would be better if we came back with a light. I can prepare—"

"Just a little way in," Spencer pleaded. "We'll be careful."

"Xing," Kuyuk sighed.

So forming a line, they crept inside.

Lin was worming into the irregular opening behind the others, stooped over. He looked back around to her and gave her his hand. *"Lai."*

Farther. They inched over the uneven rock floor. Loud

breathing, crunching rocks. They passed through the dense over-hanging shadow, and the darkness was almost total.

"This is a bad idea," Kuyuk protested from somewhere up ahead. "Let's return later!"

"Just a little way." Spencer's voice from somewhere, insisting.

"Yidian," she translated, noticing that the voices sounded far-ther away from her now. But what was this? She felt Lin squeeze her hand and pull her to him in the blackness. Her nose bumped the front of his shirt. She froze. His hands moved to either side of her waist, touching her softly, experimentally. They moved up, taking the measure of her rib cage. Outlining her torso. Avoiding her breasts.

She held her breath.

The warm hands drifted up her shoulders, her neck. Fingers waved through her hair, curious.

"Wait, I think I have a match," Kuyuk called.

The hands vanished.

The scrape and flare, the sulfur, and in an instant of flickering light and shadow she saw the damp irregular cave walls, just where they ought to be, the rocks and boulders, the others stand-ing there.

And Lin. He stood facing her, eyes boring into her. Had he really touched her?

"See that?" Kong said, in a wondering voice. There was a petroglyph carved into the wall. The monkey sun god.

"The rock art!"

"Is it not?"

"It is!"

Then Spencer's voice, shouting, "Jesus Christ!" and they all turned again.

In the last microsecond of the match they saw a man-made wall, the dark burnished gleam of metal. The cave passage ahead was completely closed off. There was a steel wall, and a giant submarinelike wheel-lock glimmering in its center.

The match went dead. The snuff of darkness.

"I have only one more," Kuyuk whispered.

Through the pounding of her heart Alice heard the papery sounds of him fumbling, and then the chuffing hiss, and then light again. Lin had moved away from her. He knelt by the metal door, the same brown hands that had just explored her now tracing along the metal wall.

"See those characters?" Kong pointed to an incised marking down in the corner.

"It says, 'Installation forty-eight, Alashan Base six,' " Lin read. "People's Liberation Army."

"Anything else?"

Lin peered closer, dropped to a whisper. *"Yuanzidanchangku."* She whispered this in English. "Nuclear silo."

"Damn!" spat Spencer.

The match went out.

She lay in bed on her back, heart pounding, staring at the ceiling. He had touched her. In the cave, in the moment of total darkness, despite the possibility that Peking Man was near—he had done it. It was already as unreal to her as a dream. She put her own hands on her waist, trailed them up. Wasn't this what he had done? She touched her neck, her hair. Lin had never made a sound. He just touched her. He was telling her he wanted her. Wasn't he? The thought made her ache. What would it be like with him? She put her hand between her legs and began to move, arching her back, imagining it. How would he do it? How?

12

SHE SLID INTO her chair at the sun-pooled breakfast table. No one was there but Lin. "Dr. Kong's not up yet?"

"No. Dr. Spencer?"

"The same."

"Are you excited about today?" he asked.

"Oh, yes," she said, wondering which way he meant it.

"I am too." He began serving her, lovingly, the way family members serve each other at home, selecting the finest-looking morsels and piling them on her small plate.

"You needn't," she murmured, and hurried to reciprocate.

But he stopped her. "No," he smiled. "you must let me. Set your heart at ease." He surveyed the table and scooped up a few more things for her plate. "Eat now, girl child," he said gently. He chose food for his own plate and started in.

She chewed slowly. He appeared relaxed, happy, as if they had been eating breakfast together for years.

"I believe we'll have success today." He glanced at her.

"I hope so."

"Peking Man is certain to be in the cave. Is it not so? Not only do we know the French priest went there—to the lamasery—but there, in the cave entrance, was the rock art."

She nodded.

"It should not be so difficult to meet with the military head of Alashan." Lin paused, thinking about it. "He will make time for us. Peking Man is a matter of importance."

"It's so." And we're in another autonomous region now, too, she thought in a quick flood of relief; far away from that horrible Lieutenant Shan in Yinchuan.

He poured her tea.

She started to eat, then, feeling his eyes on her, looked up. He was not eating. Instead he was watching her, playing with one of his chopsticks.

His fingers moved deliberately up and down the wooden utensil. He watched her while he did it.

Am I imagining this? she thought.

No. He's actually doing it.

"I think, despite everything, we may be close to it." He didn't glance at his fingers stroking the *kuaizi*. His eyes stayed on hers. "Do you think so? Do you think we're close?"

"Close to what?" she whispered, barely able to speak.

"Finding *Sinanthropus*. Of course."

She could only nod, afraid to even breathe.

"I really think we are," he said, but now his voice had gone slightly hoarse.

Then an utter change clicked over him. "Eh," he said, "Dr. Spencer." He laid the chopstick down.

Adam sat noisily beside them. "So? We have a meeting with somebody?"

"Today, we hope. Someone military."

Spencer nodded. Still suffused with his new optimism, he started serving himself.

She snatched a glance at Lin. He ate as if nothing had occurred.

*　*　*

She cleared her throat gently at the empty desk. A *fuwuyuan* came out from the back room, her world, her bed and desk and basin. "Miss, I trouble you too much. Is there any phone?"

"No phone," said the tall, equine woman.

"May I ask, where is there a phone?"

The woman thought. "In Yinchuan."

"So it's like that."

The woman made the faintest affirmative expression with her eyes, high set, brilliant, and black.

Now what do I do about Horace? Alice despaired. I'm out in the middle of nowhere, there's no phone, and what if he is dying?

What if. Because the day will come, maybe soon, when I'll stand on this earth without him. He'll be gone and it'll just be me, Alice Mannegan.

Free to choose, to love.

Free to live in China, or in the United States.

No—not the United States. People will still remember. My name will still be Mannegan and people will never let me forget it. It's not worth fighting it there. But I could live here—or Hong Kong or Taipei. Nobody cares or knows or is even aware of it in Asia. And I could let my guard down, be what my instincts tell me to be. My real self. It was the same thing Pierre had wished for Lucile: *You know that nothing makes me more happy than to feel that you are living fully by the best of yourself.*

"*Hai you qita shi ma?*" the woman inquired.

Alice shook her head sadly. "No. Nothing else."

"The lieutenant will see you now," said the crisply uniformed soldier.

He held open the door.

Lieutenant Shan half rose from behind his desk, all courtesy, all controlled bearing.

Oh, God, she thought: it's him—he's in charge of the Army here too.

The lieutenant recognized her too. She saw it in his face, although he covered expertly.

Shan smiled. Everyone smiled back except Alice.

Kuyuk made introductions. "Dr. Lin, Dr. Kong of Huabei University, and the Americans, Dr. Spencer, Miss Mo."

Lieutenant Shan emitted the small hospitable sounds which were correct in such situations. These monosyllables conveyed his pleasure at meeting them, but by their brevity reminded everyone of his very busy, very superior position.

Ah, good, Alice thought, watching him. He still didn't know she spoke Chinese. Kuyuk had not identified her as the interpreter, just introduced her by name. Now Shan was directing himself entirely at Kuyuk, Lin, and Kong—ignoring her and Spencer, obviously assuming the two Americans didn't understand him. It's too good to be true, she thought. He still doesn't know.

Of course, before the meeting's over he's going to find out I speak Chinese, but I can control when it happens. When? she thought. What moment do I select to make it crystal clear that when his soldiers brought me in the other day I understood every single vulgar word he said? She drew a careful breath, kept her face neutral.

Now Kuyuk delineated their research in Chinese, explaining why they believed Peking Man to be in the cave. Shan listened, impassive.

She stepped close to Spencer and delivered a soft, discreet translation into his ear.

When Kuyuk completed his monologue Shan cleared his throat. "It is our honor to welcome you to the Alashan Banner of

Inner Mongolia. As you have surmised, the cave in question is part of our installation. It cannot be entered, I'm afraid. The equipment inside is very sensitive, highly sophisticated. Exceedingly dangerous."

Alice's lips parted in surprise. So polished! And he'd been so crude and foul-mouthed the week before. . . . Watch yourself, she thought. Be careful.

Shan took out a pack of Chinese cigarettes and offered them around. Kuyuk and Kong accepted and, along with Shan, lit up. As he had before, that other day in Yinchuan, Lieutenant Shan did not seem to inhale and exhale, but rather to take smoke into his mouth and then just begin speaking, so that the smoke drifted in and out around his words.

"You will understand, then, why I could never permit you to enter the cave," Shan finished easily. "It's impossible."

"Ask him if there's any way he'd consider us entering together with his men," Spencer whispered.

Now, she thought.

She took a step forward and cleared her throat.

"Esteemed Lieutenant," she announced in her most precise, snobbish, Peking-accented Mandarin. "This miserable interpreter would speak. The American scientist asks if our team may search the cave under the protection and guidance of your technicians. Of course we would follow their instructions in every particular."

Shan's mouth fell slightly slack. Smoke eddied out.

Yes! she thought.

The lieutenant stubbed out his cigarette hurriedly. He lit another.

"I beg you to forgive my execrable Chinese," she added gleefully. "I'm nothing but a foreigner. My Mandarin is hopelessly inadequate."

"It's excellent," he murmured.

You bet your sorry ass it is! "Lieutenant. Have you not heard it said? The superior man is well versed in both polite letters *and* military affairs. I, a mere outsider, can claim neither. Unlike *your* honorable self."

Lin Shiyang stared at the little russet-haired foreigner. It was all he could do not to throw his head back and laugh, right in front of all of them, from sheer delight. How many women would do such a thing? "It's true," he put in to support her. "The lieutenant is an exalted official of high sensibilities."

"Ni shuo shenmo?" What are you saying? Kong whispered urgently in his ear.

"Just listen," Lin whispered back.

"I will have to take this request of yours under advisement," Shan said, his control slipping.

"Lieutenant," Kuyuk put in, attempting to steer the conversation back where it belonged, "if you would consider. The recovery of Peking Man will bring glory to our country."

"I know." Shan ground out his second cigarette.

"Esteemed sir," Alice cut in boldly. "I note by your accent that you are from the South. You're Cantonese?"

Now Lin stared at her.

She held him off with the tiniest movement of her head.

"Yes," Shan answered her reluctantly. "I'm Cantonese."

"So far away! Your mother—she's still living?"

"Yes . . ."

"You must think of her often," Alice said sweetly. "With every sentence you speak."

Understanding, knowing the Cantonese phrase in question, Lin broke into a grin. The other Chinese speakers stood confounded.

"Anyway," she concluded, "we hope you will consider our request yourself. Personally. It is so tiresome to have to report everything to Beijing. I mean *everything*. Isn't it so?"

"You will have to forgive me," the lieutenant blurted finally. "I have another appointment. As to the matter of entering the cave, I will see what can be done. Give me a little time. A technical escort would have to be very, very carefully arranged. I will think back and forth."

Alice repeated this in English, trying to keep triumph out of her voice.

"Jesus and Mary." Spencer squeezed his eyes shut. "What was that, anyway? What did you say?"

"I negotiated." She laughed. "Chinese style."

As they walked out of the building into the white desert sunlight, Lin stepped close to her. "The final stroke of *jia chi bu dian,* playing stupid while being smart." His face was radiant. "Well done. Truly, Mo Ai-li, you are more than Mu-lan. You surpass her."

"To you I must seem"—she swallowed. Was she too aggressive for him, too un-Chinese?—"too direct," she finished.

"But that is you, Interpreter Mo," he said, surprised.

That is me. She thought of Pierre's letter to Lucile: *Why do you ask me to forgive you anything about it? You are so true in what you say,—so yourself,—*"si belle," *dearest. . . .* She looked at Lin now, climbing into the jeep, fitting himself into the backseat. He glanced down at her, happy, face open. Did he actually see her, the real Alice?

Back at the guesthouse, washed, refreshed, she left her room thinking about the real reason she had bested Shan. It was because she had thought as a Chinese: know your enemy, conceal your knowledge, then when the time is right feint to the east and attack to the west. An ancient technique, one she had absorbed, living here, almost without knowing it. Still effective.

Oh, she loved the haze, the hallucinogenic dream that came over her when she managed to merge, for even an instant, with the Chinese way of thinking. Usually it was when she was alone in China for long periods, speaking, thinking, dreaming, only in Mandarin. She would imagine herself part of it. An illusion, of course. She knew that.

As she came down the stairs she heard the wind groaning. It rattled the windows.

"Xiao Mo!"

She blinked. Lin's voice, imperative. But from where?

She walked out across the empty floor.

"Xiao Mo."

Behind her. She turned. He stood in an alcove behind the staircase.

She glanced around, confused. No one else there.

"Guolai," he whispered, Come here.

She strode quickly to him and he took a step back, grasping her by the elbows, drawing her into the shadows with him.

From in front of the building erupted the babble of Chinese voices, rising over the wind.

The door clattered open.

Lin laid one dark finger on her lips, shook his head.

Along with the jumble of shoes on stone she heard the spurt of Mandarin: the nasal, deliberate tones of Kong and the harsher-sounding Mongol-accented banter of Kuyuk.

She pressed against Lin's white-shirted chest, laid her cheek against the cloth. Why doesn't he put his arms around me? she thought.

The noisy footsteps passed them, clattered on up the steps, faded into the hallway above their heads. The voices grew smaller and smaller until they were gone.

Lin stood staring down at her, still holding her lightly by the elbows.

She opened her mouth. Nothing came out.

"Shenmo?" he whispered, noticing the change in her face and raising his own eyebrows in inquiry.

"Why did you call me over here?"

He released her elbows. Uncertainty shadowed his face. "*Duibuqi*. Maybe I shouldn't have. I guess I just wanted to see if you'd come."

Longing rose up in her throat. He was releasing his reserve so gradually, with such infinite control. Would he let it go completely? What would happen when he did? If he did. She dropped her arms to her side, stood stock still, her eyes in his, only a few inches separating them.

At the sound from the second floor they both looked up. The voices were back, and the footsteps, now scuffling above their heads toward the top of the stairs. She sighed. The two of them stepped apart, and walked out into the light, into the large empty hall, as if nothing had taken place.

Kuyuk took them to three canyons with monkey sun god petroglyphs. At each place they drove to where the dirt track became impassable and then hiked on farther, until they came to the rock art. The petroglyphs were small, only a few inches high, and each was carved on a boulder that sat in some spot utterly lacking in significance. Just the steep limestone canyons, the rivers of rock, and on one rock, inexplicably, the carving. They searched all around each rock. They explored the canyons. They saw nothing to suggest Peking Man was here instead of in the cave. There was only the jumble of rocks, and the petroglyphs.

"You're right about these," Spencer said to Kong. He stood staring at one of the carvings in the third canyon, his usual blue work shirt spotted with sweat. "The way the carving's worn down—it looks really old. Late Paleolithic at least. Yet it's a complex motif—sophisticated—and a monkey, which was a non-native animal. And this far up the canyon"—he paused, looked up and down the slope—"so far from the valley floor where they must have lived. Who *were* these people?"

Kong looked longingly at the rock carving while she translated. *"Shui dou bu zhidao,"* he answered, No one knows.

"A messenger brought it," she said to Spencer, holding out the single sheet of crackly onionskin paper. "I'll translate. 'Invoice to the American Dr. Spencer. For special escort services requested, including four trucks, twenty armed men, three munitions specialists, and two vault technicians—' "

"I didn't request all that!"

"Of course you didn't. Anyway: 'Please remit in advance our costs, twenty-eight thousand seven hundred and fifty-eight renminbi. Cordially, Lieutenant Shan, People's Liberation Army, Commander, Alashan Base, Inner Mongolia Autonomous Region.' "

Spencer sank down on the edge of his bed and dropped his face into his hands. "Twenty-eight thousand what? What?"

"Renminbi." She calculated. "Almost thirty-four hundred U.S. dollars."

"What!"

"That's what it says."

"But that's impossible."

"Nothing's impossible. This is how things work."

"I can't believe people stand for it."

"You know what a lot of the Chinese say about their system? *Yi pan san sha,* That China is a plate of sand. If they don't have a firm hand holding the whole thing together, it will fly off to the heavens in random pinwheels, no gravity. So they expect stuff like this. They work with it. It's the deal."

"Why didn't he bring this up in the meeting?"

"I suppose he found it difficult to ask you directly." Of course, she knew, it was also because she'd just beaten him and he'd lost unimaginable face.

"But I don't have any more money."

"I know," she sympathized.

He rubbed at his head. He took his notebook out, wrote the numbers, and stared at them. "Alice, help me out here. Is there any way around this?"

"No," she said. "Not entirely. The PLA is a business. You're a customer. You want something special and it's going to cost. Now the first price has been named. In my experience, once a bribe is demanded, it has to be satisfied. It might be negotiated down—but it must be paid. Otherwise he'll lose face again. And then you'll never get what you want."

"So how do we negotiate?"

She thought. "Entering a nuclear silo is a pretty stiff request. I think it's worth at least a thousand U.S. dollars. Let's say you aim to end up at that level—that would be about eight or nine thousand renminbi—you should start out offering say, half that. Offer four or five hundred dollars. Then there's room to compromise."

"I don't even have that much to spare."

She fell silent.

"You got a credit card?" he asked.

"Of course."

"Well?"

She looked at him sharply. "Well what? Would I put up the money?"

"We've come this far! Alice, you saw it—the monkey sun god—the cave—the fossils're in there!"

"But why should I—"

"Look, I know how this must sound to you. But I would pay you just as soon as I could."

"*Bie shuo-le,*" she said in Chinese without thinking, Don't talk like that.

"You mean you will?"

"I didn't say that."

269

"But you will?"

"I have to think."

"Alice, I would—"

"Save your breath." She cut him off.

He stopped.

Who am I really? she thought. Am I a woman who's careful, who follows the set plan, does only her duty? Because there is no need for me to go any farther than I've gone already; I've given all this time without pay. So I could stop. Or I could commit to go on, a little farther, into all this that I never expected in my wildest dreams to happen. *Breaking some respected boundaries means a torrent of new life.* And Lin. Lin wants Peking Man, wants it so badly. . . . "Anyway," she said. "That's the way to negotiate. We get a much smaller amount of cash, we show it to Shan—U.S. dollars, you never know—he just might take it."

"But where are we supposed to get actual U.S. dollars in Eren Obo?"

"Oh, *that's* no problem. That, they'll have."

"What? No phones here, no running water . . ."

She rolled her eyes. "You are so naive, Adam. You're right, there's not much here in Eren Obo. But I guarantee you, they *will* have American currency."

The next day Alice went to the village bank. She had decided to front Spencer's money and he had fallen all over himself, thanking her, the night before. "Don't thank me," she had said. "It's only a loan. And don't you think *I'm* dying to go into the cave too?" Now as she entered the single desk-crammed room inside a tiny loess-brick structure to draw money on her credit card, she noticed something odd.

"Is that a phone?" she asked.

"Does it look like a phone?" the Mongol inquired.

"Of course. Sorry."

He shrugged and went back to counting out her money in U.S. tens and twenties.

"Might I use it?"

He stared at her as if she had asked for a free camel. "This is the only telephone in the village! It is for the bank's use."

"Pitiable," she said softly.

He gazed at the amazing pile of American money, mouth working silently. Finally he said, "Of course, for a small fee, the bank might consider allowing its use. I'm not too clear. I could ask. We're talking about an emergency, of course."

"Of course," she agreed, and took her money and left.

Kong Zhen had also noted the presence of a telephone in the bank; he possessed an internal radar that guided him infallibly to available telecommunications devices. A gift of rough, sweet local wine to the bank manager came first. Then, the next day, he casually asked permission to make a call to Beijing.

Kong chose the time with care. It was early morning; the bank would be half empty. In Beijing, his cousin Vice Director Han would just be sitting down at his desk, with tea. And then the phone would ring.

"Have you eaten, elder cousin?" Kong asked amiably when first greetings had been exchanged.

"Yes, and you?"

"Yes, thank you. Your family?"

"They're well."

"Good. Then." Kong Zhen paused to signal a little shift. Ordinarily the pleasantries would have gone on longer, but the call was expensive and the bank manager's patience limited. So he plunged on: "Have you taken care of our—our surveillance problem?"

"Eh, yes," the vice director said. "I spoke to District Commander Gao. It's most regrettable what happened to the American female. The commander agrees. But you know—provincial officials—what can you do?"

"Yes. Yes of course. So the situation now . . . ?" He let the question trail off.

"Beijing Command will advise them. I think they'll discontinue. Now. What about Peking Man?"

Kong sighed. "The group is no closer to finding it. Though there have been . . . clues. Speaking frankly, the American is right about some things. But the fossils themselves? No. Nothing yet." Kong naturally downplayed how close they were to the remains, to the cave. There was no reason to build the vice director up and then disappoint him later. And there was every reason to start drawing his interest away from Peking Man so he could be made to see the incredible Late Paleolithic research that was everywhere here in the Northwest, waiting to be done. He, Kong, saw a future for himself here. Maybe a future with Dr. Spencer.

Kong liked the American. He liked working with him even though they couldn't talk without a go-between. With Dr. Spencer he felt at ease. He knew he should keep a little more distance—after all, Spencer was an outsider—but he didn't.

Eh, Kong thought, my face has always been too open. He thought of the many times his wife had complained at his lack of guile, a quality dangerous for all *zhi shi fenzi,* intellectuals, who came of age first during the famine, and then the Cultural Revolution. "You worthless bone!" she had accused him, so often—"Think before you speak! Breathe through the same nostrils as your superiors! Consider every step, every word—" Of course, she had been right, Baoling had; the slightest mistake during those years—when an idle story told by one man could instantly become fact in the mouths of ten thousand—could bring a man down, and all his family with him. Kong had been one of the lucky ones. He had survived, his wife and son had survived, and he had been allowed to continue as an archaeologist. "Elder cousin," he said now, "it is difficult to call you from this place. But be assured I will call—if anything occurs."

"Thank you," the vice director said. *"Duo bao zhong."* Guard your health.

"Bici."

When he had hung up and stepped out onto the iridescent limestone steps and down into the dirt street, Professor Kong replayed the conversation in his mind. The hunter-gatherer work, that was what he wanted now. He hoped he'd been sufficiently casual with his cousin. He hoped he'd handled it right. He wanted all his doors left open.

The soldier who had been standing stiffly at the entrance to the cave motioned to Kuyuk. "They may enter now."

They all scrambled to their feet and exchanged looks. The previous day they'd had a taut verbal struggle with Lieutenant Shan. There had been proposals and counterproposals, feinting and parrying; several times they'd prepared to walk out, ready to abandon the idea of entering the cave—and paying Lieutenant Shan—altogether. Side issues—the inconvenience of the foreigners' presence in a military area, the inevitable damage to archaeological sites and artifacts from military activity—were raised and bartered back and forth. Finally a deal was struck. Spencer counted out six hundred and sixty in American bills, money from Alice's credit card, which the lieutenant folded and stuck in his pocket. No forms, no receipts. It's called the *hou men,* Alice explained to Spencer, The back door.

Then this morning they had waited on the rocks for hours, wondering if the PLA's vault people would ever be able to get the pressure lock open. Watching while the line of uniformed soldiers faced them with their assault rifles cocked and ready. "What, do they think we're going to rush the missile bay?" Spencer had whispered.

Now they stood up trembling in the blazing light, brushing off the yellow dust and trying not to scream with excitement.

"Ready?" Kong asked.

"All backpacks and supplies remain outside!" barked the senior PLA officer, who had emerged from the mouth of the cave covered with dirt and sweat. "Only flashlights! Form a single line!"

Alice put this quietly into English. Spencer piled his day pack on the ground with the others. "Camera?" he asked her hopefully.

"You out of your mind?"

"Okay," he groused.

"*Zou!*" the officer barked.

"Move," she translated.

Kuyuk led them, Kong, Spencer, and Lin following. Then Alice. They filed cautiously into the cave, lit now by powerful hand-torches.

Alice watched Lin's back as she stepped over the rock floor. This is where he touched me in the dark the other day, she thought.

Lin caught the memory, too, turned back to her, just an instant, then looked away.

They came to the petroglyph. She gazed at it in the good light from the soldier's handheld lamps. It was small, like the others, but beautifully wrought. And protected here, in the cave. The whole head was the sun, warm rays streaming from it; the face a wide-eyed, inquisitive monkey. Just like the carvings in the other canyons. Like the picture. Like the message in the margin of Teilhard's letter, the drawing and the words *This is it*. This *was* it. She felt the thrill a pilgrim feels, crossing into the holy land.

"Come on," Spencer called from up ahead.

Armed soldiers stood rooted in a row by the submarine lock. The massively engineered door yawned open.

They stepped through one at a time.

On the other side a cavernous room opened around them, weirdly illuminated by the roving flashlight beams. In its center hulked some massive thing draped in tarpaulins.

It was box shaped, roughly the size and shape of a small truck. Alice edged away from it. A large, densely charactered sign shrieked warnings. She shivered when she recognized the characters *yuanzidan,* Nuclear. Never had she been anywhere near such a thing before.

The armed men filed in and took up posts around the missile.

Spencer spoke in the softest voice, as if more might detonate it, and Alice's translation wove in behind. "Teilhard would have wanted the bones safe, but findable. Let's look the way he would have looked around here fifty years ago. Maybe he went further than just leaving it. He might have put it behind a rock, up a side passage. Not far. Just out of sight, that's what I think. So. Rock piles, rocks small enough to have been moved by one man, clefts in the walls, side passages . . ." He played his flashlight around the room, shook his head. "It's a big space. And I don't think our friends here are going to give us too much time."

Alice glanced at each face as she finished up in Chinese. They all fanned out across the rock floor.

Except Spencer, who sidled up beside her. "It's not a missile!" he whispered.

"What?"

"It's not a missile! Check it out."

She puckered her eyebrows and ran a cautious look from one end of the draped huddle to the other. "What are you talking about?"

"Walk around the far side. That corner—" He made a small movement with his eyes. "Look around the bottom, below the edge of the tarp."

She drew her brows together.

"Just don't let them see you."

She turned to walk in the opposite direction, and started in at the opposite end of the cave wall. She swept her flashlight beam methodically, then moved and looked behind, under, around, everywhere. She got hold of rocks with all her strength, tore her fingernails, turned them over, walked them to the side, anything not to miss a crate of hominid bones.

It was not until many tense, hard-breathing minutes later that she was able to get a look at the missile. Or not-missile. She was finally in position. Now, her moment. She passed her flashlight beam in a long, steady arc—the light merely passing by on its way to someplace else—over the low corner where the tarp was not straight, where what was underneath was, for a narrow strip, entirely visible.

She almost lost her footing on the dirt floor when she saw.

He was right. This was no missile.

It was gold. Gold bars.

Gold bars cross-stacked, rows of gleaming ingots. Unmistakable. It seemed to give off the very light, the incandescence, of wealth. No nuclear missile, just money. Business. *Yi pan san sha,* China is a plate of sand.

She gave no outward sign of having seen it, just went on working, studying the wall, probing, covering every inch. She would have liked to tell Lin. Talk to him, stand next to him. Here, though, in this place, it would have been insane.

"What's this?" Kuyuk called, and since it was the fourth time in an hour or so that someone had cried out, Look, or Come over here, or Hey, Dr. Spencer, nobody looked over at first. Kuyuk moved a boulder aside, and then sank into a careful squat. He made a small pile of rocks and pebbles as he picked each out of its resting place, and then furrowed his face, angling his flashlight straight down in front of him. He touched something hesitantly. Again he cried out, *"Na shi shenmo?"*—What's this?

Now Kong trotted over to him, and Lin. A second later their excited Mandarin spurted up over the damp cave quiet and Spencer and Alice crowded up behind.

"What?"

"Look." Lin's fingers outlined something square.

Alice leaned forward. Yes, oh, unbelievable. It was something square. A perfect, man-made square. A box.

Lin burrowed in a side pocket and drew out a clean cloth. Gently he swept the crumbs of stone away from what appeared to be a large black lacquered box. Around its edges could still be seen the ghost of scrolling gilt paint.

A box.

A crate.

And just the right size to hold skulls, bones, and teeth.

Peking Man.

13

ALICE SANK HARD to her knees, pulse hammering. The voices, bursting one atop the other in a thrill of Mandarin, and Spencer's English, first "My God," and then "Can you get it open?" but she couldn't speak, in either language, because for a moment speech lay entirely outside her. She squatted in the cave, in the flashlight-riddled dark, gasping, stunned.

It's here, she thought. We found it.

"Slowly," Lin was saying to Kong, who was bent over the box. "Be careful."

She trained her flashlight straight ahead and realized, with a start, that Lin was standing directly in front of her. His khaki-wrinkled leg rose before her face. *To connect the two energies, of the body and soul* . . . Without thinking she put out her hand, slipped it under the rough cotton cuff, and slid over the smooth knob of Lin's ankle. She felt him shudder, sensed the current of surprise through him.

Lin felt it. Everything about him was focused on Peking Man, yet still he answered her touch by pressing his leg back into her hand. "It's not locked, is it?" he said to Kong simultaneously.

She squeezed his ankle once and removed her hand.

"Locked? I'm not clear," Kong was saying as his slim, brushlike fingers explored the box's rim. He fluttered down to the dirt-crusted catch on its front, tested it.

A thrill of murmured tones raced around the little group as everyone trained their flashlights on the box. "No. It's not locked." Gently Kong manipulated the clasp.

In the hush of indrawn breath the click of the latch opening filled the air around them. Then, the soft creak of the lid. From the corner of her eye Alice glimpsed Spencer's blond putty face, haggard, triumphant.

The first to speak was Lin.

"Zenmo-le?" Alice heard him croak in disbelief. She craned over the hunched shoulders of Kuyuk, trained her flashlight beam into the yellow pool with all the others. The beam shone into a bottomless black hole, large and dusty.

It was empty.

"Mei shenmo," Kuyuk breathed.

"Nothing there," she translated.

"But the bones have to be there!" Spencer insisted.

Dr. Kong tipped the box so that its interior, bare and blank, aimed mercilessly at the face of the American.

"Jesus, this is terrible." Alice touched Spencer's shoulder.

"Looted . . ." Spencer shook out, fixing the box with a glassy-eyed stare.

She sent a desperate glance to Lin. The Chinese scientist was already looking at her, his maroon lips flat with sorrow and frustration. "We'll just have to keep trying." The painful words squeezed out of him. "Won't we?"

No one answered.

"After all," Dr. Lin croaked, "water wears through a rock."

* * *

Outside in the light the soldiers, who by now understood that the artifacts had been stolen at some point, herded the group to the side of the cave entrance. "Wait," the group leader ordered.

Then he opened his cell phone and dialed the Public Security unit from his base. As soon as someone answered he started shouting angrily into the little phone he clutched to his face.

"What's he saying?" Spencer hissed.

"You're not going to believe this." She shook her head. "He's reporting the theft."

"What!"

"Well . . ." She hesitated, wondering how to explain it to Spencer. Life in China always followed a particular logic, and he just didn't see it yet. "From his point of view, there's been a crime. Now he has to go through the appropriate steps. Relax. He doesn't think *we* took it."

"I should hope not! Does he realize it's probably been gone for thirty or forty years?"

"Maybe," she said. "Not that it would matter."

Spencer emitted a croak of disbelief and buried his head in his hands. Kuyuk stood off to the side, studiously ignoring things. Kong and Lin simply tolerated it. They didn't bother arguing with the soldiers or suggesting that an investigation would waste everyone's time. Instead they stood, staring out over the ledge to the canyon below, lost in their regret and frustration, waiting for these military functionaries—who, Kong and Lin being scholars, were naturally beneath them in the general hierarchy of things— to finish their job.

Half an hour later the Public Security men arrived, exhausted and annoyed at the long climb from the lamasery. They were taken quickly inside to see the scene of the crime, and then hustled right back out by the soldiers.

A lengthy and heated discussion ensued between Public Security and the soldiers as to who bore responsibility for the theft. The soldiers insisted that the police should have taken better

precautions with such a National Cultural Treasure; the officers
retorted that the cave was a nuclear missile silo and therefore
under the purview of the Army; moreover, who knew Peking
Man was in there in the first place? Everyone unburdened themselves of blame. No resolution was reached. The loud voices
gradually died down. Kong, Lin, and Kuyuk waited in patient
silence, while Alice translated quietly for Spencer.

Finally the officers drafted a statement, read it aloud, and had
everyone initial it. In a last flare of self-righteous fury they
handed the empty box to Dr. Spencer and stomped away back
down the mountain.

"All right," the military group leader said at last when the
police were out of sight, "you may go."

At the lamasery they piled into their jeep and bounced back in
silence. Spencer slumped on the window. "Adam," Alice tried
once, touching his arm, and he said in reply: "What am I going
to do now?"

"I'm so sorry," she said quietly, feeling for him. And on the
other side of her was Lin, burning with his own pain and loss.
She knew how he'd longed for this. She saw. They jolted in
silence all the way to Eren Obo.

At the guesthouse Kuyuk said good-night. Dr. Kong and Dr.
Lin showed as little as possible, though the veneer of hurt in their
faces was clear. Spencer hardly spoke at all.

Lin and Kong said the box should be left overnight in Spencer's room, but Spencer made a barring gesture. "Don't bring
that thing near me!"

So Dr. Kong shrugged and carried it upstairs. Spencer followed. It was just Lin and her. He started to say good-night, then
stopped. "Do you remember when we sat on the bridge in the
middle of the night in Yinchuan?" he asked.

"Of course," she said quietly.

"You asked me—do you remember or not—had I ever wished my life could be different?"

"Yes," she said, mesmerized.

"I did not tell you the truth. The truth is, I wish it." He looked miserable. "I wish we had found the bones today. I wish we could have brought our ancient ancestor back. I wish I either had my wife or else I—I knew her fate."

She felt numb when she heard the last sentence, so full of yearning. "I know it's hard for you."

"Yes." He sighed. She felt his eyes moving over her. "You're a good woman, Mo Ai-li. I'm not sure if you understand how it is with me, with my commitments. I wouldn't want to hurt you."

Maybe you wouldn't have to hurt me, she thought.

He turned resolutely and walked up the stairs.

"Peaceful night," she called softly, but he did not hear.

Alice awoke. For a moment she clung to the void, and then remembered. Crash. Peking Man stolen from the cave. Who did it? When? How many decades?

And another thing.

What if she let herself fall in love with Lin Shiyang?

If they kept going like this, they were going to sleep together. She closed her eyes, imagining how it would be to let herself go with him, to have him inside her and wrapped around her and to come: the high tide, the Chinese called it, the flooding instant without a mind or heart. To come with him. Oh, God. What if she let it happen?

Then again *he* might not let it happen, because of Meiyan. Or he might let it happen only partway. *Keep free of myself, if possible, Lucile, in having me.*

Yet Lucile had taken the chance, hadn't she? She had loved Pierre Teilhard de Chardin anyway.

And what had she gotten for it, actually? Too little. In the end she grew old alone. Alice's eyes strayed to the little altar she had half hidden behind a stack of Teilhard's books. She should do more for her ancestors, she thought guiltily. Lucile would probably help her if Alice served her better in the world of ghosts. It came to Alice that she should go out and get some ritual objects. Things like incense, fruit. Well-omened characters on silk ribbons. Paper money.

There was a store in the town that sold such objects, Alice recalled suddenly, feeling almost inspired. This was the thing to do. She got up and washed quickly, climbed into her jeans, dug around for her wallet, and went out.

Several miles from the town, in the clutch of loess-brick administrative buildings he used as his headquarters to command both Yinchuan and the area around Eren Obo, Lieutenant Shan called his subordinates together.

"Listen, you whores. The west-ocean outsiders have failed. They found the box in which Peking Man was hidden, but some clever fornicating person had already stolen it. Huh! And sold it profitably, I'm sure. Anyway, it's obvious now the foreigners will not find the ape-man. They may keep trying, but all they'll do is squat in the outhouse—squat and produce nothing." He chuckled and lit a cigarette, drew in deeply.

"Moreover," he continued. "I've received word from Beijing. They have no further interest. So—do your mothers. As of now the surveillance is canceled." Smoke drifted from his mouth. "I don't have any more time to waste on these foreigners anyway." He looked around the room. "Go on, out."

* * *

Lin Shiyang spent a long time by his window that morning, watching the dark ridgeline change along the mountain crest. First dawn, the sun screaming from behind the mountains. Then the brilliant blue bowl of midday. He stared unhappily at the world's transformation.

What was more brutal than the loss of hope? Now they would not restore Peking Man to China after all. Would not attract the money to excavate new sites, even to finally sort and catalog and properly store the appalling disarray of *Homo erectus* fossils which still remained from the Zhoukoudian site. Would not clean up the mess which had begun when most of the Peking Man bones disappeared in 1941 and whirled out of control when the Cultural Revolution came, and the students seized what bones were left and poured them out on the floor and ground them under their feet—if only, now, they could have borne back the original Peking Man. That would have reversed things.

They had started in such hope. He recalled as if it had just occurred the electrically charged scene three weeks before in Zhengzhou, when the department head had given them this assignment. How shocked he had been when the man mentioned Yinchuan, and Inner Mongolia! How he had gaped at his director—the stocky little man with the receding chin and the bottle-thick glasses and the perpetual stacks of files on his desk—who'd had no idea that Lin's wife had vanished in this remote place twenty-two years before.

But she did, and she's gone.

Then admit that she's dead.

Meiyan dead.

Lin couldn't bear this thought, this black door. Inside was a pain so sharp, so barbed with guilt, he could not go near it. So he thought: Out! Must go out. Paralyzing, these four walls. He hurried down to the street, then up the hill and to the intersection. The monochromatic labyrinth of buildings, the dark wall of mountain—somehow it comforted him. It couldn't really be said that she was dead, he reassured himself. No. Her fate was simply unknown. He could approach Mo Ai-li.

Then what of the promise you made?

He twisted uncomfortably into a faster walk. "You don't have to wait for me," Meiyan had told him. "But I will," he'd replied, even as he sensed the far-off foreboding of doom. How could he have said otherwise? She was, of the two of them, the superior being. The better Chinese. Where she had upheld the truth, he had swayed with the wind. So since she'd been taken he waited, which seemed the least he could do. His liaisons with women allowed the *yang* part of him to flower once in a while, but they never disturbed his true self. His true self rested intact.

Yet now he'd looked for Meiyan and found nothing. It was if his wife had never been here.

And now the line was drawn and the stage was set with an outside woman, an aware woman, a woman who could hear one thing yet grasp ten others. It was a kind of intellect and soul the Chinese prized. He walked harder, picturing the small freckled face and the blunt-bottomed red hair. The way she sat right down out in the desert, sat shockingly the way a Westerner does, her ass in the dirt, her blue jean legs crossed. The way she talked directly into his face.

All of him, his mind, his heart, his *yang,* could not stop dwelling on it.

He paused in front of a small brick store that sold death-ritual objects. Its huge, brilliantly colored displays of paper flowers held his gaze. Silk ribbons of every color ran from the standing wreaths like tears. Poles, tented with tasseled white paper, hung down their curtains of white streamers. This was lamaistic, Mongolian. It was different from the stores in Shanghai he remembered his mother going into when he was a child. That had been another world, the twilight of another time. Now he would never enter such a store. He was not some *tu*, backward peasant, but a modern man.

So he felt it as a shocking drop in his midsection when he heard the female voice that had been enthralling his imagination, flattened by its American accent, call out to him sharply from within the store:

"Eh, Lin Boshi!"

It was Alice, running out, taking his hand impulsively and then dropping it. "See who I've walked into—Ssanang, the Leader's daughter."

The Mongol woman, taller than Mo Ai-li, stepped out. "I came here to buy things. It is the first anniversary of my aunt's death."

"Lin, listen," Alice burst in. "She has a photograph!"

Eh, those eyes. Inhuman nearly. "Of what?"

"Of Teilhard!" she cried. "And Lucile!"

"Lucile Swan?" he repeated.

"Don't you understand?" Mo Ai-li demanded. Her hand slipped out to touch his again. "It means Lucile must have come here with him in 1945. She was here in Eren Obo."

"But the Leader did not tell us this."

"It was not asked," Ssanang explained. She took a small book from her pocket, extracted a tattered picture, and handed it to him.

He bent over it with Mo Ai-li. The priest and the American woman stood small and wartime serious in the frame, arms folded, by a low cluster of buildings. Behind them a strange W-shaped cleft marked the mountain ridge.

"What is this place?"

"No one knows. One of the Leader's men went with them and made the photo. It was a place the priest asked to be taken. That is all we knew."

"It looks like someone's home."

"The Mongol family?" Alice asked.

He met her eyes briefly and then turned the picture over, as if some clue might be on the back. It was empty, crisscrossed only with a web of fine sepia crack-lines. "What about the men who accompanied them to this place?"

"Dead many years."

He blinked.

"I heard what happened in the cave yesterday," Ssanang said quickly. "That you found the box, and someone had removed Peking Man. Pitiable! Keep the picture. It has no use for us."

"Do you think we can find this place?" Alice asked.

"If you look"—Ssanang paused—"be careful. The Army is everywhere. Now I must go. My aunt's memorial."

They watched her carry her purchases away down the hill.

Mo Ai-li stood close to him. He could feel the radiant warmth from her body, see her small chest heaving. If they were not in public he would have only to raise his hands and slip them around her shoulders, turn her toward him. . . . He closed his eyes a second. He wanted to slide his hands under her shirt and feel her. Would he do it? Would he? Yes. If they were alone.

"Lin Boshi," she was saying. "Suppose Peking Man was actually removed by someone who was supposed to remove it? Who had been asked to do so by Teilhard?"

"What?" He looked down. "Interpreter Mo. In archaeology, when artifacts are taken, it is always by looters. Thieves. Why, Dr. Spencer has said in your own country, the Native American sites—"

She shook her head. "This is different, out here. And Lucile came here with Teilhard, don't you see? That changes everything."

"How?" he asked, wanting to listen to her talk.

"Well. It proves Teilhard confided everything in her. And she would have wanted to make sure Peking Man was never lost. It was the key to his legacy. So I think, she might have seen to it that he arranged for someone to come and remove it. Later. It was because she loved him," she said.

"Ni shuo ta ai shenfu?"

"Of course she loved him. These people." She turned back to the photograph. "This house. *This* could be the Mongol family."

"Yet even the Leader and his men do not know where it is."

"I bet they didn't really try to find out."

"Mo Ai-li." He allowed himself to run his hand once over her hair. He saw her eyes soften. *"Wo kan ni zai zuo meng,"* I see you are still dreaming. "Listen. Since the separation of heaven and earth, men have sought glory. And this, to find Peking Man again, would be the greatest glory to me. It is our ancestor. It is a thing beyond price. But I think it is not on my road."

"Can't a road be changed?"

No, he thought sadly, it cannot; only a fool would even imagine that it could. But this he dared not say. She might take it to mean they could not try love together either—and that he could not bear to rule out. So he shrugged and said nothing.

She only smiled. "Let's tell the others."

They turned to walk back. He didn't ask—somehow he didn't really want to know—what she had been doing inside a death-ritual store in the first place, a feudal place for ignorant *tu* people, out here in Eren Obo.

They huddled over the photo in the guesthouse lobby.

"I know Alashan Banner, every step of its earth," Kuyuk insisted again. "How is it I cannot recognize this place?"

"Maybe it's outside the Banner," Kong said.

"Yet one of the Leader's men took them here."

"What do you think, Adam?" Alice asked.

"I think it's gone," he said flatly. "We found Teilhard's box, right in the cave, near the rock art, right where it was supposed to be. But Peking Man had been taken."

"But now we have a new lead," she insisted.

"You call that a lead? It's a picture."

"But . . ." She looked at the photo. "Okay, yesterday we were at a dead end. I admit that. But things change."

"Do they?" Spencer looked at her. His eyes said, Look at you, look at your life, has anything ever changed? "You think so."

"Yes," she said defensively, "I do." She turned to Dr. Lin. *"Ni shuo zenmoyang?"*

"I think we should continue on. Of course! This is something very important. We must keep looking."

She smiled at him. *"Wo tongyi,"* I agree. "Dr. Kong?"

Kong thought. "It's like this," he said slowly. "Is there a chance to find the relics now? Yes. Perhaps. But it is a thing so distant now, so unlikely. . . ." He paused. *"Ke yu er bu ke qiu,"* Only blind luck will bring us upon it, not searching. "Therefore. Since we have found an undreamed-of quantity of hunter-gatherer artifacts, of the highest quality under heaven—enough to support research for many years—I for one would prefer to continue surveying these sites and collecting artifacts." He looked at Adam. "Are you with me, Dr. Spencer?"

Adam listened to Alice's translation and nodded decisively to Kong. "Yes. Let's do it—survey, plan, come up with a good research design. It's true. The Late Paleolithic opportunities out here are beyond anything I ever imagined." He opened his book and made a note. Alice could see him blocking Peking Man from his mind, putting another beacon in its place.

"Of course"—Kong looked at Alice and Lin—"if you two wish to continue to look for Peking Man, I invite you. Please."

Alice and Lin exchanged glances. Be alone together, all day? Quickly they looked away.

*　*　*

After the meeting broke up she walked by herself to the edge of the town. At its boundary Eren Obo's hard-won civilization vanished all at once in the rock-strewn dirt. Then there was rolling yellow earth, ascending ever so gradually to the brown apron of mountain in the distance. Winded, scratching at the rivulets of sweat inching down through her hair, she slumped down by the side of the road.

She didn't have to wait long. A truck came roaring out from the village. She jumped up and signaled.

It ground to a stop.

"Elder brother." The Mongol in the truck held on to the wheel with one callused hand, and with the other clutched the groaning gearstick. "I beg help. You are going to Yinchuan?"

He nodded, and spat casually onto the ground.

"I need a message delivered to someone there." She held up the envelope. "I will gladly pay you ten dollars American to do this thing which is so important to me." She passed him the envelope with a U.S. bill, noting that his eyes widened in a favorable way. "The address is written on the outside."

He looked at it and froze.

Oh, she thought, he can't read characters. She rushed to explain. "The man's name is Guo Wenxiang. It is one seventy-eight Gansu Street, the Chinese quarter. Can this be remembered?"

He secreted what she'd given him in his clothing, creased his dark face into a grin. *"Ni fang xin hao,"* Put your heart at rest. No further pleasantries, then, as there would have been with a Chinese; he simply nodded, gunned the engine, and drove off.

She watched the dust spit up behind him, watched until he was a distant drone and then a moving dot miles away, in and out of sight among the switchbacks on the first flank of mountain. Then finally, the dot entered the sunbaked pass and vanished. She thought about what she had written in the note to Guo Wenxiang. How to find them in Eren Obo should he need to. Was there any news of the Mongol family—and, oh, yes, most privately important to her: had Guo learned anything of the fate of Zhang Meiyan?

14

PEKING MAN.

Alice envisioned the creature's skull for the hundredth time: the flat brainpan, the thrusting underbite, the staring eyeholes of death.

What had Kong said of Peking Man? *Ke yu er bu ke qiu,* It cannot be found through effort now, only by chance. And remote chance at that.

She pulled the *ling-pai* from the drawer and chose a new spot for it, the rickety bedside table. She had bought a few bright paper cards in the death-ritual store, and she propped those before the plaque. What else? No food, no incense—she looked around. Tea. She opened up the little box by the thermos, crumbled some of the leaves off the tea brick, and piled them in front of the tablet. It wasn't much, but it would do. She bowed her head.

Meng Shaowen, Lucile Swan. Help me.

She sat there numbly, aware that she didn't really know what she asked. Help her find Peking Man—was that what she wanted? Or help her with Lin Shiyang?

Teilhard said all things happened in relationship to each other. Life and matter, like one single organism. You had only to look at it, to be in it.

If only.

She sat silently, emptying her mind, waiting. Mother Meng, you loved your husband. Lucile, you loved Pierre. Guide me.

But she felt nothing from the *ling-pai,* nothing. It was just a wood plaque inscribed with some characters and marked with a dried-up blotch of her blood. Her knees hurt from sitting so long. The sounds outside distracted her, the scattered voices in Mongolian, the far-off clanking of machinery. She couldn't rid herself of an image, a thing she seen earlier in the courtyard: a girl, singing to herself, using a glowing-hot poker to singe the shaved, pearl-colored skin of a just-slaughtered lamb.

She knocked on Lin's door but he had vanished, gone somewhere, and so she took the photograph and left by herself. She paced up the wide, half-empty main street. A few twisty, scrubby trees had been planted, but mostly it was the low, unrelieved ocher boxes of buildings, the repeating power poles, the packed earth and desert sky. She walked past hardware stalls, produce and meat markets, with the open space and noise level of small airplane hangars. She passed a crude beauty shop: two seats, two tin basins. In wind-rattled windows she saw herself. She was short, autumn colored, shockingly different from the dark, erect, self-possessed people of the town. In America she'd always been called cute. Here she just looked different. She hated cute. Different was better.

She climbed down the shallow bank to the creek and sat by the trickling water for a while. Where was Lin? She had no right to ask him where he went, she knew that, but she still yearned to know. As if he were hers already. Foolish girl.

She stared at the stream. It was no more than a thin little gully, but spread out all around it in a blessed alluvial strip was a carpet of deep green. Even just the tiny sound of the water, and the rippling of the breeze in the grass, relieved something parched in her. She never had enough to drink in Eren Obo. Water was strictly apportioned, and she got only one boiled thermosful a day. Strange how she'd adjusted down to it. Hoarded aside enough for washing, and measured out the rest. It was just enough. But it always left her wanting more.

Should he give up? Lin asked himself. He sat on a pile of smooth white limestone rocks in a grove of poplars, looking at a clear pebbled stream. He'd caught a ride to this village called Long Bin. Behind him was the one dirt-road intersection and a single stucco building, directions to other villages painted on it in big red characters. The building fronted a big sunbaked open space that served as the village square. He'd been talking to a man who now stood at the top of the bank, wearing a straw fedora, sunglasses, and a loose white shirt. "It's regrettable we knew nothing of your wife," the man said.

"Never mind. I've troubled you too much, elder brother."

"Don't talk polite. Old Yuan is leaving soon for Eren Obo. He'll give you a lift back."

"Thank you."

"Nothing. A trifle."

Lin looked up through the columns of poplars. It was so hot. The sky was so pale, almost white—baked of color. Exhausted, like this settlement, with its one whitewashed building and its paths, radiating out to its irregular spattering of mud huts.

Like his idea of ever finding out what had happened to his *airen*. No one seemed to know. No one anywhere he went.

* * *

They met back at the guesthouse. He didn't say where he had been. She didn't ask.

They went out and walked in the waning sun up to Eren Obo's plaza—a brick circle, concentrically ringed with pink hollyhocks. In the center stood a statue of a camel, head and foreleg nobly raised.

Some Mongol men were playing on the bricks, hitching up their loose cotton pants and haggling over their chesslike game. Their playing board was a square of paper marked in a strange, complex geometric pattern. A player moved a piece. All the men cheered.

"Excuse me." She squatted next to one of the Mongol men and spoke in slow, clear Chinese.

"Outside woman!" he squawked, his accent heavy. He looked up at her and Lin.

"Do any of you know this place?" She extended the photograph. The men craned over it and erupted in their own language. Alice and Lin listened, exchanging looks. The Mongols didn't know. The hesitant, speculative rhythm of their speech was obvious.

"Sorry, foreign lady," one concluded in Chinese.

"It's nothing. Thank you," Lin said. By the time they had turned back into the rings of hollyhocks the men were playing again, exhorting one another, laughing.

As they walked she wondered when Lin was going to tell her about his family. She was waiting for him to reveal more about himself. Talking about families signaled serious intent in Chinese erotic relations. It brought honor to the equation.

And what was honor for her? Taking Lin home to meet Horace? Never. Although she loved her father in her own way— even needed him—she knew enough now to keep a man like Lin far away from him. She was older now, stronger. She'd never cave in to Horace again, not like she had with Jian. She would live according to the center of herself, and Horace would not be permitted to have an opinion.

Startling, how simple it sounded.

In this daze of realization she walked beside Lin for most of the afternoon, feeling calm. They talked only a little. As Teilhard had written to Lucile, *let us not discuss too much about words.* . . .

But they found nothing. By now everyone in the town knew what they were looking for before they approached. "Let me see the picture!" the townspeople would bark. They would study it and, almost to a man and woman, be crossed by an instant of genuine pain and forfeiture—this small chance to be a hero, lost—before they shook their heads, and said no, truly a pity!— but they did not know this place.

Back at the guesthouse, they separated to rest before dinner. She addressed him lightly as Dr. Lin, Lin Boshi, and then wondered about the word. *"Boshi,"* she said. "Doesn't that mean 'Ph.D. doctor' as opposed to 'medical doctor'?"

"It does. To earn the Ph.D. is one of the highest goals in our society. We say: *Wanban jie xia pin weiyou dushugao,*" Except for attaining a higher education, all pursuits are lowly.

"It's always been that way, hasn't it?" she asked. "Since the Imperial Examination system."

"But the role of the court academician was different from the role of the Ph.D. today," he clarified. "The court academician was more than a scholar—he was an exemplary figure. He held the highest responsibility to adhere to the codes and rules."

"Yes, I know. The codes and rules." This had always fascinated her, China's massive, nuanced structure of obligations and principles. Though where all the codes and rules ended in China, the precise point at which they dissolved into secret sex and a ruthless gulag and rampant bribery and a million other knife-points, including the Chaos—that was the thing that had always *really* intrigued her. All that lay behind China's ordered, polite, honorific veil.

Lin Boshi.

"See you at dinner then," she said.

In her room, she decided to put away the *ling-pai*. It was starting to seem like a bad idea to have it out. She studied the characters as she moved the folded clothes aside, placed the tablet at the bottom of a drawer. *Meng Shaowen, passed over July 14* . . . Yet where was Meng Shaowen? In these last few weeks, despite all her rituals, the old woman had only slipped farther and farther away from her. Meng was gone from this world. Face it, she thought. You'll never have a mother. Not Meng. Not Lucile Swan.

You have only one ancestor. Your father, Horace.

Underneath the *ling-pai* she saw a glimmer of color, and recognized the silk stomach-protector. Her heart raced. What if Lin were to see this? She crumpled the bit of silk into the smallest possible ball, and pushed it to the farthest, jumbled corner of the drawer. No, Lin wouldn't see it. She would never let that happen.

They walked after dinner and questioned people until the daylight began to fail. *"Lei-le ma?"* he asked.

She nodded. He was right, she was tired. But not from the walking. From failing. Someone had to know something, and yet no one did.

She glanced at Lin. "Do you remember when we were in the cave? Did you notice anything strange about the missile?"

His eyes met hers sidelong. "You mean, that it was not a missile?"

"Yes! Did you see—did you—"

He made a sound to cut her off, to stop her from defining everything so much. "We sometimes say in Chinese: you simply wait until the fog lifts, then—*ni renshi lu shan zhen mian-mu,* You see the true face of Lu Shan Mountain. Do you understand me or not, Mo Ai-li? We have lived in our Chinese world always. To us this true face of things is not so mysterious."

"I see," she insisted. She knew with this inference he was touching on all that the masses had feared, and learned, and come to painfully accept, about their government and their military. All she had never had to live through herself, but had read about, analyzed, mulled over countless times. "I understand."

"Though truly, how can you?" he countered sadly.

Pain rose, hot and prickly, behind her eyes. So close to him, to China, yet always shut out. "Please don't do that," she said softly.

"Oh, yes." He closed his eyes, remembering. "*Duibuqi.* Forgive me. I didn't intend to hurt you. It's just—you're a strange story from beyond the seas, Interpreter Mo. Sometimes I don't know where I am, who I am, talking to you."

"*Bici,*" she answered, which meant she felt the same.

"There is so much I did not know—did not do—before I met you. Ah," he said, "*Daole.*" We're here.

And they said good-night.

It was hotter than usual in Alice's room. The still air pressed in through the wide-flung windows and brought all the life of the night from outside: a squealing night raptor flapping down on some prey, the distant roaring engines of motorcycles from across the town, finally a jeepload of young soldiers careening up and parking in the courtyard beneath her window. As they drank beer, their voices detonated off in laughter and Chinese songs from the distant provinces. Finally the soldiers gunned their vehicle to life again and blared away, leaving their bubbles of talking and giggling and the roar of their engines to evaporate in the air. Alice looked at her watch. Ten forty-five. Useless. She'd never go to sleep.

She dressed and walked quietly down the hall. All the doors were closed, the lights were out. Everyone was sleeping. She brushed quickly out into the street. Immediately she felt a lift. Like all desert places, Eren Obo had a second life in its late summer evenings. There was a pleasant breeze. People were walking around.

She hurried up the main street and turned off into the low monochromatic labyrinth that radiated away from it. The creek was nearby, she could hear it. She scuffed along a row of dusty oleasters, listening to the water gurgling down below. This was the older part of town. Instead of the methodical yellow two-story buildings, with their rows of square-paned windows and flat roofs, here strode the lumpy, hand-built loess houses, like the ones she had seen out in the country, thatched roofs over their rafters, the houses that had stood as misshapen parts of the desert landscape for hundreds of years. There was a temple complex too. Its ornate pagoda design was all out of place in the town. Yet it was lovingly kept. Water was spared on it. Its courtyards were profuse and miraculous with potted trees and flowers.

She stood to one side of the moon gate under an electric light, looking in. The gate wasn't closed, but she knew that the hour was too late to go in.

"Younger sister," said a male voice behind her, crumbly with age. She turned and stared into an old man's deep-etched, hooded eyes.

"Is it true as I've heard, you can speak?"

"Elder brother, I don't know what you have heard. Whatever it is, I'm unworthy." Outdated politeness.

He gave the breath of a wrinkled smile, lifted his scraggly white brows. "The talk's like this. A west-ocean girl, red hair, an apparition—who can speak."

She laughed. *"Narde hua."* It meant "Nonsense," literally, but she said it with a smile.

"I have not seen a foreigner in so many years. Trouble you to tell. Is the outside the same?"

"No, the world's changed. It's a telling that would have no end."

"Really."

"Yes."

He gave a quiet old puff of a laugh. Then he studied her, storing, she felt, every pore, every fleck of off-color in her eyes. "And you, American girl child? What caused you to learn our tongue? I don't suppose you can read?"

"Yes. Inadequately, but modern and classical Chinese both."

He tilted his head. "Remarkable."

"It's nothing, old uncle. But I ask you a question. I—I beg you a question. This place—" She dug out the photograph, and handed it to him. Don't get your hopes up, she warned herself. He examined it. "Do you know it?" she asked.

"I may travel a thousand *li* from my native place, but I would never forget it," he quoted dreamily, his gaze lost in the photograph.

What? She felt like a fish flapping in a dry gulch. "Does that mean—you say—I guess you're saying you don't know it."

"Know it?" He looked at her sharply. "Of course I do. It's my sister's farm."

A bolt of wonder jolted through her. Had he spoken those words? Had he? Or was she lost in an idiot's daydream? "Did you say you know this place?"

"Well, it's not my sister's, precisely," he clarified. "I am Chinese. This family's Mongol. But my sister married one of the sons, long ago." He fell silent, staring at it. "This is an old picture. Where did you get this?"

"Ah. From these people"—she pointed to Teilhard and Lucile with a trembling finger—"you see, they're outside people. They are . . ."

"Your relatives?" he prompted. He was glancing from the picture to her, Alice noted, no doubt comparing her to Teilhard and Lucile. To the Chinese, all white people looked alike.

"Well . . ." *Lie.* "Yes. My relatives. I must contact the Mongol family that lives here." She pointed to the building behind Teilhard and Lucile. "They are old friends. And I bear a—a message."

"How can it be? Such a coincidence."

"Can you give me directions to this place?"

"The pleasure's on my side." He turned over the photograph and wrote quick, looping characters across the back, sketched a simple map. "Imagine! I do not usually come out in the night air. In my lungs there is cold. This evening I decided to go out. What if I had not?" He finished writing down the directions and handed her back the picture. "Eh, my regards to them. Now forgive me, I return home. Level road. Peaceful journey."

"*Bici,*" she said to his dignified, old-man nod, and then to his back as he turned and walked away from her, again, "*bici.*" When he had moved out of her sight around the corner she realized she was clenching the photograph in a trembling, white-knuckled fist.

She knocked softly. Lin's room was silent.

She knocked again. Of course, she had to wake him up, she had to—her hand darted out and tried the knob.

The door opened.

Inside all was dark.

A moment she stood still, then slowly under a faint cold wash from the slice of moon, all the room's shapes swam into view. The vinyl chair, the wood desk, the bed. In the bed the long huddled form, still.

She walked softly and knelt beside him. *"Lin Boshi,"* she whispered, allowing her left hand to touch his cheek. Dr. Lin. *Where all the rules dissolve into a million knifepoints.*

He breathed in with a faint groan. He did not rise up or cry out. He merely said her name, "Xiao Mo," plainly, as if her coming to him in the dark was a foreseeable fact of nature.

His hands came out from the warmth of the bed and took her face between them, exploring it as if to make sure, yes, it was really her, Little Mo. Then the hands fell away. *"Shenmo?"* he breathed, in the tiniest whisper, What is it?

She bent and whispered she had found someone who knew the photograph.

"Zhen-de ma?" Definitely?

She nodded.

"Deng yixia," Wait.

She stood back. He rose and dressed swiftly in the dark, right in front of her, while she held her breath and watched his gracefully moving shadow.

"Zou," he said, snapping his belt. Let's go.

They hurried outside, she relating quickly how she had met the old man outside the temple. They huddled under the lit front door of the guesthouse and studied the writing and the sketch on the back of the photo. There was the name of the valley, Purabanduk, and the few words explaining the road to take and where the canyons intersected. "Do you know where this is?"

"I think so," he said. "See here. This is the road we came in on. It's an ancient road, I heard the driver talking about it, it's surely the same one. And there's the pass, and here he seems to mark an opening in the foothills. There was a gap there, in the Great Wall, I remember. Perhaps we should see a dirt track leading off into this valley, Purabanduk."

She stared at the map. "Should we go there, right now?"

"Without the others?"

"Just to see if we can find it. Suppose there is a house? Just like in this picture? We don't have to approach it. We could all return together, tomorrow."

He smiled down at the photograph.

"But we need a car," she said.

"A car?" He shook his head. "No. What we need is a driver."

She looked at him strangely. "What are you talking about? I can drive."

"You can?" He stared.

"Of course, everybody in America can drive. It's not like here. We all learn. Driving's great, it's—" She stopped herself. The joy of the blacktop, the long desert view, the blood sunsets, the filling-station map on the seat next to you—he wouldn't understand. "Look, this might be the Mongol family. Could we take the jeep?"

His smile was wider now. "Why not? It is for our research, isn't it so?"

"Yes, but the keys . . ."

"Ah, I know where the driver leaves them. I have seen. He puts them on the right front tire."

She stared at him. "Isn't he afraid someone will take it?"

"Take it? Take the car? Unlikely. First, not many people can drive. Second, the penalty for stealing a car's severe. You could go to the *laogai*. You could be shot. Why between heaven and earth would you do it? How could it be worth the price?"

"I see," she agreed, though what she really saw was that it was crazy: his own wife had gotten herself into the camps for what, a scholarly article? Was *that* worth the price? It was a kind of commitment, though, Alice knew; one of the time-honored Chinese ways of being a hero. A quality she, Alice, did not have.

"So you will drive to this valley?" He touched the photo.

"Of course."

"*Zou-ba,*" Then let's go.

The jeep waited in the hard-dirt yard behind the guesthouse. They went to it, climbed in quietly, and started it up. She checked the gas and water levels, then puttered quickly to the edge of the settlement. In the manner of all outpost towns, civilization—buildings, people, lights—fell away from them with unnerving suddenness when they hit the main road. In an instant it was all empty, the silty sea of desert and black mountains.

They bounced painfully on the first long stretch, a deep-rutted, unforgiving dirt track. But then they hit smooth pavement, and the road settled to silk and looped through the night. They were in the other realm now, in a car with a dark highway in front of them and the Tengger Desert all around.

"Don't you love it?" She crooked her left arm out in the night wind.

"Driving?" He drew his brows together, confused.

"Sure. I used to drive all the way to Laredo, all the way across Texas. Imagine. It's so hot you could die. And then Customs, the little linoleum room and the man with the shark-pressed khaki uniform, but fat, beer roll, the uniform's too tight, he checks your driver's license, he asks you the questions, you answer correctly because you know what to say and they send you out of the room and through a gate and you have left your country, you are over the border, now it's Nuevo Laredo. Mexico. Everything looks different. The houses are all these wild colors. The light is strange. It smells primeval. You're on Mars."

"You are talking about driving?" Lin attempted to clarify.

"About wanderlust," she answered, using the inadequate Chinese phrase, *re-ai luxing,* and pointing out the windshield. "This is it, the open road."

He stared at her.

"Wo shi yige luxing aihao-zhe," she tried again: I'm a wanderer. But still he did not click in. Texas—the road—he'd never know. How could he? Yet the strange thing was she had the same feeling right now that she'd had all those years ago, driving out west, to Tonopah. A free feeling. Leaving her old life behind. Becoming herself. Teilhard had done it: *Make me more myself, as I dream to make you reaching the best of yourself.*

She watched Lin switch on a small light inside the glove box and peer at the back of the photo again.

"You should start watching for a dirt turnoff on the left," he told her.

When they came to it she drove past, but he spotted it and she turned the jeep around. When she caught sight of the track she saw that it was little more than a faint tamped disturbance in the great prairie of loess, but a track it was, definitely, and it wound away from them toward the black foothills. She cut her speed and lurched onto it. The surface was rough. She braked more.

"A few miles, I would guess." His voice was tight, his hands gripped his knees.

Some small marmot-looking animal darted across their path, eyes refracting brilliantly in their headlights, then shot off into the darkness.

"See that?"

He nodded.

She concentrated on the bad road. To either side of them, piles of rock stood sentrylike on the desert floor.

"Soon we'll be climbing the ridge," he whispered.

Bumps, painful pitching jolts, each threatening to tear off the muffler or bend a tie rod. They bounced and rolled, gaining elevation. Finally in front of them the track curved gracefully to the right and swept through a break in the humped-up hills, and there, in that astonished second before the car dipped nose-down into the deep falling grade, they glimpsed the spreading valley, the sheep pens, the jumble of dwellings and outbuildings. It looked just like the picture, it *was* the picture. And up behind it, the strangely notched black ridgeline of the Helan Shan.

There were lights on in the house.

She and Lin exchanged glances, triumphant. Lights down below. That meant people. The Mongol family.

15

THEY TURNED OFF the car and stared at the valley below for a long, speechless while, then finally she started it up again, turned it around, and bounced away, back down through the pass. A dog had started barking. If they sat there any longer someone would notice.

"Lin," she said, her voice low with excitement, downshifting into the grade. She glanced over and saw that he was staring at her too. "Think it's the Mongol family? Can we hope?"

"I don't hope," he answered, eyes on her. "I never hope. I just live in gratitude for what comes."

It felt strange to be the open object of his gaze. She felt as if everything about her was lit up. She sat as erect and still as she could in the driver's seat, wishing she were tall and beautiful. He kept watching her while she eased the jeep down the hill and into the long flat stretch, steered through the scattered piles of rock.

"Xiao Mo," he said.

She glanced over. "Eh?"

"*Ting che.*" Stop the car.

"*Shenmo?*" What? She'd heard him, of course she'd heard

him, but it was too shocking, too unforeseen suddenly, and she had to pretend she hadn't heard. She had to make him say it again.

"Stop the car."

She oversteered on the narrow track, corrected. Okay. Stop. She pressed a long, steady foot on the brake and then rolled off a little ways into the dirt and cut the engine. The *craaack* of the emergency brake seemed to split the night and the desert in two. In the silence she felt the endless dry air around them, a universe of it, no one for miles. Emptier than Nevada, emptier than Death Valley. Tartary.

Lin climbed out. He took the old blanket from behind the backseat and spread it on the flat ground next to a pile of boulders.

She watched, hypnotized.

He walked back and opened the door on her side.

"Lin—"

He stopped her. "My name is Shiyang."

She caught her breath. This was the first time he had offered his given name. "I am called Alice."

"Alice."

She nodded. She followed him to the blanket, and lowered herself to sit on the ground opposite him, cross-legged. He sat studying her without a word for what seemed an endless time, then eventually reached over and grasped her gently by the hips, pulled her close to him, almost to his lap, carefully moving her legs until they were wrapped around his midsection.

She placed her hands on his shoulders. Fear erupted and she fought it down.

He only had to lean forward a few inches to brush her lips with his. His mouth was soft and dry like the mouth of a young boy. She kissed him back the same way, gentle, the way an inexperienced girl would, but with all the tender feeling she'd been keeping inside.

He paused, then kissed her again. This time he entered her mouth and touched her once, delicately. She bit his lower lip a little. Yes, she meant to say, I want it. So he came into her mouth again, but confidently now, and keeping a rhythm.

They kissed this way for a long time. She moved her hands over his back, his neck, his shoulders, but he sat very still. He used only his mouth. She felt she was going to explode. Then finally his hands left her waist, slid over her neck and through her hair, dropping to her chest and her small breasts.

"Shiyang," she breathed, enchanted by his name, the softness of his mouth, the longed-for feeling at last of him touching her. She arched her back to press herself into his hands. Finally after a long time his hand arrived between her legs and grasped her there, hard, right through her clothes. *"Pan-wangle hao jiu,"* he whispered, I've wanted it such a long time. He squeezed gently and her whole body cramped.

Ah, they would do it now, she knew; no more turning back. When she had been a young girl, learning about sex, there had been times when she had kissed a man like this, and touched and been touched, through her clothes, and then stopped. Not anymore. She understood now that kissing like this made all the promises, gave out all the rhythms of the love that was to follow. She knew that after kissing like this a man and woman didn't say no. They undressed each other, and lay down in the infinite night air, and did everything to each other they could imagine.

When, some hours later, they arrived back at the Eren Obo guesthouse, they slipped quietly into Lin's room together, and spent the rest of the night in his bed. They did not actually sleep until close to dawn, and then only for what seemed like a few minutes.

When she opened her eyes the light was growing stronger in

the room. She slid off and stood nude by the bed. *"Wo gai zou-le,"* she whispered, I should go. She pulled her T-shirt over her head, stepped into her jeans. She was probing his face. Was he happy? Did he regret it? Were they just beginning, or would he, having attained her, now get scared? As she had always done herself, with every man save Jian and then, finally—admit it— with Jian too. "Shiyang?" she asked.

"Go on," he whispered, and she could read in his face nothing but the mixture of awe, joy, and painful terror to which she knew, in her most honest heart, he had every right.

"You found this house?" Spencer stared at the picture. "You actually found this house?"

"I told you things could change," she said triumphantly, and repeated the story yet again—glossing quickly over the fact that she and Lin had taken the jeep and driven out there in the middle of the night.

Spencer didn't seem to fix on this anyway. Instead he was locked into the image of Teilhard de Chardin and Lucile Swan, as they had stood and soberly spoken to the camera with their eyes fifty years before. "Is everybody finished eating?" He looked up, excitement pulling his face into a grin, across the breakfast table from Lin to Kong to Alice. "Why are we waiting around?"

There was a sea change in the group. A whiff of hope had returned. Kong and Spencer postponed their search for new hunter-gatherer sites, even though Kong still insisted on sitting in the front passenger seat so he could watch the landscape for possible signs of Paleolithic habitation. Spencer shuffled through his notebook, reviewing all he'd written, tapping his pen against the spiral-bound pages.

In the backseat, Alice tried to focus on a Teilhard book but found herself unable to think about anything but Lin, next to her. Was he it, then? Her *true* Chinese man?

They crested the hill through the pass and saw, spread below them, the hamlet and the house.

Smoke curled from its chimney.

"Daole," Lin breathed, but no one answered, or saw any need to, for it was indeed the place from the photograph. In the spread of daylight, at the spot where Pierre and Lucile had stood for the picture, in front of some animal pens, there now toiled a garden. A complicated pipe arrangement fed it from the stream. More outbuildings had been added. But there was no doubt; it was the place.

Only one person was home: a woman. She was older, but not old enough to remember 1945. No, sorry, she had no knowledge of the visit these two white people had made here. They would have to return and talk to her old father. He would come back from Yinchuan in a few days. He had been a young man at that time. He would know.

They were dumbfounded. This was the first time someone had not told them the person is dead, or the records are lost, or no one knows. Here there was actually someone who knew. And he was coming back in a few days.

Alice wondered as they bounced back to Eren Obo, Lin next to her, their legs pressed together, if she should let herself believe it was possible. That they might find Peking Man. That she might trade in all her shame, let it go, forget it, and only worship her new ancestors, Meng Shaowen and Lucile Swan. She stole a look at the tall Chinese man next to her. That this might be real.

* * *

She lay in his arms. The bed was as narrow as a cot in a monastic cell, but to them it was as wide and joyous as any sumptuous bower. They were alone, safe and undisturbed. She moved against him, closer. "Did you ever think this would happen?"

"Before I met you? How could I dream it?"

"After, I mean."

"I hoped so." His hands moved over her, memorizing. No matter how much he touched her and grasped her and kneaded her, the different feel of her skin remained something he could barely comprehend. The tiny network of pores and freckles, the down on her arms and legs, her clean dusky smell.

"I thought you said you never hoped."

He laughed. Of course he had said that, but it had not been the truth. Sometimes, he hoped. He had hoped on the way out here, to the Northwest, that they might learn what happened to Peking Man. And he had hoped to find Meiyan. He had looked, he had asked people, had even made "gifts" to a few local district administrators to lubricate his casual-seeming inquiries. But nothing.

Had he done enough? Perhaps he should have found a way to leave the group for a couple of days, make his way somehow to Camp Fourteen, or at least the site of Camp Fourteen, for everyone said that it had been closed down in the late seventies. All the inmates, those still living, reassigned.

Reassigned. Her housing registration could be anywhere. Yet he knew that usually local authorities made the choices that were convenient. That meant assignment to nearby towns and villages. And now he was back at the beginning of the circle. For nowhere, anywhere he had gone, had he located a person who had heard of Zhang Meiyan.

And yet a foreign woman lay in his arms now, wide open to him, her legs twined through his—a creature more fascinating than any he had dreamed of since his wife vanished. *This is now*.

He smiled down at her. "No, I don't hope," he teased her. "But do you remember what else I said? I do practice gratitude."

"For what?" she said immediately. Ah, he knew, looking into her green gaze, that she wanted him to say it was for her. And was it not? He *was* thankful—thankful that she risked all this with him. That she was *shi yu yuan wei,* So physically direct. That unlike a Chinese woman, whenever she laughed it was true and unconstrained, it rose right up out of her the same way her high tide did during sex. And so this erupting, rolling laugh of hers, at any time, even—especially—when they were fully dressed, in public, pretending to be no more than colleagues, seemed to excite him in a way that connected him to the base of life itself.

"Grateful for what?" she pressed again.

"For you, of course. Foreign female! You don't know how to wait for anything, do you? Eh?" He smiled. "I'm going to have to teach you."

"No you're not."

"What? Why not?"

"Because I'm a foreigner, that's why."

"You don't seem like a foreigner. In fact, you talk like someone from my home province. Do you realize you speak with a *nanfang* accent?"

She grinned. "No, no. It's just right now, because I'm talking to you, and that's *your* accent. I can't help but repeat it back to you."

"Ah, so you mirror me. And where is the real you?"

"Behind the mirror." It was a flip answer, but she longed for him to come in after her.

He pulled back in play exasperation, though he kept a tight hold on the lower half of her body with his legs. "Behind the mirror, eh? Your talk is too clever. You should have been a high official. Perhaps a professor of philosophy! Or maybe—"

"An interpreter. I'm an interpreter, Shiyang."

He studied her face. He had wondered about this. She was so intelligent, so perceptive. Why had she not aimed higher? She could have attained any degree she wanted. She could have been a *zhuanmenjia*—An expert. "Did you always wish to be a translator?" he asked softly.

"Not really. It just happened that way." She looked away from him, knowing that at thirty-six she was little more than a go-between. She'd done nothing she could call her own. It was her fault. She had let herself drift here in China, allowed herself to be fascinated by the surfaces, the stereotypes of Chinese life. She had let sex carry her to the center of things.

"It's all right," he told her. "It's a good job."

"No, it's not."

He tightened his arms around her, then reminded her of that basic rule of Chinese life. "Boundless is the bitter sea."

"*Wo zhidao,*" she whispered, I know.

Adam Spencer sat in his room, looking at his son's photograph. Tyler James Spencer, ruffled blond hair, suspicious of the camera. Roaring down the street on his bicycle one minute, climbing up his father's leg the next. Adam had gone to California, to Stockton where Ellen and Tyler now lived, just before leaving the United States. It was Tyler's birthday and he took the boy for the weekend. He'd had high hopes, big plans, but after a desultory tour of the town sights they'd ended up in Adam's motel room, eating grocery-store cake and watching cable TV. Adam had felt awful. He knew that he should have handled it better somehow, made it magical. Found a swimming pool or miniature golf, something. As it was he only lay late into the night holding the sleeping child, his heart pounding. He saw no way to get back into his son's life. All he could do was go to

China. He could recover the original ancestor, find it, and leave the Spencer name on it. He could do that for Tyler.

Spencer wondered what the boy was doing, at this very moment, on the other side of the world. He might be sailing ships in the bath, reading Batman comics in the dusty crook under the stairs, or perhaps standing at quiveringly brave attention, bat in hand, on home plate.

Adam's eyes drifted from the photo to the pile of Teilhard books on his desk. There were editions of letters; biographies; and then Teilhard's own books of spirituality, geology, and archaeology. There was a lifetime's thought, painstakingly worked out, copiously set down. Thousands of pages, opining the unity of all things.

Spencer walked across the room and propped his child's picture atop the pile of books. Now the trail was warm once again. In two days they'd drive back out to the Mongol homestead and meet the old man. There was a chance, still a chance, they might recover Peking Man.

But what if they failed? He considered the question, gazing at Tyler's simple smile. *Yo, Dad!* he could almost hear his son say. *Catch!* I'm such an idiot, he thought suddenly. Tyler could care less.

It was even better between Alice and Lin that night. They had been together a few times, and by now felt free enough to adjust each other's bodies with their hands and mouths. To try things.

He held her back from coming. When she was close he pulled out and lay over her, whispering in her ear in gentle, Yangtze-accented Chinese while she squirmed beneath him, alternately laughing and begging.

"All around us right now the Tengger is full of microliths," he told her. "Arrowheads, the tips of spears—men were whittling them out there ten thousand years ago. Twenty thousand. Carving stone, shells, animal bones.''

"Are you trying to distract me?" she whispered, trying to maneuver her hips under him.

"No. I'm telling you something. We are fucking now in the center of the anvil." He used the crude slang, *cao,* fuck.

She found this departure from his usual polite speech unimaginably exciting and struggled to pull him to her. "So this was the beginning of the world?"

He laughed and pinned her hips down so she couldn't move. "No. The world began with Gun and his son Yu. Don't you know this? Everybody knows this. They were gods who could change into any animal they liked. The world was covered by water then. Gun and Yu had the secret of soil—earth which could contain water and dam it up"—he pushed lightly against her—"and they used the magic soil to create land masses. Do you want it, Ai-li? Do you? Then once Gun and Yu had made the earth, they gave the earth to men."

"Please!"

"Xing," he whispered hoarsely, okay, and drove in again. He moved inside her for a minute. "Now you tell me," he said into her ear.

"What?"

"How the world began."

"In the beginning was the word—and the word was with God—then in six days—in seven days—I don't know, Shiyang." She couldn't do this like he could, with words, not now, not when she felt herself rising rising rising. All she knew was, the whole of China was concentrated in him, moving with him, flowing into her. "The true Chinese man," she whispered, barely audible.

He looked down at her, his breathing ragged. He was a man, just a man, what did she mean?

But she could say no more. His rhythm had reached a perfect

frequency, brought him to some ultimate spot in the center of her. The great Tengger all around them, the dark room, the bed, even his face now, just above hers, swam away into darkness.

Later they lay open, waiting for a breeze, and he said: "I really do want to know."

"What? How the world began?"

"Aiya! Shuode shi ni de wenhua!" I'm talking about your culture!

She swallowed. The hot Houston nights, the radiant, space-colony skyscrapers, the forms of upthrusting light. Country music. Men in boots and hats. The bars and juke joints. Shame of her childhood. *Oh, you must be Horace Mannegan's daughter.* "I wouldn't know where to start."

"Start here. Where are you from?"

"I told you, Texas."

"I'm saying what country are you from? Before America."

"Oh. Different ones came from different places. Ireland, Germany, England."

He looked confused. "But what do you consider yourself?"

She hesitated. "I don't know. The truth is, I don't really think of myself as having a culture."

"But you are American."

"Not really."

"But of course you are American," he insisted. "And you are white. Not Chinese. That's the way of things." But he gathered her close to him as he said this, and held her protectively, as if to console her for her whiteness, her misfortune in not being Chinese. She had the sense that he forgave her all that she was. That there was a chance that she—her true self—might be acceptable to him.

*   *   *

319

Later she closed the door to her room, took out *The Phenomenon of Man,* and read once again the words written by Father Teilhard more than fifty years before: *Nowhere either is the need more urgent of building a bridge between the two banks of our existence—the physical and the moral. . . . To connect the two energies, of the body and soul, in a coherent manner. . . .* Well, then. The body and soul. The self and the other. *Settle down, Mother Meng said. With a strong Chinese man.*

The past was locked in behind her, barbed with mistakes. She hadn't stood up to Horace when she should have. But that was changed now. The future was up to her.

Could she do it? Could she keep house for Lin in Zhengzhou?

She thought it over. He would probably have a two-room cinder-block apartment, companionably lined with books, but cold and at the top of endless stairs and ringed by dozens of avidly nosy neighbors. Their lives would be ruled by his *danwei*—Zhengzhou University. A better work unit than most, maybe, but a monolithic institution nonetheless, one to which they would have to submit for every decision: when and where they might travel, what research he might undertake, what work she'd be permitted, even whether or not they might try to have a child.

Yet they'd be together. She could sleep in his arms. And every night and every morning, she could have him inside her again.

How long will *that* last?

Or, they could leave China.

They could live in America—but the thought seemed almost unimaginable to Alice. Whatever she was, she wasn't American any longer.

Could Lin even live there? She envisioned him in Houston, on the hot, dewy street, along Buffalo Bayou with its cicadas swelling in summer. This was the Houston of her childhood, the one that persisted in her mind. Then there was Houston now: the chaotic commercial growth, all the nouveau business rich, the white-collar army clogging streets and freeways every morning and afternoon, the young women with their overdressed hair, the men in their discount suits. All this perhaps Shiyang could learn to accept.

But in America, who would he be? It would take him eight or ten years just to master enough English to work in his field, and by then he'd be in his mid-fifties. Too old. Ah, he would wither there. He was too much *zhi shi fenzi,* an intellectual.

Zhi shi fenzi. Even the Chinese phrase emphasized his other-ness. It did not mean intellectual in the individual sense, but a member of the intellectual element. Like so many things in China, it was only spoken of in reference to its position in some-thing much larger. I guess that's a thing I've never had, Alice thought. A secure place in some larger mosaic.

The next day they drove back to the Mongol house in the Purabanduk Valley.

"This is the picture," Dr. Spencer said. "We know they vis-ited Eren Obo in the winter of 1945. The Leader has records of this. And look—it is your property. They must have come here."

He handed the picture to the Mongol patriarch, Ogatai.

"I remember. It was at the end of the Japan War."

The old man handed it back. His varnished face was flattened around the cheekbones, his eyes narrowed to almost nothing. A hanging mustache and bit of beard, white. "I was young then. The French scientist came here with the woman, from Peking."

"This Frenchman—did your family know him?"

"Know him? He was like one of us!"

With his dark eyes Lin threw silent congratulations to Dr. Spencer.

"We used to live on the other side of the Helan Shan," Ogatai explained. "By the Border River. The same place where the

Frenchman found the Shuidonggou site. He stayed with our family many months then, in 1923. We moved over here, but he always wrote letters to us."

Thousands of volts were running between Kong, Lin, Alice, and Spencer.

Spencer reached for the edge of a rough table that stood nearby; he looked as if he was having trouble standing. "Alice, ask him. Did Teilhard say anything about Peking Man? About the bones he brought with him?"

Alice's Chinese rendering dropped into a void of sucking silence. No one dared to draw the next breath.

Silence.

They waited.

Finally Ogatai spoke. "It is no good man who accepts guests, especially those with some connection to the family, without proper welcome. Since you have come, take your ease." He turned aside and addressed the two women in the doorway. Instantly they disappeared behind the whitewashed wall of beaten earth and returned with dried fruit and small, bright-colored plastic liquor cups.

They poured out the familiar red spirits, sweet, powerful. Everyone drank.

Ogatai said they should all come sit on the *kang*, the most pleasant spot in any northern home, winter or summer—but there was not enough room on the *kang* for everyone. Kong and Lin crowded onto a wooden bench opposite.

"Yes, the Frenchman did bring a box of bones," Ogatai said slowly. He dropped himself on the seat of honor, center back wall of the platform, facing the door, and settled comfortably on his heels. "It was to be left in this region until the war situation stabilized. By that time the Japan War was in its last gasp—but the civil war, that was just starting. He knew the bones would not be safe in Peking. And he didn't think he could get them out of the country. Here the fossils would be secure. He said scientists would come for them. Scientists he would send." He examined them carefully.

All eyes locked. Even Kong was twitching on his seat.

"We are scientists," Lin said carefully.

"We continue this work the Frenchman started," Spencer added.

Ogatai considered. One of the women fetched more wine, poured it, and sat down with them.

Finally Ogatai said: "You must remember, we made a promise to the Frenchman. To us, this is most serious. The Frenchman had a long history with our family."

"Did you take Peking Man from the cave?" Alice blurted.

Lin and Kong raised their eyebrows at her; way too fast, too direct, not Chinese.

But Ogatai did not flinch. "Yes. According to our promise. Which was to remove the remains after thirty years if the scientists did not come."

"Do you have it?" Kong wheezed.

Next to him Lin looked as if he was going to bite all the way through his lip.

"But you have not even told me who you are!" Ogatai cried. "What is your relation to the Frenchman?"

"His fellow scientists," Spencer said. He closed his eyes, reining back his churning feelings. "He did not instruct us himself to come here. He died a few years after this picture was taken. It was still too soon to be able to return here. Aside from the woman who came here with him, he told only one person, as far as we know."

"Then how—?" Ogatai asked.

"That other person was my grandfather," Spencer said.

Ogatai stared.

"And so we studied the French scientist's life, all his writings—everything—and by guessing"—he glanced at Kong, Lin, and Alice—"and by luck, we followed his trail—which led to you. No, he did not send us himself. But, Ogatai. Truly. *We are the scientists.*"

Ogatai studied them, and a glimmer of acceptance played around his eyes.

Oh, yes, trust us, Alice begged in her heart.

The old Mongol shook his head. "So he told your grandfather. But I had always thought he would send his own son. Or his grandson."

"Oh, no!" Lin jumped in. "It is impossible. Teilhard could not have any sons. He was a Catholic priest. Did you not know?"

Ogatai froze. "It's so?"

"Yes!" Kong said.

"But he brought a woman with him! Never did he say he was a priest."

"In fact," Alice said, "he became quite famous after his death—as a Catholic theologian." A very alternative Catholic theologian, of course, but no need to detail that.

"You say he wrote books about the ape-man?" Ogatai asked.

"Well—in a way. He wrote about evolution and God."

"That's the Catholic church for you!" Ogatai slammed down his hand. "They teach their priests they are descended from monkeys—"

"No, no!" she cried, "that's not what the Catholics think—"

"—While our shamans are taught they are descended from the rocks and the sky! Well! Who's right?" He laughed the uproarious laugh of one who wants to divert the conversation away from some mounting tension, wiped at his watering eyes, and raised his glass. Everyone drank again.

"Anyway." He cleared his throat. "It is not here, you know. Peking Man. We do not keep it anymore."

"What?" They all sank as if shot.

"Where is it?" Lin managed.

"I can give you the address."

"You mean you're keeping it someplace else?" Alice burst.

Lin quieted her with a look. "Ogatai," he said more formally. "It is not even necessary for us to take the bones—if we could photograph them—catalog them—"

"Extract a small tissue sample from one of the teeth," Kong gasped.

Alice whispered these promises to Spencer in English. She saw him swallow, nervously, knowing this was a lie, knowing they would never see Peking Man, lay eyes on it, touch it, take it out in the sunlight and gasp at the wonder of the flat skulls, the receding jaws, the heavy femurs—and then hand it back to Ogatai and walk away. But no need to say so now. "Right," Spencer agreed nervously.

"*Dui,*" she translated.

"Eh," grunted Ogatai.

A premonition sharp as ice passed through Alice as she watched the old man's face growing tighter and tighter.

"So sorry," Ogatai said faintly. "You say you want the bones?"

"Yes!" blurted Kong. "Of course!"

Awash in horror, Alice gripped Spencer's hand.

"The ape-man bones?" Ogatai said.

"Yes!" Lin shouted. "Yes!"

A pulled-out silence, made longer by the screaming shreds of hope.

"But I tell you we sold it," Ogatai said finally.

"You what!" Spencer shouted. "What!"

"You gave it to someone for money?" Kong said in his slowest, most excruciatingly pinpoint tone.

"Yes," the woman suddenly spoke up, as if talking to children who did not see the obvious. "And why not? We have eighty-four *mu* of land now."

"Congratulations," Spencer breathed miserably. "Oh, my God."

"What does the American say?" Lin called over to Alice, watching Spencer.

She closed her eyes and shook her head.

Lin leaned forward and fixed directly on Ogatai. "*When* did you sell it?"

"Nineteen seventy-six. One year after we took it from the cave."

"According to our promise," the woman emphasized.

"Oh, God," Spencer said again.

"It's no problem," Ogatai said kindly. "We kept the address of the place. We always thought you might still come." He said something to the woman in Mongolian, and she left the room.

She came back with a dog-eared envelope, which she passed to Ogatai. With great seriousness he leaned forward and gave it to the American scientist.

Kong, Lin, and Alice watched in horror.

Spencer took the envelope and closed his hands around it without looking at it. It was the NSF rejection letter all over again, the custody papers, the empty box. "I'm screwed," he mumbled. "Completely screwed."

She did not translate.

16

SPENCER OPENED his door a crack. He saw her and looked away. She knew he hadn't been crying, American men never cried. But his face was pinched with misery.

"What was in the envelope?" she asked him, peering over his shoulder and seeing the bed barely disturbed. Had he stayed up all night?

"I didn't open it."

"How could you not open it?"

He closed his eyes briefly against her obstinacy. "Alice, it's over. They sold Peking Man."

"But they gave us the address! It's not like it vanished."

"What's wrong with you? They sold it nineteen years ago! And in case you haven't noticed, Alice, you of all people, China's been a bit—shall we say, chaotic?—in the intervening time."

She shrugged. What did he know about Chaos?

Spencer let out a hard, defeated breath. "That's it for me with Peking Man, Alice. This was my shot. I don't even have any money left."

"But you have the envelope."

"Wrong," he said acidly. "*You* have the envelope." He crossed the room and dug into his jeans pocket from the night before, returned, and handed it to her. "I don't even want to know what's in it."

She tore it open, scanned it, looked back up at him. "Sure?"

"No. Yes! For Christ's sake, tell me."

She showed it to him. On the right, there were two lines of Mongolian, the strange looping vertical script, like Arabic turned on its side. Then two vertical rows of Chinese.

"Come on, Alice. Translate."

"The Chinese is an address in Yinchuan. Six hundred and forty-two Drum Tower Road, ground floor. You know I don't read Mongolian. It probably says the same thing." She held it out to him.

"You keep it." He blinked wearily and shut the door in her face.

Lin Shiyang poured tea in his room. "It's only cheap Fujian bottom leaves, stored in bricks too long by the smell of it, but it's tea. Drink, girl child." He held the cup out to her with both hands.

She smiled, and took the cup the way she was supposed to, with two hands, in the old way. She had read her novels, read her history. "Please," she said, and indicated his own tea with her eyes.

He smiled at her manners. "In Zhengzhou we have wonderful tea. Jasmine tea, red lichee, chrysanthemum flower, all the best ones. And did you know there are ruins of an ancient city from the Shang era there? Very interesting excavations. You should come."

"Should I?" she said, turning it around, eyeing him over the rim of her cup.

"*Wei shenmo bu?*" he said, Why not. Then he sighed, drank from his cup, and set it heavily on the table. "Ai-li, I don't know how I should talk to you about these things. In my world, it's like this. When a man and woman do together what you and I have done—I mean the way you and I have done it—our hearts all the way open, do you understand me or not?—we know each other, gradually. We spend a long time. And eventually we talk about love."

Her heart leapt. A permanent relationship, that's what he meant.

"But my life is complicated. I was married. And—you know this, Ai-li—I have never been able to find out what happened to my wife. If I could only find out—if I could be sure . . ."

The pain swelled up behind Alice's eyes. They had felt so much in the last few nights. Yet still he clung to this.

"And another thing," he said. "You're a foreign woman! Foreigners are different. I don't know"—he looked at her beseechingly—"I don't know what we would do."

"*Wo ye bu zhidao,*" I don't know either. But Alice did know, or at least she thought she did: they should forget everything from before and go forward. They should try. But she didn't say this. She knew Lin had to realize it for himself.

They drank in silence.

He had his sleeves rolled up his hairless forearms. He stretched over to put his teacup on the dresser, settled his long body back down. "For example, your family. What would your father think if we talked about love?"

She closed her eyes. "My God, Shiyang, I can't even imagine. My father is famous for his racism, remember?" She paused at the word for racism, *zhongzu zhuyi,* knowing what it implied in English, not sure if it carried the same weight in Chinese. "He is obsessed by the past, by a time in history when laws—not just attitudes—gave white people all the privileges. He thinks that's how it should be."

"Yes, you told me. He thinks whites are superior to Chinese!"
She nodded.

Lin shook his head. "He's confused."

"That's one way of putting it."

"So. You are saying he would not then accept me as your—as your—"

She broke over him, seeing he was having trouble committing himself even to the words. "I'm saying it doesn't matter. If you and I agree to love each other, and he doesn't like it, that will be his problem. I don't care what he thinks. I don't care about him."

"Of course you care about him. He's your father."

"No, I'm ashamed of him—everything about him."

"That has nothing to do with it," Lin corrected her. "Whether parents do good or bad, they are still one's parents. One respects them. Loves them. Forgives them the bad that they've done."

She stared. How could he just cut through it all like that? "You're right, Shiyang. I do care—of course I care—in a way. In fact, the truth is I'm worried—worried he might be sick."

His eyes darkened in concern. "Is he?"

"I don't know. They don't have a clear diagnosis yet. But it might be something bad."

"In that case, you should certainly put aside your anger. We have a saying: *Renzi jiang-si qi yen ye san*." Before a man dies you must forgive him everything.

She nodded. Feelings she had been holding down for so long surged up and welled in her eyes.

Lin reached for her hand. He sat, holding it, staring at their fingers, hers white. His dark ivory.

"Despite everything, I could not bear to lose him—"

"Whenever that comes, it must be endured."

"And what about you?" she said, blinking. "You haven't told me about your parents."

"Only my brother living, and my old mother—in Shanghai."

"What would she think of me?"

He smiled faintly. His mother was old fashioned. When his father had died she had observed his passing the old way, for three years. Except that it had been during the Chaos, and she'd had to confine her rituals to what could be concealed. Like the white strip of linen she wore around her arm, inside her jacket. Like talking to the elder Lin's picture every New Year's. "Of you," he said now to Ai-li, "my mother would not know what to think. But she is like all mothers. She wants my happiness."

"I never had a mother." She sighed.

"Guolai," he whispered, and pulled her to her feet and over to him. Guiding her with his hands he settled her on his lap, then placed his hand over her chest and pressed gently. Alice rested her head. The way her bones seemed to collapse, weightless, against him gave her the greatest comfort imaginable. As if she were home.

That night he came into her room instead of waiting for her in his. He couldn't see much as he closed the door behind him, but he could hear her footsteps moving toward him. She surprised him by dropping low and grasping him by the ankle, the way she had done in the cave. He let out a tiny laugh, not enough for any of the others to hear in their rooms, where they would be just now settling down to sleep, just enough for her, to let her know he remembered. And as he had done in the cave, he responded by pressing his leg back into her hand.

Her hands slid up and opened his pants. He drew in a sharp breath. She was so immediate, so without artifice. He leaned his head back, closed his eyes at the sensation of her mouth picking him up and pulling him in—eh, he had to reach behind him now, find something to steady him. There. The rim of the bureau. Bracing his arms this way he was able to move against her mouth, just the small movements, just the first quickening. He twined one hand in her hair, gripped her head, moved more boldly in her. Ah, this woman. He remembered the first night, kissing in the desert, the way he had used only his mouth on her, the way she used her mouth on him now— Ah, the high tide. "Ai-li," he breathed, warning her.

But she tightened her hands on his hips, refusing to release him. At the same majestic moment that he felt his force rising he felt a flowering of trust as well, and so knew, for this moment anyway, that he could fully let himself go in her.

When the barest quickening of light was seeping into the room there was a small, urgent knocking on the door.

She was awake, instantly, stumbling across the floor. Suddenly, she remembered *he* was there. "Lin!" she turned and hissed.

But he had already heard, sat up.

She pointed to the bathroom; he slipped quickly across the room and shut himself inside.

The knocking again. Spencer sick? Some problem with Kong? A telegram about Horace? Her heart thudded as she crossed to the door.

"*Shui-a?*"

"Mo Ai-li?" A Chinese voice. It was a man, a voice she knew. But . . . She hesitated. Who?

"Is it you, Mo Ai-li? Please! I've driven half the night."

Guo Wenxiang! She unlatched the door and cracked it a few inches; impatiently he pushed it wide.

"Sorry to come to your place so early! Eh, it's not easy to come by a ride to this village! Eren Obo's truly not on the well-traveled road! But I have good connections. And last night luck favored me. I met some PLA officers from my home province, men stationed here in Eren Obo. As fellow Sichuanese, they naturally offered me a ride from Yinchuan."

"You learned something about Peking Man?"

"Not exactly," he evaded. He shot his gaze around the room. "May I trouble you for tea?"

"Oh. Of course." She watched him collapse into the wood-and-vinyl armchair, his bony frame a bag of strung-together sticks under wrinkled clothes. He closed his narrow eyes as if sleeping, laid his knotty bronze hands on his lap. He smiled faintly when he heard the familiar pop of the thermos, the gurgling of hot water into the cup.

"It's been difficult for you to travel here," she said, a little sharply, handing him the steaming cup. "Could you not have sent a message?"

"News such as I have brought I would entrust to no messenger! Do you remember what I told you, Mo Ai-li? Think back and forth. Be discreet. They are watching you."

"Ah." She clamped her mouth shut and poured tea, then glanced nervously at the bathroom door. How long would Shiyang have to wait?

Guo blew gratefully across his teacup. Loose leaves danced across the water's surface. He sipped, and picked a few leaf-crumbles off his lip. These he rolled into an infinitesimal ball and deposited in his shirt pocket.

She drank. "What news do you bring, then, Guo Wenxiang?" She said this a little loudly, for Lin.

Guo, alert as a twitching mouse, looked up at her. "Is someone here?" He trained his sharp awareness around the room. There were the men's athletic shoes, the trousers and belt crumpled on the floor. Guo smiled slyly. "You should speak frankly to me, Mo Ai-li. Drop your guard. I am not old fashioned!"

But still nosy as hell. Aloud she said: "I'll choose what I tell you and what I don't. Now. What about your news?"

Now that Guo had the stage, he was maddeningly slow. He

brought the teacup back to his sharp-boned face, looked dolefully at it. "This tea is terrible. But a man with an empty cup does not question. Anyway. I've made inquiries."

"Yes?"

"I uncovered news of the Mongol family. They moved. They left Shuidonggou during the Japan War. Before the Liberation, we should say! Yes, before the Liberation—that's the proper phrase. Anyway. They moved to the Nei Meng side."

"Rather close to here?"

"Yes!" He widened his eyes.

"In a valley called Purabanduk, that one?"

"Ah, Mo Ai-li, you are keen as a knife blade! I am not often matched! And you a foreigner too. Congratulations."

She heard the familiar derision under the compliment, and returned it with a rude look. "What else did you find out?"

"That the family has lived here ever since, and prospered. Nineteen years ago they started buying more land. They've kept on buying. They're rich now."

She pushed aside nausea. Nineteen years ago, buying more land! The sale of Peking Man.

But Guo was searching through his dignity-rumpled pockets for a smoke. "*Mei-le,*" he muttered, and shot her his most unctuous smile. "Mo Ai-li. Trouble you. You have a cigarette?"

"I don't smoke."

He looked pointedly at the shoes on the floor, the male trousers which might very well—he made this clear with his knowing shrug—have had a pack in one pocket. But he said nothing. With a long sigh he folded back into the chair. "Let us ascend to the summit of our discussion, then. Mo Ai-li. I have other news. You asked me to learn what became of the professor's wife, do you remember it or not? I have done what you asked. I have attained the answer."

"Later!" She dropped her voice. "We should meet at another time to talk on this."

But Lin heard.

And the bathroom door crashed open.

He stumbled out, clutching a white towel to his waist. He looked blazingly at Guo Wenxiang, and pounced on each syllable. *"Mafan ni zai shuo yibian,"* Trouble you to say that again.

"Eh, it's you." Guo gave his larded smile. "Dr. Lin! Good morning. It's my pleasure to see that you and the American woman have become intimate friends. I was just talking about news of your . . . wife. Eh, my sympathies! It's been a bad road. Truly! But time passes. Is it not so? In spring, the orchid; in autumn"—he glanced meaningfully at Alice—"the chrysanthemum."

The blaze of fury crept palpably up her face. The condescension to say this right in front of her!

But Lin would not be sidetracked. "Who asked you to look for my wife?"

"Don't you know, Dr. Lin?" Guo said creamily. "Your colleague!" He gestured to Alice.

"Ai-li?" Lin blinked back astonishment. "You engaged him to look for Zhang Meiyan?"

"Yes."

His face darkened in a way she found terrible, unreadable.

"It's true, I asked him to look for her."

"Why?"

"What do you mean, why! *You* were looking for her. Were you not? I thought this would help."

"This was my search, Ai-li," he said evenly. "Not yours."

"Please, Shiyang, I didn't think there was anything wrong with it—"

"But you did it in secret!"

"Yes . . ." She looked down, yes, okay, so in a way she'd deceived him. But why would Lin not welcome help? From her, from anyone?

"Don't stand on ceremony!" Guo cut in. "It's of no import!

What's certain is this: I have gained news of the woman Zhang Meiyan from Camp Fourteen." He shrugged as if uncovering this secret were a trifle, no more than another job well done. He patted his pockets conspicuously. *"Eh, Lin Boshi, you yan meiyou?"* Do you have a cigarette or not?

"I do not."

"Pitiable." Guo rummaged around in his clothes one last hopeful time.

"Guo Wenxiang," Lin ordered, "whatever it is. Say it."

Oh, God, Alice thought. Zhang Meiyan is alive! Waiting in some desert hut or some apartment in some desert town, waiting for Lin, still in love with him, waiting. . . .

But Guo was speaking. "Bitter the river. Bitter the lake. Forgive me for carrying this news. She has been dead for nineteen years."

17

ALL THE AIR seemed to blow out of Alice at once. From her core burst the shameful thought: *Dead? Thank God!*

"Are you sure of this?" Lin's gaze pried at Guo Wenxiang's face.

"Certain as the moon in the sky."

"And how do you know?"

"*Shi zheyangde.* I've talked to people who remember things in that camp. It was bad for some years. Not enough to eat. And other years, sickness."

Lin Shiyang's eyes filled.

Alice felt she would burst, looking at his life pain, the boards and nails that had defined him all these years, flooding out. The archaeology of his heart. His eyes spilled over. Unlike Western men, Chinese men cried when they needed to, free of shame. Yet another thing she loved. *Ge you ge de tedian.* . . .

"You will excuse me. I need to get dressed." Lin stumbled past them, snatched up his clothes, slammed into the bathroom.

"*Congshi zhaolai!*" she spat at Guo.

"Of course I'm telling the truth."

"Your information's good?"

"Miss Mo, *dangran-le,* Hasn't it always been good?"

She nodded. "Yes." She steadied her breathing. "It has. . . ."

Lin came out. "Now, tell me everything."

"Eh, all right, I'll speak frankly." Guo relaxed into his self-important smile. "To be honest, I know only the general line of events."

Lin waited.

"Your wife's name was Zhang Meiyan. Is it not so?" Guo paused as if this was a masterful stroke of detective work, when in fact it was only information given him by Alice.

"Yes."

"So. Two different people told me this story. Each was in Camp Fourteen with your wife. Each said they knew her fate."

"And her fate was?" Lin's voice was deadly quiet.

"That she fell ill with cholera in 1976. Some who got sick recovered. A few, at least. Not her. She went away. That is all! I can direct you to the place where she is buried. It would not be difficult—if you want to go."

"You say there is no question, she is dead?"

"It's a certainty! She is dead. Of course the *laogai* bosses, I am not surprised they never gave you this information! Many people, when they try to go through official channels to learn someone's fate, are only told: this or that prisoner committed suicide. Eh! Well! How can it be! Do so many millions of those arrested as *fan geming,* then perhaps interrogated, perhaps worse, *actually* commit suicide? Of course not! Eh! Lin Boshi. *Shi-ma?*"

"*Shi.*" Lin looked battered, as if these words themselves were the struggle sessions, the torture, the beatings, the starvation and sickness.

"Is that what they told you, then, when you made your inquiries—that she had committed suicide? Or did they tell you"—Guo twisted his mouth derisively at this particular evasion—"that they did not know her outcome?"

"I did not make those kinds of inquiries."

A balloon of silence dropped awkwardly over the room.

"But, Lin." Alice stumbled. "Why wouldn't you have done that? Isn't that the first thing everybody does? I thought you had done that years ago."

"Maybe I should have done it," Lin said softly. "But I didn't. *Wo pa wo renshoubuliao*," I didn't think I could bear it. "And how could I believe what they told me anyway? For that matter"—he turned his searching gaze to Guo—"how can I believe what you are telling me now?"

Guo's face, for a moment, was as open and wondering as that of a child. "But, Professor Lin, why should you *not* believe me? It is not as if you have heard competing accounts of your wife's fate! In fact, all the evidence is on the same side—the two versions I was given of Zhang Meiyan's ending were completely alike. And, as I told you"—he stopped and nodded sympathetically—"you can go to the place where she is buried. You can see for yourself."

"Even then I could not be sure it was really she who was buried there."

"Ah, Lin . . ." Alice whispered, though he did not seem to hear.

Guo drew his brows together. Until this moment he had been controlling the conversation. Now it had careened into the not quite rational. "But, Lin Shiyang. How can you tell if *any* person's grave truly holds their remains? Eh? You can't! You merely take it on faith. Faith! It's what all people—"

"That's enough, Guo," Alice said softly.

The thin man shrugged.

Lin stood like a stone, not answering.

"Well," Guo said, turning to Alice, "I've done what was asked—and more. Have I not? Now. It is my admittedly indiscreet but inescapable duty to remind you that we did not specifically discuss payment for this particular—"

"Stop it." She jabbed a finger at her lips.

He raised his palms in acquiescence.

She yanked out a desk drawer, rifled through the special small folder where she kept her passport. There; some twenty-dollar U.S. bills. She took a couple out. "Take this." She shoved it into his hands. "Now go!"

She propelled him toward the door.

He craned around. "Dr. Lin! A thousand tears of sympathy!"

Lin had lowered himself heavily to the floor. His eyes were closed.

"May the bitter sea grow sweet!"

Alice shut the door hard. She heard Guo's tinkle of face-saving laughter from the hall, and then the sound of his footsteps, at last, receding.

"Lin," she said softly to him.

He seemed not to hear.

She sank beside him, touched his shoulder.

He twisted his body away.

She laced her hands over her forehead and held it, hard, as if otherwise it might fly apart. *Zhongguo yi pan san sha,* China is a plate of sand. "Do you believe it now, Shiyang? About Zhang Meiyan?"

"Why do you always press me! Can you not defer your impulses, even once—"

"I'm sorry," she said, suddenly small.

His voice softened. "One hears stories—one never knows. . . ."

"Shiyang."

He was silent. She wanted to touch him but knew, right now, she should not. "You can go on your whole life like this, you know. You can grow old this way. It's your choice."

He said nothing.

"Or you can accept it."

He nodded reluctantly.

A half-nauseous hook tugged at her, deep down, as she studied his face. He might never change. He seemed to have something inside him that was not on the track the rest of the world was on. Be aware, her senses hissed. Yet within, at the same moment, her heart turned over in tender revolt. She could just handle it, couldn't she? Accept him, *Quan xin, quan yi*. She felt a spurt of release. Even with Jian, with all the love, she had not felt this.

Because Lin was just a man, anyway. Damaged. But doing the best he could.

"I should go," he said. "Get dressed."

"Yes."

When the door closed she felt all limp and pulled apart. It seemed like forever before she could get up and start moving around the room, tidying up.

Meiyan was dead.

And she and Lin had only to get through this nightmare.

She snapped the cover up on the bed, straightened the pillow. Of course Meiyan was dead. She'd been gone so many years. Lin just had this wall inside him.

Like me, Alice thought guiltily. On the one side America, English, my childhood, on the other side China and Chinese and life as a woman. No *kai fang*, no open doors. The wall massive, thick, medieval, like the walls that enclosed the Forbidden City and guarded its secrets and wrapped its emperors in the dreams and illusions which were ultimately to bring down their dynasties. The Great Within.

How many times, in Beijing, she'd contemplated those walls. This was how she and Lin were alike.

She washed, dressed, sat on the bed, and waited for him to come back. He'd come back in a while, they'd talk, the air would clear. Everything would be all right.

* * *

There was a knock on the door. "Lin?" She crossed the room in a few quick steps, yanked open the door.

A *fuwuyuan*. One she had never seen before.

"You are"—the woman glanced down at a paper she was holding, struggled to pronounce—"Aliss—Manwa-gen—"

"Alice Mannegan?" Her heart sank. "Yes."

The *fuwuyuan* thrust the folded paper at her. *"Dianbao."* Telegram.

Alice tore it open. It was from Roger.

Tests back. Prostate cancer. Advanced. Sorry. Advise your travel plans ASAP.

Alice stared at the paper.

"Huidian-ma?" the *fuwuyuan* said impatiently, Will you reply?

Alice swallowed. The floor was opening up under her. "Not right now. I have to think."

The young woman's bean-shaped Tartar face was empty. "When you want to reply, contact the cable office. In the bank." Then she turned, closed the door, and was gone.

Alice read the telegram over and over, as if maybe the horror would change into something else. It didn't. It still read death. Shaking, she opened the drawer, pulled the *ling-pai* out from under the clothes. She read the inscription through again. How could it be real? First Meng Shaowen. Now Horace.

The door clicked open and Lin Shiyang walked in.

"Lin." She stepped toward him, still clutching the *ling-pai* and the telegram. "I need to talk to you. I'm going to be leaving, as soon as possible—"

"That doesn't surprise me," he interrupted coldly. He shut the

door behind him, leaned against it. She saw his eyes were dark, furious. "But first I need to know if it's true."

"If what is true?"

"What Guo Wenxiang has just told me! I met him in the courtyard outside. We talked. Is it true, then?"

"You mean Zhang Meiyan? How can I be the one to say? Listen, my heart—"

"You call me your heart! Is that just honey in your mouth? I am not talking about Zhang Meiyan! I am talking about you— Mo Ai-li! I am talking about your secrets. Well! Is it true?"

She froze, a concrete ball of fear plummeting her to the ocean floor. *Was what true? That houses were burned in her name, for Alice, for Alice Mannegan? Children murdered?* When she spoke it was in the tiniest voice. "I don't know what you mean."

"Eh, well then, I'll speak frankly! Do you follow convenience?"

She shrank from his words, from his eyes boring into her. *Suibian,* Follow convenience, the horrible euphemism, the woman who goes here and there as she pleases, her legs open, her promises unkept.

"Well?"

"What are you talking about?"

"Guo says that on July nineteenth you went to Ningxia University and picked up a man! A strange man! You talked with him for a few minutes and then went with him to his home! Well?"

"Who says this! How do you know!"

"Please, Ai-li." He blinked scornfully. "This is China! Eyes are everywhere! Secrets jump from one to another in a flash! *Ni mei tingshuo-guo ma? Zhi bao bu zhu huo.*" Haven't you heard it said? You can't wrap a fire in paper.

How? The PLA? The pedicab driver? People paid by Guo? But it didn't matter. He knew.

"Well?"

"Lin, it is true, I met a man and I went with him to his home.

But nothing happened! We talked, for no more than a short time, and I left! Surely your"—she paused to lay a scornful emphasis on the word—"*informant* told you this as well!"

His voice faltered. "Yes, it was said that you left the man's apartment quickly. But, Ai-li, why would you do this thing? Why would you follow convenience with a stranger? Does a man like me not hold your interest?"

She paused, wondering how she could possibly explain herself to him. There was the *within* of things—she was the Alice from the Alice Speech, the daughter of Horace Mannegan—and there was the pragmatic side of things too. She was a woman of unique sensibilities. How many men had she met in her life, her whole life, who could truly match her? Ten? Twelve? Cut that down to those who had been single and available, and the total shrank to six or eight. Counting Jian. Counting Lin. And in between meeting such men, years had gone by. What was she supposed to do? Wait alone? Shrivel? Men did not wait alone. Even Lin, she guessed, had not gone without all these years.

But all this, she could not begin to confide. So she chose the obvious excuse. "Shiyang, of course you hold my interest. You more than hold my interest! You have my whole heart. I haven't really told you yet, Shiyang, how I feel, but believe me . . ." She swallowed. "The thing is, at that time we were not lovers. Don't you remember? We had barely begun to talk! We were—"

"Force words and twist logic! Were we not *talking* as a man and a woman? Was not the journey between us begun?"

She hesitated. "Yes."

He squeezed his eyes shut. "Everyone says this is the way Western women are! That when they fuck you they open up everything for you, so you think you are making love to their heart, their true heart—when in fact it is merely their sex, which is nothing more than a well-traveled road!"

Tears sprang to her eyes. "That's so unfair! I'm an individual, I'm Alice, Mo Ai-li, I'm someone who—who"—she closed her eyes. *Just say it* "—who loves you." She paused. "Judge me on myself. Don't treat me like I'm all Western women."

The softening that had come over his face when he heard the word *ai*, Love, dissolved quickly back into anger. "Why not, when that is how you treat me? Remember the other night when we were, we were"—he paused, as if the word were suddenly distasteful to him—"*fucking*, you said I was the true Chinese man? At the time I did not know what you meant. But now I understand. Because Guo did some checking on you. You *do* follow convenience! Everywhere you go. And only with Chinese men! As if we're all the same, we're all . . ." He swallowed, stopped. His bottomless black eyes widened in astonishment. "Eh! What! What is that thing you're holding?"

The cliff of shock gave way under her and she realized she was still holding the *ling-pai*. She stood speechless.

"Well?"

Finally words came, but they were words in English. "I needed a better ancestor."

"Speak reasonably, Ai-li. You know I cannot understand your language."

"It's not my language"—she switched to Chinese—"it's never been mine. It's theirs."

He looked at her strangely.

"And this"—she took a deep breath and raised the tablet—"it was made for an old woman I loved, a woman who's just died. She had one son. He will never practice filial piety. Not in the old way. And she loved me as a daughter. So I—I had it made."

His face sagged in disbelief. Quickly he scanned the characters, gaped up at her again. *"So you made her an ancestor?"*

She nodded.

"Mo Ai-li, that's—that's ignorant!"

"Well—"

"It's not done now! Not by people like us. Those are ancient customs."

"I like old things," she said defensively.

"But culture evolves! You say you care for China! Is this all you care for, this vanished miasma of—of paintings and poems? Of mandarins and"—he finished with chilly contempt—"women with bound feet?"

"No!" She laid the *ling-pai* on the table, her heart banging in her ears.

"Have you not seen me at all, Ai-li? What do you think I am?"

"I think you are a man!"

"The 'true Chinese man,' " he mocked her. "Shall I wear a silk robe and practice martial arts? Spout Confucian phrases for you?"

"How can you say such things!" she cried, tears spilling.

"Because suddenly you are as clear as water to me! You say you are leaving! Eh, go ahead—leave!"

"No, Shiyang, that's because—"

"What? Found something better? Another man?"

"I don't want any other man."

"No, only a new set of ancestors! Forget it. You can't be Chinese."

"You're not being fair. Just because I've devoted my whole life to China—" she said, her voice breaking.

"To your dream of China!"

"But I respect and admire you—all of you—I've done everything to learn your language, literature, culture—"

"Ai-li," he said bluntly. "You are who you are. An interpreter. An American woman who speaks Chinese. No more. Don't you know what we say? You can move mountains and alter the course of rivers more easily than you can change a person's nature! This"—he gestured derisively to the plaque—"is ridiculous! A cliché."

Silence.

"Next you are going to tell me you went to some street corner and burned grave goods!"

Oh, God. She didn't answer.

"Well?"

"Shiyang—I don't know—maybe I see China incorrectly. But to say I can't be faithful to you is wrong! I swear, if you and I took our road together I would be true to you." She turned her streaming sea-colored eyes to him and felt, for once, that she was wearing all of herself on the outside. "I'd come to Zhengzhou, if you wanted. I would live with you. Or near you. And whatever vow I made to you, I would keep."

"You'd vow to what? To see my culture—which even a foreigner must admit is the most highly developed one on earth—as some cartoon of dragons and red silk?"

"No, I wouldn't, of course not—" She yanked open the drawer and stuffed the plaque inside, slammed it shut.

"Or swear to be a foreign female who loves me until she is bored and then follows convenience?"

"No!" she screamed. "I'm not perfect! Okay! But I'm trying! Why are you making it so damn impossible?"

"Mo Ai-li!" His face changed. "Calm yourself! Be more quiet! Every one of our colleagues can hear you!"

"I don't give a fuck!" she screamed in English.

"Ai-li!" He stepped to her and wrapped his arms around her, but not to embrace her—to contain her. His powerful arms pinned her to him while he squeezed her face into his chest.

Her tears flooded onto his shirt, her shoulders shaking.

He held her stiffly.

She burrowed into him, wrapped her arms around and pressed her body against him. Any moment, any moment, he would soften and return her embrace, he would hold her, show his love to her through his body the way he had been doing for days. "Shiyang?"

But he did not answer. He only kept a secure hold on her.

347

"Shiyang, please," she begged, looking up. "Don't cut it off like this!"

Pain and regret and confusion roared across his face. But still he did not return her touch.

"Shiyang!"

He began, with no more than a soft and minute motion, to shake his head.

From outside the door, footsteps. Voices.

"Alice!" English—the voice of Spencer. "Are you all right?"

"Interpreter Mo!" Dr. Kong chimed in.

"Don't open it," she whispered in English to Lin Shiyang. "Please! *Bie kai men.*"

He dropped his arms and stepped away from her. There was a cold, unhappy cast to his face.

"Jiu zheyang jiesu-le ma?" Is that it, then?

He didn't answer, but turned and opened the door. There hovered the balloon faces of Spencer, frightened, concerned; and Kong, who looked from Lin to Alice and gave a nod of infinite sadness and understanding.

"Excuse me," Lin said shortly, and pushed past them.

"Alice?" Spencer said. Across his open blond face marched fascination, pity, kindness. "Hey! Are you okay?"

Not even bothering to wipe at the tears that now made an ugly river on her face, she hiccupped, "Just leave me alone," and slammed the door.

18

THE WORLD SHOULD have stopped. Everything ought to have gone dark and shrunk into some permanent nuclear winter. But the routine morning light appeared anyway and advanced across the plain stones of the lobby floor as if this were just another cruel quotidian turn of the wheel. She walked across the lobby, dead. She was dimly aware of Spencer, bent over some papers in the side sitting room.

"You all right, Alice?" he asked.

She stopped and stood motionless, her eyes closed.

"You don't have to answer." He sighed. "I just wanted to say, you know, I'm sorry." He resettled the papers on his lap and went on with what he was writing.

She nodded and walked on. She needed to go out. To walk. Even if everything else was a stinging piano wire of pain, she could still move her body. It was a thing that sometimes got her through.

So she walked Eren Obo for a long, uncounted time, until the sun was far and hot across the sky. The desert light, in which she had once taken pleasure, now seemed to beat on her relentlessly.

Horace was going to die. He was going to leave her.

And Lin didn't want her after all.

She trudged up the meandering creek through the scattered houses, past the temple complex. She ignored her thirst until it was a screaming need, and then she walked back to the center of town and bought an orange soda, loosely bottled, of extremely dubious hygiene. She drank it frantically. I'm Alice Mannegan, not Mo Ai-li, she thought. An American obsessed with China. Is that why I loved Lin, because he is China? No. Because he is Lin, a man. Not that it matters now. He's gone. And I'm alone again.

At the edge of Eren Obo, where the town dissolved into bare desert that rolled gently to the edge of the mountains, Dr. Kong Zhen was walking too. He kept his eyes moving in a practiced sweep over the ground. He knew how to spot the microliths, the flakes and detritus and the tools themselves, the scrapers and hammers and points. So like plain rocks to the ordinary eye. To him, relics beyond price.

He stopped suddenly, at the edge of a crudely dug hole. He studied the hole, about a meter deep, and three or four meters long—a trench, actually. There was a creek not far away. Probably, he thought, the ditch had been started as an irrigation sluice. Begun—when? Ten years ago? Fifty?—partly dug, then abandoned.

Dr. Kong dropped into the hole and examined it. A dark horizontal streak, four inches thick—could it be? His pulse picked up. Stay calm, he told himself, running his fingers over the darkened earth. Was it ash? When one excavated cross-sections of primitive huts they looked like this, from the years and years of fires inside. Trembling he turned to the trench wall, to the pebbles and rocks studding it. With practiced care, despite the anticipation roaring in his brain, he removed these objects from the ash layer one by one and examined them. Each breath caught in his throat. A flake. Another flake. A cobble. Had this been a hunter-gatherer dwelling? Oh, yes. Yes it had. He stuffed the artifacts in his pocket, scrambled out of the trench, and hurried back to find Spencer.

She went to the bank and begged the manager to let her call her father's office. On the other side of the world, in Washington, the secretary recognized her voice and called Roger to the phone at once.

"How bad is it? Tell me."

"Bad, Alice."

"So he's having surgery? Chemotherapy? What?"

A tiny but perceptible pause. "Neither of those is indicated right now. They're mainly trying to make him comfortable—"

"What?" She heard her voice rising. "Why aren't they doing anything?"

"Alice, . . ." Roger sighed. His voice was flat, exhausted. "Look, he's desperate to speak to you himself. He'll be back here in four or five hours. Can you call again then?"

She looked frantically around. "No, the bank'll be closed then. This is the only phone in the town."

"I see." Roger sounded deflated.

"I'll keep trying, though. I will. And I'll come right home, of course."

"Good. He's stepping down from Congress on Friday, Alice. We'll make the public announcement then."

"Friday! Are you kidding?"

"Can you be here by then?"

"I don't know—I'll try. . . ." She calculated quickly. It was Monday. They were supposed to drive back to Yinchuan tomorrow. The next flight from Yinchuan to Beijing wasn't until Tuesday night anyway. If she could get on that flight, it might be possible. She knew enough people in Beijing to get a quick ticket from Beijing to Hong Kong or Tokyo. Once she got to Hong Kong or Tokyo, it'd be a clear shot. "I'll try," she repeated. "If not Friday, I can definitely get there before the weekend's out."

"Good."

"Roger? How long does he have? A month? Six months?"

Silence again. "I'd rather he talked to you himself, Alice, so when you call back—"

"Roger, please. You know how hard it's going to be for me to get him on the phone. Just tell me. How long."

She heard a long, defeated exhalation. "Alice," Roger said at last, "just get here as quickly as you can."

When Kong Zhen found Adam Spencer, he had no language to tell him what he had just found. So he made a quick sketch of the landscape, the canyon mouth, the alluvial fan, and then drew the trench. Speaking rapidly in Chinese even though he knew the American couldn't understand, he colored in the ash layer and tapped the pen against it for emphasis.

"An ash layer?" Spencer said. "Are you kidding?" He stared at the page.

Kong pulled double handfuls of microliths from his pockets and scattered them on the table between them. He pointed to the microliths and then the ash layer.

"You found these in the ash? Oh, my God."

"*Zou-ba,*" Kong said, indicating the door.

"I'm with you," Spencer agreed, looking around for his hat. "Let's go take a look."

*   *   *

"Thank you, elder brother," Lin said, climbing down from the truck.

"Will you be all right?" the Mongol asked him, hands on the steering wheel.

"Yes. I have water, some food. So this was the place they called Camp Fourteen?"

"Across that ridge." The Mongol pointed up the winding dirt track that led away from them and disappeared over the boulder-strewn hills. "But I believe there's nothing left now—"

"I know," Lin cut him off heavily. "It's all right. I know."

The Mongol raised a hand and drove away.

Lin trudged up the path to the top of the ridge and then used the map Guo Wenxiang had drawn, walking over the pass, along an ancient landslide of jumbled rocks, and through a cleft which showed him, in a depressing sun-battered sweep, the valley down below where the camp had been. Although Lin could see the remains of a road, and the broken-down huddle of mud build-ings, he did not descend into the valley. Instead he followed the face of the dirt mountain around to his left, as he'd been in-structed, and came to a small, jutting butte, protected behind by piles of rock.

Guo had said this was where they were buried.

Yes. Lin narrowed his eyes against the sun. He could see the row of shallow, regular swellings in the earth. He started at the right, as Guo had told him to do, and counted back seven.

Then he stood a long time in the beating blue glare, looking down at it.

This is my Meiyan at last, he thought in a clutch of misery. He unhooked the water bottle from his belt, set it on the ground, and lay down in the dust beside her, curled into a ball, his knees pressed up to his chest.

*　*　*

Alice stood in her room by the curtain, staring dully out the window. The courtyard behind the guesthouse was empty, shimmering in the oven of midday. The hot sage fragrance of the brush along the base of the building rose to her.

All she felt was emptiness. There was an ache in her chest where love had been. It had been love, hadn't it? The real thing. Sometimes one didn't know until after. Now she knew.

It was gone, though. All in the past.

"I can't get a line to Beijing now," the Yinchuan operator told her. "Perhaps you should try later."

"It's so important," Alice pleaded. "I really have to get this call through to Washington—"

"I'm sorry. There are no lines now."

"What's the problem?" the bank manager said. He was at an adjacent desk, checking through some papers. It had been kind of him to let her use the phone again. But she could feel him wanting her to be finished and gone.

"Dabutong-le," she answered desperately, trying to keep the tears out of her voice, I can't get through.

The manager moved his shoulders in sympathetic resignation.

"I'm sorry." She swallowed, replacing the receiver. "I'll come back later."

"I hope your father will be better," the manager said.

But he won't, she thought, walking out of the bank into the harsh sunlight. I'm losing him. Losing Horace. Is that really who he is to me, Horace? The man in the Capitol, the man on TV, the champion of hate? But he's my father, my family. My ancestor. *I love you, sweetheart*—she could hear his voice, the softness in it, the constancy.

Horace had made her what she was. She was his daughter through and through. From him she got her intelligence, and her pluck. Also the pale skin on her legs, her small knotty hands, her slight body and forest-colored eyes. She pushed through the crowd of young Mongol men loitering outside the bank and stepped into the dirt-packed street.

Yes. It was Horace who'd endowed her with intuition and sensitivity and then—cruelly—put her on national display. *I have a little girl named Alice.* She winced at the memory of his voice, the words caught in countless recordings and documentaries and now distilled in the minds of people everywhere. Because of this she'd lived all her life inversely: always the foreigner, the other, forever pretending to be something apart from what she truly was. Unloved and unloving. It all went back to Horace.

Suddenly everything around her jolted into sharper focus. How could she have ever expected to be a part of Asia? She saw how people moving in the road stepped carefully around her, avoiding her, turning their faces and their eyes away from her. She was the redheaded outsider. She always would be.

Of course, Horace hadn't intended to do all this. *Renzi jiang-si qi yen ye san.* Before a man dies you must forgive him. That was what Lin said.

Forgive him. Forgive him. The word was a drumbeat of agony in her head. Impossible. It was all too big, too crushing, too many years of shame that never should have been hers in the first place. Anger made more sense than forgiveness. Didn't it? Rage, thundering fury—to these feelings she had every right. *Ke bu shi ma?* Yes. Anyone would say so.

Yet at the same moment, under this current of emotion, she knew that neither vengeance nor absolution would work. She had to find some middle way to acknowledge the past and free up the future. Some way to choose her own life, for herself.

And meanwhile he's going to die, she thought. Whatever else I do—whether I succeed or fail—I have to travel to him and say good-bye.

She walked quickly away down the street, conscious of the crowd's awareness of her, conscious of the tears seeping from her eyes. The saving breath of his love, the death grip of his power. When he passed on it was all going to drain away from her at once.

She pushed through the front door of the guesthouse and saw Spencer and Kong bent over a pile of flakes, cobbles, and hammerstones in the lobby sitting-room. "Alice!" Spencer cried. "Just the person! Come and help us!"

"With what?" she whispered.

"You won't believe what Dr. Kong has found! Look at this!" He held up a piece of incised bone.

Alice walked over, took it, tried to focus her swollen eyes on the etched design of an animal face surrounded by streaming sun-rays. "Is it—"

"It's the monkey sun god!"

"But where—"

"Kong dug it out of the ash layer! In an irrigation trench he found!"

"But it's what—a tool? A piece of a tool? What does it mean?"

"Don't you see?" He stared at her. "It means we've found the monkey sun god people! We can excavate the site, we can get a firm date on their culture—this is bone, you see, it's been buried all this time and not exposed to the air, so we can carbon-date it—Alice! A whole world of research just opened up here—articles—books—conferences—"

"*Dicheng yidian ye mei dajiao-ne,*" Kong put in excitedly.

"And the site is totally undisturbed," Alice translated.

Spencer laughed. "Amazing, isn't it? People walk away from their homesteads twenty thousand years ago. The climate keeps everything perfect. Nobody disturbs it, nobody knows it's there—hell, nobody even passes by it for all these centuries except a couple of shepherds and to them, it's nothing but some rocks!" He looked radiantly at the small prize in front of him, then turned to Alice. "Will you help us?"

"With what?"

"Well, we've got at least one monkey sun god site here and I'm sure there're dozens more. We'll be the first to survey and the first to identify and date the culture. Kong and I. We're going to do it together." He pointed to Kong.

The Chinese scientist nodded.

"These notes here—we're starting to frame out a grant for NSF. I am *sure* they'll go for this. It's airtight. We have a few hours left before we leave for Yinchuan. Will you help us, Alice? Translate some of Kong's ideas while I'm drafting it? I mean"— he colored again—"hey. You've given me more than I had a right to ask for already. I know that. I just mean, if you're here and you're feeling, well, you know, terrible, and maybe focusing on something else might help you—" He broke off. "God, Alice. You look awful. Listen. I'm sorry about the thing with Lin. I'd really like it if things went well for you. You know—as a friend—if there's anything I can do—" He stopped, nodding wordlessly at the papers in front of him. "You know."

"Yeah," she said. "I know. But something else has happened."

"What?" He looked at her.

"My father's sick."

"How sick?"

"Dying sick."

"What! Horace Mannegan? What's wrong?"

"Prostate cancer."

"Oh, God—" His eyes filled with feeling. "Alice—what are you going to do?"

"I'm going straight back to Beijing, as soon as we get to Yinchuan. Fly to Washington."

Spencer reached out and gripped her hand. He didn't know what to say.

Neither did she. "Thanks," she managed.

Kong had sat while they spoke English, seeing that their exchange was emotional, but not understanding, thinking her unhappiness was all over Lin, waiting to say something in Mandarin. "Interpreter Mo," he put in kindly. "I am sorry for your sadness. I hope your happiness returns. Now come, see the marvelous quality of this hammerstone from the trench. The monkey sun god people made it! Hold it in the palm of your hand!" He extended a perfectly, lovingly worn stone tool.

She closed her hand around it. He was right, it had such a comforting weight. Like the heaviness of wool blankets on a cold night. Like the lead apron in the dentist's office. She closed her eyes. Thousands of years ago, long before she had lived this life and felt this pain, this stone had pounded grain. *"Meizhile,"* she said softly, the Beijing street slang for incredible, marvelous, and handed it back to him.

Kong laughed at her unexpected colloquialism and then turned serious. "You know," he said, "the French priest was right. There is a treasure here. The Helan Shan is close to heaven!"

"I guess it is," she agreed. There was death inside her, death all around, but maybe it would feel better to work. "Okay," she said. She sat down. "Tell me what you want in the grant proposal, Dr. Kong. I'll translate it for Dr. Spencer."

"What are you saying?" Hope danced in Spencer's face.

She switched into English. "I'll interpret." She sighed.

And the American man broke into a smile.

* * *

When Lin woke up it was nearing sunset. He was cold, stiff, curled up in the dirt next to Meiyan's grave.

How had he fallen asleep? He rolled to his back and sat up. He rotated his head slowly from one side to another. The light was lengthening. The boulders all around him had dropped their growing shadows onto the hard ground.

Was she here? Was she next to him? Though he'd slept he hadn't dreamed of her. He tried to imagine her now, Meiyan, his wife, his *airen,* but all he could see in his mind was the way she'd looked when she was young. She wouldn't be young now. Impossible. He looked down at his hand, the worn skin pulling tight, no longer marble-smooth and poreless the way it had once been. He, his friends, everyone he knew, had grown older. None of them was young anymore.

Yet Meiyan was frozen young. By death.

He touched the slight swelling in the ground next to him.

And then in a rush of warmth he saw the redheaded west-ocean woman in his mind. He remembered her arms and legs around him. Why had she used him? Why had she not treated him as a man—a man with a heart—

Because I have no heart, he thought suddenly, staring at the shallow grave. I lost it a long time ago. He could feel his face burn as the truth came clear.

Somehow he understood that he still wanted Mo Ai-li. He wanted her here, wanted her to sit beside him staring at the desert, wanted to shed a thousand tears into her neck. He wanted to describe to her the cruel twisted road of his life, the walls, the beams and girders hammered in around him. And he wanted to see her face exalted again by the high tide, her sea-colored eyes open to him, transported. He couldn't simply forget her. Her shadow was still on him.

He climbed awkwardly to his feet and brushed some of the dirt from his clothes. Evening would be here soon. He had to walk back to the road and get a ride to Eren Obo.

At the end of the day, when they'd finished roughing out the NSF proposal, she realized she had not eaten since the night before. She forced herself to go down for dinner. Only Kong was there.

He smiled at her with great kindness. "Eat, girl child," he said, and placed tidbits of his choosing on her plate.

She looked at him and her eyes brimmed with tears.

"Ah, come, Interpreter Mo! Do not cry! I cannot face you in such sorrow. Eh. Come, eat. The river of life flows on."

He picked up his own chopsticks.

"I don't deserve your kindness," she said numbly, automatically reverting to the old manners.

"Don't talk polite." Kong sighed. "It's so tiresome. No one does that anymore. Look." He dug in his pocket and produced the hammerstone she had held earlier. "I saw how you took to this. It's so, isn't it? You liked this relic. It's all right! It's well and good! I want you to have it."

He pressed it into her hand.

Alice stared.

"Take it. Such a thing few modern humans own! A tool from twenty thousand years ago, eh, it's a wonder." He turned, embarrassed, back to his plate.

"Oh, Dr. Kong." She sighed. "I'd love to have this thing. You are right, it's a wonder. But I cannot remove this from China. It is *wei-fa*," against the law.

"Eh, of course. You are right."

She placed it carefully back on the table in front of him.

"I could send it to you—"

"Thank you. No. I would not want to break the law in any form."

"Eh," he assented, expressing the requisite disappointment in her refusal and yet revealing, in the Chinese manner, his relief at her graceful withdrawal. "Eat," he commanded her.

She took a few bites. Strange, she didn't feel like eating. The hunger that had dogged her for years now seemed absent.

"Where will you go now?" he asked. "Do you have another interpreting job?"

She shook her head. "I must return home as quickly as possible. To America. My father—you see—I've just learned my father is very sick. To speak frankly he is dying."

"Bitter and deep is the sea!" Kong said, shocked. "Interpreter Mo, I am so sorry."

She nodded, almost overwhelmed by his empathy.

"Level road," he told her with feeling. "Peaceful journey."

On her way out of the dining room she was surprised by Guo Wenxiang.

"I thought you'd left," she said, her distaste plain.

"Leaving soon. I wanted to say good-bye."

"That's hardly necessary."

"Still, between friends—Ah!" He snapped his fingers in a shallow, calculated parody of having just remembered something. "Mo Ai-li!"

"What?" she said tiredly.

"There *is* something I must give you! Something for Lin Shiyang. Blame me, for I almost forgot!" He reached inside his shirt collar and withdrew a black silk cord, then pulled it off over his head. Hanging from it was an ancient, human-looking tooth.

"What is it?" She stared.

"Dr. Lin will know." Guo handed it to her. "One of the women untied it from his wife after she went away. When I told her I was working for the husband"—Guo shot Alice a wry smile; this was not true, of course, but it was close enough— "she gave it to me. She had kept it all this time in case he ever came."

"Why didn't you give it to him before, when you told him his wife was dead?" she asked suspiciously. "Why did you say nothing about it then?"

He looked away from her. "I suppose I forgot."

"You forgot! You were keeping it to sell. Right?"

"Come, Miss Mo, why stand on this unpleasant point? What does it matter? I am giving it to you now, am I not?"

"You should have told Dr. Lin about it before."

"Look." He made his voice small, intense, almost honest. "I know what you think of me. But I'm outside the system. I have no iron rice bowl. I have to deal any way I can. And people like me are the future in this country: remember that. Now good-bye, Mo Ai-li. Level road." He turned and walked away from her.

She glanced down at the tiny, yellow-cracked bit of bone in her hand—a tooth, of course, it was a tooth—and wondered if it was as old as it appeared to be. When she looked up again, questions on her lips, he was out the door and stepping into a waiting car.

Finally, at the bank, she got through to him.

"Horace, I know," she blurted. "Roger told me."

"Sweetheart, are you coming home now?"

"Yes." She took a long, deep breath. "I'm on my way."

"I'm sorry, darling. I know you're on a job—"

"Don't worry about that," she hushed him. "It's not impor-tant. Anyway, it's finished, the job."

"Well, Alice," he began, and then paused, looking for words. "I guess I'm coming to the end too. You know that, right?"

"Yes." She tried to keep tears out of her voice, for his sake. "I know that."

"I've been thinking." She heard his breathing, a heavy, labored sound. "I feel bad about—I was wrong about that boyfriend of yours. What was his name?"

She closed her eyes. "Jian."

"Right. Jian. I thought you'd find somebody else easily—"

"Horace, please. You don't have to—"

"No, I want to say this. I never meant for you to be alone."

"I know that. I know you didn't." Everything she had thought about, all the fury and forgiveness, swirled to a hurricane inside her. With an effort she mastered herself, made her voice gentle. "Anyway," she told her father, "it was a long time ago."

He was silent for a moment. Only the sound of his breathing. "Horace?"

"So you'll come as soon as you can, Alice?"

"Yes. Of course. I told you—I'm on my way." She twisted the phone cord around and around her finger, feeling she was about to break. She wanted so badly to get there in time, to be near him, at least, for the end. Then she would deal with the rest.

"Alice?"

"Horace," she said softly, "hang on."

When she got back to her room Lin was there. His face was scraped, his hair matted, his clothes streaked with dirt. "Where have you been? I've been waiting for you!" His voice was urgent. "I know why you are leaving—your father. Kong told me. Ah, Mo Ai-li, it's a sadness."

"Yes," she managed. Why had he come back? Out of sympathy? He'd already made it clear he didn't want her anymore.

"I hope your father will be all right," Lin said quietly, trying to pin her with his eyes.

"He won't." She looked away. "He's going to die."

His face softened. "I'm so sorry. You are going back right away?"

"As soon as we get to Yinchuan."

"Xiao Mo," he said, his voice gentle but insistent. "*Dating yixia*. I'm sorry for the things I said when you told me you were leaving. If I had known . . ."

"Of course," she said, looking into his face, tearing apart inside. "I know that. But there were other things you said, Dr. Lin. Remember?" Her chin trembled slightly as she reverted to the old, distant form of address they'd used at first.

"Yes, I remember. Please. Don't call me that."

"But you did say those things, Lin. Come on. You had a right to say them. Though on some of them you were wrong." Her voice grew hard. "So there is a point I'd like to make. Just one. If I may."

"Ai-li."

"No, please. Let me. About following convenience. Yes, I led a free life. But the past is the past. And I meant what I said about the future. If you and I had taken our road together I would have been true to you. I'd never have been unfaithful. I don't know if you heard me when I told you, or if you even care anymore, but I meant it, it's true, with all my heart I tell you it's true, I loved you."

His mouth fell slack at those words, which carried so much weight in Chinese. Love. He felt it, too, he knew he did. It hadn't happened to him in so long. "Why do you use the past tense?" he whispered. "Why do you say 'loved'? Is it finished for you? You don't feel it anymore?"

She hesitated. "It's not that. It's that I have to go back. I have to say good-bye to my father. And there are so many things I have to sort out. Then maybe I can really know love."

He studied her hard. "Maybe?"

"Oh, Shiyang, I—I wish it, of course, the same way I've always wished it. But I see now that it's not something I can simply reach out and take." She looked up at him and held his gaze. "It's true for you, too, Shiyang. You know it is. Otherwise you wouldn't still be searching for traces of your wife."

"But I've found her now," he said heavily. "She's gone."

"Ah. I have something for you." Alice opened her suitcase, packed and ready for the drive back to Yinchuan, and removed a small square of padded green silk. "Guo Wenxiang gave it to me. He claimed he had forgotten about it before. Of course he was probably just planning to keep it, and sell it. But at the last moment he changed his mind." With the greatest respect, using both hands, she extended it.

In silence he took it. And unwrapped it.

The look on his face, the gasp that trembled through him when he saw the tooth, told her he knew it very well. He stared at it, eyes glistening.

"It was hers, yes?" She zipped the suitcase shut.

He nodded, unable to speak.

"Shiyang," she whispered. "You're a man of great commitment. I admire that. Perhaps I was wrong to think I could take you away from your memories."

He stared at her, everything battling inside him, then looked down at the million-year-old tooth in his brown, hollow palm. He raised his eyes back to hers. These things she kept saying, these equivocations—"Are you letting me go?" he asked her bluntly. "Are you telling me you want the rest of your life without me?"

Hurt flared. Isn't that what you told me? she thought. Yet at the same moment she saw him standing in front of her, a man, shimmering with feeling. Half of her wanted only to step into his arms. "It's not that I want my life without you," she said in a rough whisper. "It's just that I can't see anything, right now, except what I have to do. I have to go back. Beyond that"—she looked up at him, blinked back pain—"I just don't know."

After he left she took the Teilhard books off her desk, leafed through them, then closed them firmly and buried them in her suitcase. She still had a little time remaining.

So she walked out of Eren Obo into the sudden, all-powerful desert, and climbed high enough to gain a good, unfettered view of the alluvial plain and the town. Its grid of loess buildings glinted in the sun. This was a place my life changed, she thought.

She found a good spot marked by a little jumble of boulders, just off the path. Everything behind her, all of her past, seemed dead. Lucile was dead. Meng Shaowen. Teilhard de Chardin. And soon her father would die, too, Horace Mannegan. She'd be alone again. Always alone.

It was time to leave the *ling-pai* behind.

And the stomach-protector too.

She knelt and, using a stone from beside the path just as a Paleolithic woman would once have done, she dug a hole several inches deep.

In it she placed the *ling-pai*.

She dug the antique red silk stomach-protector out of her pocket and threw it into the hole on top of the *ling-pai*. She never wanted to see it again.

Staring at the two mismatched objects in the hole, she felt a weird kind of clarity. She should say a prayer. What had the Chinese words been, when she had said the *jiao-hun*, the calling of the soul that night on the street corner in Yinchuan?

She sighed. She couldn't remember. "Ashes to ashes," she said in English into the empty desert air, "dust to dust." She swept the loose dirt back into the hole and patted it down. *Good-bye, Mother Meng. I loved you. Good-bye, Lucile.*

She slowly raised herself and walked back down the path.

The first thing she did when they arrived in Yinchuan was call her father again. "Horace? I was just calling to—"

"You're still coming home, aren't you?" His voice sounded weak.

"Yes! I have a flight to Beijing tonight. From there it'll take about twenty-four hours."

"Thank you, sweetheart. Thank you." He sounded so tired, so far away.

"Get some rest," she said, not knowing what else to say. "I'll be there soon." She hung up.

In Yinchuan, in his room, Lin sat on his bed holding the tooth. In the next building Mo Ai-li was preparing to leave. She would leave and she might never come back.

Pain sliced through him at the thought.

He pushed the tooth in his pocket and walked quickly out of the room, down the hall, picking up speed, footsteps clattering, down the stairs, out of Building Two and across the courtyard.

He found her in her room, sitting beside her suitcase. "Can I do anything for you?"

"No," she said in an empty voice. "Nothing."

"Have you talked to your father again?"

She nodded.

"How is he?"

"Bad," she said, and now her voice was uneven, on the point of breaking. She dropped her head forward, stared at her hands in her blue-jeaned lap.

"When's your flight?"

"Eight o'clock tonight," she said, not moving.

"Ai-li," he said.

She looked up.

"Listen to me. I can't call back all the words that were said, but I can say this. Are you listening?"

She nodded.

"Go on. Go to your father and do what must be done. I came back to tell you I'll wait for you. Do you hear me? I will wait in Zhengzhou. I won't wait forever, but I'll wait."

She reached for his hand and brought it to her face.

Realizing there could be no promise now, that their future was unknown, she whispered the one thing she did know: *"Wo kongpa wode xin yi jiao gei le ni."* I'm afraid my heart's been given to you.

Gently he pressed her cheek in reply.

That afternoon, late, Alice Mannegan and Adam Spencer stood on the corner of Erqi Lu and Huimin Lu in Yinchuan.

"You really don't have to do this," Spencer repeated, peering over her shoulder at the small paper she held with its lines of Chinese and Mongolian writing.

"We've come all this way. Let's just put this thing to rest."

"I've already put it to rest," he reminded her. "I'm on to something else."

She faced east, down the clattery cobbled side street. "Should be this way."

He followed her, sidestepping a red-cheeked Mongol girl with a toddler and an impossibly large cloth bundle, and then a group of white-capped Muslim men hurrying, laughing, up the alley the opposite way.

"And I am going to pay you," he said. "When I get my NSF grant for the monkey sun god project, I'll send you the money."

"I don't care about it," she said.

"You going to stay in America awhile?"

"Awhile, yes. Then after that—I'm not sure where I'm going to end up, but I think it's time to settle down somewhere. Stop traveling all the time."

"Aha." He looked at her, smiling.

"We're here," she said softly. She had come to an abrupt stop and was gazing into a dark store-window, checking and rechecking the ancient number scratched into the stone. The door, secured with a rusted padlock, appeared not to have been opened for many years. Above their heads a hanging wooden sign creaked faintly. On it were carved age-darkened Chinese characters.

"This is it? You're sure?"

She nodded.

"But what kind of place was it?" He looked up at the sign.

"It was an apothecary." Her voice was small and final.

"What? Why would they sell the remains to—"

"Adam. Don't you see? It's an old Chinese belief. Men would pay a lot of money for potions made from ground-up fossils, or dragon bones, they called them. It was supposed to give you— you know, power. Potency."

His soft face lost all its color. "You don't mean they ground up the bones and they—they—"

She stopped and listened to the teeming sounds of the city all around. "Let's just say Peking Man has been—reabsorbed into the population."

He stared at the ground, mouth open, breathing strangely. She thought he might be sick, but after a time he slowly straightened up.

"Ready?" she said.

He closed his eyes and nodded.

They turned together to walk back. She had just enough time to make her flight to Beijing.

Historical Note

This is a work of fiction. All the characters who actually appear in the story are imagined. The historical aspects that form its backdrop, however, are based on real people and events.

The life and thought of Pierre Teilhard de Chardin (1881–1955) are well documented through his many books as well as biographies and editions of his letters. All the quotes herein attributed to Father Teilhard and Lucile Swan (1890–1965) are from published sources.

Teilhard de Chardin did live in semiexile in China for twenty-three years, did write many of his major works there including *The Phenomenon of Man*, did journey to northwest China in the early 1920s with Émile Licent, and did discover the site at Shuidonggou. He made important contributions in his era to Western understanding of the geology and archaeology of China. He worked closely over a long period with the multinational group excavating the Peking Man site at Zhoukoudian. During his China years he formulated and refined many of the ideas that were later to inform his works of Christian mysticism and philosophy.

Teilhard's profound and enduring relationship with Lucile Swan is mentioned in the memoirs of other foreigners who lived in Peking during those decades but is best described in *The Letters of Teilhard de Chardin and Lucile Swan*, published in 1993.

All the settings and places in this book do exist, and are presented as accurately as possible. The monkey sun god petroglyphs are real (and remain unexplained). Only one place name has been changed—that of Eren Obo, the Inner Mongolian town.

Liberties *have* been taken with the sequence of events surrounding Peking Man itself. Teilhard did not get Peking Man back from the Japanese at the end of the war. And although Teilhard made multiple journeys to northwest China and Mongolia, he is not known to have ever actually visited the town called Eren Obo in the book. Certainly after the war broke out he is not thought to have returned to the Northwest. He remained mostly in Peking until he was able to leave China in March 1946. And by that time Lucile was already gone, for she'd managed to get out and return to America in August 1941.

As for Peking Man, it really did vanish in 1941 as described in these pages; it vanished utterly and completely. It has never been found.

Acknowledgments

To my agent, Bonnie Nadell, and her colleague, Frederick Hill, my great thanks for believing in this book and working so hard to improve it.

I am deeply grateful to my editor, Leslie Schnur, not only for the vision and intelligence of her editing, but also for the remarkable depth of her commitment to this first novel. My appreciation also to Diane Bartoli for always being there to help.

My gratitude to the archaeologists David Madsen, Evelyn Seelinger, Robert Bettinger, and Robert Elston for allowing me to translate on their 1991 expedition to Ningxia and Inner Mongolia. Special thanks to Dr. Madsen whose advice on matters related to archaeology continued through the final draft.

To Bai Xiaobei, for her thoughtful review of the Chinese phrases in the book and her wonderful insights into its Chinese characters, my unending appreciation. A grateful salute to Zhang Jian for helping.

Thanks to the friends and fellow writers who read drafts: Peter Elbling, Liza Taylor, Tarabu Betserai Kirkland, Brian Cullman, Jill Peacock, Daniel Cano, Diane Sherry, Marjorie David, Jamie Bernstein Thomas, George Madarasz, Anita Witt, and—my China Trade partner—Cyndi Crabtree. Thanks to Mona Simpson for her early support. Thanks to my teacher Jim Krusoe, in whose class this novel was begun. Thanks to my other teachers, especially Mary Wong, Lin Duan, and the remarkable Dr. Ger-bei Lee for opening the door into Chinese. Thanks to Nobuko Miyamoto for the inspiration of her work and for years of fruitful discussion of some of the issues in this book.

My deepest appreciation to the countless people I've met and known in China over the past twenty-one years who have candidly related their hopes, regrets, and life histories to me. Thank you, all. Without you the Chinese characters in this book could never have been imagined.

I am indebted to many secondary sources in addition to those, cited at the front of the book, from which previously published material is quoted. Chief among these additional sources are *Death Ritual in Late Imperial and Modern China*, James L. Watson and Evelyn S. Rawski, editors; *The Cambridge Encyclopedia of China*, Brian Hook, editor, and Denis Twitchett, consultant editor; *Half of Man Is Woman* and *Getting Used to Dying* by Zhang Xianliang; *A Photographer in Old Peking* by Hedda Morrison; *China Pop* by Jianying Zha; *China Wakes* by Nicholas Kristof and Sheryl WuDunn; *In Search of Old Peking* by L. C. Arlington and William Lewisohn; and *The Years That Were Fat* by George Kates.

Finally, the greatest thanks are due to my husband, Paul Mones. Without his support, encouragement, constant stream of great ideas, and general all-around valorous partnership, I'd never have written this book at all.